Tünde Farrand grew up in Debrecen, Hungary, and lived, studied and worked in several countries before settling in the UK in 2005. She has continued to work in this country as a language specialist and modern languages teacher. She has an MA in Creative Writing from Sheffield Hallam University, and lives with her husband in Sheffield.

Published by
Lightning Books Ltd
Imprint of EyeStorm Media
312 Uxbridge Road
Rickmansworth
Hertfordshire
WD3 8YL

www.lightning-books.com

First Edition 2019
Copyright © Tünde Farrand
Cover design by Ifan Bates

British Library Cataloguing in Publication Data
A catalogue record for this book is available from the British Library

Printed by CPI Group (UK) Ltd, Croydon CR0 4YY

ISBN: 9781785630927

WOLF COUNTRY

TÜNDE FARRAND

To Nick, with love

PROLOGUE

It must have begun when my apple tree flourished and Sofia's withered and died. Perhaps that was when Sofia first had an inkling that she didn't belong. Dad used to say war begins at home, in the family. It was not his own idea; he must have read it somewhere and felt obliged to pass the wisdom on to his daughters. It took me twenty years to grasp its meaning, the realisation coming only yesterday after I put the phone down, an entirely changed person from the one who picked it up a minute earlier. I wonder what Dad would say now, if he saw me – saw us – like this, preparing for the final battle, a battle too painful and far too unequal to be fought in the sanctuary of the family.

16 JUNE, 2050

I've never been alone at a monorail station before. It's a peculiar feeling I can't put my finger on. The sense of luxury, the absence of sound. Like I have my own piece of Earth.

In the passenger lounge the pebble-shaped sofas are empty and waiting, the dimly lit wood-panelled bar silent. A fragrance of orchid is released and, for a moment, I'm fooled into thinking it's real.

Ten minutes ago, when we arrived from London, my fellow passengers left the monorail in haste. They hurried out to the square without stopping in the nineteenth-century station building. They wore well-cut clothes in the finest fabric, leather shoes soft as butter, but none of these could conceal their vacant stares, the servitude dried on their faces. A line of minibuses with tinted windows swallowed them up like a hungry mouth. The Owners must pay them well to make the long commute worthwhile. Apart from the financial remuneration, of course, there is the privilege of working directly in the service of the Owners. A privilege you can't put a price on.

The square is just as abandoned as the station. There is a high street running through the small town, and little side streets off it, all lined with original Victorian terraced houses, now functioning as traditional pastry shops and tearooms. It is not my first time away from a megacity, but the serenity still comes as a surprise. There's not a soul apart from me. The tourists don't tend to arrive before 10am.

It's a perfect English summer day, which usually lifts my spirits, though today it fails to do so. To kill time and avoid thinking about the ordeal I'm about to face, I watch the advert screens. There's one on my left, another attached to the station building, and a third one across the road. The same video is playing on each screen. It shows an elderly lady, wearing a pale pink blouse, sitting comfortably in a Chesterfield-style armchair. Behind her, a flowery curtain is drawn open to reveal a breathtaking view. Roses are climbing up the windowsill, while in the distance rolling hills create the impression of heaven on earth. The lady, wearing gold-framed spectacles, leans closer to the camera. She says she could not be happier, and all the things Dignitorium residents usually say. I don't want to watch it, and yet I can't keep my eyes off the screen. Now there's a new resident, from another Dignitorium, then another. The names and faces keep changing, only their message remains the same.

Checking the time, I'm starting to worry I've been forgotten when a long black car pulls up in front of me. There's an RR emblem on its front and a tiny statue of a winged woman. In the old system, these so-called limousines were used mostly by presidents and film stars. I'm flattered, even a bit excited, but I'm not sure about getting into the vehicle. The archive footage of fatal car accidents shown on the Globe always horrifies me.

The last time I was in a car, I was seven. It was still in the old system, when everyone had cars. Now only the Owners do. They say they need them against the wolves. For everyone else there's the monorail.

The chauffeur gets out and looks around, squinting in the sunlight. He's in his fifties, with deep wrinkles across his forehead; he seems a trustworthy type. In his immaculate black suit, with matching hat and white gloves, he oozes professionalism. Like the butlers I have seen in period dramas, he seems to have trouble turning his head, as if he had swallowed a stick. He greets me with a courteous bow, avoiding eye contact. If only he knew that I'm more afraid of his Owner employer than he is; that I am not a fellow Owner but a helpless person desperately trying not to blow her very last chance of survival.

'Mrs Alice Brunelli?' he asks, and when I nod he checks my identity on his ID Phone. The official photo of me was taken three years ago, and I wonder if – after the past few months – I still resemble that young woman with honey-blond hair, porcelain skin and a lively, elfish smile. Or has my face – carrying pain like an antiquity carries the mark of centuries – become unrecognisable?

He nods and opens the car door for me. He must enjoy watching me struggle to get in. The door seems to be in the way. I do my best to mimic what I've seen in old films, to climb in sideways, without hitting my head or tripping over. I refuse his offer of help. 'Are you comfortable, madam?' he asks. There's a slight hint of friendliness in his tone, now that he's realised I'm one of his kind, a mere mortal.

Inside the vehicle a gentle blue light illuminates the jet-black interior. The cool leather seat stings my arms, the cold seeping through my linen trousers and my blouse. The scent opens up a new dimension, a realm of privilege and opulence. In any other circumstances, I would be excited, but instead I'm ill at ease. This is an alien world, alien and hostile.

As the limousine reaches a high-security red fence, the gate slides open, then closes immediately behind us. We're entering the infamous wolf country. I peer through the tinted window, trying to spot some wolves, but then remember that they don't like coming close to vehicles. The landscape changes as the town disappears behind us. The road begins to climb and soon we reach the top of a hill; looking down, I realise how near we are to the coast, only a few miles from the silvery blue that seems to flow beyond the horizon. It shouldn't surprise me; even as a child, Sofia was attracted to the sea. There's something surreal about the car's motion – like being able to fly – seeing the road ahead, running, bending, then we're snaking our way through a forest. I don't like the speed, though, and I'm on the verge of begging the chauffeur to slow down. Again I remember the bodies shown on the Globe, broken and blood-soaked, and a recent documentary illustrating how much living space roads used to take up and how cars had a disastrous impact on the environment. There is a sharp curve; I have to hold on to the seat. I press a button to my left and speak into the intercom.

'Could you slow down a bit, please?'

His expression in the mirror suggests he doesn't understand.

'I'm not used to this speed.'

For a second it seems he wants to say something but then his face returns to a rigid mask and he slows the car down. It is still a little fast but I don't want to ask him again.

'When will we get there?'

'We'll be there in approximately twenty minutes, madam.'

I check the map on my ID Phone but all areas that belong to the Owners – everything behind the red fence – is blanked out. The closer we get to our destination, the faster my heart beats, and my palms are so sweaty they leave wet patches on the soft leather.

How did I ever dare to dream that my sister would help me? I think back to that evening, more than two decades ago. That was the day when Sofia and I, the enemies, became something much worse than that, something I don't have the words for. That was the last time we saw each other. In the past, whenever I thought of Sofia, I was always overcome with anger, but now the questions overwhelm me. Does she regret what happened? Has she been thinking of that day? And when I manage to forget about the pain, just for a few seconds – usually early in the morning, when I'm between sleep and waking, and my mind is still enveloped in a white, thick fog – I catch myself asking: how has her life been for the past twenty years? Has she – like all of us – been moulded and mellowed by inevitable hardships, or have wealth and status shielded her? I know that for most of us, time smooths over the rough patches and casts a rose tint over everything. However, I am not one of those lucky ones.

Eventually the floating sensation of the car calms my nerves, and another story, an earlier one, emerges from the cloud of memories. I was only nine; Sofia was twelve.

It was about a year after the new system was introduced, though the transition was far from complete. Dramatic changes of that scale take years to implement, delayed by those who oppose them. The opponents were a minority of the retired population, those wealthy enough to escape the notorious retirement homes. They were clinging to an old, failed system like children to their abusive parents or Stockholm syndrome sufferers to their kidnappers. They rejected the new society and many went into hiding.

Our grandmother, in her mid-sixties and bursting with joie de vivre, was horrified by the new system. She said she would rather face prosecution from the authorities than have a tracker installed. I, for one, was excited about the trackers, and Sofia, fascinated by the science behind them, was even more so, but Grandma's reaction was understandable; she and her peers had grown up in a very different world. No matter how much Mum tried to explain, Grandma couldn't understand that it was for the good of everyone, that if ever something happened to her, we would be able to locate her immediately. Apart from Grandma, we had all had the trackers shot under the skin behind the left ear when the new system started, gladly and voluntarily. It took only a second, and I immediately felt safe, protected, and even proud.

It was reported in the media that with the help of the trackers, criminals were arrested within hours of committing a crime. As expected, this brought about a rapid fall in crime and won us over to the new system. But not Grandma. She – having been a homeowner, a rarity in her generation – even joined a demonstration outside the Houses of Parliament, but it was stopped, and some participants were arrested; Grandma had a narrow escape. It was reported on the Globe that the authorities were looking for the 'troublemakers'.

Mum gently tried to convince Grandma that she would have a wonderful retirement in the Dignitorium, reaping the fruits of her life's work until she felt she was ready. Mum even brought her a shiny prospectus printed with golden letters, but she tore it up. Later that day, Sofia and I spent hours piecing together the fragments, imagining ourselves living like royalty between the walls of the grand Victorian mansion.

'I'm loving this new system,' she said. I nearly said I agreed when Grandma's tearful face came to mind.

'Yeah. But poor Grandma...'

'Don't tell me you wouldn't like to retire in a place like that?'

'I don't know.' I shrugged.

'How do you want to die then?'

'I've never thought about it. I don't want to die.'

'It's not a choice, princess,' she said and I felt – as usual when

11

getting into a conversation with her – like a complete idiot. She excelled in sciences at school and had won a national competition. She even had a tiny room in our attic, which was her 'laboratory'. Her ambition was to become a scientist. I, until my early adulthood, had no idea what I wanted to do.

Grandma fled her old house the night before the authorities began the evictions. Her house – like most built in the old system – was not nice or practical enough to be kept; they rebuilt that district into a beautiful area for High Spenders.

Grandma stayed with us. She came with just one suitcase of clothes and her wedding album. Everything else was left behind. We still lived in our old house, awaiting the completion of our new Mid-Spender area. I kept picturing our future place; Mum said the new homes would be more attractive and convenient than any accommodation in the history of mankind. We were overjoyed about the brand-new semi we would be given once it was built. Dad tried to explain to me and Sofia on our own level why the old world had collapsed. Even as a nine-year-old I understood that the increasing demands put upon the welfare system by the old and sick had led to the impoverishment of the hard-working majority. I can still feel the excitement in the air about getting free housing; I remember the constant media coverage, strangers hugging each other in the street, grown men crying with joy that the economic and housing crisis had been tackled for good. All we had to do in return was consume.

In the old system our family was lucky because Dad had inherited a house, but when I visited some of my friends I saw the poverty they lived in, two to three families sharing a house, mothers and babies crammed into tiny bedsits. Apart from well-to-do non-profit people like Grandma, everyone hailed the new system. The majority of the working population, who were previously rent slaves, praised the gift of secure employment and accommodation in the regenerated megacities. The pensioners were set free from the subhuman conditions of the retirement homes, in which they had been kept like animals, up to ten of them sharing a room, all crammed onto two large piss- and vomit-soaked mattresses, starved and even beaten by staff. After the change of system, they were given an unprecedented quality of life in the newly completed Dignitoriums.

Grandma refused to be called a non-profit person, though we kept telling her we loved her nonetheless. She had been with us for two days, occupying Sofia's laboratory, when the authorities visited us, enquiring about Grandma. She was in fact out that evening at a meeting with other non-profit people. They asked us to contact them once she returned, thanked us politely and left.

Of course, Mum and Dad knew that Grandma's fear was totally unfounded – we all knew it – but strangely we couldn't bring ourselves to turn her in. When we looked into her eyes, the terror we saw was very real indeed. I suppose it's like taking a little bird in your hands. Though you know you won't harm it, the bird does not. Aged nine, I learned to appreciate the power of fear.

We were prepared to defend Grandma if we had to, but they didn't return. We hoped they had forgotten about her. In the evenings, after school, we would play cards or have dinner together. We did our best to make her happy, but she always said she felt like a prisoner. One day in the kitchen, when Grandma couldn't hear, Mum said to Dad that Grandma was not a real prisoner, only a prisoner of her fear. That evening I asked Sofia what being the prisoner of fear meant.

'You wouldn't understand,' she replied. 'But I can tell you it's far worse than being locked up in a real prison.'

Grandma must have been with us for two months when, one afternoon, the authorities returned. The three young female officers

– kind and softly spoken – came in, and after a warm greeting they went straight upstairs to her room. Paralysed, I hid on the landing while they stood in the doorway, smiling at Grandma. Her face turned white, but her fear was unnecessary, for they were very understanding. Their leader, a petite woman with a heart-shaped face, sat down next to Grandma on the bed, and patiently explained to her why they had come.

'It's in your own interest, Mrs King, that you make a choice now. Start to earn your Right To Reside, like everyone else, or retire to the Dignitorium. It's totally up to you. I'm happy to announce that we have just completed a cosy little Low-Spender area, where the Right To Reside in a lovely studio is very affordable. I'm sure that with your family's support you could spend some wonderful years there before you retire. You could even do a little part-time work.' Grandma nearly exploded.

'How dare you! I have been working all my life! I paid into a decent pension for forty years. We had our own house. I want my home and my pension back!'

'I'm sorry to see how it upsets you, Mrs King,' the chief officer said with genuine concern in her voice. 'You, like many people of your age group, fail to understand – and I don't blame you for it – that those times are gone. Now we have a new, more sustainable system. Ask me any questions you like. We are here to help you make the right decision.'

'I don't want to live in a flat, and is the Government going to compensate me for taking my home?'

'My dear Mrs King,' said the officer patiently, 'if we compensated everyone, we wouldn't have any resources for our new, improved society. We would be right back where we were before. Surely you don't want that.'

'Of course that's what I want. I want it just how it was.'

The woman sighed and exchanged glances with the rest of us.

'How can you say you want things how they were? Mrs King, I agree that you were very fortunate in the old system, but surely you must be aware of how the majority suffered? How people were denied a decent life, the country bankrupted trying to care for the elderly, unemployed and the sick? Think of the future of your family, think of your granddaughters', she said, nodding at me and Sofia.

Grandma looked confused and was still unable to make a decision.

The officer took a device that resembled a chunky plastic pistol out of a bag. Grandma screamed that they wouldn't put that thing near her. I wanted to go to her, cuddle her and tell her that the tracker wouldn't hurt, but Dad gently held me back. Mum asked to have a few words with her in private, so we all left the attic.

While we were waiting down in the living room, the officers showed us a short film that had been made with families in mind. The documentary started by explaining the psychology of fear of the unknown and that this kind of fear – like all manner of degradation – increases with old age. It told us about what happens to the human body and brain as we age. Halfway through, an officer asked me and Sofia to turn our heads away, as we might find the images disturbing. I did so but Sofia didn't; she gazed with interest at the many centenarians lying helpless and half-naked in their own waste. I know this because I turned my head back for a second when Dad didn't see. 'We don't let animals suffer, why would we do it to our own parents?' This slogan was repeated many times, and it made my heart contract in pain for what would soon happen to Grandma's aged body.

'At what age does it strike?' Sofia asked.

'We never know for sure but it gets considerably worse after the age of sixty.'

Grandma's age, I thought.

'And is the deterioration gradual or sudden?' Sofia asked.

The woman was evidently surprised by a twelve-year-old using such language. She glanced at Dad.

'Sofia is our little scientist, with big plans, aren't you?' He patted her shoulder, and Sofia shone like a crown jewel, then started boasting about her hope to find a cure against ageing. I felt acid filling my stomach.

Finally, Grandma made a decision. After a lengthy discussion she reluctantly agreed to move into the Dignitorium. She had to leave immediately, so they offered to take us in their helicopter to a nearby one, in MW12. The roads had just been converted into pedestrian zones and cycle routes but the monorail hadn't been completed yet.

As we flew over the city, it was fascinating to look down on London beneath us. Our city, just like the whole country and indeed the whole world, was undergoing a total transformation. It was still our city, the city we loved. Big Ben stood proudly next to the Houses of Parliament, boats on the Thames headed up towards Tower Bridge, and in the distance the dome of St Paul's rose up majestically. But a new earth was about to be born from the ashes of the old one. From the air we could see the rows of back-to-back terraced houses, the narrow streets; a total disorder. A few miles away, the vision of the new system had already materialised, in the form of wide tree-lined promenades alongside which ran the bicycle routes and the monorail track. We marvelled at the very first monorail we saw, a glittering red metallic snake, an improved replica of those originally used in Disneyland.

'Not bad, but I have better ideas,' Sofia commented.

Though she wouldn't admit it, I could see she was spellbound, her eyes widening as she drank up the view.

'Those are Low-Spender buildings. Ours will be much better,' Sofia said, pointing at the six- and eight-storey blocks, painted magnolia and terracotta, complete with balconies.

'Mid Spenders get a proper house with a garden,' she continued. 'And what if I want a flat?'

'They're not called flats any more, silly. They're apartments!'

'Okay, so what if a Mid Spender wants an apartment?'

'They can get one. Those will be in four-storey condos. They will each have roof gardens and an inner courtyard with a playground and swimming pool.'

I didn't know where Sofia had got all this information from, but later she was proven right. Dad had requested a semi with a pleasant garden at the front and back, near our new school, and we were given just that.

Sofia pressed her nose to the window, her breath creating steam on the glass surface. I watched her for a long time. I was admiring her profile, the straight nose I so envied, her almond-shaped eyes and long dark hair that framed her face. Her immaculate white skin had never been blemished by the sun. She was studying something in the far distance, mesmerised. I followed her gaze through the window to a slim, snow-white, windowless skyscraper. It was only half-finished but it already dominated the city's skyline, like a watchtower.

'What's that?' I asked her with awe.

'The Primavera Club. The Owners' playground. Cool, isn't it?'

'What's in there?'

'No idea.' She shrugged.

If I look back to our childhood, this was one of the few things she ever admitted to not knowing.

'The Owners go there to relax,' she added, confidence returning to her voice. 'After the responsible work they do.'

'What work?'

'Everything. Creating new cities, looking after the countryside, and most importantly, protecting us from the wolves.' At the mention of wolves, I shivered.

17

Despite the ride being a cool adventure, I couldn't wait to arrive. I could tell Grandma had already regretted her decision. She was trying to avoid looking down on the new London, but when we pointed something out in admiration, she looked at it with fearful disgust. I hoped once we arrived and she saw the gorgeous building and gardens of the Dignitorium, she would calm down. She kept staring ahead solemnly then suddenly looked at me and Sofia: 'Do you girls agree with that woman?'

'Agree about what, Grandma?' I asked.

'That I'm selfish. For wanting the old system back.'

'Oh, Mum.' Mum patted her hand. 'Forget about that woman. We are your family. We love you. We all understand how difficult it is to accept change.' Sofia and I nodded at the same time and sent her a sweet smile.

'I … I love you girls,' Grandma said with a serious face. 'And the last thing I want is for you to think otherwise.'

Mum laughed out and cuddled Grandma. 'You have made the right decision, that's the only thing that counts.

'You two really want this new system, right?' she asked, brooding, with a strange resignation in her voice.

We arrived above the Dignitorium. The grand Victorian brick mansion was stunningly beautiful in the middle of the magical gardens and lush old trees. Even Grandma looked down with curiosity and when we arrived and said goodbye, she was calmer. What we saw – the gardens, the reception hall, the Salon where we said goodbye to Grandma before she was led away – fascinated all of us. I couldn't wait to return to visit her and hear all her adventures.

On our journey home, we all were silent. Mum was trying hard to conceal that she was wiping her eyes. The last image of Grandma, looking back from the door of the Salon with an encouraging but somewhat forced smile, made us realise she wouldn't be a part of our everyday life any more. There was this sense of loss until Mum broke it and got Sofia and me to plan a lovely gift for Grandma that we would take her on our next visit. Sofia wasn't paying much attention – she was admiring the view of the new London below – but I loved the idea. I said we could have bespoke doll versions of ourselves made for her so she would feel we're with her all the time. Mum loved the idea and ordered the dolls once we got home.

But Dad couldn't stop wondering why the authorities had gone straight upstairs to Sofia's laboratory, how they knew she was there.

'It doesn't matter now,' Mum said while dishing out plates of pasta.

'It does matter,' Dad replied. He didn't touch his fork. 'If they are monitoring us in our own home, I'll report them.'

I looked at Sofia, who was browsing on her ID Phone, entirely uninterested in the conversation. Mum slammed the cheese grater down on the table. 'Ben, I think you're overreacting. Mum is now in a safe place, let's just drop it and enjoy our meal,' she said.

Dad didn't reply. He stared ahead into the empty air for what felt like ages. When he spoke his voice was unusually quiet.

'It's not just about finding the bugs, Evelyn,' he said. 'If they're really spying on us, this is more serious than I thought. And this new system is more dangerous than they tell us.' I felt goose bumps rising all over my skin.

'There are no bugs,' Sofia said, not even looking up from her ID phone. 'It was me who reported Grandma.' Her words hung in the air. We all looked at her.

'What are you saying?' my father asked.

'I reported her to the authorities. In fact, I don't know what took them so long. I did it two months ago.' She glanced up. 'Why are you staring at me like that? She was cheating the system. I would report anyone for it.' I saw something unnatural in Mum's gaze, like she'd been hit with a hammer but was trying to conceal the pain. Dad looked at Sofia with disbelief, then at Mum, then back at Sofia. I think something broke in him for good that evening.

Sadly, Grandma didn't enjoy the Dignitorium; she wanted to go out and do the things she was used to doing, like wandering around the local flea market or hiking in the hills with her walking group. The fact that her body would soon start to deteriorate didn't seem to bother her. Grandma insisted she could easily live a full life for another twenty years. There were moments when I nearly believed her and was confused, but once Citizenship classes were introduced at school, they explained how it was in human nature to resist the process of ageing. We were given numerous examples of retired people in the old system not accepting their deterioration and even becoming a danger to society. One was driving a car almost blind, and killed a group of school children. Once I heard that, I understood that it was better for all of us – especially Grandma – if she accepted the new system and even tried to enjoy the luxurious retirement she was being offered.

But when Mum, Dad and I visited Grandma in the Dignitorium, she looked old and thin. I noticed how she tried to conceal her shaking hands. She told us she was organising a little group of fellow residents to write to the Prime Minister and some important Globe broadcasters in protest against their situation. She didn't have time to follow through with her plan.

Just two weeks after she moved in, we were given an emergency call to go to the Dignitorium. They told us Grandma had been diagnosed with a very advanced cancer. She had requested instant euthanasia and her body had already been cremated. We were in shock. We knew Grandma wouldn't have done anything like this, not without wanting to see us first. They showed us her diagnosis and explained her illness to us in great detail. Then we saw her Farewell Video in which she sat in a chair, smiling, saying goodbye to us, telling us this was what she wanted. She explained that she wished to avoid the pain of cancer. She hoped to save us the trouble, the heartache.

Her name, etched on a silver plaque on the memory wall in the Dignitorium's garden, was the only trace left of her, apart from her suitcase and the wedding album. All we could do was to return to the wall with flowers and mourn. Sofia never expressed any desire to come with us, and I had a feeling Dad wouldn't have taken her even if she had. From the day her betrayal came to light, Dad was cautious around Sofia. Sometimes it was more than caution. I could swear it was fear.

The limousine slows down as we descend a steep hill. I can see dozens of narrow chimneys on an ancient rooftop surrounded by lofty trees. So it's a Victorian mansion, a grand place. Within the vast grounds a snow-white chopper stands on a helipad. Even from this distance, it all radiates Sofia's arrogance and obsession with luxury. Suddenly I start to shiver. She won't help me.

Dad is not here to warn her that war begins in the family and that – despite the crippling interval of two decades since we have seen each other – I am still family. The only reason she has agreed to meet me is because she wants to humiliate me. She'll listen, raising my hopes, just to laugh in my face the next moment. She'll bring up the past, condemning me for that day when we parted, when I said things I shouldn't have said. I want to go back to London. I bend forward, trying to form the words to tell the chauffeur to stop and turn around. It's not too late yet. But then my survival instinct kicks in, followed by an image of Philip, and I feel ashamed for my momentary weakness. I'm ready to meet my fate, if there is just the slightest hope. Today, I will rise or fall.

SEVEN WEEKS EARLIER...

BOOK ONE

ONE

It's already May, my favourite month. But instead of strolling in the park, I am at home, feeling suffocated, yet unable to leave. On the news they announce that the Paradise shopping centre is ready to be reopened. They rebuilt it brick by brick in the hope that people might forget the fact that it was blown to pieces less than five months ago. The reporter is standing in the rooftop garden with dozens of waving customers behind her. With her shoulder-length hair flying in the wind, her waterproof puffed up, she reminds me of an astronaut floating in space. She exudes an air of triumph as she keeps repeating the words 'bigger and better', like a mantra.

A year ago I would have been the first to enter, eager to explore the cave of treasures. The new me couldn't care less. I'm trapped in time, still reliving that Boxing Day five months ago when Philip didn't come home from work. Just when we were about to become High Spenders, on the verge of starting a family... Now not only is he gone, but – as I discovered soon after his disappearance – so are the considerable savings from his bank account.

I switch off the Globe and go to my favourite place at the window. I spend more time here than is healthy, watching people in the inner courtyard. The obligatory ingredients of Mid-Spender community living – a neat lawn with a barbecue area, the heated swimming pool in the far right corner and the winding path, bordered with flowers, that circles around the fountain – are supposed to raise the spirits, but instead they fill me with a gnawing loneliness. Still, it's too addictive to stop. When the courtyard is empty – in bad weather or at night – my eyes are often drawn to the windows of the apartments opposite mine and stay there longer than they should.

This morning I went to the police station again. By now everyone there knows me. I wonder what they really think behind their compassionate smiles. 'You're wasting your time,' the officer said. 'These days, with such technology, who can be more dead than the officially dead?' They probably think me a lunatic. Sometimes I'm worried they're right. This foolish hope that Philip is still alive only prolongs my suffering, conserving it until it becomes a part of my body, and seeps permanently into my bones.

On my way to work, struggling for air during rush hour on the monorail; in the staffroom, while my colleagues are gossiping away, I think of Philip. He's still there on my way home, when I leave the monorail and pick up the ingredients for a quick, lonely dinner. Wherever I go, I can't help searching for his eyes in the crowd of unknown faces.

In February I was given the evacuation order. It came as a shock, even though I knew that one day I would have to move into a single apartment. At the council I pretended not to see the dread-ridden faces in the queue, the faces of those who were being downgraded to Low Spenders. I kept telling myself it could be worse. I could be one of them. The council officer's words were sympathetic but businesslike.

'Your husband is not coming back. A newly married couple will need your apartment, Mrs Brunelli. You must move out within three days.' She scanned my ID phone and typed something into her computer. 'It's done,' she said. 'From now on you will be able to enter your new home. Don't worry, it's just as lovely as your old one, the perfect size for a single person.' She gave me a charming smile. I wanted to reply but my tongue was tied. 'The entry code for your old home will soon be de-activated. So it's in your interest to move all your belongings as quickly as possible.' She gave me another smile of encouragement, the equivalent of a hug had we been friends. I walked home like an automaton, the frost-covered street and the people around me blurred.

I know the police officer was right. If a person's tracker is deactivated, there are only three – equally hopeless – possibilities. Upon retiring to the Dignitorium, residents have their trackers removed, cut out of their bodies, leaving a barely visible mark behind the left ear. The same happens to those unfortunates who, not qualifying for the Dignitorium, are forced to withdraw from society and are dumped in the Zone, to await their miserable end, either by starvation or attack from other unfortunates. The third possibility is that they are already dead. The tracker switches itself off because of a lack of energy from the living body to fuel it.

The breeze blows gently at the muslin curtain. I prefer hiding behind it; if I am to be a voyeur, better to do it invisibly. The playground below is becoming interesting, now that families are finishing their Sunday lunch and are ready to walk it off. I wonder, if we had had any children, would they have been girls or boys. For some reason, I always thought the first one would be a girl. What would she play with now? Would she sit on the mini-carousel? Or would she be more adventurous and climb the artificial tree? Would she be shooting glances up at the window, waving and shouting: 'Hi, Mummy'?

It's getting busier – only the secluded smaller playground for non-profit children is empty as usual. Fathers are watching their children playing on the swings, mums are sunk deep in the jacuzzi, holding one wrist above the water, the wrist with the ID Phone, which they almost never take their eyes off. I would have been a different mother. More attentive, less frivolous. This is all that is left to me now, watching from high up, with the soft muslin curtain tickling the tip of my nose.

Recently I started to make excuses when friends called, inviting me for a birthday bash or a weekend shopping in another city. By now the calls and invitations have stopped. Hi-hello-how're-yous are scattered around in the staffroom, but it rarely goes any further than that. I can hardly bear other people's company any more.

Tired of the family scenes, I look across at the apartment opposite. The woman who lives there is always reading on her balcony, and today is no exception. She's young and beautiful. All she ever does is read, either down in the courtyard on a lounger or on her balcony, swinging in an orange hammock. In the beginning, I kept asking myself how she could earn her Right To Reside. Not any more, now that I know the answer.

I wonder what Philip would make of her, given his recent disillusionment with everything under the sun. He used to say that only idiots read fiction; weak and unfit people who choose to escape from reality instead of confronting it. It seemed he'd forgotten the days when, years ago, we used to read books together, cuddled up, one of us reading aloud, the other listening with closed eyes. Then we would swap.

'Books are gateways to other dimensions,' Philip said on our honeymoon in Madeira, out of the blue as we were coasting in a hired boat across the turquoise water of the bay. 'Once you start reading, the gate opens up, and the other world behind draws you in.'

'Sometimes I wish I could close the gate and stay trapped in that world,' I replied jokingly, but he remained serious.

'We would be separated then,' he said.

'Or we could be trapped together.' I laughed and when the sweet wind blew in my face and sent my hair flying back, my heart nearly burst.

It's not an imaginary dimension I'm trapped in now, but this harsh, cold and dreadful world. Even worse, I'm trapped alone. Those who counted have gone. We never know how the death of our parents will affect us. I can testify that the adult orphan suffers no less than the child. Mum and Dad often return in my dreams, sometimes in the form of nightmares. I see Mum crouching above someone. It's Dad, lying face down. Mum starts screaming. At this point I always wake up in a sweat, my heart rate up in the sky. Fortunately this dream only haunts me rarely. Usually I see them as I did for the very last time, on that autumn day four years ago when their retirement in the Dignitorium came to an end and I stayed on the bench in front of the main building. Dad didn't want me to escort them to the entrance of the T-wing. They said they were ready to go, and had their heads held high, but they never stopped holding each other's hands. As if they were hanging on to the only certain thing. That's how I see them when I dream, walking away from me, hand in hand, and the further they walk, the brighter they appear, until they shine like a diamond star.

A breeze is coming through the window and the little living room quickly loses heat. In my old home I could sit out on our private roof terrace if I needed the sun. There were so many things I couldn't bring from the old apartment, such as Philip's exercise bike. Maybe it's better that way, so I don't have to see it sitting unused. I glance at the clock and my stomach contracts. I'm getting closer to tomorrow by the hour, to the dreaded Monday when the nightmare at work begins again.

On Friday, Leo Sullivan, the head teacher, called me into his office. I had expected it, after I failed to notice that three children hadn't returned to class from break. Even security couldn't find them, and they had to call in the police to locate their trackers. For a short time they feared a repetition of the notorious kidnappings – it was the first thing that came to everyone's minds – but luckily it wasn't the case. They found them playing truant in a nearby shopping centre. Leo, an exemplary family man, the type who wears a freshly starched shirt every day and decorates his desk with family photos, had warned me in the past weeks to get some help; I thought there was nothing new to say. This time his tone was more severe.

'What happened today in Year 8 will cost you three penalty points.'

'I'm sorry, Leo.'

'With these three points, now you have thirteen.'

'That's impossible!' I stared at him in disbelief. He pointed at his computer screen for me to see. It can't be true! In September, at the start of the new school year, I had only five points that had accumulated over the years.

'Look, Alice, I don't judge you; in fact, I deeply sympathise with you. But if a parent reports the school, it's not you but me who will be in trouble.'

'I'm really sorry. These days I'm just…not well.'

'I know.'

'You don't know what an effort it is to get out of bed every morning, how I struggle to cope with even simple tasks.'

'I have to tell you something, but it must remain between us.' His tone mellowed to a friendly one. 'My wife has been diagnosed with multiple sclerosis.' He lowered his voice even though there was no one around. 'Her condition is deteriorating, it seems she'll never be able to earn her Right To Reside. I can't afford to lose my credit in this job.'

At this stage he sounded like he was begging me to sort myself out.

'I understand,' I said. 'The last thing I want is to get you into trouble.'

'Get some help then.'

'Even if I could afford therapy, it wouldn't give me the answers.'

He promised to see what he could do. When he got back to me in the afternoon, he gave me a list of crisis advisors, available from the council free of charge. I applied straightaway . It suggested that in the meantime I get additional help from the Mini-doc.

Mini-doc again! For God's sake, this is not a common flu or infection I have – how could an app possibly understand what I'm going through?

I close the blinds as if it could shield me from the outside world. Tomorrow it's back to school again. With my thirteen penalty points, I'm dangerously close to the maximum of twenty, which would mean suspension. I can't afford another mistake. I'm eyeing my ID Phone on the table, flirting with it. For some reason I have always been against the idea of using the Mini-doc for non-physical symptoms. But what harm can it do? Like everyone else, I pay for it anyway. For a monthly subscription we have this high-tech doctor available to us, day and night. I was a child when the old system collapsed, so I have only vague memories of visiting a doctor. However, Mum would often bring up its horrors: waiting for hours in a confined, badly lit space, having to share it with other sick people, mostly children and the elderly.

I pick my ID phone up and turn on the Mini-doc. A greying man in a white coat greets me. 'Good afternoon, Alice.' He introduces himself as Doctor Graham. His manner is professional, and only the lack of any fluctuation in his tone betrays the fact that he's not real. As I'm trying to explain my problem in a few sentences, narrowing it down, there are more focused questions popping up. My blood pressure and other body functions are measured. Then after a short wait, the results are processed. The diagnosis is depression and exhaustion of medium severity. Four different types of medicine are recommended, but I can't bring myself to go through the lengthy descriptions so I let Mini-doc choose. It selects one and I pay. Doctor Graham reappears on the screen. 'Your medicine will arrive within two hours. To aid your recovery, I'd recommend a compilation of relaxing classical music. Please see the available selection on your Globe. Goodbye, Alice, and thank you for using Mini-doc.'

When the Globe comes on, its spherical 3D projection is beamed down from the ceiling into the room. I switch to music mode and type in Johann Sebastian Bach. Dad brought us up listening to music, so unlike most people these days I know many of the great composers. It was one of the things I had in common with Philip. We were rare in that respect, anomalies.

BOXING DAY

Christine, our neighbour, poked her head out of the door to our roof terrace but once she looked down, she grimaced and retreated back into the living room. It amused me, but I was not as cruel as her husband, Paul, who would push her towards the edge of the terrace until her face went deathly pale, and she gripped his arm, her fingers leaving red marks. Christine's vertigo didn't allow her to join me. I knew it; that's why I'd gone outside. I stood there taking in the fresh air, with my elbows pressed to the icy rail, trying to get Christine's words out of my head.

'Last night there was a chat show on the Globe about women who don't have children,' she'd said the previous evening, and I knew I didn't want to hear what was coming next.

'So what?'

'The survey concluded that ninety-five per cent of them regret not starting a family by the time it's too late.' She shot me a meaningful look. I swallowed hard.

'Where are you going with this, Christine?'

'Nowhere. Honestly. It's fine if you don't want to talk about it.' Her voice was filled with curiosity, her eyes widened with excitement as she waited for me to start lamenting – as once, in a moment of weakness, I did – about the fact that Philip didn't want to have children.

On the balcony I inhaled deeply and reminded myself not to confide in Christine in the future.

It was only 2pm. The street was silent under the thick blanket of virgin snow. Far away, above the roofs of the city, the London Eye was turning slowly, but gracefully, many tiny pairs of legs dangling from the seats. This new, giant London Eye had just been installed, to replace the original one with capsules. Customers craved ever bigger thrills. Now they sat between earth and sky, uncovered, unprotected. Even the sight of it gave me the shivers and I shifted so that it was concealed by the roof opposite.

Christine, like me, was enjoying the two-week winter break all non-teachers were so jealous of – those who had never experienced the sensation of a lead-heavy brain after months in the classroom, who had never felt the numbing stress when, every afternoon, the results of likeability votes from the students appeared on all teacher's computer screens. I pulled my coat around me; the cold was biting but I needed more time to myself. This was one of the moments when I thought it would be good to be a smoker. It would feel pleasant to do something with my fingers and release smoke circles into the crisp air.

It was a very special Boxing Day. Christine and I had been so excited about it. We had discussed whether Philip would change his mind and, as the chief architect of the Paradise project, make a speech, and if so, how he would look on the Globe in the silky white shirt I had bought him for the occasion. It brought out his Mediterranean complexion. Secretly, I hoped he would make the speech so that everyone in the country could see him handsome and bright, and I would burst with pride.

After ten minutes of quiet time, I went in. The combined smell of roasted vegetables and pine needles hit my nostrils. Christine was sprawled across our sofa as if she was at home. She was absorbed in her favourite programme, in which a celebrity offers one of her designer gowns for a charity auction. Only this is no ordinary auction. It is a battle. The ten women who are ready to pay the highest price for the gown have to fight for it, physically. First they must search for the dress, which is packed up in a box and hidden on a closed-off section on the promenade. The real excitement for onlookers and Globe viewers, however, begins when the box is found. The contestants can fight each other without restrictions, including using teeth and nails. There are several ambulance helicopters on the scene, waiting for those with the weakest teeth and shortest nails. Christine was loudly cheering on the woman she was rooting for. I tried to keep my eyes off the screen.

It was still two hours until the Paradise opening ceremony, and Christine was starting to tire me with all her chatter. She was a great shopping partner but not exactly a close friend. I was looking forward to our shopping spree the next day, when we would get to the Paradise by 7am. The first thousand customers would be given a free e-trolley with the words 'My Paradise' on it. We planned to stay all day, and round it off with dinner in a rotating restaurant on the roof. New mini-trains had been introduced to carry shoppers around. We would spend a lot, I knew; the Paradise was in a High-Spender area, targeting High Spenders and those aspiring to join their ranks. I wasn't usually the type to go beyond my budget, but Christine had convinced me I deserved it after an exceptionally difficult term at school.

Christine's conversation was of limited interest; it started and ended with shopping. I was glad when she found a film to watch;

it was a silly rom-com, not really funny, but at least she shut up. I fell into a light doze; the sound of people giggling on the Globe and Christine's occasional remarks always pulling me back.

'So, your father-in-law actually lives in the Zone? Or was that just a joke?' Christine's voice came from the other end of the sofa. She put the Globe on mute. I was surprised that she mentioned the Zone without her usual tone of contempt. The Zone is a segregated, abandoned area on the eastern periphery of London, where the most deprived quarters used to be. A high concrete wall, built at the beginning of the new system, separates it from the rest of the city. It's a no man's land, the only place remaining where life is miserable and death is slow and unassisted. All criminals are exiled there and those non-profit people who – having been active consumers for less than ten years – don't qualify for the Dignitorium.

'Philip is not the type to joke around these days,' I replied, 'and I don't think he would joke about his own father. Yes, Antonio has been living there for years now.'

'How come he's still alive?'

'He took over a large house and formed a self-sustaining community. There are about thirty of them now.'

'Self-sustaining?' Christine snorted. 'Without us providing free water, he and his community wouldn't survive for a day.'

Christine, when sober, was a fairly nice person, but I could see she'd had her fair share of drink by then. Philip, who was far less indulgent than I, would say this was her real personality, freed of any inhibitions by the alcohol, and now I started to see her through his eyes.

'Don't get me wrong,' she said in a conciliatory tone. 'I fully support the Zone residents getting free water.'

I nodded, forcing a half-smile.

'Are those armoured buses as safe as they say?' she asked after a short pause. 'I've been thinking of a visit as a special birthday gift for Paul. We're both dying to know what it's like there. But what if the gangs, you know, attack the bus?'

'It's not for fun, Christine. Most people go there out of necessity. They want to make sure their loved ones are OK.'

Christine rolled her unnaturally blue eyes.

'I mean, relatively OK,' I said. 'That's why we usually go only to the Visitor's Centre. It's been years since we were fully inside the Zone.'

And I don't mean to return there, ever, I thought. We were lucky, yes, that nothing happened last time Philip and I visited Antonio. But in a place abandoned by civilisation, where humans are each other's greatest enemies, anything could have happened to us.

'It's that or the Red Carpet Treatment in Cannes.' Christine's voice brought me back to my living room. 'I think I've decided. Hello, Cannes! At least we're guaranteed to come back in one piece.'

We ate and chatted and wrote a list of what to do in the Paradise the next day. Minutes before 4pm we were ready to watch the live broadcast.

'Philip is an oaf, excuse me for saying so, if he doesn't make this speech. What's his problem exactly?' she asked.

'It's complicated. The area where the Paradise is used to be part of the Zone.'

'So?'

'And hundreds of inhabitants were evicted to make space for the new High-Spender area.'

'I know, there was nothing else on the news for weeks. I still don't see the problem.' She pulled a face.

'You must have heard that many of the evicted froze to death in the streets. Others were killed by the gangs.'

'Oh, those rumours.' She rolled her eyes. 'I mean, look at the Zone, it's still huge; even if we had taken half of it away, there would still be space for thousands. Those who died could have found some shelter if they really wanted to.'

'Philip's father says it's not a rumour. He tried to save–'

'So what's Philip's problem?'

'He doesn't want to give his name to a project that takes away from the disadvantaged and gives to the already rich.'

'For god's sake. Let's not enjoy a meal because there are people out there in the world who are starving, eh?'

'Well, that's not exactly–'

'He accepted the job, didn't he? And the money and status that come with it?' She gave me a piercing look.

'Well…to be honest–'

'Did he?'

'He had no choice but–'

'Hypocrisy, thy name is man!' She let out an exaggerated groan and before I could reply she changed the subject. 'Let's just have a blast tomorrow. I can't wait.' For the sake of being a good neighbour, I said nothing.

She reached out to turn up the volume on the Globe. The reporter, an overly excited blonde woman, was wearing a white fur coat that went well with the festive background. The temperature was below zero but a crowd of hundreds had assembled nonetheless. The people were chanting and cheering, already queuing up with their My Paradise e-trolleys. For a moment they looked to me like a well-equipped and bloodthirsty army, coming closer and closer.

The reporter entered the building right after the managing director. Sparkling Christmas trees and golden-winged angels were suspended from the ceiling in the main hall. The crowd now lost all sense and direction. They flooded in like ants; a mass of miniature black figures flowing over the shiny white floor. Up on the roof terrace, dignitaries from the council, celebrities and politicians stood, holding champagne glasses, chattering away, with the magnificent London skyline stretching behind them. I was scanning their faces to find Philip in the group, but the camera moved too quickly.

I hoped Philip had left the office in time to do his speech. With his talent, he could be promoted within a few years, become a celebrity architect, and design some more iconic buildings. We could finally become High Spenders.

After we got married, Philip and I used to visit High-Spender areas. We liked looking at the mansions in the leafy streets and the exclusive boutiques. The magnitude of space was the thing that struck me the most, reminding me of what Dad had once said about the value of real land when I was a child. I didn't deny it would be good to live somewhere like this. But Philip was reluctant, even after he accepted the Paradise contract, when the possibility of becoming High Spenders was within our grasp. He had always been disgusted by the notion of spending on useless, throw-away stuff just to become and stay High Spenders. I suggested we could do it for just a few months, treat it like a holiday, enjoying the luxury while it lasted and then gladly return to our normal Mid-Spender life afterwards. But in the end we never did.

We never talked about it, but it lingered in the air between us, unsaid but always present. I wasn't sure I would have been able to move back to the Mid-Spender area once I got used to the high life. Downgrading is bad – the twin sister of decay and destitution. It's what old people do when their health deteriorates and they are forced to become Low Spenders. The final step before retiring to the Dignitorium. Downgrading is like dying in slow motion.

I cursed the camera again for moving so quickly. All the men were wearing suits and white shirts, making it impossible to spot Philip. The mayor had just turned to the camera and handed his champagne over to his assistant when the explosion happened. It was so loud and unexpected that for a moment I thought it was the Globe that had exploded in the room. Christine and I jumped up at the same time. The smoke prevented us from seeing anything. We stood there, not knowing whether to stay or run, whether to turn away or keep watching. My blood ran cold. Philip!

I called him immediately but he didn't answer. I tried again and again, hysterically pressing the repeat button on my ID Phone until Christine gently took it out of my hand and helped me to sit down. She made me a strong coffee while I kept watching the Globe for news updates.

'Could you just leave me alone?' I asked her after a while.

She stood there, hesitant, opening her mouth to protest.

'Christine, please.'

I heard her faffing around in the kitchen, then she quietly slipped out of the living room while I was fixed to the screen.

'Call me if you need anything, OK?' she whispered.

I heard her close the apartment door.

I became edgy when the news didn't mention anything about the victims. The news reporter, usually collected and professional, was fighting back tears. Philip still didn't answer his ID phone. I went out to the monorail stop, roamed the streets. People were coming and going, with fear on their faces. All they were talking about was the 'terrorist attack'. I hesitated over where to go first – to Philip's office or to the Paradise. Hoping he hadn't left work, I hurried to his office, a black glass-walled skyscraper in the city centre.

'Everyone left, it's Boxing Day,' the receptionist said. With a trembling voice, I asked him to check what time Philip had left to attend the Paradise opening ceremony.

'Let me see, madam.' While he was searching on his computer, I prayed he would say Philip had gone out earlier, somewhere else, to a building site, perhaps. Or that he was still up in his office and there was a practical reason for him not answering his phone. The receptionist was searching for ages and I started to lose my patience.

'I'm sorry, madam, he didn't come to work today.'

'That's not possible. Could you check it again, please?'

'I checked it three times, madam.'

'What if there's a problem with the system?'

'There's never anything wrong with the system, madam. But if you call tomorrow after nine, one of my colleagues may be able to assist you further.'

I felt goose bumps rising on my skin. He'd left for work that morning after eight, as usual. While on my way to the Paradise, I kept on dialling his number, my hands shaking all the while, but there was no answer.

When I arrived I was hit once more by the scene of destruction. Where the Paradise had stood gleaming, chaos now ruled. The fire had already been extinguished but the scene was still painful to look at. People were being rescued from the debris of the blackened building. The sound of sirens and helicopters mixed with the cries of survivors and family members. The police had formed a human shield around the area, so I couldn't get closer. Dead bodies covered with blankets were carried on stretchers out from the heavy smoke, but when I ran towards one of them I was pulled away by strong arms. A camera was pushed into my face, the reporter asking what I was doing there. I tried to form a coherent sentence but all I could repeat was Philip's name. An announcement asked us to register our missing loved ones, then return home. Half an hour later, the crowd had dissipated, and only a few of us remained, gathering in a park nearby. I kept calling Philip's number and I repeatedly returned yet was always sent away. It was three in the morning when the freezing cold forced me to go home, but I didn't sleep a wink.

On the news they announced that there were forty-two dead and hundreds injured. They believed there had been four suicide bombers, but the numbers were unconfirmed. The 'Warriors' had taken responsibility for the attack. They were on a mission to bring 'traditional' values back to society, murdering those who went shopping on Boxing Day instead of spending Christmas in the 'appropriate' way.

The Prime Minister, Edward Finch, made an emergency appearance on the Globe, broadcast live from his holiday retreat in South Africa. 'We will not allow our enemies to destroy our values,' he said. 'Values of abundance and opportunity, values of wellbeing and fulfilment. We, as a nation, have been through far too much of the opposite.' He paused for effect. 'My family, like so many others in the old system, would queue at the food banks. When the new system began, I swore this would never happen to my children. Since then I have become your Prime Minister, so I extend this promise to future generations. I promise the old times will never return.'

After a sleepless night I went to the police station, increasingly convinced that Philip had been one of the victims of the attack. When I enquired about his final route, they said they had no information. 'What do you mean? You must be able to see his tracker. You can see everyone's.' I was nearly crying. 'It's been de-activated,' they said. When I tried calling him again, his number was no longer in use.

Losing a loved one is nothing like they portray it in films. It tears you apart and leaves you a walking skeleton. The worst part was getting back to the daily routine. It started when I spotted Philip's mug – a chunky white one with a caricature of Beethoven on it – in the sink, waiting to be washed and put away, ready for the next cup of Earl Grey with a dash of full-fat milk. His belongings – his clothes, his towel, his toothbrush – were like extensions of his body, widening the aching gap inside me. The initial shock lessened after the first unbearable week, but it took months before hope, that stubborn little flame, began to fade away. I tried to revive it, but it shrank to a faint glow.

TWO

Sunday mornings are busy on the promenade, especially on days like this when the sun is smiling down on the earth. All week I've been trying to shake off a fear that something terrible is about to happen. Not that my situation could be much worse. My grief gnaws away at me, but if I manage to get over the night, when it's the worst, I can get through the day. Dizzy and exhausted from the medication, but fuelled by coffee, I drag myself along towards my oasis. The bright red monorail to my left slides away with a smooth rumble. The vibrant advert screens are encouraging pedestrians to buy this sofa or that tub of ice-cream, the word 'family' used everywhere to indicate communal joy. To me, the word means nothing.

The walk invigorates me, but I find the growing crowd and the noise of the adverts irritating. I step onto a passing monorail. I'm the only passenger in the carriage. Sitting at the window, I can observe the Sunday faces as the monorail glides alongside the promenade, which, true to its slogan, is a place where life happens.

When I get off the monorail, my feet instinctively carry me faster than before. Just straight down this street, then turn right at the oak tree. It will do me good to switch off after the shock of the past few days. It's already too much. The thought of my penalty points kept me awake all night; I had to turn to Mini-doc again. This time Doctor Graham recommended something called Friends Market, where people can hire companionship. I signed up for the trial period, and found a woman of my age in the area. We made an appointment to meet on the promenade, but when I saw her approaching, looking as if she was on her way to a job interview, I felt a sudden disgust and left. At home I ordered a stronger medication, which I started taking immediately.

I hope that by coming here I can start to heal myself. Finally I arrive at the imposing wrought-iron gate. The golden plate on the high brick wall reads:

DIGNITORIUM – RETIREMENT SOLUTIONS

It feels a bit like a homecoming. One of the guards, a beefy young man, points at a selection of flowers in steel buckets. There are bunches of lilac, freesia, tulips in all colours. I pick a bunch of red and yellow freesia, Mum's favourite. The guard scans my ID Phone, then wishes me a pleasant stay, as if I've checked into a holiday complex.

Before Dignitoriums were introduced, there were other places to remember loved ones. On the outskirts of the city, there are still some old cemeteries, like outdoor museums. I once visited one out of curiosity. It was ancient, crammed with graves that were hundreds of years old, but it was not as beautiful as the Dignitoriums. It's understandable – it's only the living that require beauty.

As a teenager, I was keen to learn more about the old system and how retired people used to live. I discovered that they just lived at home – if they were lucky enough to have one – or in a hospital or, even worse, in the final decades of the old system, in miserable retirement homes, until they met their lonely, painful, and above all slow death. Once they reached a certain age, they were entitled to a government pension, but there was no way they could afford the standards of a Dignitorium. In fact, it provided them with very little. Despite the warnings, I searched for photos of centenarians. I suppose it's human nature to be curious about such morbid things. It's wrong and yet, from time to time, we all search for the pictures.

On seeing the photos my first reaction was disgust, then pity and compassion, and finally a rush of gratitude. Even as an adult the photos gave me nightmares – the poor sods looked like zombies from those horror films shown on the late-night Globe. They suffered a multitude of incurable, debilitating illnesses like dementia before they died, trapped in a decaying body for twenty, thirty, even forty years. They were begging for death but their loved ones could do absolutely nothing to end their suffering; euthanasia was illegal. I consider myself extremely lucky to have been born after those barbaric times.

Although it fascinates me, I don't think I'll return to a cemetery. There was a smell of decay, slightly sweet but with a putrid undertone. It was so strong I could still smell it on my clothes for days. Here in the Dignitorium, there's only the soothing fragrance of lilac.

As I enter the gate and hear it click shut behind me, something otherworldly washes over my exhausted spirit and body. The blossoming trees sway gracefully in the breeze. Flowerbeds carpet the ground in all the colours of the rainbow. A narrow stream coils through ornate gardens, creating tiny islands that are connected by carved wooden bridges. I hear a variety of bird song; Dad once counted eleven different species. This peace and harmony can't be found anywhere else in the city. Here and there, residents with a carer, or visitor, are strolling as if they have all the time in the world. The carers wear grass-green uniforms. The frantic speed of the outside world doesn't penetrate these walls. To my left a group of elderly female residents are practising Tai chi; a young Chinese girl instructor faces the group making the poses, which they all mimic in unison. A grey-haired couple sit on a blanket on the hillside with a picnic basket, enjoying the view. They remind me of my parents.

I make my way to the memory wall which is nearly full with plaques. The names stretch up to the very top; there are sturdy wooden stools in the corner for those who can't reach the name of their loved one. Most names are written on silver plaques, given that this Dignitorium – like the majority of them – is mixed class but caters mostly for Mid Spenders. There are still some names on golden plaques and a significant number on simple bronze ones, too.

It's good I came early on a Saturday morning, for there's no one else here. I try to avoid busy times. When there is a crowd, they all want to be near the wall and touch it, so I have to stand in the second or third row. The hysterical cries disturb my quiet reflection and soon someone else puts their bunch of flowers on top of mine. I don't stand a chance of getting close enough to touch my parents' names. Now I put my left palm over the letters that read 'Evelyn and Ben Walker'; it feels like it's pulsing, Mum and Dad's spirit flowing into me.

I search for a photo of my parents on my ID Phone, and zoom in on their smiling faces. Now we are together. Apart from Sofia. But I don't consider her family. I don't even want to think about her. Where was I? Yes, with Mum and Dad, all together now. I treasure this rare occasion when I'm the closest I can be to feeling connected to them.

I don't know how long I've been here – my palm is ice-cold from the plaque but still pressed to my parents' names. It's starting to get busier. Another hand is reaching out just above my head, and I have to bend down to make room. It feels like an intrusion. I slip out from under the arm and move away, my body numb. My eyes are searching for the bench. That bench. When I find it, in front of a giant hydrangea bush, my eyes rest on it for a long time. I walk closer. This is the nearest bench to the T-wing. It hasn't changed over the years, though the timbers painted in sunny yellow must have witnessed many farewell tears and kisses.

I sit down on it as I did on that autumn day, four years ago. Mum and Dad are with me again. I recall how we embraced each other for the last time before they turned around and left for the T-wing. It was an uplifting moment, so I don't understand why there are tears rolling down my cheeks. I wipe my face with the back of my hand and stand up. I'd like to see the tulip beds in all their kaleidoscopic colours. I walk up the hill. From here I have a lovely view down the lawn, with the lake in the middle sparkling like an oversized crystal. I know for a fact that it's not natural. With Mum and Dad, we saw once how they poured a sack of powder into it that immediately transformed the greyish water into a deep blue.

In the distance, I see the familiar delicate figure of an elderly lady, linking arms with a tall young man. It's Nurse Vogel, who used to look after my parents. If not for her green uniform, one would assume it was the healthy youth taking the fragile older lady for a walk, not the other way around. A small gesture reveals the truth in the next moment when she reaches out for his arm to make sure he doesn't fall as he sits down on the bench. With her lithe movements, Nurse Vogel is the picture of eternal youth. Despite her tiny figure, she radiates an inner strength I have always admired.

The pair are a picture of tranquillity; I can't keep my eyes off them as they relax on the ornate bench in the silvery glow of the early morning sun.

These days all older ladies dye their hair, mostly a blond colour, or a shade of burgundy red for those with a darker complexion. When Dad introduced Nurse Vogel to me shortly after their retirement, it was the first time I had seen grey hair on a woman. Up near the roots it's almost white, while down at the ends it's a darker grey, and slightly frizzy. At first, I found it really quite ugly. But I quickly got used to it. I have to admit that her soft, ash-grey hair, which is tied up in a bun today, suits her. I couldn't begin to imagine her with one of those undulating, golden-blond hairstyles Mum had. The other thing that surprised me back then was her face. There's no sign of any make-up or the skin improvement therapy that older ladies are so keen on. She doesn't even try.

Nurse Vogel and her patient are half-hidden by a bush heavy with yellow roses. In the background, on top of a hill stands the main building, an imposing white mansion. It looks as if cream had been poured all over it. It's the only white Dignitorium in London, a rarity. Elegant sash windows and stuccoed façade invite the visitor hundreds of years back in time. I know that the house is authentic, unlike many of those 'period' mansions in the High-Spender areas. In the old system, before they turned it into a Dignitorium, it functioned as a museum and was called Kenwood House. People could only visit for a few hours before they returned to their shabby homes. They couldn't even dream of living in a place like this.

Finally Nurse Vogel notices me, waves in my direction and I stroll down the hill.

'Alice, I wasn't sure from the distance if it was you.'

'It must be years since we met. This place looks more beautiful than ever!'

'They are trying hard to outdo other Dignitoriums,' she says, sarcasm lacing her voice. 'In my view they are all quite similar. The management easily forgets that they all use the same architects and garden designers.'

She stands up and we give each other a warm hug. I'm afraid she might break in my embrace. Her wise, curious eyes examine me with delight. The playful sparkle hasn't faded one bit. In her mid-seventies, the oldest person I've ever met, Nurse Vogel looks much less hideous than the elderly people featured in history programmes. Amazingly, she still has all her teeth, despite the fact that most people start losing them soon after the age of sixty. Perhaps they are false. Does she have the smell, too? I try not to sit too close. I know it's not her fault; it's what old age does to all of us. Nurse Vogel, born in the seventies of the last century, could be my grandmother.

'How are you these days?' I ask her.

'What can I say?' She shrugs. 'Work, work and more work, all over again. Here, please meet Owen.'

The tall, stocky man on her left flashes a seductive smile in my direction, but his deep brown eyes betray the fact that he is floating somewhere between the real world and another. In his late twenties, he's much younger than the average resident.

'Hello,' he says, grinning. Not waiting for my response, he gives me a big bear-like hug and kisses my cheek.

'Now, Owen, let me find you a lovely game,' Nurse Vogel tells him gently.

'Combat boys, please,' he tells her, still clinging on to me and chuckling.

'Owen, let Alice go, you're suffocating her,' Nurse Vogel says and quickly starts peeling Owen off me.

'It's OK,' I say, smiling back at Owen. 'It's just a happier version of him,' I blurt out before I realise I'm parroting the adverts.

Nurse Vogel holds a mini-screen in front of him and puts a pair of headphones over his ears.

'I love you,' he shouts at me from under the headphones, waving, then buries himself in the video game.

'Isn't he a bit young to be here?' I ask in disbelief.

'More and more of the young end up with us, mostly executives who are on top of the world one day, and for one reason or another the next day are…well, here.' Nurse Vogel pats Owen on the shoulder as if he's a high-achieving schoolboy, and sits down next to him. It's funny, he is more than double her size.

'Tell me, how have you been coping?' she asks, offering me a seat on her right.

'I'm OK now, thank you.'

'I remember how it wore you out. It's not easy to lose one's parents, at any age. It reminds us that it will soon be our turn.'

'And you? How is your back? Did you manage to get the money for the operation?'

'Not yet. By the time I save up for it, I probably won't need the operation any more.' She laughs and I'm shocked at how she can be so light-hearted about it. 'But it's bearable.'

'I was quite surprised to see you here,' I blurt out. 'I assumed you'd be…retired by now.'

'Oh, no. When I go, I'll go quickly.'

'Yes, but…why avoid the pleasurable part? There must be a reason why ninety-six per cent of people choose retirement over instant euthanasia. They said it on the Globe. It must be a dream to live in a place like this, starting every day in the spa, then off to Eternal Peace classes, then having a four-course meal for dinner.'

'It's not really—'

'Mum couldn't stop raving about the food. She told me how she and Dad would go to the open-air restaurant overlooking the lake, where the jazz band on the terrace began to play and when the waiter lit the candle on their table, Mum always took Dad's hand. They had just such a perfect moment, every single evening. They completely understood why the first six months are called the honeymoon period.'

'That's the slang for it, yes. Officially it's called Pre-Sedation Period.'

'And when their Sedation Period began, it was great, too. They remained themselves, just a happier version.' I glance at Owen, who is still giggling and fervently pushing the buttons on the mini-screen. 'When the sedation stopped for their last day, so that we could say our goodbyes, even with a clear mind they weren't afraid of death any more. They knew, just as I did, that they were going to a wonderful place.'

Nurse Vogel's eyes turn darker. She watches a tree branch stirring in the wind.

'How is Philip?'

I don't respond.

'I still remember how good you and he were together. The way he looked at you.'

I'm unsure of what to say, whether to burden her with my problems. Nurse Vogel turns to me and I'm forced to look into her eyes.

'What's wrong, Alice?'

'He disappeared.'

'Disappeared?'

'It was on Boxing Day.'

'In the explosion?'

I nod, but can't say a word. We are quiet for several moments, and she probably senses that I might break down if she asks any more.

'Poor soul, you have only his eccentric father now.' She exhales deeply. 'Mind you, I quite liked him, I thought he was a true independent.'

'He's gone completely off the rails since then. He moved to the Zone. Voluntarily.'

She pulls a face of disbelief then shuffles closer and gives me a hug, a long and heartfelt one; her compassion is heart-warming.

'So you have no one left now.'

'No one.'

'If you need to talk, anytime, let me know,' she says, patting my shoulder. 'Just call me.'

'It would mean a lot. But you're so busy–'

'Helping others is what keeps me alive. Try to see it that way.'

We sit there quietly, enjoying the silence, when suddenly her gaze moves up to the dense canopy of an elm tree opposite us. My gaze follows hers.

'Don't! Please, don't look that way,' she whispers.

'Why?'

Ignoring my question, she checks the time on her watch and stands up gracefully.

'Give me a ring tonight,' she tells me, avoiding meeting my eye, before turning to Owen. 'Time to go in, darling,' she tells him, like a mother to her child.

I don't understand what's happened but I know she's on duty so I don't want to hold her up.

'What about working here?' she asks, hurriedly bidding me goodbye. 'It's much less stressful than teaching.'

'I've already thought about it, Nurse Vogel. But I'm not as strong as you are. I couldn't do…this.' And I steal a side-glance at Owen.

Seeing my parents' names on the memory wall and the little chat with Nurse Vogel has made me feel a bit lighter as I make my way back home along the promenade. I'm bewitched by the Sunday lunchtime cavalcade, how it swirls and dances and fuels itself with the energy of pleasure. I don't see a single sad face. Everyone smiles as if it's the default human condition. Just by walking here, just by being myself, I'm a killjoy. An aching loneliness settles in my bones.

I leave the promenade and walk across the lawn. The first building on my right is our old home, the one I had to leave in February. It's a sleek four-storey condo surfaced in deep-red brick and wooden panels. It doesn't let me forget. Whenever I pass it, I can't help but look up to the roof terrace. Our terrace. Usually I take another route, to avoid the building, but today I feel like facing it. The silver paint on the rail is sparkling in the sun; Philip repainted it just last year. The new inhabitants must have discovered the sunniest spot, as I can see the top of a lounger in the corner, the same place where I used to sit.

The ash-blond woman is on my terrace again; the woman who took our home. She put up that boring grey-blue curtain in our bedroom, which I feel like tearing down. I want to tell her it's our home, Philip's and mine. But there's no Philip, he might be just a pile of grey dust, and I don't even have the solace of seeing his name written on a commemorative plaque.

I don't stop and after passing three condos I arrive at mine. When I was a child we still used keys. Mum could never find them in her bag. I remember one winter when we arrived home and she had to throw everything from her bag onto the frozen pavement. It took her minutes to find the keys but then her hands were so stiff she couldn't hold them. I can still see her blowing hot air onto her palms, rubbing her hands together before she could turn the key in the lock.

All that is in the past now. By lifting my left wrist to the scanner, I open the gate with my ID Phone and make my way upstairs. From my usual spot by the window, I see that the courtyard is almost empty – even the reading woman seems to be away. I have a perfect view of the apartment right under hers. It's painful to watch but I can't help it. The young girl on the balcony, no older than nineteen, is wearing white sensory sunglasses for the blind while feeling for the clothes she hangs on the line. She hangs them as neatly as anyone with normal eyesight. His jeans, his shirts, his underwear. At first I thought they were grandfather and daughter, but I've seen far too much. Gratitude and respect are reflected in her every move – just for being alive.

My thoughts return to Nurse Vogel's behaviour this morning. It's strange how nervous she became all of a sudden. I know she was on duty but there was something else. She looked like she was afraid. No doubt it's age-related paranoia.

I'm unsure whether to trust her with my problems. I know she asked me to call her but I don't know how strongly she's affected by old age. Maybe – unbeknown to her – she will do more harm than good.

Once I see her smiling eyes on my screen, I know I've done the right thing. She's nestling in a large puffy armchair, and her room is lit by a cosy subdued light. She's back to her normal self, there's no sign of the earlier fear on her face. I feel warm comfort spreading through my body.

'Right,' she says, sighing with relief. 'Now we can talk undisturbed.'

'Undisturbed by whom?'

'Dignitorium staff are not supposed to get into conversation with visitors while on duty.'

'Were you being watched?'

'We are all being watched, my dear.'

'But it's for the residents' safety.'

'It is indeed.'

'Since we met, I haven't been able to get Owen out of my head. As a successful executive, how could he end up in the Dignitorium?'

'When his firm went bankrupt, he lost everything, including his mental health. He couldn't earn his Right To Reside any more. It sounds so terrifyingly easy, doesn't it?'

'But it's so… I don't know.'

'I know, my dear. I've done this for decades, but it's still heartbreaking when a young one comes to us. Sometimes, however, I think it's still the best option for them.'

'At least in the Dignitorium he's safe from the abductions,' I say with unease.

'Oh, don't even get me started on that,' she waves dismissively. 'I have been campaigning for years to have the Zone restructured. If more of those criminals get out, who knows what could happen to us?'

I can't help but admire Nurse Vogel's strength, being able to campaign for what she believes in at her age. But she's right. The number of abductions in the Low-Spender areas has doubled in the past few years and it is an open secret that the High Spenders are behind it, earning a fortune by trading in human organs. They wouldn't do the work themselves, of course. They employ corruptible Zone residents, most of whom are so desperate they would do anything to survive. Not having trackers, they are perfect for the job.

'You have no reason to worry as a Mid Spender, it was a one-off,' she says.

It's easy for her to think like this. But I'm still disturbed by the horrible event that shook the foundations of our society a few years ago, when three Mid-Spender children were abducted on their way home from school. From my school. I'm about to tell her this when all of a sudden her face turns a deathly white. Her eyes are fixed on something above the camera.

'Is something wrong?' I ask.

'Hang on a minute,' she says. She must have put her ID Phone on the table, because all I can see now is the wall with a painting hanging askew. I try to listen for noises, but all I hear is Nurse Vogel shuffling around the room. When her face finally reappears on the screen, she's like a different person.

'What's happened, Nurse Vogel?'

'I'm not sure. It's probably nothing.'

'Nurse Vogel, are you all right? You look like you've seen a ghost.'

'I wish it was a ghost, Alice,' she mumbles, her eyes darting around the room. 'I must put this down.' I don't know if she's talking to me or to herself.

She apologises and, without waiting for my reply, hangs up. I have no idea what frightened her. I hesitate over whether I should call her back, to ask if she needs any help. Finally I decide to drop her a message. She replies immediately. 'Please don't worry about me!'

WOLF COUNTRY

The deep humming of the monorail lulled me into a dreamlike state. Through half-closed eyes I watched the running lines of trees and sheep grazing in the fields. I supposed Dad was also snoozing next to me, but I was too sleepy to turn my head. This was my very first time in the countryside – a birthday gift from my parents and I was fizzing with excitement. That week I turned sixteen, the same age as Sofia when she'd left us three years earlier, for good. Voices rose from the seats behind me. An older lady was travelling with her daughter to Chatsworth House, where she would be retiring. I overheard her saying that it used to be the private home of an aristocrat, but had been converted into a grand Dignitorium for the cream of High Spenders.

The two women stood up, the older lady giddy with anticipation as she walked down the corridor to the restaurant car. She was wearing a short-sleeved summer dress, decorated with flowers, and a purple fascinator in her hair. But the youthful clothes couldn't hide her sagging skin and the disgusting brown spots on her hands and arms. She must be over seventy, I thought. A rarity, probably a privileged High Spender who could afford to live forever. But even she couldn't buy her way out of a rotting, decaying body. Dad nudged me gently with his elbow.

'Good morning, Princess Alice. Don't miss out on the view.'

I sat up and bent forward to have a closer look at the landscape I had seen only on the Globe. I touched the cold surface, as if I wanted to make sure it was real.

'This is incredible, Dad. It's huge, it's everywhere.'

My head was still filled with the conversation I'd just overheard. I was wondering how I would feel when the time came for my parents to retire and I escorted them to their Dignitorium. My stomach turned. Sofia was right about my being selfish: it was selfish wanting them to stay with me in their miserable old age instead of letting them enjoy the most beautiful months of their lives, preparing for their final departure in a dignified way. I scolded myself for letting such bleak thoughts even cross my mind when Mum and Dad were only in their early forties.

Dad was lost in thought.

'What are you thinking about?'

'I'm planning the day ahead. Look…' and he took a folded paper out of his pocket. On the cover it said: Map of the Peak District.

'This is what people used before the digital age.' The map smelled funny, like it had been rescued from an ancient attic.

'I've booked two lovely rooms in a guesthouse called Rose Cottage.'

'Thanks, Dad.' I patted his hand.

I couldn't believe the majesty of the landscape. This is how the Owners live! This is how Sofia lives! I pushed the bitterness away. I couldn't let Sofia ruin my day – not this day that I'd been looking forward to all month.

The further your destination was from a mega-city, the more expensive the fare. Tickets to settlements with countryside-access such as Bakewell cost a small fortune, but when it came to me, Dad didn't care about the price. The landscape outside changed, turning dark. Heavy clouds filled the sky, threatening rain. In the distance, I spotted rolling hills embracing a city. Dad was staring out of the window with a look of yearning in his eyes. For a moment I could see him as a little boy, running over these hills, or riding his bike on these streets. Soon the monorail arrived in Sheffield. The station was built into the side of a hill, providing a full view of the city's ultramodern skyline.

'Have you ever thought of moving back here?' I asked Dad.

'Sometimes. We could have been given a three-storey detached villa here. But your mother wouldn't even consider it.'

'Why?'

'There's not much of the high life here.'

The monorail halted in a glass-covered tunnel and we got off. I looked around me on the platform. This was my first time in the north of England and it was clear this was a very different world from London.

Soon we embarked on the next monorail. Once we left Sheffield, the buffet-belt under the window started moving, carrying drinks, sandwiches, sweets and newspapers. I took two sandwiches out and we ate quietly. When Dad had finished, he suddenly said: 'I wasn't a good father to her, Ali. I'm sorry, but it's the truth.'

I sat there, petrified, until I realised Dad was talking about Sofia.

'Dad, you were and still are the perfect father.'

'No, no, you don't understand. Let me explain. I failed to hide how I felt about her, and she knew it. For example, when we learned that she had betrayed Grandma. I stopped caring for her that day.'

His serious tone was starting to scare me.

'Dad, don't be harsh on yourself. You were in shock.'

'I've never told anyone about this. That day when she admitted to betraying Grandma, I was relieved. I was afraid the house had been bugged. You were only small, but maybe you remember. There were certain things that worried me when the new system came in. I was terrified for you.'

'For me?'

'I didn't want you to grow up in a world that is rotten to the core. When Sofia admitted the truth, my faith in the new system was restored. I could believe in a future for you after all.'

'You doubted I had a future?'

He sighed and hugged me.

'For a father it is the most important thing in the world – you'll understand when you become a parent yourself. Your happiness and safety was the only measure. But not hers. That didn't even cross my mind.'

He looked away and fumbled with his jacket sleeve.

'And I can tell you, Ali, that she sensed my relief. In that moment she understood that from the depth of my heart I cared only for you. I can't shake off the sense that I was responsible for what she became after that. No wonder they say war begins at home, in the family. It was I who–'

'Don't let her make you feel guilty, Dad. She's very good at that, you know. Meanwhile, she's enjoying the high life as an Owner.'

He was staring ahead and held my hand tightly in his. I would have done anything to have a magic sponge to wipe away his misery.

'I've never been so excited. Thank you for planning all this.'

His face lit up, and I could see he had decided not to ruin my special day by bringing up Sofia again.

To me, Sofia's betrayal of Nana hadn't come as a shock. I had always sensed she had a kind of emotional disability. The day after

Grandma retired, I knocked on Sofia's laboratory door. When she let me in, without the slightest sign of guilt on her face, I didn't beat around the bush.

'Why did you betray Grandma?' I asked.

'Go away!' she said, not looking up from her microscope.

'I just don't get it. You've always wanted to help old people. You wanted to stop ageing.'

'No. I wanted to stop them being a burden on society.'

'How can you say that? They're not a burden. They…they just live, like all of us.'

'I can see Dad explained it in vain,' she said.

'Explained what?'

'Why the old system collapsed.'

'Grandma didn't do anything!' I cried out.

She rolled her eyes, then stood up and started pushing me towards the door.

'Tell me what Grandma did!'

'You wouldn't understand,' she said, and slammed the door in my face.

Our monorail arrived in Bakewell, a former village. We had learned at school that villages used to be little settlements, much less convenient than cities, whose inhabitants lived in primitive conditions, many of them having been forced out of cities by the high living costs. In the new system, with everyone assigned free accommodation in the megacities, the village became completely unnecessary. Farmers and agricultural workers were delighted that, thanks to the new high-speed transport, they could travel out to the countryside in no time, and return to civilisation at the end of the working day.

Village-dwellers who didn't work on the land had been at a great disadvantage, for there were few job opportunities and very little entertainment. I couldn't believe people really had to put up with living in such isolated and backward places. By now the remaining villages were fully commercialised: visitors accustomed to city life could stay in the cottages that had been converted into guesthouses; others had been made into restaurants, museums and, most importantly, souvenir shops. Once we got off the monorail, we were transported into the past. I marvelled at the rustic bakeries, tea rooms and antique shops, and posed for photos.

The veteran car-taxi was a whole new experience. The one we hired was blood-red and allegedly from the 1950s. We were driven really slowly and attracted looks of astonishment from the pedestrians around us. The taxi took us around Bakewell, but the end of the village was closed off with a red wire fence and a plaque that read: 'Warning! Predatory wolves beyond this point.' We got out of the taxi and gazed beyond the fence. There was no sign of any human dwelling, only the vast green of hills and valleys stretching out, untouched, before us.

'This is one of the rare places where you can walk in the countryside before you get to the fence,' Dad said. 'Not too far, about a square mile, but it will do.'

'Will we see wolves?'

'We might.'

There was a sign indicating a narrow path on the left. The taxi driver advised us to walk for five minutes alongside the fence and then we would get to the open countryside. Once there, we saw a few other families who had come to the furthest point of the safe area, some of them standing just next to the fence. They had cameras ready; Dad said they were waiting for wolves. I wanted to see the wolves too, but first we took a long walk. It was a new experience for me, as I ran up and down the meadow, feeling the crisp air on my skin. I got tired after an hour and we sat on top of a huge rock, which was the highest point in sight, and felt as if we were suspended between earth and sky. Dad was very quiet all day. I think he was still torturing himself about Sofia, although he was trying hard to conceal it.

The silence was shattered by the sound of a helicopter, cutting through the air like thunder. The whirring became louder and soon we saw it hovering over the woods down in the valley, approaching the meadow. It was about to land. I wondered who would want to land in the middle of the fields. Dad said it was probably a High Spender who felt he was above taking the monorail. He pulled a face; I found it funny how he never even tried to hide his feelings about High Spenders. I hated them too, and now they were about to ruin the quiet beauty of our trip. I wanted to suggest that we return to the guesthouse and come back later, when I saw the helicopter prepare for landing beyond the fence.

'Dad! Look, they're going to land in the wolf zone.'

'No way! What is that crazy pilot doing?'

The other families stopped their barbecues or whatever they were doing, ran to the fence and held up their ID Phones to record the incident.

'Don't worry, sweetie,' Dad said. 'They probably have guns. It might be an Owner surrounded by soldiers.'

The helicopter landed and we held our breath and waited. Soon a dark green jeep appeared on the road beyond and stopped near the helicopter. Three men in military-style uniforms jumped out of the vehicle with some equipment and disappeared into the depths of the forest. My heart stopped beating; they didn't have any guns with them. Some minutes later, they returned, and I was shocked to see that two of them were carrying a stretcher with a bloody bundle on it. The onlookers gasped in horror and began taking photos. The third man was pushing a broken bicycle out of the woods. It must have belonged to the dead man, probably a reckless biker, tempting fate despite the warnings. We assumed the three men would be in a rush to put the body and the bike in the van and get in before the wolves could return. But they just kept messing around. A few spectators began yelling to the guys to hurry up. I nearly started screaming. Dad said they might have guns in their pockets, but I looked very closely and couldn't see any evidence of it. And what if a wolf attacks unexpectedly, I thought; the men might not have enough time to react and shoot.

The next moment a man emerged from the forest. He was middle-aged, with dark blond hair, and victory written across his tanned face. He wore a dark green uniform in the same colour as the jeep. On his back he carried a long rifle. Dad and I sighed with relief. The other onlookers calmed down, too. So that's why the three men were so relaxed: they knew the guy with the rifle, probably a hobby hunter, was behind them and would protect them. Dad and I went to the nearest part of the fence to get a better view. Everyone else was there, chatting excitedly. The three men finally put the body and the bicycle into the vehicle. The hunter stayed speaking for a while with the jeep driver. We all expected to see the wolf's carcass carried out of the forest shortly. Everyone pointed their cameras, ready to start recording. Even Dad turned the camera of his ID Phone on. Someone whispered there might be more than one wolf. People said that the police would come soon, some even suggested an ambulance, but this was unlikely as it was clearly too late.

Still, nothing happened. After a few minutes of conversation, the driver closed the van door and drove away. The hunter climbed aboard the helicopter and left. Dad said they had probably left the wolf's carcass in the forest so the other wolves could feed on it. I could sense people's disappointment that they hadn't seen the dead wolf. I felt the same way and couldn't stop thinking about the accident even when we walked back to the guesthouse.

At dinner, the waiter served my favourite, a rocky road cake with my name written on it in tiny marshmallows, but my mind was still on the bloody bundle on the stretcher. In the meantime, I was relieved by the fact that I was not the only one tortured by Sofia and even a strong, grown-up man like Dad could be hurt by her.

The next morning we visited a farm where animals were kept for demonstration purposes. I was disgusted by the horrible smell and by how boring and dirty the cow was. I couldn't believe that milk came from such a sickening place. Then we went to the farm shop where we bought Mum a plastic cow the size of a toaster, in which to store milk. Its oversized udders were made to look and feel like real ones and had to be milked. I thought Mum would love it, and she did indeed. None of her friends had anything like it, but when they saw ours, they all decided to get one.

The sense of freedom I'd experienced in the countryside was new to me and I craved more of it. When we returned to London the next day, I told Dad I wanted to become a doctor or a lawyer to earn a lot of money and come to the countryside every weekend. Dad chuckled and said that those sorts of people didn't have proper weekends and I'd do better to become a gardener if I liked the outdoors.

THREE

This room feels familiar. Maybe it's the way the declining sun shines in through the sash window, just as it does on my balcony at home. My eyes are drawn to the pots of cacti Ms Hayashi, the crisis advisor, crams into her little office. They are everywhere, on the windowsill, on the bookshelf, on the edge of her desk. Hundreds of tiny thorns, directed at me. Ms Hayashi resembles an ostrich, her head balancing on top of a long thin neck. Most of her little consulting room is taken up by two oversized armchairs facing each other. The armchairs are covered with soft orange and yellow blankets, inviting the person in crisis to sink into sunny comfort.

All it takes is Ms Hayashi asking 'How can I help?' and all the pain of the last few months comes pouring out. The conversation is recorded so that she can pay full attention without having to make notes. A lovely gesture. She looks at me attentively with her bright green eyes as I tell her my sad story of husband lost, home downgraded, work jeopardised, and dreams shattered. She leans slightly closer to examine me.

'If I understand correctly, Alice, it was the loss of your husband that triggered all this. It seems to me that after the death of your parents, your relationship with Philip was still strong.'

'For a while, yes, but lately we had drifted apart. The stress at work didn't help either – you know how it is. He became more and more withdrawn.'

'Do you have any idea why?'

'He began to isolate himself. For example, he stopped his early morning gym and his weekend cycling club, without which he couldn't have coped before. He bought himself an exercise bike to use at home, an expensive one that simulates outdoor cycling. But he used it less and less frequently.'

'How did you react?'

'I kept asking what was wrong but he didn't reply. I hoped one day he would overcome his inner demons. I hoped that we could start a family, have a future.'

'Did you do anything else? Apart from hoping?'

'I'm sorry?'

'Never mind,' she says and holds out a tray of chocolate biscuits. 'Let's be realistic, Alice. If he can't be tracked, I know it hurts, but it's very likely he's dead. And if he's dead, you need to sort out your life. On your own. A crisis advisor is not a counsellor, this one-off session wouldn't be enough for that, I hope you understand. Also, I'm afraid you're running out of time.'

'If I move into a Low-Spender area–'

She gives me a sharp look, as piercing as the spines of one of her cacti.

'Of course, I would like to avoid it,' I murmur.

She nods.

'Going downhill, becoming a Low Spender is something that happens to the elderly and the terminally ill, not to someone of your age, Alice. You should be aiming higher. Why not spend your savings on an excellent psychologist?'

'Would it bring my husband back? Would it give me the answers I need?'

She holds my gaze.

'If you can't get up, Alice, there's only one way out. I'm really ashamed to even mention this to a young lady like you.'

'Do you mean…the Dignitorium?'

'Have you been working for at least ten years?'

'I started working when I was twenty-one. Thirteen years ago.'

'Good. So you're eligible for retirement in the Dignitorium. But are you aware there is an alternative to retirement?'

'Instant euthanasia?'

'You would feel nothing.'

'Hang on, Ms Hayashi.' I can hear the anxiety distorting my voice. 'You're telling a 34-year-old woman, who came to you for help, that death is the only option?'

'Don't get so upset, Alice. Quite the contrary! I'm trying to tell you that either you stand up and carry on or you let yourself go and fall. If you fall, instant euthanasia is an option. But I wholeheartedly wish you will be able to get yourself together. Recover and keep on working, consuming, enjoying life. Maybe if you could find a boyfriend–'

'But…I'm married.'

'You don't have to love him. Just find someone to keep contributing for your Right To Reside. That should be your priority. If you really want to live, of course.'

I'm struggling to speak.

'Many other women do it, Alice.' The woman who is always reading in my condo comes to mind. I feel sick.

'You can't be serious.'

She gets up and walks over to the window. She looks down

at me, a mixture of patronising authority and compassion in her bulging eyes. The cacti on the shelf behind her are watching me intently, like a miniature army, sharpening their thorns. I should just go.

'I'm only talking from a realistic point of view, Alice. I know the rules of this world, it seems, better than you do.'

My whole body is shaking and I'm unable to hold the tears back. I have to turn away, I don't want this woman to see me cry. She pushes a box of tissues in front of me. Her voice sounds slightly softer now.

'It doesn't have to be a psychologist. Do you really not have anyone to talk to? A close friend?'

'Philip and my parents were the only people I was close to. I don't have anyone else but…'

'Yes?'

'There is Philip's father. But he is useless. He lives in the Zone.' She snorts.

'Any brothers, sisters, cousins?'

I hesitate for a moment as if I need to think about the answer. Do I have a sister? Or do I not? I shake my head and stand up, ready to go. I'm going to be sick.

'One more thing, Alice,' she says when I'm at the door.

I make an effort to turn around.

'I really hope I'm wrong, but have you ever considered that Philip was not a victim of the explosion?'

'What do you mean?'

'You said yourself that he despised the custom of Boxing Day shopping. And he didn't turn up at work that day. What if he wasn't a victim? What if he was involved in the terrorist attacks?'

'That is…impossible.'

'It could also explain why there was so little money left in his account.'

'You don't know him! How can you –?'

'Was Philip an anti-consumerist, a freedom seeker, the type who secretly disappeared, allegedly to enjoy nature, for a whole weekend? And then came home more withdrawn than ever, but with a glint of something indescribable in his eyes?'

Philip used to say Boxing Day shoppers were feeding this rotten system. It's on the tip of my tongue, as a part of me is desperate to pour my heart out to this woman, but I have enough sense to hold back.

'Leave him out of this. Please.' I drag myself out of the room, but my legs won't carry me beyond the waiting area. Blurred faces follow me as I collapse into an armchair in the corner. I try to get up but drop back into the seat. I can't see through my tears anyway.

Looking out of the window from my apartment, watching the more capable part of the world go by, only makes me feel worse, but it's addictive. The courtyard is swimming in the sunshine and my eyes wander idly over to the apartments on the opposite side. The reading woman looks as if she's on holiday, the way she's sprawling in her hammock, wearing white hot pants and a bikini top. There's something comforting in watching her; she's one of the few certainties in my life right now, though I've never met her and she doesn't even know I exist. Out of the blue, she slams her book down and runs inside. Not long after, she closes the balcony door and draws the heavy curtain. It's rare that she has a visitor in the daytime; most of them come in the evening. I try to ignore the pinch of jealousy in my gut; it can't be real, I can't be jealous of a woman like that. But then I have to admit there are moments when I would swap this icy loneliness for any company at all.

I look back at the courtyard. Two older ladies are chatting away on the bench, their purple shoes matching their handbags. The confidence that oozes from a young woman in a leather mini-skirt irritates me; her highlighted hair and designer sunglasses make me feel like an outcast, like someone who doesn't belong to the club any more. I feel less envious when my eyes fall on her ankle, still wrapped in a plaster cast from last month when she fell and injured herself in a two-minute All You Can Grab competition at the supermarket.

Ms Hayashi's words are still gnawing at me. What a strange woman, as contradictory as her office, welcoming and thorny at the same time. How dare she accuse Philip of being one of the Boxing Day terrorists…

How did I end up like this, in danger of premature retirement or instant euthanasia? I mustn't even consider what Ms Hayashi said. I turn on the Mini-doc on my wrist and re-take the test. Doctor Graham says that my condition has deteriorated. I'm more depressed, more anxious. It takes about two weeks for the medicine to kick in, he says, and suggests that I wait and try to relax. If only.

I make myself a cup of tea and sit down on the sofa with the warm mug between my palms, trying to gain comfort from the heat. But I can't sit still. Ms Hayashi's question keeps running through my head. 'Was he an anti-consumerist, a freedom seeker…?'

Philip was a good person, not capable of hurting anyone. The tea burns my throat. '…the type who secretly disappeared, allegedly to nature, for a whole weekend…?'

I have an urge to speak to someone other than Ms Hayashi. Before I know it, I'm calling the only person I feel I can confide in. Soon Nurse Vogel's familiar smiling face appears on the screen of my ID Phone, the twinkle in her eyes as fresh as ever. Behind her the room is filled with bookshelves, but there's no Globe in sight and when I ask her she tells me she doesn't need one. Today she is back to her old self, full of life and relaxed, wearing her hair down.

'What happened to you yesterday?' I ask. 'Did you see something?'

'Never mind, my dear. I'm just a silly old woman.'

'No, you're not. Was it something you saw in your flat?'

'There are some peculiar things happening here,' she looks around, lowering her voice. 'Small objects – chairs, dishes – are moved, things like that. Little things that are meant to make me doubt my sanity.'

'The authorities?'

She nods.

'One of my favourite photos of my late husband disappeared from the bookshelf. I noticed it was missing when we were talking.'

'But how is that possible?'

'It's not the first time. Anyway, I don't want to burden you with my troubles,' she says, and I can see I won't be able to get any more out of her. 'But there's something I forgot to ask about Philip. What did his tracker show?'

'Nothing; it was disabled,' I reply. 'His body has never been found. Or that's what they tell me. To conceal the truth.'

'What truth?'

'That he was one of the terrorists.'

'Of course Philip was not a terrorist.'

'I don't know any more, to be honest. He always disliked people who went shopping on Boxing Day. Maybe at weekends he secretly went to 'Warriors' meetings.'

'Have you spoken to someone about this?' Her voice suddenly drops to a whisper.

'What do you mean?'

'In your right mind you'd never assume Philip was a terrorist.'

'Yes, when she mentioned it first, it sounded mad. But then I thought about it and I came to the conclusion–'

'Who did you speak to, Alice?'

'I went to the crisis advisor this morning, that's all.'

She exhales deeply and rolls her eyes.

'Can you promise me something?' Her voice is barely louder than a murmur but there's an edge to it. 'Don't go there again. If they get in touch, tell them you feel much better. Lie that you've recovered. Say that you've confided in a friend who helped a lot. Feel free to mention my name.'

'Why?'

'More and more of our patients come to us from crisis advisors.' I have to lean closer to hear what she's saying. 'Dignitorium agents, that's what we call them.'

'But…I just had a chat with her.'

'They are there to assess your state, and if they find you weak and unlikely to recover, they frighten you with nonsense like Philip being a terrorist. To push you further towards the abyss you're heading for anyway.'

I don't see the point of this. I try to keep a straight face but I'm sure working at the Dignitorium too long must have gone to Nurse Vogel's head. Has her age finally started to take its toll? I wouldn't hold it against her. Yes, Ms Hayashi really upset me but recently everything upsets me. It's ridiculous.

'Are you taking medication?' She breaks the silence. Next, she'll say my pills are poisoned. Nurse Vogel is kind but this is going too far.

'No. I'm not a fan of Mini-doc.'

'Good. Keep it that way.'

'OK.'

'And for once and for all, get it out of your head that Philip was a terrorist.'

THE ARTIST'S SON

When I was eighteen, the long-awaited Prom Night marked the start of adult life. During the ceremony they declared that we were now contributors. After the performances and a long-winded speech by the head teacher, we were each given a grown-up version of the ID Phone with a fully licensed Buy-O-Meter app on it. This phone looked serious in comparison to the plastic toy-like gadgets we were now putting back in a huge basket. Most importantly, it didn't have a spending limit set by our parents any more.

My skin protested as the smooth, ice-cold steel was attached to my wrist. For a moment the click and grip felt like handcuffs, but I shrugged off the thought and reminded myself of the gravity of the occasion. The government had kindly topped up our Buy-O-Meters with enough for a month's consumption to qualify as a Mid Spender, just to get us started. Everyone around me was elated. For some reason, the thought of unlimited consuming frightened rather than pleased me; even though it was in reality far from unlimited, it felt that way to us. Like children in a candy shop, we all went mad shopping and bought heaps of clothes and accessories. At the same time, I was aware that the golden days of carefree adolescence were over and that I was expected to earn my Right To Reside.

My first job was in a nursery. During lunchtime, while all the other staff snuck out to post something or chat on Yap!, I watched the toddlers from the corner. I would imagine myself as a mother, coming to pick my child up, standing at the door at 5pm, feeling the tiny soft palms on the back of my neck, the weight in my arms, even the little knees kicking into my belly. Something was missing, though, apart from a boyfriend. For over a year I couldn't work out what it was. All I knew was that I craved more. New clothes, new restaurants, the odd holiday – nothing quite filled the gap. When I saw an advert for an evening teaching course at Central London University, I realised it was the intellectual stimulation that I had been missing in the nursery work. My parents were really proud of my ambitions and Dad was happy to help me out with the course fee. They said that with a degree, my Mid Spender future would now be guaranteed.

I did my training at a primary school in a Low-Spender area on the outskirts of London. I felt an aura of safety in the building, as if it was padded with cotton wool to shield pupils from the outside world. One spring afternoon, not long before my twenty-first birthday, I went into the staff room after lunch to get a hot drink. Aisha, the teacher in charge of training me, and the head teacher, Sudir, were discussing the Everyday Heroes. Once a month they would invite in someone who had done something heroic, as a positive example to the children. This time they were struggling to find anyone.

'I have someone in mind,' Aisha said, between two bites of her cucumber sandwich.

'Hope it's not another kitten saver,' Sudir joked.

'No, this one's a real hero for a change,' Aisha replied, and her eyes lit up with excitement. 'I saw it in the morning paper. An older man attempted suicide by jumping into the Thames during a storm and this younger guy leapt in after him despite the weather and poor visibility, risking his own life.'

I was about to join in and share my enthusiasm for the idea, but Sudir shook his head.

'It's too harsh for our kids, learning about suicide at such an early age.'

'Look, Sudir.' Aisha was not the type who gave up easily. 'They'll have to face the real world one day. Many of them already know about euthanasia, Dignitoriums and the Zone. Some of them know about things that are far worse.'

There was a short silence. I could hear a fly buzzing at the window and then hitting it hard and dropping onto the table below.

'Not in my school.'

'I keep telling you guys I've got this firefighter neighbour,' a teacher called John piped up from the corner of the room. 'He doesn't mind coming back for a second round.'

'There's no point inviting the same person twice, John.' Aisha rolled her eyes.

'We could leave the suicide part out,' I suggested. 'We could just say it was a boating accident.'

Sudir looked at me. I could see he was considering it. He nodded.

'Cool,' Aisha exclaimed. 'I'll contact the paper where I saw the article.'

'What's his name?' John called out.

'Philip Brunelli. That's the lifesaver. And the guy he saved is his father.'

When, a few days later, Aisha brought the article in, I saw a dark, wavy-haired man in his late-twenties, lean and attractive despite the sadness in his eyes. Soaking wet, his hair and clothes sticking to his body, he was hugging an older man with a similarly dark complexion and an empty look in his eyes. The hero turned out to be an up-and-coming architect responsible for the design of many of the city's newest buildings. Whenever Philip Brunelli's name was mentioned in the staffroom, I couldn't help listening in.

The day of Philip's visit arrived, and the pupils and teachers gathered in the sports hall. Pupils sat on the parqueted floor, while the staff took folding chairs along the wall.

Philip immediately caught my attention as he stood at the side of the stage, chatting to Aisha. There was something about him, the way he was listening so attentively, nodding occasionally, standing with a straight back in corduroy trousers and a black turtle-neck jumper. When he spoke into the microphone, his voice was rich and husky.

'I had arranged to meet my dad that morning but I arrived way earlier,' he said. 'It's pure coincidence that I looked down at the river as I was crossing over, for we were supposed to meet on the opposite bank. At that moment, when I saw him from the bridge, turning over in his hobby boat, nothing else mattered but to save him. Normally I wouldn't call myself a brave person, but something came over me.' It sounded like a confession. 'I didn't even think about my own safety.'

His eyes didn't blink when he said the words 'hobby boat'. My idea.

The kids were captivated by him; I hadn't seen them this engaged before, even when the firefighter came. They watched him with their mouths open, their heads tilted. He replied with genuine kindness, even to the silly questions like 'Would you save him again?' He was a natural. The way he patiently waited until they finished their questions, and the warmth that radiated from him, told me this was a good man. I noticed that he didn't have a wedding ring, and nor was he wearing his ID Phone, which was unusual.

When Philip left the stage, all the teachers stood up to take their students back to the classrooms. I watched him as he was escorted out of the sports hall, waving back to the pupils, and the door softly being closed behind him. I felt as if a spell had been broken.

Philip lingered in my thoughts over the next few days. I kept wondering about his ID Phone. He must have had it with him in his bag, otherwise he couldn't even lock or open the door to his home. So why didn't he wear it? Like everyone else, he could have just muted it for the duration of the speech. It didn't make sense, unless – and the thought kept picking at my mind – he didn't wear it on purpose, because he disagreed with what it represented. I was sorry I had missed the opportunity to meet him in person and that he was now gone from my life, as quickly as he had appeared.

Less than a month later, I had booked tickets for myself and my parents at the Wigmore Hall, to celebrate Dad's birthday. Mendelssohn's Violin Concerto would be performed by Montgomery X, the eccentric virtuoso violinist. Most people of my age weren't into classical music, but I was passionate about it, thanks to Dad's early efforts. It turned out Mum had already booked a holiday to St Petersburg for the two of them, so I was left with two extra tickets. I really wanted to go, but not alone, so I asked around at school. Only Aisha was interested in coming with me, if only to keep me company. I knew I could rely on her: she was a kind soul.

The Wigmore Hall was one of the few Victorian institutions that had been preserved from the old system due to its historic heritage. It was still used for its original purpose, which was to host classical and chamber music concerts. Dad used to take Mum there occasionally, and I would often go with them. This time, I was surprised to see that less than half of the seats were occupied.

'It's like being in a Dignitorium,' Aisha remarked. 'Seriously, not even there have I seen so many old people. And they don't even care to hide their age.'

She was right. Strangely, most of the visitors were dressed for their age, in elegant, tasteful, if slightly old-fashioned clothes. In the sea of grey and silver heads, there was only one figure that stood out.

'Look who's there!'

Aisha pulled me closer. Philip Brunelli was sitting in the first row, wearing an immaculate black suit, his head buried in the concert programme. An unexpected joy filled my chest but I hid it from Aisha and we sat down in the middle row, from where I had a clear view of the stage. And luckily of Philip, too.

The music was played with Montgomery X's distinctively buoyant style, but it was painful to watch his desperate expression, how he was almost begging the audience for attention. He had always been known for his eccentric clothing – vaguely Napoleonic – and parrot-like hairstyle dyed in multiple bright colours. But this time he outdid himself, and as he stood there, grimacing and perspiring as he played, he reminded me of an old circus clown. I couldn't help glancing over to where Philip sat, seemingly without company.

I hoped Aisha wouldn't go home at the interval, as I had seen her pulling faces during the performance and even secretly using her ID Phone. She reassured me she wouldn't let me down. When we stood up and made our way out of the auditorium, a lady with white hair asked me where the toilets were, and didn't believe me when I told her I was a visitor, not an usher.

'Did you see the look on her face?' Aisha whispered. 'You must be the only person under fifty in the whole of London who ever sets foot in here.'

It took us several minutes to get out of the hall, due to the people inching slowly ahead of us. We headed straight to the bar. Aisha ordered a glass of champagne, while I stuck to mineral water.

'I wonder what our everyday hero is doing,' Aisha said. 'Being as saintly as he is, he must be staying in his seat all through the interval.'

'Why do you think he is saintly?'

'I just have a feeling.' She shrugged. 'Shall we find out?' Without waiting for my reply, Aisha stood up. 'I'll go and check if he's still in his seat. He's probably memorising the names of all the secondary musicians.' She rolled her eyes.

The champagne had made her even more curious and giggly than usual. I was glad she had come with me. As I looked around in the wood-panelled bar, I saw that everyone had company. They were mostly in small groups or couples; nobody was alone, even the oldest people, some nearing seventy.

It came as a slight shock when Aisha returned to the table along with Philip.

'I told you, Ali. He would have been left there alone, if I hadn't come to his rescue. Philip, this is Alice, my colleague. Alice was in the audience during your Everyday Hero speech and was sorry not to meet you properly.'

We shook hands, and when our palms, touched, I felt myself blushing deeply, and it took all my courage to hold his gaze. Philip sat down on my left, and I found myself struggling for words. Luckily Aisha saved the day.

'I was about to leave, but it's quite a show, I have to admit,' she remarked. 'Montgomery X is not as boring as I expected.'

'I would never say classical music is boring,' Philip said. 'Even if it's played by a simple musician in a simple black suit.'

'Do you play yourself?'

'I did as a child. But I had to stop.' I sensed anxiety in his voice, and his fingers were furiously rolling a paper napkin into a ball. I couldn't help noticing he wasn't wearing his ID Phone again.

'I'm not too fond of the concert to be honest,' he continued. 'He plays it far too quickly.'

'It's more enjoyable this way.'

'But it's not how Mendelssohn wrote it.'

'Hah,' Aisha scoffed. 'Mendelssohn! When? Some three hundred years ago?'

'Only 210.' Philip said, then suddenly looked at me. 'What do you think?'

'I like it both ways. But if you ask me, I definitely prefer the original version. The one I heard years ago with my parents, when Sokolowski performed it. It still gives me goosebumps. I was so sad when he retired.'

'I saw him live too, in Warsaw, at the Chopin Festival. But that was ten years ago. When the festival still existed.'

Aisha glanced at her ID phone to check the time, excused herself and left for the bathroom. I hoped there would be a long queue, and luckily there was. By the time she returned, Philip and I were deep into a conversation about our favourite music, our knees almost touching. I was so mesmerised, I almost missed the bell for the second part. During the performance I couldn't focus on Montgomery X, I kept watching Philip and afterwards I left the row deliberately slowly so that we would meet in the aisle.

'Why did you come tonight if you don't like Montgomery X's style?' Aisha asked him, while we remained stuck in the middle of the slow-moving crowd.

'These are the final weeks of classical concerts at the Wigmore Hall. Next month it will be converted.'

'Refurbished? It could do with it, to be honest.'

'No, not refurbished. Converted into a cabaret venue. It will cease to be a concert hall. So I take every opportunity to come here while I can.'

'How sad!' I said.

'I'm not surprised,' said Aisha, casting her eyes over the audience which was still not moving, due to an elderly man blocking the way with his walking frame. 'But how do you know about this?'

'We architects know everything about each other's projects.' His eyes were filled with nostalgia as he gazed around him.

Outside, Aisha blew a kiss dramatically to both of us, while pushing herself forward to get on her monorail, in a rush to get home and feed her puppy. Mine was due in four minutes.

'Are you waiting for yours, too?' I asked Philip.

'No. I'm walking.'

'Well, it was a lovely night.'

'It was. And thanks for taking my side against Aisha.'

'Don't judge her too harshly. She doesn't know any better. She didn't have the parents I had.'

'She certainly didn't.' There was appreciation in his voice and I was grateful that in the dim evening light he couldn't see my cheeks redden.

I expected him to say goodbye and turn on his heels but he didn't.

'How sad about the hall!' I said, trying to keep my voice level.

'It is.'

I checked again, he still wasn't wearing his ID Phone. He must have noticed my eyes on his naked wrist.

'I like the touch of fresh air on my skin, I like to feel… Never mind.'

I had a sudden thought that what he wanted to say was 'free'. The growing crowd around us, the noise and the biting cold seemed to have disappeared. I stared at him, not knowing what to say. All I knew was that I couldn't bear the thought of saying goodbye and not seeing him again. Then he spoke.

'The very last concert will be next Friday. Just before they close the hall down. Mozart's Clarinet Concerto. I definitely want to go. I wonder if you…'

'It's one of my favourite pieces ever,' I lied.

'Would you…would you like to join me?'

'I'd love to,' I smiled.

He opened his bag and took out his ID Phone to enter my contact details. When he had finished, he put it back in his bag. I watched him astonished, burning to ask him more about it, but good manners held me back. My monorail rolled into the station, and I leapt on it before I could say anything that might ruin the moment. From my seat I glanced at the platform, but all I saw was his dark hair and the back of his black overcoat as he was swallowed by the billowing crowd.

FOUR

Before my first lesson starts, there's already a lump in my throat. In the staffroom this morning I bumped into Linda who is a governor, a High Spender on the school board of directors. She must have noticed my lethargy as she looked me up and down and began spouting her usual condescending platitudes: 'You see, if you had had kids, you wouldn't be completely alone now. I'm so sorry for poor Philip, Alice, but you know, life goes on.' It took all my willpower to give her a polite smile.

Everything is set up, minutes now before my Year 8 students come in. I can't think of anything but my penalty points. I quickly check them on the computer. No, they haven't gone up. It's Citizenship class with a fascinating topic: non-profit people. I keep reminding myself that I just need to survive the next hour, then there's the commemoration until lunchtime and I only have one more lesson in the afternoon.

In my mind's eye, all I can see is my bed and the soft velvety duvet cover, decorated with rows of light brown elephants marching on sand-coloured dunes. In the middle there's a baby one I adore. Last night I spent a long time studying the elephant pattern. I slid into my leggings and an oversized jumper – an old Christmas present from Philip – and lay on the sofa, hugging the duvet, breathing in its familiar scent. The fabric is tired in places, the surface slightly fluffy from years of washing. Philip said he would get us another one, but I refused. The elephants fill my heart with warmth, bring back days filled with joy, the feeling of happiness just to be alive. It all feels a lifetime ago.

I'm torn out of my reverie by the sound of girls screaming and doors slamming. My students are approaching. They are fighting and calling each other's mums non-profit. To my surprise, Charlie leads the way. Usually he's the very last one to arrive, but knowing that the subject of today's class is non-profit people, he's eager to learn. I straighten my back, attempting to appear stronger and in control.

I start the video. It has a positive, supportive approach that I like. Instead of focusing on the non-profitable side of non-profit people, it highlights the humanity with which we should treat them. It also encourages us to do our best to contribute towards their Right To Reside, if possible, and if not possible, to make those final years as enjoyable as we can. The video talks about the importance of supporting the Zone and urges us to contribute unwanted goods to its Distribution Centre. It shows how tirelessly the government is working on maintaining the free water system there, despite the residents not paying a penny for it.

'They shouldn't be getting water. They should all be left to die of dehydration,' Charlie shouts out. 'Fucking useless freeloaders.' Other children start giggling.

'Quiet, Charlie!' I shout.

'But that's the truth, miss. My dad always says no one should get anything for free. We don't get water for free.'

'Enough, Charlie.'

'Do you get water for free, miss?'

He stares at me insolently. A cold silence settles on the room. I can hear the humming of the lamp overhead.

'Charlie, we'll discuss—'

'Do you get water for free, miss?'

'No, but—'

'You see, so why should the Zone get free water? It's us who are paying for it.'

'That's what this video is about, Charlie. It teaches us compassion.'

The video ends by emphasising the fact that almost all of us will cease to be profitable at some stage in our lives. It's a powerful ending that moves students every year, resulting in a deep silence long after the video has finished playing.

'I'll never end up like that.' Charlie shouts out. 'That only happens to fucking losers.'

'Charlie!'

He jumps up and grabs Joanna, the girl who sits in front of him, by the hair.

'You're keeping a non-profit bastard at home, aren't you?'

Everyone knows she has a sister who was born deaf. He holds Joanna down, so that she can't escape. She starts crying. I press the emergency button under my desk then run to separate them. Very soon the door swings open and two guards enter. The moment Charlie sees them, he releases Joanna. They take him away but bring him back ten minutes later. He has a chip on his shoulder, I can see that. He doesn't say a word, but his eyes are boring into me. I ignore him. Only fifteen minutes left.

Now I give the students an opportunity to ask anything they want about the Zone. They are very interested, hands are popping up in the air. They ask clever questions, like how the waste-disposal system works. One girl refers back to the video which stated that residents live up to a year in the Zone before dying either of starvation, illness or violence. 'But how do they know? How do they measure such things if there are no cameras there?' she asks.

'It's a very good question,' I say. 'I suppose these are just estimates. They might not apply to everyone. I happen to know someone who has lived there for three years and is still alive.'

The moment this leaves my lips, I know I've made a terrible mistake. I take a deep breath and maintain a professional demeanour. I shoot a quick glance towards the camera opposite me. I feel it's rebuking me. Now more hands are up in the air, asking more questions, again and again. For a fraction of a second my gaze falls upon Charlie. His eyes are still on me, giving me goose bumps. Despite many years of experience, it's hard to keep a straight face when things like this happen. I struggle to find my voice; I stand there gawping like a dying fish, but nothing comes out. The class stops, hands drop down. It's deadly quiet. Thirty pairs of eyes stare at me in confusion. I must do something. I go to the window, open it and breathe in the cool, crisp air. Then I'm back at my desk.

'Carry on, everyone,' I call out with a false air of confidence. But inside my chest I can feel my rapid heartbeat, fuelled by an unpronounceable fear.

'Right. Now can you tell me who we define as non-profit people?'

A dozen hands shoot up. I force a smile and keep nodding. I'm grateful for my twelve years of experience that allow me to function on autopilot if I need to. Less than ten minutes to go now.

I'm leading my class down the corridor, to the sports hall. Today they're more fidgety: they know the commemoration is coming, when we'll pay tribute to the three students who were abducted while walking home from school a few years ago.

Seeing the festive preparations – flowers, cards, decorations on the walls – I find myself wondering whether we celebrate the abductions instead of paying tribute to those who were abducted. If I didn't know it was Linda who organised the decoration, I would have guessed it by now. The three children are looked upon as martyrs, like sacrifices that were tragic but also necessary in order to raise awareness. As a result, armed security was introduced at schools throughout the country.

By 10am we are all assembled in the sports hall, with security guards holding down some of the kids, who are kicking, fighting, swearing and spitting, desperate to run around. On the stage, Leo Sullivan stands in a ceremonial manner, lowering the microphone, for he's a small man, smaller than many of the female teachers. His grey blazer bulges on one side, reminding us of who he is: the only person in the school allowed to carry a gun – apart from the security guards, of course.

'Welcome.' His rich voice cuts into the air, commanding immediate attention.

'I don't have to remind you what a sad occasion it is we are remembering today. Joshua Robinson, Aliya Khan, Samir Khan. They are our heroes who will never be forgotten. I want you to consider and be aware of the fact that you are probably alive because they are not.'

The next half an hour is an emotional commemoration, with the three children's photos projected on the wall, then poems read by students, some by well-known poets, some by the students themselves. There is singing, clapping, nodding and plenty of tear-wiping followed by praise for the security guards, who parade around on stage, displaying their guns, promising what everyone craves: protection.

Leo returns to the microphone. He stands there waiting for the noise to die down. There's more to come, and knowing Leo I assume he'll say something impromptu, like the good pastor who is unable to let his herd go without imparting some final words of wisdom.

'As you all know, I appreciate the positive measures that have been introduced since this tragic event. Despite all this, we keep hearing news of youth abductions in the Low-Spender areas. If they don't target children on their way to or from school, they target them in other places, in the playground, for example.'

I sense unrest in the audience, some whispering from the back.

'I know you're told that it's nothing to worry about, that it happens only in the Low-Spender areas. We keep being reassured how safe, secure and wonderful our lives are here, as Mid Spenders.'

He speaks louder now and I fear what's about to come.

'However, I'm afraid the horrible event we are remembering today might not be the last abduction in the Mid-Spender areas. I can't conclude this commemoration without warning you all: despite being told we're safe now, we are not. If it happened once, it could happen again.'

The murmuring from the audience is getting louder. Teachers are exchanging horrified glances.

'No one will protect us if we don't protect ourselves. Not the government, not the cameras, not the police. Not even the armed guards, despite their best efforts. The moment you leave school territory, you are potential victims.'

Mrs Galloway, the deputy head, runs up onto the stage, switches off Leo's microphone and whispers something to him, pointing at the audience with her long crimson nails. Leo hesitates, and turns his back on us while they talk. Mrs Galloway is nervously wringing her hands. When she finally returns to her seat, Leo switches the microphone back on.

'What I meant to say is be aware, be vigilant. Look after yourselves.' The fire has disappeared from his voice. He swiftly wraps up his speech by wishing us good luck. There is an eerie silence in the hall; the only sound is the ticking of the large, old-fashioned clock on the wall. Leo leaves the stage, but it seems the whole audience has been paralysed by his words. Someone should tell the kids to stand up. Everyone is looking at someone else, waiting for a signal. Finally, Mrs Galloway comes and shouts in her high-pitched voice: 'Up you get, everyone! Time to go back to class.'

In the staffroom Linda's perfume is more offensive than ever. Her words this morning are still nagging at me, but my curiosity is piqued and I drop down on a sofa near her inner circle. The teachers are discussing the commemoration, and mainly Leo's speech. The general opinion is that it was outrageous; Leo must be overworked – he has been under a lot of pressure recently. Some are harsher, saying no head teacher should be allowed to spread these kinds of views and that he should have been stopped. I don't understand the fuss. I'm proud of Leo for what he said. Just because we Mid Spenders are relatively safe, I can't sleep peacefully at night knowing children and young people are in danger. Even if they are only Low Spenders.

Linda leaves, probably for the bathroom. The moment she is gone, the conversation shifts onto organ robberies, the poor kids who were abducted and how the High Spenders were able to get away with it. This leads to a discussion about who is more dangerous, the smooth criminal in a High-Spender villa who masterminds the crime, or the perpetrator, the destitute Zone resident who can run about and do anything he is commissioned to do because he can't be tracked and caught. We don't notice when Linda returns until her violent fragrance begins to creep back into our nostrils. And then it's too late. Her voice is less sugar-coated than normal, her eyes are like darting arrows.

'I wish I was able to find the person who started this stupid gossip.'

'It's not gossip, Linda,' Mrs Galloway says. 'It's on the Globe, it's everywhere. It's a fact.'

'But it's a lie. You simply don't understand how—'

'Linda, you don't have to take it personally. No one is accusing you of organ theft. But it does happen.'

'If you hadn't interrupted me I would have been able to tell you that it's totally impossible,' Linda says, her face turning purple. 'Why would we do that? We can get organ transplants – if we need them – in hospitals. It's the hospital's job to find donors. Contrary to popular belief – because the truth is always less romantic than fiction – the donors are voluntary Dignitorium residents.'

'So how do you explain the abductions?'

'What am I, a detective? I can't explain everything. Crime is as old as humanity. I have never said that all High Spenders are angels. Some of them are involved in the drug trade, I imagine. But I can tell you that High Spenders don't need illegal organs.'

Everyone nods and the conversation moves back to Leo's speech. No one believes Linda, I can see it in their eyes. We are born with an innate suspicion of the more privileged. I can't blame my colleagues; I feel the same way. I don't believe a word Linda said. She would never accept a transplant from a Dignitorium resident – aged and medicated – into her perfectly groomed body.

The corridor feels colder and more abandoned than usual as I walk towards Leo Sullivan's office, my shoes echoing on the tiled floor. During lunch break he called, asking me to see him. It's not the best time; the afternoon lesson starts very soon. I'll definitely let him know that I agree with his speech. I always have a sense of heaviness when I see the fake smiling faces on the Globe, trying to reassure us that Mid and High Spenders are safe. On the other hand, nothing is said about Low Spenders, or how they are protected. I'm pretty certain they aren't.

When I knock and enter Leo's little office, it takes a few moments to locate him among the piles of books on his desk. The long-forgotten sweet scent of printed books immediately calms my nerves. The hustle of the schoolyard seems miles away.

'I want you to know, Leo, that I agree with every word you said during the commemoration,' I start.

He sighs deeply, as if he's carrying the weight of the world, and puts his half-finished sandwich down.

'Thank you, Alice,' he says in a melancholy tone. 'I appreciate it. However, I asked to see you for an entirely different reason. Charlie reported you.'

I bury my face in my palms.

'I've checked the cameras.' His voice is genuinely sad. 'I listened to the audio twice. Unfortunately it can't be a misunderstanding.'

'I expected this,' I explode. 'But you have to know, it just slipped out. Charlie was intimidating me, I swear, until he found a mistake, any mistake.'

Leo stands up and starts walking slowly to the window and back.

'I want you to understand that I believe you. From the first day Charlie entered this school, he has been nothing but trouble. But my hands are tied. I wish you the best.'

A cold sweat breaks out on the nape of my neck.

'I'm so sorry, Alice. But there's also the fact that you've reached twenty penalty points.'

'This…this must be a misunderstanding. I had only thirteen points. I have earned thirteen over the past twelve years, for minor things adding up.'

'Teaching something this wrong earns you eight points. If the school is taken to court–'

'But it's true, Leo. I didn't lie. My father-in-law has been in the Zone for three years and he's still alive.'

His face turns deathly pale.

'I didn't hear that, OK?' he whispers.

'I'll take it back, then. I'll tell them I made a mistake. That I was

91

not prepared for a question like that, that I didn't know what to say. They can send me to a training session, teach me what to say next time.'

'I've tried it, trust me.'

'What do you mean?'

'During lunch break. I've already spoken to the authorities, and I told them you'd take it back. They accepted it.'

'Oh, thank God!' Relief and gratitude for Leo's support floods through me. But Leo's frown hasn't changed.

'They accepted it but then called back fifteen minutes later. They found out about your depression and that you're taking medication. You started a stronger one yesterday, which makes the situation even worse.'

'For God's sake, Leo, I was trying to do my work, to keep myself alive. Of course I tried to find a way. That's what Mini-doc is for.'

'I know.'

'Everyone is taking some kind of medicine.'

'It's just a very unfortunate coincidence, Alice. I'm sorry. You're declared unsuitable for work for the next twelve months. For any work. In a year's time they'll examine your suitability again.'

I try to take a deep breath but I feel as if I'm suffocating.

'But I'll lose my Right To Reside, for God's sake!'

I stare at him, pleading. He avoids meeting my eye and turns to the window, looking out for a while before he turns around again.

'Don't you have any savings?' he asks softly.

'If I move to a Low-Spender Area – the very thing I wanted to avoid – I may be able to survive on my savings for a few months. But definitely not for a year.'

'It'll be temporary, you'll see. Once you recover, you'll come back to us and you can move back to the Mid-Spender area.'

'You don't understand. I won't be able to recuperate. I have to know what happened to Philip or I'll just get worse and end up in the Dignitorium.'

'You really have to calm down or you'll make yourself ill. There's no way you'll end up in the Dignitorium just yet. Not for another thirty years.'

I don't have the strength to explain.

'Look, Leo, I've been a teacher for twelve years, is there really no way of protecting myself?'

His eyes give me the answer. He beckons me to sit down next to him behind his desk. He points at the screen.

'What's this?'

'Just read it.'

It's the chart showing my likeability ratings for the whole term, based on the votes of all my students. It has plummeted in the past few months.

'This has also contributed to the authorities' decision. You need a break, Alice.'

I make a final attempt.

'Who is going to teach the handwriting class?'

He clears his throat.

'Who will do it without me?'

'Alice, the handwriting class is not required any more.'

'But I had six students in that class! They were devoted—'

'I have to tell you,' he says, wiping sweat from his forehead with his hand, 'that the only reason it was run was because I thought it was such a wonderful idea. And I wanted to keep you happy.'

'But I had six regular students.'

'I had to bribe them by cancelling their detentions. I struggled to find the six of them. No kid wants to learn handwriting any more. I'm sorry that I had to tell you this in such circumstances.'

The people I pass on the promenade could be ghosts, just shadows and colours all blurred and distorted. Hoping for even the smallest sign of human compassion, I try to catch a genuine gaze, but all I see are smiles and laughter, worn as a shield or as a weapon. There's no way to get to the person behind them. It makes me want to get away from the crowd, but it's rush hour and the open-air bars, restaurants and pubs are buzzing. I cross the lawn to get to a narrow pavement where it's quieter. I can't explain the sudden urge to see my old home, a home I find hard to believe was ever mine.

I'm unemployed. It sounds like someone else, not me. I have been disabled. Or discarded. There's no difference really. I must go home and count my remaining money, if I have the courage. I know I don't have enough to live off for a year. Not even in a Low-Spender area.

I shouldn't look up at the third floor terrace, but I can't help it. She's there, again. I can see her ash-blond hair tied up with a clip; wavy ends are falling on the back of her neck. She's wearing a white sleeveless top, an expensive one; despite its simplicity I can tell it from the material, the way it ripples on her back and shoulder. She's china-white, protected; not even the rays of the sun are allowed to fall upon her without her consent. I can see her doll-like face, as she turns her head for a moment, then types something into her ID Phone. Her carefree gestures make me seethe. I recognise this type, an excellent education paid for with daddy's money, a husband from the same circle, a good career promising a glittering future. My old home is just a stepping-stone for them. In a few years they will be High Spenders.

I couldn't keep quiet forever, just nod and agree in order to keep my job or whatever is at stake. Finally, I snort, nothing is at stake. I have nothing and they must know it. They must see what became of me while they were enjoying themselves in our home. I don't wish to make a scene; they could report me for that. But they have to know. They have to know how easy it is to find oneself fallen from grace, from having it all to having nothing at all.

I walk back to the building, climb the steps, stare at the intercom. Number 33. I could ask them to come down and talk to me.

Looking at it rationally, I know it was not their fault. By law a single person is not allowed to occupy a home for a whole family. If not to them, my home would have been given to someone else in February, to another family. I must have done the same to someone when I moved into my new place, without knowing it. And when Philip and I moved into Number 33 many years ago, someone had already lived there before us. It never occurred to me to think about it, about where these people go, those who leave their homes for us.

I'm eyeing buzzer number 33, trying to prepare what to say that will make them come down and listen to me. I'm aware I must look strange on the security cameras, standing here with my finger reaching out towards the intercom. I go back to the lawn, where I will look less suspicious. I put on my sunglasses and keep my eyes fixed on her. Should I say I left something in the apartment? No, they would have thrown everything out on the first day. Could I pretend we know each other from school? I need to come up with something believable, otherwise she will just hang up.

She is still there, on her ID Phone. Her husband, a dark blond, tanned guy, straight out of a tennis racket advert, brings her out a glass of orange juice. My stomach churns with envy. She takes a few sips then leans back against the lounger. Soon she is ready to get up, and he reaches out an arm for her. Spoilt brat. She stands up, with her back to me, and takes another sip of juice. As she turns to the table, I can see her figure from the hips upwards. She's pregnant. About six months. Or five.

I start to run as if I'm in the middle of a burning field, not turning back, not looking once at my past. I can't help it but the image of her in her full pregnant glory is already blazoned in my mind. All I have now is a sickly bitter taste in my mouth. The taste of ultimate defeat.

In the corner of the courtyard the evening is colder and darker than ever, despite the last rays of the sun warming my skin. This is the last evening I can sit here. It's time to go in and start packing, for the second time this year. But I find I can't focus on clothes and dishes and suitcases. Instead I'm dialling Nurse Vogel, and through my tears I tell her what has happened.

'I'm so sorry to hear that, my dear,' she says with compassion. 'But you shouldn't let it destroy you.'

'It's not up to me. My savings are enough for seven months. If I don't recover–'

'You will recover, I'll make sure of it.'

'And how about you? Did they bother you again?'

She stands up and goes to her mantelpiece. She lifts up a small oval-shaped orange vase.

'This is a vase my husband bought me from a work trip in Spain. Red is my favourite colour. Whenever he saw something nice in red, he bought it for me.'

'But it's…it's not red.'

She nods with a tortured expression on her face.

'Exactly. Yesterday, when I arrived home from work, I spotted it straight away. They changed it.'

I feel cold tingle running up my spine.

'They returned, then.'

'The worst thing is, Alice, there are moments when I start to doubt my own state of mind. They are really good at this.'

'But you're so respectable and you do such wonderful work.'

She lowers her voice and looks me straight in the eye.

'I'm everything they deny the existence of. I'm at the age that people should be dreading but I defy everything they claim. So far they've let me get away with it, out of consideration for my decades of experience and the fact that they can't fault me. I earn my Right To Reside so I'm not a non-profit person. But they watch me constantly.'

'What can you do to protect yourself?'

'I'll keep going, like before. I complain more and more at the health check-ups, despite not having any serious health concerns. That has saved my life, I think.'

'Really?'

I'm unsure again whether to believe what she says or if it is all part of the mental deterioration that comes with old age. What if these 'changes' in her flat are just the product of her crumbling sanity? But the fear and sadness in her eyes are so real. Just as they were in Grandma's. I despise old age; how our loved ones fall apart in front of our very eyes. And how it makes them blind with denial.

'Oh, Alice,' her voice turns into a whisper, 'did you really believe I had horrible back pain? I made up that story years ago so they would be satisfied that I'm deteriorating like I'm supposed to. Like everyone else. I have some back pain, of course, but it's nothing serious. I need to keep telling people how much I suffer.'

'What a clever idea!'

'The problem is, the medical checks don't show anything serious. That's what raised their suspicion recently, I guess. They might have sussed out that I had made it up just to prolong my life.'

I still can't see the point of this. Why would anyone have a problem with Nurse Vogel if she's not non-profit?

'I'm sure no harm will come to you, Nurse Vogel. You're a useful member of society.'

'This is what I keep telling myself, but I have a hunch they are about to get me, very soon. Don't forget, just by being alive at this age I'm a rebel, an enemy.'

DATE

After the clarinet concerto, Philip accompanied me to the monorail. Standing on the platform in the falling snow, he kissed my cheek and held my hand in his. Then he asked me if he could see me again soon. Two days later, we met for lunch at my favourite Italian restaurant. To break the ice, I brought up his Everyday Hero speech. 'I was so impressed by the way you spoke to our pupils. It gave the impression you'd had a loving dad as a child.'

He frowned and took a long sip of red wine. He stood out as solemn among the other diners, who were mostly quite tipsy. This just made him even more enigmatic in my eyes.

'You couldn't be further from the truth.'

'What was he like, then?'

'Difficult,' he said after a long pause.

'He must have been in great trouble if he attempted suicide.'

'He has been in great trouble all his life.'

Something told me I had entered forbidden territory and I

quickly changed the subject to my own dad. He sat, listening intently while I talked about my life, sharing my hopes and dreams and, as the wine took effect, sharing my fears too, including those caused by Sofia, our own family devil. After our first date I was not sure he would want to see me again, but he messaged the same night.

As the weeks went by, despite seeing each other almost every day, I sensed he had built a protective wall around himself, following some traumatic experience that he seemed unable to share. On the other hand, he spoke freely about his views on society and his career. He was hugely critical of the system in which he was determined to become an important architect.

'Important?' I asked, looking down from the Millennium Bridge at the panorama, both sides of the river built up with futuristic skyscrapers. 'You mean you'd like to win awards?'

'I'm not interested in awards,' he said defensively. 'People don't realise that architecture is much more than just creating buildings for people to live and work in, or showing off the latest mad ideas when it comes to structure.'

He stopped and I waited to hear what he thought architecture was, but he simply stared into the distance, as if he was miles away from the hordes of tourists around us.

When I tried to find out more about his mum, I was not much luckier.

'She died. I was just eighteen.' Bitterness laced his voice and I started to ask questions, but he was tight-lipped. 'She had to retire too early. She would still be fairly young today.'

We'd been dating for three weeks when, one evening, during a walk along the promenade , he asked me:

'What's your favourite cuisine? Apart from Italian?'

'I love Greek. But to get it right, you need the best ingredients.'

'Leave it to me. Come visit me at home tomorrow.'

'We can cook together!'

He loved the idea and we kissed goodbye.

The next evening, I arrived at his attic apartment in MS05. I was ready to help him cook, when I noticed the small round dining table was already set, with a vase of red roses and a lit candle in the middle. Philip pulled a chair out for me. He served a three-course Greek meal with wine paired to each course. It was all just perfect, but something was gnawing at me.

'How is it?' he asked, when I was a few bites into the *spanakopita*.

'It's wonderful Philip, thank you!'

'What's wrong then?'

'Nothing at all.'

'You seem buried in your thoughts.'

'I'm just tired. It's been a long week,' I said. 'Next time, we could cook together,' I blurted out.

'Is it what's troubling you? That I didn't wait for you?'

I nodded and gently took his hand across the table.

'You don't have to prove anything to me, Phil. Maybe in the past you had to deal with things on your own.' I pulled my chair over to his side of the table and took his face in my hands. 'You are not alone any more. We are together now.'

'I'd like you to teach me togetherness,' he said, and that's when I saw how vulnerable he was. A feeling of deep concern hit me in the heart, and I swore to myself I would never let him down. That I'd rather have him, in all his grumpiness, darkness and reserve, than an average Joe with no emotional baggage. I finally had someone to look after.

One month into my relationship with Philip, we had agreed to meet at a rooftop bar called The Calypso. I still knew nothing about his father or the reason for his suicide attempt. Whenever I brought it up, he changed the subject and frowned, so after a while

I stopped asking.

The Calypso was frequented by people who liked to take their time and enjoyed the small things in life, such as the view over the city – Big Ben, for example, was visible in the distance. I don't know if I belonged to that crowd or just desperately wanted to.

From above, the city looked surprisingly peaceful. Not too far away, a new skyscraper was being built, slowly creeping upwards. I knew when it was complete, it would block out the sun and I would have to find a new favourite bar.

I thought of Philip. Despite having met several times now, I found him a puzzle. I had no idea how he felt for me or where exactly our relationship was going. It felt as if I was sitting in a boat, not knowing which way the current would carry me. When Philip arrived at the Calypso, he brought an air of seriousness with him. I sensed his disapproval of the bar, and began justifying myself.

'You know, I like coming here,' I said. 'I feel as if a weight has been lifted from my shoulders when I'm up here.'

'You seem to be the picture of perfect harmony and satisfaction.' He kept watching me. 'In your padded little life, filled with cute schoolchildren, what do you have to worry about, exactly?'

Sarcasm can feel like an arrow tinged with malice, sometimes.

'You have no idea how much effort it takes me to–' I stopped. 'It doesn't matter.'

His eyes were now piercing through me. I turned towards the entrance, and pretended to watch the group of people who had just come in. I quickly wiped the corners of my eyes. I felt as if I'd just been opened up from head to toe with a giant scalpel.

On the terrace, men in immaculate white shirts and perfectly tailored suits, were deeply engaged in discussion. Women in halter-neck dresses and wide-brimmed hats chatted and sipped at cocktails. I was wondering whether their conversations were as heavy as ours, and the trendy appearances merely disguised something more profound. Or were they exactly what they seemed to be? This feeling of being a spy among my own kind was new to me. I'd never experienced this, not until I met Philip.

After some time, I spoke.

'Next time maybe we could go to Sunday Mass together.'

He didn't even try to conceal a grimace.

'I wouldn't waste our time together there. I almost never go to Mass. My father calls it the mass of the masses who are in a huge mess.'

I smiled.

'Neither do I, but once a month I have to. The extra money is a big help.'

Suddenly his voice deepened.

'Do you know why they give you that extra money?'

'I suppose to encourage us to buy.'

'Yes, in part, but there's more to it than that.'

The severity of his voice made me put my drink down. Unintentionally I leaned closer, as if he was about to share a secret.

'Brainwashing is far more effective with a crowd,' he said with a sinister calm. 'The more often you go, the more you'll become like them. In the long term, you'll be spending far more this way than in isolation, and you'll be less likely to complain.'

'So how do you keep your Right To Reside if you're so careful about what you spend?' I asked.

'I save up for countryside visits.'

'I wish I could afford them more often.'

'Getting to the countryside costs a fortune for a reason.' His eyes were sparkling and he leaned closer to me.

'But it's worth it, for my own sanity. I don't mind living more modestly during the rest of the week.'

'When I was a teenager, my dad took me to the north, to the Peak District,' I said. 'That was my first time in the countryside and

I've never felt that free. So I know the feeling.'

Suddenly I remembered the bloody corpse carried on a stretcher out of the woods and I shivered. He noticed my change of mood and I shared my sad experience.

'Luckily I've never seen such things. You must come with me one day, Alice. Trust me, there's nothing more uplifting than walking across the open fields on a summer's day, with your ID Phone off, free from all this.'

'Aren't you afraid?'

'Of the wolves?'

'Of the authorities. Your tracker can show them the frequency of your visits.'

Finishing his drink, he put the glass down on the table.

'There's nothing to be afraid of. What can they do, really? I work hard, I consume. As a Mid Spender I'm a useful member of society. You're welcome to join me next Sunday.'

'That's when I planned to go to Mass. I wonder what will happen if I don't.'

'I don't think that is the question here. The question is whether you're ready to give up on Mid-Spender comfort to experience something extraordinary.'

His smile transformed him; I could swear, for just a moment, that he was carefree.

'Where would we go?'

'There's a beautiful lake in Somerset, which I visit regularly. You have an area of a square mile before you get to the fence. The peace and quiet is otherworldly. It helps me clear my head.'

'The exact opposite of what Sunday Mass does,' I said, broodily.

'You know what?' he said. 'Let me show you something. Once you've finished your drink.'

I downed my drink in one gulp and stood up.

We were out in the busy street, and I wanted to ask him where he was taking me, but I couldn't shout loud enough over the hustle and bustle, the invasive adverts and the tooting of e-trolleys. On the crowded monorail, we both kept quiet. We left the city centre, travelled past a suburban high street and then got off at Hampstead Monorail Station.

'I don't know about you, but I find it increasingly hard to cope with the pollution in the city.' He fanned his face and inhaled deeply.

'Air pollution? There are no cars any more.'

'Not that kind of pollution. The pollution from the adverts, from the constant aggression and stress accumulated in the air around us.'

I didn't say anything, but strangely, for the first time, I felt its presence in the air.

We walked along a wide, tree-lined pavement; the street was built up with ultramodern glass palaces that housed offices and banks. At the corner of an authentic Victorian brick building, we turned left and found ourselves in a hidden paradise. Philip's sense of relief was evident. I had blurred memories of this suburb of London, usually referred to as the English Montmartre.

Construction signs were up everywhere, marring the unique beauty of the place, but the jungle-like feel of it still reminded me of a fairy-tale. There was no one else there, and we let the peace and quiet envelop us. The street lamps were bent, and the old shop windows were all broken, some of them victims of arson. The local landmark, a painting of a man on the tiny bridge, painting himself standing on the same bridge, had been ruined by graffiti. Philip sat down on a nearby bench, his gaze fixed on the painting that had seen better days.

'I heard this place is going down the drain due to the lack of financial support,' I said.

He shrugged. 'They are going to demolish all this and add it to the High-Spender area.'

'How sad it is!' I exclaimed. 'This must have been such a wonderful little park.'

'There's worse to come. There is talk of more luxurious High-Spender areas to be developed. Where do you think they will take the land from?'

'The Zone?'

He nodded. Suddenly his eyes were filled with sadness.

'Try not to think about it.' I put my hand on his arm.

'It's not really an option.' He snorted. 'I've been asked to design the next one.'

'Oh, God. Do you have to?'

'No. And I won't. I'd rather take jobs that pay half, and still be able to look at myself in the mirror.'

I had no idea how to console him.

'Do you like it?' He pointed at the painting on the bridge.

'It's magical.'

'I think you'd look beautiful painted. You have very distinctive features.'

'Ugly, you mean? I know, I hate my dimples. I'll have them removed one day.'

'Please don't! They give your face character.' Suddenly he was shy, like a schoolboy.

'Any other gems around here?' I asked.

'What about that?' He pointed at a bench in the distance, behind the trees. I stood up and made my way to the bench, which had something on it. As I got closer I saw what it was – a kind of group sculpture, a family. Shoes, hats, gloves and bags were held together by thin, almost invisible wires, while between them there was only empty space. Still, the way the tiny shoes of the children were turned towards the adults', and the implied gestures of the parents' protective hands made it feel alive.

'What do you see?' he asked.

'The younger child, probably a girl, is sitting on her mother's lap. The bigger one, a boy, is cuddling up to his father. This is one of the most beautiful things I've ever seen!'

A gentle smile lit up his face. 'As they say, beauty is in the eye of the beholder,' he said. 'You fill the void with what you are inside.'

He touched the imaginary boy's red hat with the tip of his fingers. 'Dad meant for it to be this way. To hold up a mirror to people.'

'Your dad? Did your dad make this?'

He nodded.

'He's an incredible artist,' I whispered.

'He's a weak person. It took me a while to realise he's nothing but a delusional fool.'

'How can you say that?'

'To me he has lost all credibility to make family-themed art.'

'Why?'

'He has always been a dissenter. He couldn't cope with the new system; he became so disillusioned he simply left us one day. I was eleven. He chose his art and politics over us, and moved in with a community of other losers.' The memories were now flowing freely from him. 'My mother could never get over it, and had such severe depression she had to retire when I was eighteen. Some years later my father returned and apologised, blaming the system, as usual.'

'So his suicide attempt was not unexpected at all,' I said gently.

He took my hand. 'I swear to you, I'll never be like him.' There was passion in his voice; this was not the reserved Philip I knew. 'I'll be able to make it in this world.'

He gazed into my eyes with unusual intensity.

'Would you like to be my partner in this, Alice?'

We didn't even know each other really. I wanted to ask him if this meant we were serious from now on, after just four weeks of dating, and find out what he meant by partner, and partner in what, exactly, but all I could say was: yes.

FIVE

It will be a week tomorrow since I became a Low Spender. At the council I was given my new address and told to move within twenty-four hours. I fled like a wild animal, my face burning, not even looking around me on the promenade. I didn't belong there any more.

Nurse Vogel came over to comfort me. She had unexpectedly become a friend. After our meeting in the Dignitorium, her sixth sense had shown her I was only holding it together on the surface, while on the inside I was close to collapse. Being the kind soul she is, she says she was really worried something might happen to me and she wanted to remain in touch to keep an eye on me. She started to come over regularly, in the evenings, after work, and we chatted and drank tea in as much harmony as if we were of the same generation. It turned out there was one thing she missed about not having a Globe: cartoons. So she got hooked on them during her visits, and we watched old-fashioned cartoons, with talking animals. But later we always chatted, and I spilled my heart out as if it were a bottomless pit that could never be emptied. It's not an exaggeration to say that she saved me.

My new home is on the third floor of an eight-storey block in LN11, painted mint green. When I opened the front door to the flat, my eyes fell on the square little studio. Sorrow seeped out and hit me right in the face. The previous resident had left unwashed dishes in the sink. The drain was blocked and there was a stagnant smell in the air. The dirty fingerprints on the kitchen cupboard doors, judging by their size, must have belonged to a man. On the wall there was a large poster depicting a Dignitorium in North London. Its surface had been touched so many times that in places the paper had become shiny. The poster must have been torn to pieces then put back together, with Sellotape that ran across the surface like a river. Whoever my predecessor was, I hope he made it to his dream Dignitorium and is enjoying himself. I can empathise with him; after my parents retired, I also had a short period when I loved and loathed the institution at the same time.

I have good days, but mostly bad ones. On good days I hope I'll hear something about Philip that will give me peace of mind. I'm prepared to hear the worst, that I'm a widow, to be shattered; anything is better than this state of uncertainty. On bad days I fear I'll never recover and my savings will dwindle away until I have nothing, leaving me with the unhappy choice between instant euthanasia or a delayed death after nine months of retirement. Or less, if they cut it again.

What I find worst about moving to a Low-Spender area is not the act of downgrading, but the fact that I no longer feel safe. Although I know abductions are rare and that most of the victims are young people, I can't stop comparing this place to where I came from, to the safety of the Mid-Spender area. I miss the courtyard. My high-rise building overlooks a park and playground, but anyone can go there – it's not a community. I also miss watching my neighbours. I wonder what they're doing now.

When I was dismissed, I was cut off from my students and colleagues too suddenly. I stopped belonging there. It's funny, I never thought I would miss Linda's company, her irritating voice, her pungent perfume. I don't even remember the last time I used perfume. Or had my hair done. I'd never imagined that one could be so isolated despite sharing the same air, the same ground beneath our feet. The only thing that comforts me is the elephant blanket, which I clutch at during the night, sleepless until I get up at 3am to find some old photos and immerse myself in memories.

I have just understood what Dad meant when he said that the land is so priceless that we have no right to occupy it if we become disadvantaged. It was a few weeks before Dad requested the new, free semi under the new system. I asked him why we wouldn't have a swimming pool like the Mid Spenders in the condos, and he explained that one couldn't have everything. 'As occupants of a house with a garden, we will be taking up more space than a family in a condo. With the swimming pool they are compensated for not using so much land. We'll get real land, which is the most precious thing on Earth.' He watched Sofia and me for a while then asked: 'Or would you prefer an apartment instead?'

'No, I prefer a house with a garden,' I said.

'Gardens are boring,' Sofia moaned. 'I want to live in a condo with a swimming pool.'

'But I can't replant my tree in a flat.'

'Apartment. Not flat. No one gives a shit about your tree, anyway.'

'Language, Sofia,' Dad warned her.

I could see she was hurt because she didn't have an apple tree. Dad had planted one for her too on the day she was born, but it died within a year. It was only my tree that was growing and blooming and I didn't want to part with it.

'We'll see about our new home. We'll discuss it later,' Dad said after some hesitation, but he never mentioned it again and we moved into the house with the garden. Since then I've lived in several different types of accommodation, but Dad's words about land being the most precious thing on Earth have always remained with me.

On my first day as a Low Spender, I called Christine and some of my other friends or I would say ex-friends. Only Christine answered the phone, the others just sent a message saying 'Get Well Soon' and 'Kisses'. Christine was brief and distant and we had nothing to talk about. 'You must be really under the weather in that horrible gloomy place,' she said, and all I could do was nod. She asked me to show her around the flat and I rotated my ID Phone around the small room. 'You're kidding me,' she said in an exaggerated voice. 'I mean, you don't even have space for wardrobes to store your clothes.' I didn't have time to tell her that I had given away most of my stuff to the Zone Distribution Centre, because she waved me farewell and hung up.

Not having much to do, I'm in the park, just outside my block. I have time to rethink my life, the pleasures I had, the mistakes I made. I'm bathing in the early afternoon sunshine, waiting for families to arrive. To trick myself into feeling connected, though in reality it seems there is less and less that can connect me to others. I've come to realise Philip was right. I have thought through his words, his behaviour over the years, his resistance to starting a family, his bleak view of this society. What I interpreted as pessimism, I now see as wisdom; what seemed selfishness, I realise was caring. How lonely he must have been! Married to me but unable to find solace, to share the terror he felt.

In the distance a woman, slightly younger than I am, is

approaching the playground slowly, to give her daughter time to catch up. The girl has Down syndrome. They walk to the corner of the playground, to the secluded, fenced area half-hidden by the bushes. On the gate is a large non-profit sign. The first thought that runs through my head is how lonely it must be for that poor girl, having to play alone. But the wooden fence, with colourful baby animals, birds and yellow suns painted on it, will probably cheer her up.

As I see them approaching, I turn my head away, as any decent person would. It's not proper to stare. Of course, there are people who will not only stare but openly jeer. Fortunately, they're a small minority.

I, like millions in the country, regularly watch a show called *Heartless*, which reveals the shocking facts of how handicapped children live. It always brings tears to my eyes, and thousands of viewers call in after each show, protesting against the parents, asking for stricter measures. Money is not the most important thing, as the presenters of *Heartless* always take care to emphasise. These parents work hard, especially the single mothers, to support their children. They are misguided, believing that if they contribute to their child's Right To Reside, they can solve the problem. They don't understand that it's not about being non-profit, it's not about money at all.

At the beginning of the new system, many of these children were placed straight in Junior Dignitoriums. Thousands of parents protested and demanded the demolition of Junior Dignitoriums and equal treatment for their children. Of course, this couldn't be granted, given that the new system is based on fairness. Non-profit people can't just exploit useful members of society; otherwise we would end up back in the old system. No one wants that. But their wishes were taken seriously and another option was introduced. Kids who will never grow up to be useful contributors can be supported by their parents, even when they grow up, so long as their families are earning their Right To Reside. If the parent doesn't want the child or can't afford it, the child is sent to the Junior Dignitorium. It's like earthly paradise there, as they say in *Heartless*.

It's clear that this woman is one of those who are selfish enough to let her child suffer. I take a good look at her. Her pale face shows signs of exhaustion, but there's a sparkle of joy in her eyes. It's strange, she doesn't look like a bad person at all. Quite the opposite – the way she is holding her daughter's hand and bending down so that they can walk together shows she really does care. The mothers shown in Heartless are very different from her, much more aggressive, though they still claim to love their children.

I turn away from them, and then I hear the tapping of footsteps and feel a soft little palm on my arm. It's so gentle I'm not sure if it's real or just the tickle of the warm breeze. It's the little girl, smiling widely up at me. Her mother comes running over, her face burning with embarrassment.

'I'm really sorry about this. She's too small to understand.' She gently tries to lead her daughter away from me, in the direction of the non-profit playground.

I ask her how old the girl is; she says she's five. The girl is still in front of me, trying to pull the leather flower off my handbag. I hold the bag in front of her, and let her play with it.

'She goes mad if she sees flowers,' the mother says apologetically. 'Even if they're not real.'

The girl's face is flushed; she is glowing with joy. I have never seen a child with Down syndrome so close up before. I lift the girl up and sit her on my knee. I can sense her mother's surprise, just for a moment, but then she sits down next to me.

'Do you…do you have the same? A child like her?'

'No,' I say. 'I don't have any children.' I turn to her. 'Alice,' I say, and hold out my hand.

She says her name is Ruth, her daughter is Felicity. When Felicity hears her name, she stops playing with the leather flower and looks up at her mum, smiling again. It's an infectious smile, and soon the three of us are laughing, though we have no idea what about. Suddenly I see Ruth's eyes turn dark. She has noticed some other families approaching across the lawn. They have normal children.

'Excuse me,' she mumbles. She quickly picks up Felicity and carries her over to the non-profit playground.

The families are now on the edge of the playground. Their children are running towards the swing, the bigger ones making their way to the basketball pitch. I stand up to look behind the painted fence. Felicity is sitting in the sand pit, Ruth is kneeling next to her. I open the little gate and join them. I kneel on the sand beside Felicity and show her how to build a sand castle. Halfway through she always demolishes it, laughing so hard that I can't hear properly what Ruth is saying.

'She is usually asleep by eight. If you don't mind, come over for a cup of tea.'

We agree that I'll visit her tonight. It might do me good to get to know people in my new neighbourhood.

We're sitting at the little table in front of the only window in her flat.

'Thank you,' I say to Ruth as she places a cup of tea down on the sunflower-patterned coaster. Her home is the same size and layout as mine, but it feels smaller because of the mountains of toys all over the place.

'Sorry about the mess,' Ruth says while stroking Felicity's soft blonde hair. 'It just keeps on growing every month.'

'Is it because you have to contribute for Felicity's Right To Reside?'

She nods.

'I don't have time to go shopping,' she says. 'All I can buy is cuddly toys, which keep popping up while I'm doing my food shopping online.'

'Cuddly toys are not that bad. I had a High Spender colleague, Linda, who suffers from the same problem, but she uses SpendItAll and has numerous portraits painted of herself.'

'How does she have the time then to sit as a model?'

'She doesn't. She just gives a photo to the artist. You should see her living room, there's no space left on the wall.'

She snorts and rolls her eyes.

'I couldn't even fit a miniature in here,' she says.

We burst out laughing and Felicity, hearing us, joins in.

'She's so full of life,' I say to Ruth.

'She has always been that way, even as a baby. After she was born they tried to convince me to take her to the Junior Dignitorium, for instant euthanasia. I have to admit, I thought about it. I used to watch *Heartless*, and I wasn't sure what to think. Please, believe me, the last thing I want is for her to suffer.'

'I know.' I reach out to squeeze her hand.

'So, they didn't ask me to name her for a few days, not knowing what would happen. I grew more attached to her by the hour. Finally I decided to keep her.'

'Where did the name come from?'

'She could have been Rachel, like my sister, or Janet, like my mother. She could have been anyone, but whenever I looked into her eyes, I knew she would be Felicity.'

Felicity, hearing her name again, runs to her mother, buries her face in her skirt and giggles so hard I'm afraid she'll choke. Then she glances at me and runs over and embraces me too. I bend down and hold her close to my chest. I feel as if my very bones are melting with affection. Ruth chuckles.

'She loves everyone but it seems she has a special connection with you.'

'If you feel you need help, looking after her, just let me know,' I tell her. 'I have plenty of time. In fact, that's all I have at the moment.'

She thinks I'm being polite, I can see that. She asks me about myself. I tell her about Philip, about being left alone. I don't know whether to tell her the truth about myself, my sudden downhill journey. Would I trust my child with a stranger with mental illness?

'I've been made redundant. There weren't enough students at the school,' I lie. 'I moved here to save costs, until I find another job.'

Felicity has fallen asleep on the top of the pile of plush toys. With her rosy cheeks and golden hair she looks like one of her dolls. Ruth is making another cup of tea.

'There aren't many children like her, almost none in fact, in the Mid-Spender areas,' I remark.

'Almost all parents of these kids are Low Spenders.' Ruth nods. 'Even those who start off as Mid or High Spenders downgrade as their priorities change.'

We don't say anything for a while and I just enjoy the cosiness of the room.

'Would you really not mind?' Ruth asks out of the blue.

'It would be a pleasure.'

Ruth has two jobs, one during the day, one in the evening. The non-profit kids' nursery is open day and night because the parents – having to earn an extra Right To Reside – all work long night shifts or several jobs. We agree that I'll come and look after Felicity in the evenings, while Ruth is wiping down gym equipment after each guest in a luxury leisure centre built on a bridge over the Thames. The average High Spender spends more in the spa's health bar on a given evening than Ruth earns every month just to keep Felicity alive.

THE FIGHT

The wind went mad that morning. I woke to the branches tapping and scraping on the windowpane as if desperate to come in. I sat up in my bed, slowly coming around, my head heavy as lead. The bitter taste of heartache filled my mouth as memories of the previous day came seeping back. It was a low-grade heartache, nothing unbearable for a thirteen-year-old girl. My very first boyfriend, Luke, had broken up with me, with no explanation.

Trying to forget the humiliation, I got out of bed and dragged myself to the window. The familiar softness of the carpet beneath my feet reminded me that I was home, and I was loved. I pressed my nose to the cold windowpane. There was not a soul out in the street, only an advert screen flashing in the distance. The houses opposite looked so quiet they could have been abandoned. It seemed the storm was going to uproot the trees from the earth.

My eyes fell on my apple tree under my window. It was the first thing I saw every morning, long before I greeted any human being, and the last thing at night before I crawled into bed.

I stood in front of the mirror, holding another, smaller mirror in my hand so that I could see my profile. Yes, I thought, no wonder nobody wants me with this nose. I honestly couldn't tell which part of my face I hated more: my upturned nose that made me look like a silly child, or the dimples on my cheeks which the school bullies loved to tease me about. 'The girl with the holes in her face,' some of them called me. Mum and Dad never mentioned it in my presence; or else they tried to flatter me and said the dimples gave my face character. Other adults said how cute the dimples were; I know they were trying not to hurt my feelings. I didn't want to be cute, I wanted to be beautiful like Sofia. Turning slightly to have a better view of my profile, I decided to have a nose job once I was eighteen.

The cold foggy weather sent me back to the comfort of my bed, where I pulled the duvet up to my neck and indulged myself in grumpiness. Dad came in later, wearing the dark green bathrobe he always wore on Sundays, when he did nothing but lounge around the house. Mum followed soon, her hair freshly highlighted, her landmark blood-red lipstick already on. They sat on the side of my bed like bodyguards, ready to defend their girl. I felt like an only child. I desperately wanted to believe I was one.

Six months after Sofia's elopement, we'd stopped speaking about her. I think my parents found it easier to cope with the loss by pretending it never happened. Why build castles of hope every morning, just to see them demolished by the end of the day? She would never come back. Who would return from the glamour and privilege of an Owner's lifestyle to the Mid-Spender boredom she'd always detested; from being admired by the elite to a family she'd never connected with? Even the police's initial helpfulness vanished once they learned she had gone to her Owner boyfriend. 'Owners are untraceable,' the police officer said with a serious expression.

'Sofia wasn't born an Owner.' Mum protested. 'She has a tracker in her body.'

The police officer shrugged. 'She's sixteen, she left of her own free will,' he said. 'There's nothing we can do.'

The problems with Sofia had started when the intelligent, ambitious child grew into a mysterious teenager. She abandoned her laboratory and went out instead. I found some pictures of her on Yap! showing her hanging out with friends – none of the friends were from school. They seemed a bit older and much wealthier. She looked stunning – dangerously seductive. I recognised the logos of the places and looked them up. One of them was St Paul's Nightclub; for centuries it had been a cathedral but in the new system it had been converted. Sofia had access to the most exclusive bars where even High Spenders were not allowed, only Owners. But when I asked Sofia about it, she was offhand and wouldn't be drawn into conversation. 'Mind your own business' was all I could get out of her. She came home with diamond earrings and extravagant designer clothes, all of which made Mum worry. Sofia didn't hide the fact that she had an Owner for a boyfriend, but my parents didn't believe it until they saw him. His name was Sebastian.

'Something feels wrong about all this,' Mum said to Dad during a dinner when Sofia was away again, allegedly with Sebastian.

'Do you mean she's lying? Dad asked. 'That this Sebastian is an imposter?'

'I suspect worse than that.' Mum lowered her voice. 'I think she got these luxury objects and jewellery in an…illegal way.'

'What do you mean?'

'You know what I mean,' said Mum, shooting sideways glances at me.

'You can't be serious! You mean she gained them by working as a…'

Dad had difficulty saying what he meant, though I was old enough to know that prostitution existed.

'I'm afraid so, Ben. And that this Sebastian doesn't even exist.'

When, a few weeks later, Sebastian was introduced, it came as an enormous relief to Mum. He was real and he was wealthy indeed. When the two of them arrived in his private helicopter, my parents and I were staring out of the window. Sebastian was incredibly shy, clearly an introvert and very plain to look at, so it was clear Sofia was only interested in him for his money. Even the blind could tell they had absolutely nothing in common. Seeing them walking through the gate, Dad didn't think this could be Sebastian: he just couldn't imagine that Sofia, who had always been attracted to sporty, confident and charismatic boys, would even look at someone so far from her type. But Mum knew it straight away. 'It's him. Look at his clothes! All immaculate! The highest quality,' she exclaimed. I wasn't as naïve as Dad. I immediately understood. 'How clever of Sofia!' I thought. 'And how low!'

That evening Dad sat there with disbelief written all over his face, staring at Sofia, trying and failing to find the daughter he knew. As for Mum, the giant bouquet of rare exotic flowers delivered by a private butler swept her off her feet. She treated Sebastian like a long-lost son, the two of them chatted and enjoyed the shepherd's pie Mum had made especially to show Sebastian something other than the trendy food he was used to eating in the world's top restaurants. She was deliberately going for this cosy, home-made family style, knowing it would appeal to someone who had seen it all.

Sebastian became a regular visitor. Mum was almost grateful that he appreciated our modest home, picked up objects with curiosity, listened to everyone intently. Seeing his humble personality, Dad and I quickly warmed to him.

Soon Sebastian's initial shyness melted and a warm-hearted young man with a great sense of humour was revealed. I liked it when he came over. Our home was transformed by his laughter and we entertained him as if it was our duty to keep him laughing. What was painful for me was to see Sofia's ever-growing sense of superiority. As if she already knew that she'd be the lady of the manor. Besotted, Sebastian would stare at her with his huge, round blue eyes, a benevolent smile on his pudgy face, his white, sausage-like fingers always around her waist like an ever-tightening belt. He always smelt of talcum powder.

My envy rose to new levels, seeing how effortlessly Sofia's dream was coming true, while nothing was happening for me. Among our friends and family she became almost like a celebrity. The fact that she had taken advantage of a kind, sensitive boy just for his status didn't bother anyone. She seemed beyond moral responsibility.

Sebastian had a penthouse pad on the banks of the Thames, in a glass-walled apartment block surrounded by a laser fence and guarded by an elite security team. It was one of the few places in the city where Owners had accommodation. If I were an Owner I would prefer the countryside. Like Sebastian's parents, I would have a Victorian mansion near the Cornwall coast.

The Owners came to London to visit the Primavera Club, to enjoy the high life, and do some shopping, but after a few days they inevitably retreated to their country homes. Sebastian would come to London to see Sofia. Then one day it was Sofia who went to him, leaving us a venom-filled note on the kitchen table, saying she was finished with us and our pitiful Mid-Spender lifestyle for good. Mum and Dad didn't give up hope that after the initial fascination with luxury she would start missing us and come home. I secretly hoped she wouldn't return. We were the perfect family now, without her there to make me feel less pretty and less cool.

The first few months my parents constantly worried about her whereabouts and Dad's hair began to turn grey. 'She'll come back, she's just got into bad company,' he would say, and I had to bite my lip. I tried to be the good daughter and did everything I could to please my parents, to ease their heartache and soak up their love to the last drop, to bathe in it every day. I was glad I didn't have to share it with Sofia; she didn't want it anyway.

Still in bed, with the weather rapidly changing between sunny spells and storms, I felt sorry for myself. Eventually I got bored with flicking through the channels on the Globe and forced myself to get up and eat the sandwich Mum had prepared for me. When Mum asked what was wrong, I blamed it on the weather.

'You know, it won't hurt for too long,' she said. 'I don't even remember my first boyfriend's name.'

'I don't care. It hurts now.'

She didn't say a word but checked on me every half an hour, examining my face until I turned away. In the afternoon, all of a sudden it got really dark, because of the storm. We sat in the conservatory, watching the plants being drenched in the rain. On Yap! messages about the break-up were pouring in from my contacts; I didn't want to think about it any more, and had to switch Yap! off. I wanted a good boyfriend so badly, one who would pamper and worship me as Sebastian did Sofia. I began to share my dreams with Mum and Dad. Talking about it was almost like making it happen, their encouragement fuelling my desires, repairing my broken wings.

'I'll have a boy and a girl.' I said. 'The girl will be called May, the boy Peter.'

'Why Peter?' Mum interrupted, while adding some more lemonade to her Pimm's.

'I don't know.' I shrugged. 'It sounds intelligent.'

She nodded.

'It's a brave name. I can't see any harm coming to a Peter.'

'Regardless of the name, you'll find the perfect guy,' Dad said. 'Someone who deserves you. Now let's hear the rest.' He pulled his bathrobe tighter around his body. It was turning chilly. Mum turned up the conservatory temperature on her ID Phone.

'Carry on; just make it up,' Dad continued. 'If you keep believing it, it will happen.' I knew my parents were just being nice and they didn't mean a word of what they said. They were lying to me, just as they did about my dimples.

We enjoyed the idle atmosphere, sitting around the table, which was packed with olives and cheese, Pimm's and lemonade. Outside the sky turned a silky midnight blue. The half-moon transformed the garden into a magical place. For a fraction of a second my dreams seemed only an arm's reach away.

Mum and Dad were listening to me describing my future husband and our home. They sat with their backs to the living room door. At some point I realised that the birds had all stopped chirping at the same time, as if they had been switched off with a remote control. I sat opposite my parents and cold blood filled my veins when halfway through a sentence I saw Sofia's figure appear in the living room, moving closer like a shadow. Soon her face was right behind the glass door. She was watching intently, not making any noise. She stood there, in shock, motionless, her eyes like burning coal. The door was ajar – who knows how long she had been listening? I broke off as if I had been saying something inappropriate. The air froze and a heavy black cloud settled over the house. Sofia was back. I didn't want her there. I looked at my parents in panic as if they had the power to send the spectre away.

We all jumped up, torn from our happy conversation. My parents, overcome with joy, both gave her a long hug. She was like a stick in their arms. Dad looked at her with concern.

'You look ill. What's happened to you?'

She was much paler than usual but she just shrugged and didn't reply. Her almond-shaped eyes were shielded, guarding her secrets, but an underlying fear filtered through, something I'd never seen before in her. My parents' joy over her return was tainted by her unnatural silence. I sensed she resented me for sharing all my dreams so intimately with our parents.

All evening she treated me like an enemy. While we were eating, the food turned bitter in my mouth. Sofia didn't touch her plate, even though Mum had done everything to give her a proper celebration and had ordered her favourite take-out. Her eyes bored into me, filled with accusation.

'Where is your lovely Sebastian?' Mum asked, but met only with silence.

Dad begged Sofia for ages to say something and she still didn't, but went up to her room. Despite a strong sense of danger I couldn't help sneaking out of my room and knocking on her door. I was desperate to hear about life in the deluxe city pad on the riverside; I wanted to know what it felt like to be an Owner, whether the concierge really bowed before her, how the interior of a private jet differed from a normal one, and whether Sebastian's parents were really as posh as he'd said. Secretly gloating, I assumed she had broken up with Sebastian and so lost the privileges of the Owner lifestyle, forced back into the so despised Mid-Spender boredom. Like a small predator recklessly deciding to take on a bigger competitor, I ignored the fear swirling in my stomach.

She opened the door with a face that could have killed. Her hair was dishevelled, her eyes wild.

'What happened to Sebastian?'

'None of your business.'

'Are you ashamed to admit he's ditched you?'

'Mind your own crap. Just carry on building your family in the clouds.'

'So he ditched you.'

She slammed the door in my face. I felt glorious. Yes, Sebastian got bored with Sofia and ditched her, I thought, and now she's back to the life, the house she so despised, and penniless. A rush of superiority ran through my body. All my earlier insecurity faded.

That night I couldn't sleep. I was trying to listen for any noises from her room through the thin wall behind my head, but no sound came through. I was in two minds about Sofia's return. On the one hand, I was glad she had been proved wrong, her arrogance broken. On the other hand I felt our home was poisoned. Sofia's presence, like slowly spilt ink, had soaked into every corner of the house. I could feel it on my skin.

The next day was a Sunday. My parents were at home, pretending that we were one happy family, now that Sofia had returned to us. By noon they were starting to be concerned about her as she hadn't left her room. They crept up the stairs, to the landing. Mum put her ear to her door. Nothing. Dad was looking at her with worry.

'Sofia!' Dad shouted. 'Are you okay?'

No answer.

'Honey, are you awake?' Mum asked.

The silence behind the door wasn't like when someone is pretending that they are not in the room. It really felt empty. Dad began knocking.

'Sofia. Open up! We just want to know how you are.'

'I'm begging you, darling. Just say a word. Then we'll leave you alone,' Mum cried.

There was nothing for minutes but then suddenly we heard the door unlock and Sofia came out of her room. She ignored us completely, and hurried into the bathroom. Some minutes later she returned to her room, slammed her door and locked it. We had only seen her for a few seconds but it was enough. I could sense my parents' shock. For the first time in her life, our strong, arrogant, beautiful Sofia, was broken. With her ashen face, black circles under her eyes, the empty expression, she was a totally different person. Mum and Dad were anxious, while I was more curious.

'You never loved him. It can't be that bad,' I shouted through the door until Mum hushed me and Dad led me downstairs, shooting me several scolding looks.

'But seriously,' I protested. 'You both know I'm right.'

'Maybe she loved him. Don't assume you know other people's feelings.'

'Oh, come on, Mum, don't be ridiculous,' I kept my voice unnaturally loud, hoping she would hear me from upstairs. 'She is incapable of loving anyone and anything apart from money.' I made this last sentence louder than the rest. Dad ushered me further away.

We continued our day as usual; I helped Mum cook while Dad made some small repairs in the garden and the shed. The radio was on in the kitchen – Mum turned it up, probably to stop herself from thinking. Her mind was disturbed, I could tell. Through the window I saw Dad out in the garden, the worry on his face making him look twenty years older. I was itching to turn down the volume on the radio, to tell Mum what I was thinking; that I was sure Sofia had never loved or even liked Sebastian, so the only thing she was mourning with such melodrama was her Owner lifestyle. I was glad she would learn her lesson now; she might even become a bit humbler and more appreciative. But the empty look in her eyes was haunting me and I caught myself worrying in case she did something to harm herself. We couldn't do anything about it, with her door locked.

'Take this up to her.' Mum pushed a tray of sandwiches and a glass of water in my hand. 'But don't you dare say anything nasty to her. I'll hear it if you do.'

Of course, she didn't open no matter how much I knocked or shouted that her food was ready. It was the same empty silence glaring from her room. I put the tray on the floor.

'Room service is still there if you want it.' I went back downstairs to the kitchen. Nothing else happened that day, not on the outside, but three minds were whirring non-stop, wondering, asking, fearing, hoping. I hated to admit it but even I began to worry. This was not like Sofia at all.

'I'll find out how she is,' I said to my parents after dinner. 'I'll take this up to her.' I grabbed an apple.

'Be kind to her, sweetheart.' Dad said. I nodded and went up.

The tray with the food from earlier was still on the floor, untouched.

I was listening in front of her door before I knocked.

'Sofia, you must eat something. Mum and Dad are seriously worried.'

Nothing.

'If you don't eat, they'll call the police to break the door down.'

My empty threat worked. I heard the shuffle of clothes being moved, feet dragging on the carpet. She opened the door, looking like a ghost. The empty look in her eyes had been replaced by a deep, penetrating hatred. A hatred that could kill. I instinctively backed off. She quickly picked up the tray and placed it down in her room.

'Now get away.' She mumbled.

'You don't want the apple?'

Instead of answering she tried to close the door but I didn't let her. For some seconds I felt genuinely sorry for her. She was in a terrible state and I wanted to say something encouraging.

'Instead of rotting in here, you could go out again. I'm sure you could find someone else. Another Owner.'

It didn't come out the way I meant it. Her features were distorted by the malice in her eyes. She stood in the doorway, blocking it with her body and outstretched arms.

'What's your problem?' I burst out. 'Are you jealous?'

'Of you?'

'That I'll have the life I've always wanted. And you won't.'

Suddenly she grabbed my hand and pulled me into the room. She slammed the door behind me, and locked it with her ID Phone. I didn't have mine on me. I was trapped.

'Do you want to know what I really think of your bloody plans?' she hissed. 'They're the typical little dreams of a spoilt princess like you, for a world that only exists inside your stupid little head. I've seen the world, the real one. I've seen what's in store for you, how you'll all end up. You and your plans are pathetic, and you're a selfish idiot for wanting the same for your kids!'

'You're just jealous,' I yelled. 'How can you even compare my family plans with your useless, hedonistic lifestyle?'

Her face went dark. I'm sure she was surprised at my use of the word hedonistic and it crossed her mind that I had heard it from our parents and that it meant they were criticising her in her absence.

'I'd rather live in the Zone than be a Mid Spender!' she shouted. I wasn't listening any more.

'You might live in luxury for the rest of your life, but I don't give a shit,' I continued with victory in my voice. 'I'll be more than just a decoration. I have a future!'

I turned around to force the door open but it remained locked, and before I could start banging on it, she knocked me away. I landed on her bed, and saw her coming closer.

'Your future?' she spat. 'I can tell you about your fucking future–'

'I'm not going to listen to this.'

But I had no way of leaving the room. I scrambled up and looked her in the eye.

'At least try to accept with dignity that Mum and Dad love me more. Just go back to your Sebastian. We don't want you here.'

She stared at me for a while. For the first time, I wasn't afraid of her. I felt my parents' loving hands on my shoulders. We were three. She was on her own.

'I'd like to be there when reality hits you, you stupid fuck,' she screamed.

'My reality will be a loving family, a happy home, a fulfilled life. Yours will be nothing but empty luxury! Empty!'

I kept on shouting, hoping Dad would hear and come to my rescue. Sofia suddenly grabbed my shoulders and shook me. I wriggled out of her grip but she pushed me to the door and pulled my hair back. She looked me right in the eye. I was sure there was insanity in that gaze. For a moment I was convinced she was really going to hurt me.

'Stop playing your childish games with me,' she hissed. 'You'll never have your own family. And even if you do, you'll lose them and you will die a lonely and miserable death.'

'Let me go. Dad, help me.'

'And you'll never have any children!'

The blood drained from my face and I stopped breathing with the shock. She released her grip on my shoulders and dragged me over to the door. She scanned her ID phone and the lock released with a click.

'Now get out of my room!'

I looked at her as if she was the devil himself. Then I tore the door open and ran. Dad went up to speak to her, while I stayed with Mum in their bedroom, terrified. Mum kept asking what had happened but I couldn't stop shaking and crying. I felt as if Sofia had trampled on my delicately constructed world and it had collapsed like a tower of cards under the weight of her fury. Dad soon returned, saying her door was locked and she was playing loud music.

'She won't get away with it. I'll talk to her tomorrow,' he said grimly. The wrinkles running across his forehead became more pronounced.

In my bedroom I made sure I locked the door. That night my sleep was disturbed and in the morning I woke in a pool of sweat and tears. When I went down for breakfast, Mum told me Sofia was gone again. All she'd left behind was a message, black letters written with a marker pen on the white wall of her bedroom: 'YOU'RE ALL DEAD TO ME'.

But the main shock came when Dad went out to the garden. He saw something and tried to hide it, but I could tell he was shaken, as he stood rooted to the spot, staring out. I knew at once that it was my apple tree. Dad told me not to come any closer. He stood in the doorway so I couldn't go out, but I ran into the living room and from the window I could see it clearly. The tree had been slashed at with an axe and its bark criss-crossed with a sharp blade like the scalpel Sofia kept in her laboratory. Some of its branches lay on the ground, like severed arms.

Though relieved that Sofia had left, I didn't know how much I could believe her promise that she'd never return. With time came proof that it was true. It was the last time we saw her. After months of painful uncertainty for my parents and newly found freedom for me, a photo was uploaded on Yap! of her wedding day with Sebastian. She wore a champagne-coloured wedding gown that embraced her perfect figure. Sebastian's chubby white face radiated pride and disbelief. The photo must have been taken in an exotic location. They stood on top of a rock, the crystal blue ocean behind them. For a long time, my parents tried to get in touch with her, but it all proved fruitless. We wouldn't have known even if she had died.

SIX

Far away from the London I'm familiar with, I get off the monorail at the Zone Visitor Centre. There are no condos here, only an empty square populated with rusting statues and a fountain that no longer flows. On the right, an angular grey building looms over the square, blocking out the sunlight. From either side of it a massive concrete wall extends, farther than the eye can see. The wall enclosing the Zone is as high as a two-storey building, and smooth like a mirror, impossible to climb.

I'm dreading seeing my father-in-law. I will continue to help him, but I don't know if it's out of love or pity, or out of pure selfishness, because he's my last remaining connection to Philip.

My e-trolley follows me up the ramp, and I enter the ash-grey building that is the Visitor Centre. It's equally bleak inside and out, without any windows or decoration. Artificial light, brighter than the sun, streams from all directions but I can't identify a specific source. Endless rows of metal benches line the waiting hall, packed with visitors and their e-trolleys. I sit down in a quiet corner. The announcement keeps asking us to wait patiently until our name is called out. It could be half an hour. It could be much longer.

It's strange how Antonio and I have become closer after Philip's disappearance. We would never admit it, but now we only have each other. 'What can you have in common with her?' he asked Philip, not long after we were married. I'd just arrived home from work and wanted to surprise Philip on his birthday, sneaking quietly into the apartment with a cake, balloons and a bunch of flowers. Philip answered something in my defence, though I don't recall exactly what. It was all I could do not to drop everything. 'She is the perfect product of this rotten society. The very type of woman you always wanted to avoid,' Antonio spat. Philip was about to reply when I did drop the cake, and they both looked up in surprise. Antonio gave me a sharp look and stood up, ready to leave. 'What did I tell you?' he said to Philip, giving a final glance of disgust at the gifts I was bearing. 'Don't you know, bella, he doesn't like sweets? Or do you just not care?' Philip sent him home, and tried to reassure me that I mustn't take his father's behaviour personally, but the day was ruined.

Antonio grew up in Italy and moved to the UK as a hopeful young artist at the start of the new system. Before he lost his senses, he was a reputable painter and sculptor. But madness slowly took over. First he refused some lucrative commissions from the council, including sculptures for shopping centres. Then he refused offers from private customers. The number of commissions he received kept on shrinking until one day, three years ago, he stopped working for money. He continued painting for joy and gave his work away to schools. Philip and I begged him to find a job, any kind of job, just to keep his Right To Reside, but he didn't listen. We knew he was slipping away, but his decision to move to the Zone, still came as a shock. After that Philip worked even harder to remain a Mid

Spender, to prove his father wrong.

We both thought Antonio wouldn't last long in the Zone. I don't know how a feeble artistic soul like him, who found our spender areas unbearable, managed to stay alive in what must be the most dangerous place on Earth. The Zone is a hotbed of crime, with the convicts who are dumped there forming violent gangs. Apart from them, most Zone residents are just non-profit people – orphans, the ill and disabled, the long-term unemployed and those without savings – people who have no right to reside on this planet, but are not lucky enough to qualify for the Dignitorium. For that, you need at least ten years of employment. Despite being entitled to it, Antonio refused to retire in the Dignitorium.

On a low glass table in front of me is a pile of Zone flyers. Out of boredom I reach for one. They are there to take away, to discourage us and those we know from ending up in the Zone. It's heart-breaking to see the photos of the half-collapsed buildings, the dilapidated roads, the rat-infested squares, the bodies covered and carried away on makeshift stretchers. It's like a war zone, but worse. In war, there is at least hope that peace will one day be restored; but in the Zone, people only hope that death will come swiftly, releasing them from this netherworld. I throw the flyer back quickly, as if it were burning hot. Not that I'm much better off; I'm just as doomed as Antonio and the rest. During my sleepless nights, panic gnaws at my insides, and I'm tortured by questions about the future. How will I earn my Right To Reside if I'm not allowed to work? How will my savings, just enough for seven months, last for twelve? I still have visions of my last day at school, in which I see Charlie's malicious grin as I'm dragged to the T-wing by iron-armed nurses for instant euthanasia.

I remind myself of Pastor Obi's words at Sunday Mass, reassuring us that only one per cent of the population ends up in the Zone, contrary to the old system in which more than ninety per cent were considered poor and the number grew year by year. I firmly believe that with the government's help, it can go down even further. Building the Distribution Centre, basically a rubbish tip, was a great idea and now – I remember they said it on the Globe – thousands of items are left there every day. Of course, some people still don't understand that there's no electricity inside the Zone, so they take washing machines and other things for which the residents have no use. It's kind of the government to provide the Zone with clean water, given how much it costs to maintain the piping system. It's an act of philanthropy, of kindness, a good example for us to follow.

Twenty minutes have passed, but it feels like much longer. My body is not used to the cold metal seat. On the giant screen there's a list of things visitors are recommended to bring, like matches, blankets, footwear, medicine and so on. Antonio always asks for three bottles of red wine, the maximum amount of alcohol that visitors are allowed to bring in with them. The waiting room is filling up steadily. Some people are coming back from the meeting hall, weeping desperately, grabbing the guards by the arm and demanding answers they know they'll never get. These scenes are far too familiar; I witness them every month. Their loved ones haven't turned up to meet them and there's no way of contacting them in the Zone.

Finally I hear my name among a dozen others. We make our way to the checking room, followed by our e-trolleys. It feels like being in an airport. The checking room is illuminated with white lights that practically pierce the skin, and stern-looking officers in indigo-coloured uniforms form a line like soldiers. I'm asked to enter a little Portacabin that looks like a steel lift. Inside it's pitch dark. After only a few seconds, a flash of indigo light and a buzzing sound, the door opens to let me out. The scanner sees right inside my body, inside my very bones, and looks into the depths of my e-trolley. For a moment I wonder if it can see inside my mind.

I'm in a place that resembles a sports hall cut in two by a glass wall. Before the wall, there is a long row of cubicles. I need to wait until one is vacant. Officers are hurrying up and down; one of them grabs my e-trolley, switches off the 'follow the owner' setting and pushes it away. Wherever I look, people are wiping their eyes and kissing the glass wall where on the opposite side a loved one is weeping.

The smooth plastic seat is still warm when I sit down. While waiting, I look through the glass to the other side of the hall. In the far distance, scrawny, gaunt-faced people dressed in ragged clothes are hurrying to the mountains of rubbish, jumping at the freshly distributed sacks of clothes, bed linen and tinned food. A boy, no older than ten, picks up a bicycle, but two others seize it and push him away. They run off with the bike, leaving the unlucky boy on top of a pile of sacks, struggling to get up. A guard on the other side of the wall is placing the contents of my e-trolley on the table. Soon it is returned to me, empty.

Finally, Antonio arrives. He sits down opposite me; as usual his greying shoulder-length hair looks like he's just got out of bed. There is a sense of eagerness about him, almost busyness, which is quite absurd given his position. For a moment I feel I'm wasting his precious time. Despite being in his early sixties, he's incredibly nimble. Having a conversation with Antonio has always felt like trying to catch a butterfly by hand and unless I can fly with him, there's no way to follow his conversation.

'I wish you could bring more wine, bella,' he says, looking over the goods I've brought.

'You know that I don't make the rules here.'

'But thanks for these. Matches never last, someone must be eating them secretly. Having a cold soup is bearable but a cold bath is a big no. Everything OK? You're not looking like a happy bride-to-be.'

This is not the first time he has suggested that I should re-marry. Is he really that stupid or is he joking? I don't know any more. All I know is that I'm already losing my patience.

'You want me to stop coming?'

'Calm yourself, bella. I'm just being practical.'

You and practicality, I'm thinking, but I bite my tongue.

'You have to be practical to survive in your precious spender areas,' he says in a taunting voice. 'Filippo is out of the way. You need to find another breeder.'

I want to remind him that he's talking about his own son, but I manage to hold back.

'He was not the most ideal candidate for the role, anyway,' he remarks.

I struggle to calm my raging nerves. He's my only living family, I keep telling myself, though it's not strictly true. He's the only living family member I'm in touch with.

I check the time. Two more minutes, then I'll go.

'Are you alright?' he asks, watching me closely.

'Of course.'

'Don't bullshit me. What's happened?'

'Well…I've lost my job. And I've become a Low Spender.'

'You say this like you've been through a tsunami. Do you expect me to feel sorry for you? Me? The Zone resident?'

'At least you're free from worrying about your Right To Reside.'

'Want to swap? Just joking.' He snorts. 'I'd never let my community down.'

Really? It's on the tip of my tongue. But you didn't mind letting your family down, did you? I'm fuming inside; I can't stand his condescending expression. If he's as busy as he makes out, I don't want to hold him up. I get up from my chair.

'I just wanted to bring these in. See you in a month, Antonio.'

'I know I seem like an ungrateful jerk,' he says, 'but next time, no Cabernet Sauvignon, I beg you. Just Pinot Noir or Merlot. With my meagre diet, Cabernet is just too heavy.'

'Any other requests, sir?'

'Haha, very funny. Let me see. No, just the normal stuff. By the way, have you finally decided to have plastic surgery? It worked, if you ask me.'

'What?'

'You look younger and more relaxed than ever.'

I know he's just mocking me. I really shouldn't have shared anything about myself with him.

'Start enjoying life, bella. For the first time, you can,' he says, jumping up from the chair.

He quickly shoves everything into his shabby non-electric trolley. He waves to me in his typical light-hearted way, and vanishes. I stay seated for a bit, trying to recover, until the guard asks me to give up my seat for the next visitor.

In the distance, Antonio re-appears for a moment, pulling his trolley, swaggering towards the pile of sacks in the collection hall. The young boy who didn't get the bike is still on top of the pile, shaking out the remaining breadcrumbs from a buckled steel bread bin.

Felicity is fast asleep. She's just had her lunch – macaroni cheese, her favourite. Among the cuddly toys, rag dolls and plastic cubes, she looks like a tiny enchanted princess, her golden hair scattered all over the pillow. Occasionally she gurgles in her sleep; she must be in little girl heaven. With her left hand she's clutching my index finger. Ruth says that before I arrive – as if she can sense it – Felicity goes to the door and sits down in front of it, waiting.

Start enjoying life. For the first time, you can. Antonio's words keep haunting me. Is it possible that this time he wasn't mocking me? Was he right about my skin? I gently extract my finger from Felicity's clutch and lift my ID phone up to switch on the mirror function, when the bell rings.

On the door-cam I see a platinum blonde woman in a black two-piece outfit. I have no idea who she is.

'Hello?' I say, keeping my eyes on her.

'Who is it? Is Ruth there?'

'I'm Felicity's babysitter. Who are you?'

'I'm her grandmother. Would you let me in?'

Now it springs to mind that Ruth said her mum might pop over from time to time. When I asked more about her, Ruth didn't reply and quickly changed the subject.

This woman is in her mid-fifties, has immaculate hair, and wears bright-pink lipstick. Her black skirt and matching blazer are a perfect fit and of the softest material, beautifully complemented by a black leather handbag. Her clothes and accessories show so little wear and tear that it reminds me of the rumour about some High Spenders who wear things only once. She's a typical High Spender, I would think, from her appearance, but in her eyes there's a surprising gentleness. She keeps glancing nervously at her ID Phone.

'I don't have much time left from my lunch break. Can I have ten minutes with her?'

'She's asleep.'

'I won't wake her. I'll only be watching her.'

She checks her ID Phone again, then quickly removes it from her wrist and hands it over to me. 'If it rings, don't answer it. My husband mustn't know I'm here.'

While she carefully draws open the partition curtain behind which Felicity sleeps, I sit in the living room, eying her ID Phone on the table. Its metal body is gold-plated, telling the world it belongs to a High Spender.

When she returns, her eyes are wet, her make-up smudged. She grabs her ID Phone, hurries to the Globe on the wall and charges it up with money.

'I know she won't accept it. But please try to convince her.'

Her eyes are pleading and when I nod reassuringly, she thanks me and dashes out of the flat. I go to check on Felicity. She's in the same position as she was, but there's a pink lip-shaped stain in the middle of her forehead. From the window I can see Ruth's mother running across the lawn, her pencil skirt limiting her moves, her high heels buckling on the lumpy grass. With the help of the pilot she climbs into a golden-coloured heli-taxi. While the taxi is taking off, she holds the ID Phone close to her face, probably correcting her make-up. Now that her nervous energy has left the flat, I can hear the birds chirping outside again. Antonio's unwanted words ring in my head, Start enjoying life…

THE PARTY

I was in the staff room, making coffee and thinking about the night before. I'd dreamed about a mystery man in a hood for the third time that month. It was always the same dream: he was approaching me with a wide grin on his face that kept growing. He handed me a bundle in a blanket. When I held it in my arms, I saw it was a baby, then a door somewhere behind me slammed shut and I woke with a scream. Luckily Philip had never been woken up by it.

The staffroom was suffocating, reeking of Linda's latest perfume, which always announced her presence before anyone could actually see her. She was chatting to a group of colleagues, boasting about the film set she and her husband Mark had visited over the weekend.

When the bell rang, all the teachers hurried to their classrooms. Linda made herself another coffee. I had a free period so I stayed on. She sat down next to me, bringing a cloud of the nauseating floral scent with her.

'You know, we never have the chance to get to know one another,' she said, squirming like a cat. 'You're always in your own world.'

'Don't take it personally, Linda. I'm just tired. In between lessons I really need to clear my head.'

'We're having a little party at ours tomorrow evening. Come over with Philip.'

Thanks to Mark, who was a Globe executive, Linda lived in one of the wealthiest High-Spender areas. I must have irritated her, never joining her crowd of admirers, passing them by with a well-constructed smile but sitting as far away as possible. I knew that putting Linda and Philip together in the same room would be a recipe for disaster, but not wanting to give her more ground for gossip, I accepted the invitation.

Back home that afternoon, I was watching parents playing with their children in the park, chasing each other on the lawn, others walking and collecting the orange and yellow leaves that had fallen. Beautiful fresh ones, not yet withered. I tried hard not to think about the fact that I had turned thirty-two the previous day.

As I'd expected, Philip wasn't keen on going to the party.

'I would only ruin it for you,' he said. 'If I have to listen to them, I'll be sick.'

'It's been a long time since we met anyone new.'

'You're always saying what a bitch Linda is.' Philip sighed.

I told him to sleep on it.

An hour later Philip and I were sitting on the roof terrace, at a table packed with leftover canapés and cakes I had treated myself to for my birthday. The birthday Philip had completely forgotten about. The sun was shining, and the sky was clear. The humming of the lively crowd on the promenade rose up from below. I immediately recognised the sound of a food trolley, its wheels catching on a door frame, making the cutlery clatter. I heard a bottle of wine being corked from our neighbour's terrace, which was adjacent to ours.

'Hiya, guys.' Ted, our neighbour, waved to us over the ivy-covered wall. 'Nice day today, isn't it?'

'Lovely,' I replied. 'Celebrating something?'

Philip pretended not to have noticed him. Turning his back on Ted, he started fiddling with a candle holder on the table.

'Just life, that's all,' Ted said, raising a glass of white wine. 'The kids are away on a school excursion, you know.' June, his wife, came out to the terrace pushing a food trolley packed with silver dishes. It was just an ordinary weekday but June looked like a glamour model with her freshly highlighted hair and false eyelashes. I greeted her and sat back in my chair. The partition wall stopped them from seeing us when sitting, but I could hear the clinking of crystal glasses and muffled conversation.

Philip didn't touch any of the food. Just one day before, on my birthday, I had sworn to myself to bring life back into our marriage, and that I would not compromise on the baby issue. Now, admitting my failure, I repressed the urge to shake him. I loved Philip but I repeatedly found myself wondering why all my friends and colleagues had fun, adventure-loving husbands, while mine seemed to suck all the life out of me.

'I'm exhausted, Ali,' Philip said quietly, so the neighbours couldn't hear. 'Not just now; it's permanent and getting worse.'

'Do you want to go part-time?' I asked. 'Are you ready to pay the price for it?'

I meant it as a joke, of course; I would never have considered downgrading to the Low-Spender area, but he replied in a serious tone.

'I wouldn't mind. Tom's a Low Spender; they are OK with it.'

'I would ask Tom again when something happens to his kids.'

'Because nothing ever happens to kids in Mid-Spender areas – is that what you mean?'

His words were enough to make me shiver, despite the warm

sunshine. I was wondering if he enjoyed reminding me of that day, to torture me. I felt Philip was accusing me of forgetting too easily. But I hadn't. Joshua's seat in my class – still vacant – served as a constant reminder, as did the quiet fear in the air, and the flowers I saw every day laid around the school gate. It nearly broke my heart.

'Life goes on, Philip. It's tragic, but–'

'What kind of life do you mean?'

'Sometimes I really think you don't love me any more.'

He looked up with eyes that were filled with pain. I reached out for his hand.

'I admit things aren't perfect. But it's because we're not doing the right thing, Philip. We try to compensate with books, shopping, dinners, the Globe. But what we need – what I want – is a child.'

He was listening intently.

'What future do you imagine for that child?'

'Why did you keep promising then? For all these years?'

'I never promised anything.'

'But you were never opposed to it either. You said the time would come when you'd be ready–'

'No, I didn't. You said that, and expected me to agree.'

'And why can't you agree?'

'Because I have concerns, Ali. I'm not sure any responsible person could bring a child into this world. Can't you see that?'

I didn't know what to say for a while. I sat there, listening to the laughter seeping over from Ted's terrace, wondering what the world would come to if everyone thought like Philip.

'You're becoming more and more like your dad,' I blurted out.

I could see that this hurt him. It hurt me to say it, too. But it had to be said. Just like Antonio, Philip had become contemptuous towards the Owners and increasingly cynical about everything. I couldn't understand how it had happened, right before my eyes. But the most disturbing thing was that I had to decide whether I wanted to spend the rest of my life like this. I had lots of temptations. It would have been so easy to enter that door from my dream before it slammed shut. To take the baby from the man in the hood.

'OK, I take back what I said about your dad. But we mustn't let some homeless thugs steal our dreams away from us. We're safe here. It was a one off.'

'That's not much consolation.'

'I told you there are guards now. The school feels like a military base, with drones hovering permanently above the yard. The government has invested a huge amount in security.'

He looked up at me.

'Do you really believe they care?'

'I know it's a good initiative. Stop being so negative, I want to enjoy myself. Come.'

'Where?'

'Come, I'll show you something.'

I pulled him up from the chair and led him over to the edge of the terrace.

'Have a look at this!'

We both looked down at the park below. I started counting out loud.

'Now, there are seven children down there. Seven children whose parents chose to believe in a future. Seven children whose parents look after their own family instead of dwelling on something that can't be changed. Seven–'

'Our life is not stable right now.'

'Philip, I'm thirty-two.'

I hated raising my voice but any willingness to understand his point suddenly dissipated. I had always been so attracted to his darkness and mystery but now they merely reminded me of the distance between us. Mum's words kept ringing in my ears, that a jovial type would be more suitable for me, someone full of joy and optimism. And my impulsive reply that I didn't want anyone else.

'It's not you, Ali. But I keep seeing the faces of those abducted children.' His voice was ghostlike, melancholy.

'Phil.'

'I'm useless.'

'You'll be a wonderful father. I know it.'

The party was a disaster. The only good thing about it was that we got to see an exclusive High-Spender area and the inside of Linda's stunning Georgian villa. Even from a distance Philip could tell it was fake, a good imitation but still fake, built at the beginning of the new system. 'Look at the wall; it's perfect,' he whispered. 'It would be worn and darker if it were original.'

The streets were unusually wide and empty, and at the end of Linda's street there was a heli-taxi station with helicopters parked outside. Linda's mansion stood in a French formal garden, with a mini-waterfall at the back. When Philip saw it, he pulled a face of disgust.

'One hour, not a minute longer,' he said, checking the time on his ID phone. 'I'll shoot off, with or without you.'

Linda welcomed us with an exaggerated smile, holding an oversized champagne glass in her hand. I felt awkward and followed Philip into a corner, where we hoped to observe the party without having to make conversation with the other guests, all snobbish High Spenders. Sensing the icy superiority in the air, I regretted accepting the invitation.

The house didn't appeal to me. In the sleek, modern interior, white and gold dominated, but the lack of curtains made me miss our cosy apartment. I saw a bespoke sofa, serpentine in shape, designed for sixteen people. Among the numerous professional photos on the walls hung a life-sized painting of Linda, posing in a white fur coat.

They were all eagerly waiting for the arrival of a special guest, a certain Tiara Joy, a senior winner of that year's *Elevate!*, a programme in which participants compete to become a High-Spender celebrity. Every year the lavish lifestyle of the winner is broadcast on the Globe. There are two age groups: under and over forties. Tiara won after she walked in to her audition stark naked, but for a pink flower headband. The tabloids were full of gossip about her 'hot body'. In her mid-forties, she was still very attractive and youthful, with long platinum-blond hair. Philip and I agreed we had to flee the party before Tiara's arrival.

The conversation revolved around a new app called SpendItAll, which was designed for those who didn't have the time to spend the minimum amount to earn their Right To Reside in any given month. At the press of a button on SpendItAll, Linda ordered the painting of herself and paid for it or for any of the millions of offers on the app, and she and Mark were saved, and could remain High Spenders for the next month. Linda said in a dramatic voice that she was getting bored with paintings and from next month she needed new suggestions from SpendItAll.

I exchanged frequent glances with Philip. He was staring at the garish portrait of Linda on the wall. At this moment Mark approached Philip. His skin was unnaturally orange, but the wrinkles around his eyes and on his forehead were white. After making small talk for a few minutes, Mark offered Philip an exclusive interview slot on the Globe, an opportunity that could lead to bigger, more important contracts, and celebrity architect status for Philip. For example, to finish the Paradise project, as Mark hinted. The other guests' conversation had died away and I held my breath. Apparently the previous architect had had a heart attack, it turned out later, but Philip rejected the offer anyway, so it didn't matter.

My view of Linda as the most snobbish person on Earth changed when I realised she wasn't as bad as most of her guests. One of them, a frighteningly elderly fashion designer wearing a frilly dress and a pink fascinator as big as her head, was talking loudly and contemptuously about aspiring High Spenders. Even with her back to me, I could sense her words were addressed to us. I felt shame filling every part of my body. Philip only had to look at me once to see how I was feeling. He took my hand and dragged me out of the room, without saying goodbye.

As we were crossing the lawn, we saw a bright pink heli-taxi land in front of Linda's mansion. Two bodyguards in black suits disembarked before helping out a blonde woman in a golden mini dress. It was Tiara Joy, squeaking instructions at her staff. We scurried away as fast as we could. I expected Philip to be upset, but he was easy-going, and joked about the party on the way home.

'That ageing fashion designer looked like a walking skeleton,' he said in the street, laughing.

'A skeleton dressed up as a ballerina,' I said, giggling. We laughed and kissed and zig-zagged across the pavement, arm in arm. Philip did a brilliant imitation of the fashion designer: 'And, honestly, you can't go anywhere these days without bumping into High Spender wannabees. How thoroughly disagreeable!'

I could still see the shock on Linda's face when Philip refused the job on moral grounds. 'Moral grounds?' Philip exclaimed. 'They don't even understand the word.' We laughed so hard it hurt.

The next day, to our surprise, Mark gave Philip a ring.

'Fashion designers can be horrible. Don't take it to heart, Philip. My offer still stands.'

I don't know if it was Mark's apology, or his relaxed style, or maybe our underlying desire to become High Spenders, but Philip later agreed to finish the Paradise project; his first and last work on a shopping centre.

SEVEN

The end of the month is dangerously close now. We have only three days left to catch up with our spending to qualify for the class we are in. I am on the promenade, making my way to the monorail stop. While I feel drained by the typical end-of-month crowd, with everyone rushing to spend what is required, I can't help but find it amusing. In front of me, a middle-aged man is dragging an oversized plush crocodile, clearly bought just to increase his spending as he must have teenage children now. A mother with two small children is followed by three fully packed e-trolleys bigger than her kids. From a distance they look like five kids obediently following their mother.

I've just checked my account and I have some spending to do. Of course, the last thing on my mind this month was shopping. I still have time to do it, thank God for online shopping and instant home delivery, which is – like all transportation – done very efficiently by underground trains. But shopping for me now is a chore and I don't understand how I could have enjoyed it so much when I was an affluent Mid Spender.

I have arrived at Nurse Vogel's street. Like me, she lives in a Low-Spender area, but it's a much rougher neighbourhood than mine. Next to her building, just beyond a fenced-off area, a group of tower blocks are awaiting demolition. A mega-excavator is being driven slowly towards the first building, followed by a group of construction workers. A large billboard advertises a new luxury High Spender development.

Nurse Vogel lives in a standalone tower block, one of six that form a circle around a modest local supermarket and a little playground. Sadness lingers over the place; the people's faces are wrinkled and gaunt, their clothing drab. They keep their heads down and I feel horribly out of place, embarrassed that I might exude a superior air of pride and confidence I picked up unintentionally when I was a Mid Spender. Nurse Vogel must have a good income from the Dignitorium. She could even be a Mid Spender. So why has she chosen this place?

She lives on the ninth floor. In the tiny lift, I'm overcome with sympathy for her, as it strikes me that most of her friends and family must be gone by now. I wonder what it might feel like to be alone in the world, that everyone we have ever known is dead and we are left behind like a museum piece. But then I realise I am in exactly the same position. All my loved ones are dead and gone.

At the end of a narrow, poorly lit corridor I find her flat, Number 62. I'm shocked to see that her door is covered in graffiti: 'Non-profit scum!' The dark red paint has run on the white surface and dried like blood.

When she opens the door, I almost don't recognise her. She's wearing a loose top in vibrant purple and a pair of wide-legged turquoise trousers with Indian mandala patterns. An oversized wooden necklace is hanging around her neck and her curly hair, fully let down for once, is framed by a colourful headscarf. She greets me with a smile and when I ask about the graffiti, she only shrugs.

'I used to clean it off but it only encourages them. So now I just ignore it. Come in.'

I find myself in a square-shaped studio, lined with floor-to-ceiling bookshelves.

'But what's their problem with you?'

'I guess they're right. I should have long retired like other women of my age.' She points to an armchair under the window. 'Make yourself at home.'

'How can people be so cruel?'

'The graffiti is not the worst of the bullying, trust me.' There's no anger or bitterness in her voice. 'The subtle everyday humiliation is far more painful, for example, when my younger colleagues dismiss my advice because they think I must have lost the plot at my age.'

She drops down on the sofa, which is covered with an ancient multi-coloured blanket. I gaze around the room that she uses as her living, dining and bedroom. The flat is tiny but oozes the warmth and comfort of long-forgotten times. I wouldn't call it tidy, but the disorder lends it a special charm. I don't think I've ever visited a home without a Globe before. Seeing my face, she laughs.

'Don't be such a snob, Alice.'

'But...everything looks so...different.'

'This mix-and-match style was quite fashionable when I was young.'

My eyes wander to the mantelpiece. The vase Nurse Vogel showed me a couple of weeks ago on the phone is not orange any more. It's red.

'They changed it back,' she says when she notices me staring at it. 'But I don't care any more.'

I'm desperate to say something encouraging about the vase's

disappearance but I don't know what. I can sense a gaping loneliness, a lack of anyone who really understands her.

She leans forward and examines my face.

'Your skin is tighter and even the circles under your eyes have disappeared. I can see a twinkle returning. Am I wrong, or are you feeling better?'

I tell her about Ruth and Felicity. She keeps nodding.

'You're on the right track. I'll meet up with you anytime you need, but I've got a feeling this little Felicity will do most of the work.'

While she's in the kitchenette making jasmine tea for us, I take another look around her living room. The shelves are packed with old books, and the distinctive smell of paper hits me as I get closer. There are also framed photos everywhere. Apart from a young Nurse Vogel – her lively eyes and warm smile haven't changed over the years – there are two other people in the photos: a man with a moustache and a green-eyed, lanky boy who grew up to be a handsome young man.

She returns with two steaming mugs and places them on the low birch table between us. She notices that I'm looking at the photos.

'Your husband and son?'

She nods briefly and for a moment her face turns grave. It's strange thinking of Nurse Vogel as a wife, sister or mother. She is the epitome of the perfect carer, the rock everyone else relies on. I find it hard to imagine her with a family.

One picture is her son's graduation photo, with his name written on it: Adam MacKay.

'MacKay?' I ask, surprised. 'Not Vogel?'

'It's safer this way.'

'Safer? From what?'

'Not from what. From whom. Since the deaths of my husband and son I don't use my married name any more, so that no one will connect me to them. Of course, as the case of the vases shows, I was utterly wrong.'

Unintentionally, I turn my head to look at the vase.

'I'm fed up with putting on a brave face, Alice. I'm fed up with lying and pretending. If I tell you the truth, will you listen to me?'

I nod.

'But I'm warning you, it will go against what you were taught at school.'

Not waiting for my reply, she starts to speak, her voice more serious than I've ever heard.

'I was in my thirties when our world started to change drastically. Capitalism was out of control, the elite became greedy and ever more powerful. The gap between rich and poor grew rapidly until the very terms were meaningless. There were the ultra-rich, and then there were the rest, whose standard of living was rapidly worsening. The elite owned more than ninety per cent of the land. For me and my family just to stay in our shabby studio, we worked ourselves sick. Landlords could name any price they wanted. The home owner became the new celebrity. Men wanted to be them; women wanted to marry them. The rest of us spent our lives in meaningless drudgery. I worked so hard I had two miscarriages.'

'Two miscarriages!' I gasp.

'We lived like cattle, rent slaves, but at least we had work and an income. For the increasing part of the population that was retired, there was no way that their meagre pensions would cover the ever-rising rents, so they were dependent upon social housing and other state benefits. Of course, it couldn't go on forever, and the burden of the sick and elderly became too great to support. That's when they evicted all pensioners from their own homes and moved them to the infamous retirement homes.'

'Yes, I've heard a lot about those and how inhumane the conditions were due to the sheer number of residents.'

'I worked in them, Alice, and I wouldn't even keep a dog there. But it wasn't really the high numbers that were the problem; the elderly were simply a convenient scapegoat. In reality, if the elite had just paid their taxes, the burden on society would have been significantly reduced. Anyway, families demanded higher quality care for their loved ones, and that's when the demonisation of the old and disabled started in the media. It worked for some people, but not for most, who finally saw through the whole system, clearer than ever. Despite the fact that huge swathes of housing were newly available, after the elderly had been moved to the retirement homes, rents kept on growing. Mansions and skyscrapers stood empty while people starved on the streets. Across the world, the people started rioting. This is the real history, my dear. You won't hear it from anyone else. Those who could testify are long dead.'

She's watching me and I can't hide my confusion.

'You don't have to believe me,' she says. 'I know it must be a shock for you.'

'And your son...?'

'Adam grew up disillusioned and hopeless. He had a good job offer from Australia and he saw it as his only chance.' She quickly wipes her eye. 'I talked him out of it.'

'You make it sound like his death was your fault.'

'And probably my husband's too. Not intentionally, of course, not even directly. But if I hadn't pushed him, Adam would be still alive.'

'Pushed him to what?'

'I had only good intentions, I swear.'

These final words sound like a death sentence.

'So you talked him out of going to Australia?'

'And he listened to me. He stayed and became one of the leaders of the riots. The uprising began when his group broke into an empty skyscraper and organised the rebellion from there.'

'You must have been so proud of him.'

'I was. Until my husband joined them. And soon I lost them both.'

Her eyes are filled with tears. I go and sit down beside her, and give her a long hug. I can't believe that a fragile body like hers can hold such a strong spirit. She leaves for the bathroom. When she's back, her eyes are dry and she's back to her former self.

'What happened after the riots?' I ask.

'Little changed. The economy collapsed, and homelessness and destitution ruled. Then the elite monopolised the Earth and proclaimed themselves Owners. The new system was established in which they allowed the economically useful to stay alive for as long as they continued to support the system as consumers, and the non-productive were put into Dignitoriums. A puppet government was set up to serve solely the interests of the elite. You know the rest.'

'But then how was all this the non-profit people's fault?'

'It wasn't.'

'But... They claim that the ageing population demanded pensions and healthcare and that caused the collapse. And the disabled who demanded–'

'They teach whatever they want, my child. I don't watch their documentaries and I don't read their propaganda. All I do is remember.'

She is staring ahead and again, I'm surprised at how her playful, lively face can turn so serious. I go up to her and hold her delicate, weightless hand in mine. I really don't know what to believe now. She doesn't bear any resemblance to those poor senile people shown on the Globe and in textbooks, but her story contradicts everything I've ever known.

'I can see you are struggling to know what to believe, Alice, and I understand. Sometimes even I am taken in by the twisted reality;

it's all around us, it sucks us in.'

'Is there any documentation, or books that support this?'

'They were destroyed. Not like in the middle ages when they were burned publicly. No, the Owners are much cleverer than that,' she suddenly stands up. 'But I managed to hide some articles. You want proof? I'll show you.'

She gets a folding ladder out of the built-in wardrobe and climbs it so she can reach the uppermost compartment. I hold my breath. I will finally get to see the truth. Nurse Vogel is getting more and more nervous. 'I don't know...' she says. 'I'm quite sure it was here.' She turns to me. 'I sometimes take it out and just read it, hold it. I did it last month. But it's not here.' She rummages through the whole wardrobe, throwing clothes and bags out onto the floor.

'It doesn't matter Nurse Vogel. You can show me another time.'

'It's not about that. I have kept it here for decades. They must have broken in again. They took it.' She's so upset, I'm fearful for her safety and give her a hand getting down from the ladder. She's pale as a ghost. Her frail body is trembling.

'They've been here again,' she keeps repeating, empty dread in her gaze.

I help her to sit down and then make her a strong tea in the kitchenette. I'm utterly confused, more than ever. She is so sensible, a kind, caring, admirable person. Is it possible that she is losing her mind? Or is she right?

'In the article Adam is pictured on the front page, addressing a large crowd from the top of a car during the riots,' she explains, her eyes darting around the room as if trying to keep an eye on all of it at once. 'Behind them is the row of brand-new skyscrapers with an empty car park, closed off from non-residents, while the street is lined with tents and sleeping bags belonging to homeless families. A man holding a board with the message: "I'm a full-time teacher and homeless".'

I'd really like to see the picture but right now I'm more worried about her.

'How stupid I was to think they wouldn't return. It must have been while I was at work.'

'Do you want me to stay overnight? Would you feel better?'

She shakes her head.

'Don't worry about me. Come, there are still things I can show you.'

We walk around her room and I can't stop admiring all the bric-a-brac, most of it completely unfamiliar to me. In the centre of the room, above her sofa, is a huge poster with a baby swimming under water to get a banknote that was the symbol of money in the old system. It says 'Nirvana' in the corner. I gaze at the picture with fascination, instinctively knowing this must have been important in Nurse Vogel's youth. Like a museum curator, she tells me about the band called Nirvana and many others whose music she still keeps on dozens of so-called 'CDs'. CDs were used to store music before it could be played on the ID Phone or on the Globe.

'How do you play these?' I ask, lifting up one of the round, flat discs.

'Don't touch it like that.' She takes it away and carefully holds the edge of the disc between her fingers. Opening a glass cupboard, she shows me the player, an angular plastic box with several buttons on it. It's funny how it swallows the CD and makes strange sounds before the music comes on. This is rough music, raw and primal and energetic.

We continue our tour around the room. The numerous books on her shelves include classic novels from the nineteenth century, heavy dictionaries and books on faraway, exotic places or famous inventors. I could stay here and explore this Aladdin's cave for ages.

She picks up a photo of her husband and starts speaking to him. It's just a murmur, and all I catch are the words 'together' and 'finally'. She puts it back, sits down in an armchair and apologises.

'May I ask, what was your marriage like?' I sit back in the armchair by the window.

'We were close, despite the difficulties. He helped me through the miscarriages. If we had only an hour after work, we spent it together.'

I'd like to ask her how she survived, how one recovers from such a loss, but I don't want to open up her wounds.

'You see, it was the opposite with us,' I say, fretfully. 'Even as Mid Spenders, Philip and I drifted apart. I was a hectic wife, and instead of paying attention to him it was easier to go out for a meal, to buy something new.'

I turn away to wipe a tear from my eye. I think of Philip, my easy, comfortable life with him, the evenings in our stylish living room. Our empty, wordless evenings.

'And who can blame you?' Nurse Vogel says thoughtfully. 'When the outside world offers us endless excitement at the mere push of a button, the person next to us will always seem boring in comparison. But at least you've learned your lesson…' She bites her tongue at the end but I know what she wanted to say. That I learned it too late.

TWO OLD FOOLS

The light of the fading sun, however comforting, didn't help me relax. I loved sitting in the corner of our roof terrace, one of the few places where I always found peace. Earlier that day we'd been tidying extensively, Philip and I, sorting out decade-old junk, moving furniture that hadn't been moved for years, washing bed linen and curtains for the new room. Mum and Dad deserved a fresh start.

Philip came over and crouched down to face me. He took my hand and put his head on my lap. The slight wrinkles on his forehead seemed more pronounced than ever, a dark shadow clouded his eyes. I was about to reassure him that my parents were OK to live with. But the wrinkle seemed to have softened just by the intimacy of holding hands and I remained quiet.

Mum and Dad had finally reached the stage everyone dreaded and anticipated at the same time. They had become non-profit. Having been good contributors, never out of work, they were given the gift of one extra free year of their Right To Reside, during which they were allowed to live with relatives before retirement, as a gesture of good will from the government. We were about to collect them that evening.

We lived in MW05, which stands for Mid Spender, West London, area number five. We considered ourselves lucky to be able to live there, with its leafy streets, filled with couples looking half their age, sipping iced cappuccinos on sun-soaked café terraces beside the promenade. It made my blood boil to think of Mum and Dad in their one-bedroom apartment in LE12, the most deprived area of London – apart from the Zone, of course – where there were an average of two abductions every month. It was an area filled with budget shops, unkempt parks, residents with a liking for cheap handbags and even cheaper wine. Mum never really got used to the Low-Spender Area, and never stopped missing our old family house, the semi in MN09. The lush new growth on my apple tree was the only thing reminding the world that we had been there. Like most of us, it had not only survived the uprooting from the old system to the new one, but flourished afterwards.

Both having full-time jobs, my parents had managed to stay in that house for a good twenty years, until one day Mum broke her ankle at the CinePalace where she worked as an administrator. That was the start of a downward spiral. A month's absence from work was enough for her to be fired, without negotiation or any kind of recompense.

The next nail in the coffin was Dad's stroke. It drained the money they had saved up by making sacrifices over the years: the money from missed concerts, missed theatre shows, missed opportunities. For example, instead of celebrating their silver anniversary in Hawaii, Mum's dream place, they went to the Norfolk coast. I always admired how they could spend just enough to remain Mid Spenders and yet put some aside for an emergency. But, as was the case for most Mid Spenders, it was just a matter of time until they were forced to downgrade. In the end, the savings of the past twenty-something years were barely enough to pay off the costs of Dad's operation and aftercare. While he was recovering in hospital, dreaming of coming home to his beloved home in MN09, unbeknown to him, Philip and I helped Mum pack up the house. The only thing we couldn't pack was my tree. By the time Dad was ready to leave the hospital, Mum already lived in the small flat in LE12. I'll never forget when we opened the front door for the first time, and mum saw the tiny, confined space she and dad were supposed to call home. It was the only time I saw my resilient, spirited mother break down.

A week later we picked Dad up in a heli-taxi.

'We're going the wrong way,' he said.

We weren't flying high; wearing his glasses, he could read the street signs saying MC05, then HC03. From the position of the Primavera Club, with its white windowless surface dominating the city skyline on the south-east, Dad realised we were flying in the opposite direction to where our old house was.

'Where are you taking me?' Dad's cheerful tone nearly broke my heart. 'Was this your idea?'

He looked at me, trying to smile, though it hurt him, to thank me for the surprise trip he assumed we'd planned for him. The gratitude on his face brought tears to my eyes, and I had to turn away. How could I tell him there was no surprise-trip? He patted my hand.

'Let's do this another time, darling! I need a big rest, you know. That's all I need right now.'

Everyone stopped breathing. I took his right hand, Mum grabbed his left one, caressing it.

'Ben! It's not what you—'

'It's so kind of you. But can I go home now? I need to lie down.'

'We're going home, Ben.' Mum's voice was the softest I had ever heard.

'Yes, Dad, we're going home.'

Dad muttered something, half asleep now. His head dropped onto my shoulder.

I didn't feel like getting up from the lounger. The sun still painted the sky an opaque pink but it didn't release any more warmth. It was only Philip's head on my lap that did. He opened his eyes.

'Are you ready?' he asked.

I sighed and nodded.

'It will be good for them, you'll see. Living in a better area and having us around.'

I nodded again. Our second bedroom was large enough for Mum and Dad to live in quite comfortably. The common areas were big enough that we wouldn't be in each other's way. I'd already been making plans, like cooking with Mum the way we used to, baking her favourite carrot cake with orange zest, or dining out on the roof terrace, watching the ever-exciting Mid-Spender world go by. Mum and Dad would be living among their own kind again, forgetting about the four years of Low-Spender nightmare. We were looking forward to a good year, unlike some people who were not keen on letting their elderly parents move in with them, secretly wishing something would happen. It might sound shocking, but I've met people like that. The staff room at my school was full of them. Beyond the one free year ahead, of course, I never dared think. As far as I was concerned, it would never come.

It was already dark when we arrived in front of Mum and Dad's block. The illuminated windows of the tower block glinted down at me like a hundred-eyed giant.

'Thank God it's the last time we have to come to this place,' Philip remarked while pressing the buzzer. In the lift we stared at each other, petrified.

'It's really happening, Phil. It's not just a nightmare any more.' I felt panic threatening to overcome me until Philip drew me closer.

'It's lucky they've got us, Ali. They'll be fine.'

I almost burst out, saying this year before their retirement would fly by in a flash, but I forced my mouth shut. I nodded and fumbled for a tissue in my pocket.

Once Mum opened the door I knew something was wrong. They wore their best clothes, not what people wear for moving house. I had my long-forgotten childhood-mum in front of me, her hair freshly dyed a Scandinavian blonde, her face heavily made-up. She wore white from head to toe. As for Dad, it took a very special occasion for him to wear the exquisite lavender shirt Mum had given him for their silver wedding anniversary. Philip, ready to start packing, grabbed two boxes.

'Philip,' Mum said.

'Yes?'

'Philip, put the boxes down, please,' Dad said, in a voice that made both of us look at him.

'Can you two just sit down for a minute?' Mum said calmly.

'What's happened?' I asked, but got no reply. Mum and Dad sat on the sofa, expecting us to join them. This ugly mustard-coloured sofa had been our companion for more than twenty years. On its back I'd once secretly spread some mustard, to see if there was any difference between the colours. I knew it was the last time we would sit on it. Philip had rented an e-cart to take it to the Zone's Distribution Centre after the move.

'Before I start, I have to tell you, Alice and Philip, we are very grateful for your generous offer to let us spend our extra year with you.' Dad spoke in an almost ceremonial manner. 'However, we've decided not to. We've thought through our decision carefully and we are certain we want to go through with it. All we ask is for you to please accept it.'

'What is it, Dad?' I couldn't hide the frustration in my voice. Philip put his hand over mine. It was cold like a windowpane on winter nights.

'We've decided to move into a Dignitorium. Today.'

'Is this a joke?' Philip jumped up as if he'd been stung by a wasp. 'Of course you're not going to do that. It's out of the question!'

'Philip, what did I just ask you?' Dad asked.

Philip shut up then, but I couldn't.

'Dad, please tell me this is a joke.'

He didn't say anything. After that I became dizzy, my vision blurred. I remember bits and pieces like Mum crying, her make-up smudged and lipstick smeared around her mouth as if she had eaten a mouthful of raspberries; Philip being deathly pale, even paler than usual; Dad staring ahead without saying a word; and the taste of bile in my throat. I remember Philip helping me down the stairs, holding me tight. I wanted to scream but I didn't have the strength. At one point we said farewell to the flat and went to the monorail station, waited there like normal people, as if we'd just been out for a meal. The only difference was that we had two e-trolleys fully packed with my parents' personal belongings.

Sitting on the monorail, I looked at Dad on my right, then at Mum opposite me. Something shone through in both their faces, it was the closest thing to real relief I ever saw. Mum's face, despite the red and black smudges of make-up, looked like it had been ironed. Even the crow's feet around her eyes seemed to have melted away. Dad turned to me.

'I understand it all came a bit suddenly. But why the big protest? It's normal these days.'

'I know, Dad. But we wanted you to come back with us. Into our home, which is yours now. How can you throw away a whole year of life?'

'So tell me what we would do after the one year? Apart from what we're doing right now?'

'We would do something,' Philip replied. 'Things could get better, you could even find another job by then.'

Dad sighed. 'At our age it's impossible. You know it very well, Philip.'

'Apart from that,' said Mum, 'our medical costs would increase year by year.'

'Mum–'

'It's a burden I couldn't put on you two. I can't ask you to use up the savings you are putting aside for your children.'

'Exactly! Now you can have children.' Dad tried to look encouraging. 'You couldn't if we took up your only free room.'

'Dad, don't be ridiculous, we can have children next year, when you…'

They all stared at me, Dad with victory sparkling in his eyes.

'I mean, it's not so urgent for us to have children. That's what I meant to say.'

'Exactly,' Philip said, with an edge to his voice. I have been replaying his words in my mind recently, wondering exactly whom they were intended for.

'Darling, we've had our time.' Dad's voice was serious now. 'We know when to give way to the next generation. You and your children are far more important than two old fools like us.'

'One old fool,' Mum remarked and Dad winked at her.

After a short walk we arrived at a long brick wall. The thick canopy of trees, illuminated by a green light, hinted at the paradise beyond. We checked in at the gate and went inside. I'd never seen a Dignitorium in the moonlight before. Even through my tears I appreciated the majesty of the place. A sweet scent of roses hit my nostrils. Victorian-style streetlamps gave out a soft yellow light. The white walls of the building glowed in the floodlight. Overlooking a small lake in the middle of a park, the regal beauty seemed to be inviting and mysterious at the same time. I shivered.

'Look at this. Isn't it stunning?' Dad said. 'This is what we want, no matter how short it will be.'

'Twelve months of absolute happiness is not short, and you can visit us anytime you want to,' Mum added.

Once the gate closed behind us, I couldn't hold back my tears; I clung to Dad first, then to Mum. They kept telling me that this was the normal way of things. Even Philip said so, although I knew his real view on the subject. It's one thing to hear about others doing it and another to see your own parents entering their place of death, no matter how rose-scented it is.

We went into the registration office, where the manager served us hot drinks. Mum was bubbling with the excitement of being inside the gorgeous main building. They were given a lengthy contract to read through and had been examining it for quite some time when Dad suddenly lifted his head.

'Nine months?' he looked up at the manager, a cordial gentleman who was seated behind a heavy oak desk, his short fingers tapping on the desktop while he explained the latest changes.

'It's a brand-new measure, Mr Walker. It will be announced tomorrow.'

'I thought…we thought,' Dad was stammering, 'that it would be twelve months.' He and Mum exchanged glances.

Philip jumped up from his seat, stormed over to Dad and grabbed the contract from him. He began reading it.

'What's this?' he asked, barely repressing the fury in his voice.

'As I said, it's a brand-new measure that will be introduced unilaterally from tomorrow,' the manager said patiently, his exaggerated smile never leaving his face. 'We conducted a survey and found that Dignitorium residents on a national level–'

'Then we don't want it, thank you,' Philip barked. 'We'll come back in a year's time.' He looked at my parents, expecting them to stand up and leave the office, come home with us. But Mum and Dad remained calm.

'Just sit down, Philip,' Dad said. 'It's OK.'

'We're OK with it, Philip,' Mum chimed in and flashed a wide smile at us.

'How can you say it's OK?' Philip raised his voice. He was pacing up and down the room like a trapped lion in a cage.

'Because it is,' Mum replied. 'These people are experts, they know what they are doing and why.'

'Mrs Walker is perfectly right.' The manager didn't stop nodding. 'These new measures are the results of an extensive survey. We will show our new residents a documentary tonight that will explain everything in detail. The conclusion is that the great majority of residents prefer to enjoy a more luxurious retirement for a shorter period of time, rather than stretching it out for infinity.'

'Infinity?' Philip couldn't keep his voice down any longer. 'How can you have the nerve to call one fucking year infinity, you–'

'Philip!' Dad cut in. 'Stop it, now! Please! We're OK with it. Honestly.'

'In fact, it's better this way,' Mum nodded fervently, shooting glances at the manager. 'Am I right, sir?'

'Without giving too much away,' he said, with an air of mystery, 'I can confirm, Mr and Mrs Walker, that you won't be disappointed.'

Mum's cheeks were flushed with excitement. She leaned closer to the manager. 'Those multi-sensory capsules that are always in the adverts – have you got them?'

'Mrs Walker, I hope you're joking,' answered the manager, pretending to be insulted. 'Of course we do.' He sat up straight. 'We have purchased the finest available on the market.' Mum was over the moon and became giddy like a little girl.

Philip turned to me.

'The bastards, they cut it again.'

I couldn't say a word for the lump in my throat. Mum and Dad didn't even have a year to live.

EIGHT

This week I received a friendly reminder, politely asking me to come to the next Sunday Mass. It's today. The note says the authorities are extremely sorry about me becoming a Low Spender but they wish me a quick recovery and return to where I belong. As an act of encouragement, they allow me to attend Sunday Mass with the Mid Spenders one last time.

I don't feel like going, but I know what comes after a friendly reminder. I remember, years ago, when Philip received one and ignored it. He received another one, less friendly. Then a final note, with a bill attached.

I'm staring at the church building with the same fascination as when I saw it for the first time. It looks like a giant egg turned on its side, one quarter of it buried in the lawn. Ten years on, the sleek, cream-coloured surface is just as shiny as it was then. Its frosted glass door is wide open, and masses of colourfully-dressed figures are pouring in. People are wearing their best outfits, as if attending a fashion show instead of Mass.

I feel shamefully under-dressed in my white cotton T-shirt with plain black trousers, but looking glamorous was the last thing on my mind this morning. Even the grass around the church is greener than in other parts of the park. I can't help wondering whether Pastor Obi secretly sprays it green at night while his wife polishes the building's outer surface. The electric bell strikes eleven – it sounds like a real one in a Gothic cathedral. I feel awkward going in; people usually don't come here alone. Although I have no companion, I carry Philip within me. I can still hear his words, on those rare occasions when he attended Mass, after receiving a final warning: 'It's time to enter the zombie factory.'

In the doorway I see two rows of glittering white teeth, surrounded by curly golden hair. It's Janine, Pastor Obi's mother.

'Welcome, my dear. God bless.'

Before I can say anything, she ushers me inside and in the bright reception room a volunteer puts a glass of champagne into my hand. I take a deep breath and step into the main hall. The crowd is bursting with energy, like spectators in a Roman coliseum. Red velvet seats are organised in a giant semi-circle; they are so comfortable that once you sit down, it's nigh on impossible to get up. I take the very first seat in the back row. Other people are coming in, among them I recognise Christine from my old condo. She's with her girlfriends, who are all heavily made-up and chattering away. When I wave to her, she comes and air-kisses me without making eye contact, then apologises, saying 'I'll call you,' and joins her friends. She turns around; I see her gulp down some champagne and disappear into the crowd.

The service is about to start, and the melodic rock music playing from the speakers on the walls gets louder and faster. People are fidgeting in their seats. Total darkness falls upon the hall and behind the stage the wall-to-wall 3D screen vibrates to the increasing speed of the drums. People are stamping out the rhythm with their feet; some are standing up, with hands held up in the air. Suddenly the music stops. Two thousand people hold their breath.

With the stage lights comes an explosion of sound. In the middle of it all, like a demi-god, stands Pastor Obi. His white three-piece suit and crimson tie are eye-catching even from a distance. Now the screen behind him shows his face up close. Pastor Obi may be in his mid-fifties, but he could be a film star, not only because of his good looks – his charisma could light a fire in the middle of Siberia. A cacophony of clapping and screaming rises to an almost unbearable level and I find myself thinking it's lucky there are no windows in the hall as they would simply shatter. The pastor holds his right hand up, and the crowd is instantly quiet. The women in the choir stop singing.

'God bless you all, my brothers and sisters.'

A thick wall of screams, whistles, clapping and cheering follows.

'What did you buy today?'

Laughter.

As usual, the service starts with the Final Farewell announcements. Mrs Parker is on the screens. In her early seventies, she has immaculate golden hair and rosy cheeks.

'This is my opportunity to tell you how happy I've been all my life and how grateful I am for all I've had: for my late husband, my beloved children and grandchildren. For being able to spend nine wonderful months at this extraordinary place and prepare for my final departure' – clapping from the audience – 'maintaining my dignity and…departing with that same dignity.'

More screams of support and applause.

'I feel I'm ready to go now, and join my beloved Jack. I wish you all the same happiness and quality of life I've experienced. Goodbye.'

The audience are wiping their eyes; most of them gulp down the remains of their champagne. Next on screen is Hugo, a jovial man in his mid-sixties. He is in a wheelchair in the breathtaking garden of a Dignitorium, behind him a carpet of red and yellow tulips.

'Hello, everyone! I'm here to say goodbye. By the time you see this I won't be here. To cut it short all I can say is: Live as much as I did, enjoy it as much as I did, consume as much as I did. Then you'll go as happily as I do.'

Applause, whistles, cheers.

'One more thing: this stupid liver damage just hit me, and before coming here I went through hell, queuing for ages at the hospital, then hearing the cost of the operation just to carry on like this for two or three more years, as a Low Spender. And for what? What's the point in being alive without dignity, suffering like an animal? No way, I told them. I showed them the finger.'

Hugo lifts his right hand and shows his middle finger to the camera.

'Like this, I did. I walked out. Next day I was here. Never had a better time. See ya, guys.'

The audience starts screaming, people stand up, clapping their hands, and soon everyone is chanting: 'Hugo! Hugo!'

The pastor joins in. 'Hugo! Hugo!' He stops for a second, tilts his head up and winks at the ceiling. 'Hi Hugo!' Laughter fills the hall.

The green frame on the screen changes to pink. Weddings. A video of a young bride and groom starts in front of a dreamlike castle. I recognise it: Castle Howard in North Yorkshire, a popular wedding location for High Spenders, though Mid Spenders can also afford it if they save up for years. I have to admit the pictures are amazing, like watching a fairy-tale coming true. The couple, Richard and Amy, are over the moon.

'She is my princess, and I am the happiest man on Earth,' Richard says. Amy blushes, while women in the audience are screaming hysterically. My breakfast, meanwhile, is trying to climb up from my stomach.

Next the upcoming weddings are announced, then communal parties, and dinner with Pastor Obi, which is open to anyone, for a hefty price. A visit to Pastor Obi's home is an annual occasion strictly limited to twelve people. The pastor's wife, Eleanor, is on stage in a royal-blue silk overall that was designed for someone half her size and a third her age. She wears it with extraordinary confidence, though.

Now Pastor Obi announces the new Mid Spenders, who have just been upgraded. There's a dozen of them, lining up on the stage. They are young, hopeful and shining against the wall of applause. I know what comes next; I just hope it will be short. The pastor expresses his condolences for those who are here today for the last time as they have become Low Spenders.

'I don't want to humiliate you by calling out your names, so if you want to stand up, it's fine, if not, that's okay.'

Deadly silence. I look around, pretending to seek out the down-graders. No one stands up.

There's a change of mood now. The lights come up; red, orange, blue and green spotlights flash above our heads. The choir starts singing. People stand up and sing with the choir, and everyone is gradually drawn into a trance by the powerful music. I put my hands up dutifully in the air but I already feel exhausted and secretly glance at my wrist for the time.

After half an hour of music and dancing, the room quietens down, for the sermon is about to begin. Today's speech, on the importance of generosity, flows out of Pastor Obi's lips like melted honey. Don't break the circle, keep it flowing, he says. Be grateful for what others do, return their hard work by consuming and contributing. He constantly reminds us how lucky we are in the new system, that this is the very first society in recorded history where an exceptionally good standard of living and free accommodation is guaranteed for the majority.

'DEATH!' He yells out so loud that the microphone squeaks. 'We, my brothers and sisters, have managed to do the impossible! We have cheated death!'

On the screen pictures appear: poor-quality ones, probably taken decades ago in the old system. The audience gasp when they see the bedridden pensioners. Old people, unimaginably old, some of them in their nineties or beyond, with IV tubes hanging out of them. A pension in the old system was a stipend the elderly received from the government to keep them quiet, to delude them into believing they were cared for. But one only has to look at these photos to see how they were cared for. They wear a look of unmistakeable fear, the terror of an animal about to be shot. Some children in the audience start crying and their parents put pink glasses over their eyes. Now before them they see only Disney figures dancing in a pink light and they immediately calm down. Pastor Obi starts to list all the things that happen to the human body around the age of seventy, the signs of decay. The list is endless and I don't even want to pay attention, it's so heartbreaking.

I think of Nurse Vogel, how many of these symptoms she already has. The smell, yes, I think I smelt it when I went to her flat. It will no doubt become unbearable in a few years' time. Pastor Obi has just mentioned mental breakdown and memory loss. I haven't noticed any signs of this in her. But it raises doubts about all that she has told me. How much can I believe of what she said about the uprising?

At last, the pastor has finished and is breathing heavily. He watches his audience, waiting for their reaction.

Only when the prayers, moans and sighs die out, does he continue.

'For the first time in history, people don't have to go through this. YOU don't have to go through this, my brothers and sisters!

171

You are no longer victims waiting for a disaster to happen, helplessly witnessing your own physical and mental deterioration,' he exclaims fervently. 'You're in control of your own destiny. You are not defenceless puppets in the cruel hands of nature, you are wonderful human beings who can make a conscious decision! You have the CHOICE, the choice previous generations didn't have, the choice our ancestors would have valued more than anything, the choice to decide when and how you want to leave this world!'

His words are drowned out by the screams of the audience. By now he's panting. I fear he will faint or have a heart attack. Eleanor runs to him with a tissue and wipes his forehead and face. The pastor continues, though with less fervour now.

'What else is this, my brothers and sisters, than the living proof that God has given us so much? But do we give back?'

'Yes,' many of them shout out.

'Are we as generous as God is or are we keeping it to ourselves?'

'We are generous,' many people say.

'Amen,' others cry.

There are dark wet patches on the underarms of Pastor Obi's suit and sweat trickles down his forehead into his eyes. He can't see and he has to close his eyes, but he doesn't stop.

'Now turn to your neighbour, shake each other's hands, and say: "You deserve everything your heart desires and God will give it to you."'

The young woman on my left has a hazy expression and her hand is hot and shaking. She must be in a trance. I try to make eye contact but she doesn't acknowledge me and after the handshake she bursts into tears and praises the Lord loudly. After this the pastor sits down to recover and has a glass of water. Eleanor, beaming, announces that the opportunity to give back has started. People get excited, especially after the next round of champagne that is carried around by volunteers. Now the images of the decrepit old people disappear from the screen.

The next video shows the Obi family in a short film. We are given an insight into the pastor's life, to reassure the audience that he's one of us and give us the impression that we know him personally. Funny incidents that happened last week are shown: a family outing to the park with their three kids, a late-night shopping trip to the supermarket when their smallest, the five-year-old, led the e-trolley into a mountain of tinned food. Everyone laughs.

After the film is over, clothes, food and furniture are brought up on stage and people can see them and select on their ID Phones whatever they want to buy. The pastor doesn't stop repeating: 'Who will be our highest spender today?' The volunteers are very busy now, running around with extra-large champagne bottles. I feel a bit dizzy and don't let them refill my glass, claiming I have a headache.

Pastor Obi is prancing around on the stage, his hair shining with sweat. More and more people, mostly women, become so excited they faint. The volunteers are now even busier, trying to get them on the stretchers that are dropping down from the ceiling like oxygen masks on airplanes. Next the pastor recommends his latest book, titled *A Recipe For Success*. Then he tells us to turn to our neighbours and ask them: 'What did you buy today?'

The young woman on my left is happily showing me her ID Phone, on which she ticked all the clothes Eleanor was wearing in the video. Pastor Obi shouts: 'Let's see who our highest spender is today! Who is the winner? Three, two, one!' The music stops. I decide to make my escape, before the screaming erupts again. I am about to faint but not with excitement. Thank God I'm out.

At the exit I get extra money uploaded on my ID Phone, a reward for attending the service. At the door, Janine, showing all her teeth, says that I can stay in the restaurant because they're having a meal with the pastor soon. It's the last thing I want. As a final effort, she recommends Pastor Obi's rainbow paintings that fully cover the wall. She claims they have healing energy. I'm starting to have a real headache now, so I tell her I have already two paintings of the pastor. The fresh air outside sobers me up. I'm relieved I can tick Sunday Mass off my list. Even though I won't be returning, I can't do anything to escape the church in my new Low Spender area. But they won't be bothering me with friendly reminders for another month.

It's quiet at home, thank God, and I finally collapse on the sofa and put my feet up against the wall. I wonder what has changed in me. Why did I find the service so unbearable? I used to be one of those who danced and wept. Now I'm irritated by their empty stares and fake smiles, and can't wait to hear Felicity's genuine laughter, which melts my heart every time I see her.

It always upsets me when I see Farewell Videos at Sunday Mass. They remind me of Mum and Dad. I have a copy of their's and I often watch it, especially after I wake up from those horrible nightmares in which I see Dad on the floor and Mum leaning above him, screaming. I had the same dream last night. When I woke up, my heart kept on beating furiously for a long time. But then I watched their Farewell Video, in which they confirmed how happy they were and that the best gift was that they could do it together. They praised Nurse Vogel and how she had taken great care of them. I watched it twice to calm myself down. There was nothing like this in the old system, but Nurse Vogel clearly preferred it all the same. It's probably because of what she went through. Her story was heartbreaking, and I can completely identify with her guilt. Since I started to look after Felicity, I can't shake off the feeling that I didn't listen to Philip, didn't pay attention to him the way I should have. I'll never see him again, never have the opportunity to make it better, to tell him I'm sorry.

So many thoughts are swirling in my head; I'll go mad if I can't talk to someone. Before I know it, I'm calling Nurse Vogel.

She answers immediately. She's sitting deep in her armchair, wearing a chunky cardigan. There's something in her demeanour today – an aura of invincibility.

'Can we talk?' I ask. 'Are they not listening to your line?'

'I don't care if they do, I've got nothing to hide. Nothing to be ashamed of. This morning I escorted a dear friend of mine, Shirley, to the T-wing. I was her primary carer, and she was crying with gratitude. That's all that counts, and I will take these memories with me wherever I go if they decide to terminate me. Nothing can scare me now, my dear.'

'Have you ever worked inside the T-wing?'

From her silence I can tell she's surprised by my question. 'I was offered the chance but I didn't have the stomach for it.' She swallows hard.

'Why? There's nothing wrong with the place, is there?' I hope she won't pick up on the trembling in my voice.

'I'm grateful I never had to go there,' she says after a short pause. 'But I can tell you I don't like the colleagues who work in the T-wing. They're all, how to put it, people I don't want to be close to. Sometimes I feel – I know it makes no sense – that they lack compassion. I can't explain why.'

'They've probably been hardened by such an emotionally draining job, don't you think?'

'Well, it can't be easy to send people on their last journey. Then clean up the body half an hour later.'

'Oh, God.' I can feel the blood draining from my face.

'I'm sorry. I should have realised how traumatic it sounds to outsiders,' she says. 'I'm used to it, talking to someone, sharing a life, holding a hand, then seeing them escorted to the T-Wing, and the next day taking a flower to their name on the wall.'

'So was it better in the old system, when there were no Dignitoriums?'

'I wish I had a clear answer for you, Alice. I don't know which is better. It's definitely better to die with preparation and dignity than without. I wouldn't work there if I didn't believe that. These days I mostly look after residents in their sedation period. Like Owen, the young man you saw. When they are drugged, they are happy. When they are no longer drugged, they remember the blissful state they experienced and they stop fearing death. How could that be a bad thing?'

I'm flooded with relief.

'Even Owners have their own Dignitoriums,' she adds.

'Do they?'

'If it was painful they wouldn't choose to die this way, trust me.'

On the Globe almost every channel is showing breaking news. The red warning sign is blinking to give parents time to take their kids out of the room, so they won't see the horror that is about to be shown. Bodies of huge, mutant wolves have been found, the newsreader announces with gravity in his voice. Pictures are shown, and I notice with shock that the wolf is almost as big as the van parked next to it. The dead body of a human is being carried away on a stretcher. Suddenly the stretcher accidentally tips over and the body rolls off it onto the ground. Before the crew could turn off the camera, one of them zooms on the body. Screams of horror are heard but before the broadcasting would stop, there are a few seconds during which all the viewers in the country can see the horrible injuries up close. The body doesn't even resemble a human any more. It's a red pulp, held together with shreds of purple skin. Then the camera is switched off. Now we're back in the studio where the newsreader is deathly pale and struggles to collect his thoughts. When he continues his announcement, he says it's feared that this new kind of mutant wolf can now be found all over the country. No matter how hard he tries, he can't hide the dread on his face.

The Prime Minister, Edward Finch, is being interviewed on the Globe. He's a stern, wiry man in his mid-fifties, not too tall and with a boxer's nose. Very different from his predecessor, Vincent Lloyd, who was tanned and sporty, with a mesmerising gaze. Despite the difference in their looks I can see many similarities: they use much of the same vocabulary and the rhythm of their speech sounds alike. Philip used to mock all of them. 'All politics is a lie, a show put on for the masses,' he would say. He never even mentioned the political parties by their names, he just called them The Good – our current government, The Wrong – the socialists, The Evil – the ultranationalists and The Tree Huggers – the greens. 'Their nicknames put together sound like an old spaghetti western movie,' he said. It was the kind of joke you know you should laugh at but can't. 'Seriously, I wouldn't be surprised if most of them had an acting background,' he added. 'Probably in a puppet theatre.' I found it amusing to listen to his sarcastic comments, but always dismissed them with a smile. Sometimes I thought Philip was slightly paranoid, though nothing compared to his father.

That was until a particularly heated live debate on the Globe. Vincent Lloyd was the PM back then, and he was fervently defending our system in which hard work is appreciated, while the socialist leader argued that in not supporting non-profit people, we were denying them basic human rights. The debate escalated and the presenter didn't help by reading out heated messages from viewers. A physical brawl broke out between the two men, and it took security several long minutes to separate them.

The whole country was shocked, apart from Philip, who said, 'It was just a show. The actors were well compensated for their physical injuries.' The next morning a new scandal went viral on the Globe. Someone had shared a photo taken of the two leaders later that evening in a wine bar, guffawing, their arms wrapped around each other like the best of old friends. Their bruises were still fresh on their faces. The scandal implied the fighting had been put on to disguise the lack of real interest in their party rhetoric; to mislead voters.

Philip was victorious. I began to take his words a bit more seriously, but the same evening the mystery was solved. It was announced that the two leaders had been piss-drunk and that notorious image had been taken in a moment of reconciliation, just before they collapsed on the bar floor. Philip said the media was trying to clean up the mess and I should wait and see; Vincent Lloyd would soon be removed. We didn't have to wait too long. The following week he resigned, allegedly because of the scandal. He was replaced by our current PM, Edward Finch, who is equally well-spoken and charming. Lloyd disappeared from the public eye and the scandal was quickly forgotten. But it's taken me this long to see it clearly.

THE BRIDE

In the atrium of the early-Victorian-style city hall, there was a wall covered with mirrors. I'm not a particularly vain person but I couldn't help getting closer. I saw my own reflection along with that of three other brides, admiring themselves. I couldn't believe how well a beautiful dress, hairstyle and make-up could disguise my internal misery. Although there were moments when I wished Sofia could see me like this, on my big day, my fear was stronger. Behind me, I could see Philip, Antonio, Mum and Dad, talking excitedly. Having lost contact with their other daughter, my wedding day had taken on an even greater importance to my parents.

As usual, Antonio was the centre of attention, entertaining my parents, probably boasting light-heartedly about his artistic success. He was gesticulating wildly and pulling faces to make his story more theatrical. Dad watched him, bemused, while Mum couldn't stop laughing. 'Good,' I thought. 'At least they will be all right with him.' From the first day we had met, it was clear that my father-in-law disliked me, but today of all days he was behaving himself.

Fed up with the new system in the UK, he had gone back to his native Italy a year earlier and when, after six months, he returned, he was shattered, utterly disappointed, and looked twenty years older.

'It's no better in Italy now, the only thing that's better is the wine,' he moaned, and to demonstrate the horrors of the new Italy, he explained how he had wanted to see the Sistine chapel, his eternal source of artistic inspiration, but wasn't allowed in.

'They've converted it into a bath house for High Spenders,' he lamented. Philip and I didn't believe it until we saw the proof online. 'But the frescos will be destroyed by the humidity, for God's sake!' Philip exclaimed. 'They're covered with Plexiglas to protect them,' Antonio explained, before cursing the High Spenders, the Italian government and even the Owners themselves. 'This disease has spread all around the world now,' he kept repeating, his wild curls bouncing with every word. My parents found him amusing but I was overcome with an unexpected sadness.

Mum scurried over to the little group of my friends, girls from work, and they took some selfies and blew me a kiss. I blew one back. I thought of the dinner we would be enjoying later in an exclusive panoramic restaurant – usually only frequented by High Spenders – overlooking the Thames. A once-in-a-lifetime but well-deserved experience, Mum had said. I had told her not to worry, that a simple place would suffice, but secretly I was glad when she said she'd managed to book it. Someone else had cancelled a wedding party at the last minute, she told me, and I found myself wishing she hadn't let me know.

Months had passed during which I'd almost been able to forget about Sofia's curse. Almost. But I felt that taking the place of another couple was a sinister omen. I couldn't help wondering what had happened. Did they break up? Does one single argument have the power to sweep away years of commitment? Or did one of them back off? These days many young women dive into marriage without thinking about it, just to have their big Cinderella day. I looked at the other brides in front of the mirror, posing, pouting and twisting their bodies into unnatural shapes in order to upload the photos later on Yap! I drifted back to my family, took Philip's hand and gave a charming smile to the approaching photographer. I could feel panic rising from deep inside. Sofia wouldn't let this wedding happen. I looked at Philip, the man I'd chosen for life, but despite being a strong, handsome young man on his best form, he seemed weak compared to Sofia's curse. Philip saw my fear and pulled me over to the corner, away from the others.

'Has it come back?' he asked.

'Just for a moment,' I said. 'You know, the couple who cancelled the restaurant. It felt like an omen.'

'It doesn't mean anything.'

'I know, I know. It's nothing.'

'But you can't stop dwelling on it.'

'It was just a moment.'

He held my hand and turned to face me.

'Just hold on for another half an hour and I'm yours forever.'

We giggled and went back to the others.

'Is everything all right?' Dad asked.

Philip nodded. 'Just the old thing.'

'Sofia?' Mum asked. 'Oh, darling, don't let her ruin your big day! Soon you'll be married.'

'That's what I said,' Philip replied, squeezing my hand.

Another couple left the wedding room, the bride wiggling her hips like a catwalk model. She was in her late forties and they had about two hundred guests. It took them ages to leave. After them there was just one elderly couple, and then it would be our turn.

Thank God they had only two witnesses with them. Not long now, I thought. The photographer asked me to stand at the top of the grand staircase and started taking photos. It felt regal, but I couldn't help moving my eyes back to the clock on the wall. I waved down to my family and friends, who were all cheering, and then the photographer asked Philip to join me.

Philip was running up the stairs when we heard the explosion. A sudden thundering sound came from above and the fire alarms went off. People started screaming, and crowding to get outside. More than one bride tripped over in her long dress. Security guards appeared and ushered everyone out of the building. Three fire engines approached and we could hear the sound of sirens in the distance, meaning there were more on the way. A terrifying sight awaited us; fire and smoke poured out of the roof, which had partly fallen in. As I looked up, just next to where the flames had erupted from the hole in the roof, I saw someone waiting to be rescued. Soon it was announced a heli-taxi had accidentally crashed. Luckily there were no casualties and they managed to save the man stuck on the roof, who was apparently the heli-taxi driver. The fire was put out relatively quickly. I gripped Philip's hand harder than ever, my heart pulsing in my throat.

'Don't worry,' Philip said in a soothing voice. 'Soon everything will be back on track.'

I lost my composure, I felt I would never be able to get rid of Sofia's curse, that it would find me wherever I went. She wouldn't let me get married today, or any other day.

'It's her, Philip. It's Sofia.'

'Please.'

'She did it, I know. She arranged the helicopter crash.'

Philip gently took my hand, looked into my eyes.

'Now, listen. We'll be married today. No matter what happens, if the world collapses or London burns down, we will be married.

I promise you.'

I nodded and tried to smile. I didn't want to upset him, but an unspeakable fear came over me. What if this curse was stronger than anything, even stronger than Philip and me together?

The entrance hall was intact, so I broke through the crowd to speak to a police officer. I asked him if we could just go in and continue the ceremony. I had to hold myself back from making a scene when he said no. The next few hours were torture. We were told to wait another two hours while they made sure the building was safe to enter again. We all went to a nearby park and sat on the benches, but I soon grew sick of all the well-wishers and the fake smiles I had to produce for them. Mum did well, chatting to everyone about Madeira, where we were due to go for our honeymoon the next day. I couldn't focus on it; before that damned honeymoon, I wanted a wedding. Philip, who was talking to some of the guests, kept looking in my direction, winking at me, trying to encourage me. At one point I just wanted to slap him.

Finally, the moment came when we were allowed to go into the wedding chamber. All eyes were on me as I entered, with Dad on my left. I expected something to happen at the last moment, another crash, the end of the world, anything. My hands were shaking as I signed the register, and I was sobbing so hard I couldn't stand up from the chair. Philip held my hand and I tasted the bitterness of my streaming make-up in my mouth. The guests' hearts went out to me, thinking that my tears were tears of joy. Only Philip and my parents knew the truth.

NINE

From the window of my flat I'm watching Ruth and Felicity down in the playground. Ruth throws a blanket down on the lawn and invites Felicity to join her for a picnic. The little girl, full of energy, is not listening. She runs out of the non-profit playground to the benches, where only normal children are allowed to play, and gives another girl a hug. The girl pushes her away, then starts crying in an exaggerated, attention-seeking way. Her mother makes her way to Ruth, explains something with flailing arms. I can't hear a word but I don't want to open the window. Ruth stays calm and says something that winds up the sobbing girl's mother even more. One of the fathers is helping Felicity back to the non-profit playground, gently pulling her by the sleeve of her shirt. I keep watching this silent movie unfolding, hoping it will end well, but my stomach is in knots.

Poor Felicity! Having to live with the consequences of something that is not her fault must be hard for an adult, let alone for a little child. I'd like to run out to her and to Ruth, to show my support. Currently it looks like an unequal war, as the group of parents shoot menacing glances at the offending pair. I take a deep breath and leave the flat. As the lift goes downwards, my courage dissipates, as if a tap has been turned off. I could run out and be there with Ruth in a few seconds. But an intimidating tension emanates from the playground and my legs start to tremble. The parents outside are suddenly very real, no longer tiny figures seen from the third floor. What help would I be to Ruth? It's not as if she or Felicity have been physically threatened. It's ridiculous how panicky I've become since I moved to the Low-Spender area. I open the lift door and get back inside. I press number three and as it takes me back to my nest, the negative energy evaporates. I can breathe again. I should really start minding my own business. I'm in just as much trouble as Ruth, or will be soon.

I make myself a strong tea and return to the window. They are still in the playground. Ruth has a devoted daughter, Felicity has a loving mother, but who do I have?

I have a desire every now and then to re-visit my early childhood haunts, to walk the streets I used to walk with Mum and Dad, to dip into the lake of security. I was eight when my first childhood home was demolished, along with the entire street of terraced houses. They were deemed too small and damp, unfit for occupation in the new system.

Yesterday I went back to that street, now in MW05, with an aching heart. I wish I hadn't. I wandered like a ghost, stuck in the past. There was nothing left, not even a lamp post from the old system that I could cherish. When I came home I felt abandoned, like I had been shot out to space.

One of the bigger boys has just pushed Felicity to the ground. She's crying, and her elbow is bleeding. Ruth runs to comfort her. The other parents look at Ruth with barely disguised contempt while she and Felicity go back to the blanket, a good distance away from the others. I'm aware that we have to be careful not to let history repeat itself. But is Felicity really a dangerous freeloader who needs to be eliminated? Or the hapless victim of her mum's selfishness? How can she be deemed non-profit if she gives me so much love, and joy that heals my wounds faster than any medicine? I'm too upset to try to answer these questions. All I know is that her laughter makes me forget all my troubles. Ruth's careworn face is transformed when she tickles her daughter and they laugh together so hard that the bottle of water tips over and spills all over the blanket. The parents of the normal children pretend not to hear them, and start speaking louder to drown them out. A boy, who must be about fourteen, kicks a ball into the middle of the non-profit playground. The ball lands with a thud just inches away from Felicity's head.

I slam my cup down and leave the flat. When my fear resurfaces in the lift, I push it aside. I hurry out of the building and make my way with firm steps to the non-profit playground. When Felicity spots me, she screams with joy and runs towards me. I lift her up and give her a kiss on both cheeks. She giggles and starts fumbling with my earring. I can sense the horror of the parents watching me. Despite the invisible pull of my flat and all its safety, under the stinging looks I sit down next to Ruth on the blanket. Her eyes are overflowing with gratitude. I reach out and squeeze her hand.

'Are you OK?' I ask.

'Apart from the usual shit, yes.'

'What usual shit?'

'Someone put a Junior Dignitorium leaflet through my letterbox this morning. It was one of them.' She looks in the direction of the group in the playground.

'That's sick!'

'I'm used to it,' she says softly, looking away, 'but thank you for standing up for us. I wish I was as brave as you.'

'You have no idea, Ruth, how brave and strong you are.'

'I draw strength from your support. It's been ages since I had a friend. If I ever had any.'

'It was a noble thing to do, leaving the High-Spender lifestyle for Felicity.'

'I wasn't happy, Ali.' She looks me in the eye. 'In fact, I was so unhappy and lonely that sometimes I spent the whole day shopping just to experience some kindness from the shop assistants.'

'But that's not real kindness, is it?'

'It is if you're wealthy enough. For that money, they will be whatever you want them to be.'

I take a good look at Ruth, her gentle eyes, her flat, dry hair, her chipped nails, her rough hands, the alarming black circles under her eyes. I struggle to see her as a glamorous High Spender. She must have noticed me watching her, for she starts examining her hands.

'I used to have artificial nails, too. It was a requirement in the High Spender champagne bar.'

'Did you really work at a champagne bar?'

'I left last year. It was because of a 'prominent' guest. She was nothing but a cheap little celeb. But she left some very negative feedback.'

'And they fired you because of feedback from one customer?' I'm on the verge of admitting that this is what happened to me, but I realise Ruth still doesn't know I was suspended from school.

'What did you do to make her so angry? Did you serve the wrong drink?'

A smile runs across her face.

'Nothing. But she was convinced I'd been looking and laughing at her.'

'But the cameras showed you weren't, didn't they?'

'No one cared about watching the CCTV footage, Ali.' Her face turns dark.

'The only thing that counts is the feedback. Beforehand I worked as a waitress in an award-winning gourmet restaurant, full of prominent guests. None of them knew the truth about how we were paid.'

'How?'

'We didn't have a salary. Each five-star feedback carried a monetary value. And we were paid only after those.'

'Not even four-star feedback paid?'

She shakes her head.

'I'm so sorry, Ruth. I don't think I would have been able to put up with it. Or with the champagne bar.'

'You know, in a way I'm relieved I left. Here at the spa, they never notice me. It's unlikely they will leave negative feedback about the person who wipes down the gym equipment.' She laughs out loud, but her laughter carries a bitter edge.

My heart is singing with a long forgotten joy as I enter the flat, after spending time with Ruth and Felicity in the playground, even though it felt like a battlefield. Here I am, a Low Spender, but finally I have something I never had as a Mid Spender: true friendship. And not only one friend, but three. Not the shallow acquaintance I had with Christine and the others, who still haven't even picked up the phone to ask me if I'm alive.

At the window again, I look down at the playground, pitying those who claim to have normal children and despise Ruth for bringing a non-profit burden into this world. They have absolutely no idea about the sacrifices Ruth makes. Living in the flat underneath hers, I do. Every morning at six I hear the slam of the front door above me, followed by the sound of Ruth's footsteps hurrying away down the pavement. In the evening, she's never back before eleven. Last night it was almost midnight. She came in and then suddenly she stopped, dropped her bag and bent forward, her face distorted in pain. She was holding her hand against the middle of her chest. I jumped up to help but she shook her head. 'I'm fine. It's just the stress,' she murmured. She looked back at me, smiling through the pain. Which of us will last longer, I keep asking myself. Which of us will be the first to sink?

I look around my flat. I've been cleaning almost non-stop since I moved in but it still stinks of decay. I move away from the window and for a change I request a playlist. I choose 'Classical Music for Cleaning'. From the large selection I choose piano music. I turn it up and start to clean like a maniac, as if I can erase all the hardship from my life and from Ruth's and Felicity's lives, too. I move the sofa and the armchair and the wardrobe; all these were rearranged a week ago, but I need to mop the floor underneath, until I feel this is my home and the alien smell turns into a familiar one. It's eight in the evening when I realise I haven't stopped or eaten since breakfast. From a distance I hear the muffled ringtone of my ID Phone. I so want to pick it up, in the hope that someone out there wants to speak to me, although I'm certain it's just an advert call.

It stops ringing by the time I fish it out of my handbag. It was Nurse Vogel. She called three times this afternoon and left two video messages. I watch the first one, left at four. She's at work, it seems, she must be in the staff toilet of the Dignitorium. She leans closer to the camera and, calmly but firmly, begs me to call her straight away. Is her life in danger? Did they decide to terminate her or is it just a panic attack? The other message was left just after six. She's standing in the street, near the Dignitorium's main entrance, by the brick wall. She's more nervous than earlier, and keeps looking around before she leans closer and whispers into the phone.

'Alice. I'm worried that you haven't replied to my first message. It's very, very important that you call me immediately.' She looks around again, then leans so close that I can see the pores on her nose. Even closer, and all I see is a big mouth, filling the whole screen. 'I have news about Philip.'

Philip?

To make sure I heard correctly, I watch the last message again, in slow motion. I rush to the bathroom and wash my face with ice-cold water. My hands are eager to return her call but I hesitate. I'm not sure I'm prepared for what she'll say. She has connections through her job; maybe she has access to the police files about the Boxing Day victims. Am I ready to face Philip's death? Will I ever be?

My face is still burning; I splash more cold water over it. In the mirror I see dread in my eyes. Maybe she's mistaken. Maybe it's not my Philip but someone with the same name. I dash into the room to fetch my ID Phone. It's cold and stings my hands as I pick it up. Finally I summon enough courage to dial Nurse Vogel's number. She answers immediately. She is at home, standing in her kitchen in front of the traditional mahogany kitchen cupboard.

'Nurse Vogel, you have to tell me—'

'Alice, please, sit down.'

'Oh my God, what is it?'

'You have to sit down first.'

My knees give way and I drop onto the sofa.

'I beg you.'

'Alice, Philip is alive. He's in a Dignitorium.'

'It's…impossible. You must be mistaken. Why would he…how could he…?'

'I know it's a shock but it's him. There's no doubt. Philip Brunelli, aged 38, born 9 November 2012. Is it him?'

'My God!'

I can't say anything more, I'm trembling uncontrollably.

'Alice, you have to calm down. I'm coming over, OK?'

Questions are spinning through my head so fast they make me dizzy. Why is it taking her so long? How could Philip let me down like this? I've just calculated, he's got three weeks from his Honeymoon Period before his Sedation Period starts. There must be a mistake; it can't be my Philip. He would never retire without me. After a strong coffee, when Nurse Vogel rings the doorbell, I fly to the door and tear it open.

'I know it's a terrible shock, my child,' she says, giving me a warm hug. She smells of lilac and something medicinal. She sits down on the sofa, I keep pacing up and down until she asks me to sit.

'How did you find out?'

'I suspected it when you visited the Dignitorium, and said Philip had disappeared but couldn't be traced. I decided to check that route but it took weeks to gain access to all the Dignitoriums' patient lists.'

'But why? Why did he do it?'

'He must have had a serious reason, Alice. Don't torture yourself.'

'Jesus Christ, I don't know what else to do! Believe me, he never said anything. He must have gone insane like his father.'

'Hopefully you'll be able to ask him yourself.'

'I want to see him now.'

'This is the complicated part,' she says after a short pause. 'You can visit him only if he agrees to it, but you're not supposed to know that he's there in the first place.'

'I don't care, I'll go tonight–'

'Alice, you must be sensible.'

'Can you help me then?'

'I'll see what I can do. The thing is, he's there voluntarily and he kept it from you for a reason. I know it hurts but he might not want you to visit him.'

'He would never–!'

'Now, write this name and number down, in case you find that you can't get in touch with me any more.'

'Any more?'

'Her name is Edith, she's a friend.'

'What do you mean by 'I can't get in touch with you any more'?'

She gives me an annoyed glance, like I've interrupted her.

'They are coming for me,' she says curtly.

'Did something happen? What happened?'

'Calm down, my dear. Nothing happened.'

'So?'

'I just know.'

'Don't let them–'

'Do you want to see Philip or not?'

I nod.

'This is Edith's number. She'll help you. She works in the Dignitorium where Philip is.'

'Which one is that?'

'I can't tell you.'

'I beg you–'

'You'd ruin everything if you went there now. Just do as I say. Edith will help you if I can't.'

'Please don't talk like this. You'll be fine, I'm sure.'

She gives a deep sigh.

'Philip probably won't react if you demand to see him. But if he sees something from you, an object or a letter, he might not be able to resist. Can you handwrite?'

'I'm one of those last remaining people who can, yes. Dad would never have allowed me to grow up without it.'

'I suggest you write an honest heartfelt letter to him. Tell him how much you love him and what happened to you as a result of his decision.'

'I don't know.' I can't calm down, I pace up and down the room, my hands trembling. 'His decision can't be undone. He can't leave the Dignitorium, am I right?'

She nods.

'What if they forced him or abducted him?'

'No one forces anyone to go to the Dignitorium, Alice. It's supposed to be a privilege.'

'I'll write the letter now. When can you give it to Edith?'

'As soon as I see her. But I'm being watched, I must be careful. It might take a few days or so.'

'But there is no time left!' I can't control my rising voice. 'Couldn't you just meet up with her after work? By the way, no one is watching you. You're paranoid!'

I've crossed the line, I've realised. Nurse Vogel is not the type to raise one's voice with. She's staring at me with a hurt expression. I feel my face burning.

'Sorry, Nurse Vogel. I am really sorry.'

'Hurry up with that letter. I'm exhausted.'

OUROBOROS

It was a solid sterling-silver ring. It didn't come in a box; Philip simply opened his palm and slid it onto my finger.

'Another ring?' I didn't understand.

I loved the platinum wedding ring he'd given me, just two weeks earlier. This one was unexpected.

We had arrived back in London the day before, slightly burned and deliriously happy. The beauty and spaciousness of our new apartment took some getting used to. It felt decadent, even in its unfurnished state, eagerly waiting to start its new life as our family home. We both admired the roof-terrace. It was big enough to host barbecues and dinners, to sunbathe and even have a little herb garden. The park below and the monorail beyond it were far away enough to maintain our privacy.

The new silver ring took the form of a snake swallowing its own tail. With the tip of my finger, I could feel the ridges on the snake's skin.

'Ouroboros,' Philip said. 'The snake that swallows its own tail. The symbol of eternity.'

'Why?'

'To remind you of my eternal love.'

I wondered what he meant by this. Perhaps, out in Madeira, I had spoken a bit too often about having a baby. He told me he thought my concern was mostly fuelled by Sofia's curse, that I was desperate to defy it. He joked that if I could, I would use some magic to conceive and give birth at once. Just to prove my sister wrong. Behind the cheeky smile, there was some truth in what he said.

'Rushing beautiful things can often ruin them,' he said, holding my hand in his palm and admiring the ring.

'Like a caterpillar that has been forced open too early, revealing a freak instead of a butterfly?'

'Something like that.'

The ring was certainly elegant, though it also carried a weight and solemnity that I found reassuring. Warmth filled my chest.

These were my happiest days. I could finally leave Sofia's curse behind. Together, we were stronger than her. Sofia might be a lavish Owner, I thought, living the high life at the Primavera Club; she might travel the world with an entourage at her beck and call, but she didn't know the tender, healing joys of the heart.

Ouroboros. Eternity. It was some years before I started to reflect on the ring and what it really meant. From a symbol of our bond it gradually became one of doubt and self-torture. Was it a proof of our never-ending love? Or was it Philip's way of telling me that we had all the time in the world, and having kids could wait? Or that it might never happen at all?

TEN

Edith mutters on the other end of the line, anxiety filling her voice. Her camera is switched off, so I can't see her face. She sounds young in body but not in spirit.

'I'll pass on your letter to your husband, but you have to be patient,' she says.

I repress the urge to ask why she can't do it faster. As if sensing my question, she continues.

'Nurse Vogel will give me your letter later this week, when I go to London.'

'So Philip's not in a London Dignitorium?'

'No.'

'Where is he?'

She doesn't reply. I know I won't be able to get any more out of her. My camera is on and I smile into it; I'm the kindest I can be to this young woman upon whom everything I hold dear depends. I thank her for the hundredth time, before we hang up.

I didn't hold back in the letter. I told Philip what I was going through, how I had lost my job, my status and very nearly my sanity. How I lost all the security I had known, and become a shadow of my former self, almost a non-profit. How alone I am, abandoned by the circle I thought I belonged to. I deliberately didn't mention my new friends, to make him feel guilty. I allowed the bitterness to pour out freely. I sent him back the ring, Ouroboros, partly to reject him, partly to remind him. While waiting for his reply, to distract myself and do something positive, I'm about to embark on a dangerous mission.

The entrance gate to the Zone is a sturdy steel construction, sliding open and closed once every hour to let pass the armoured buses full of visitors. With its sheer enormity, it rules the yard, like a conqueror. We, the next bunch of reckless visitors to the Zone, are watching it in awe. This is the gate that protects us from the mortal danger behind. For one reason or another, we'll soon pass through it. My reason is altruistic: Antonio has the right to know that his son is alive.

A large white skull vibrates on the advert board to my left, warning us that what we are about to see might be extremely upsetting. It also says in small letters at the bottom that if we change our mind at this point, we don't get a refund. My eyes keep rising up to the security drones hovering above the gate.

'You may embark now,' the driver repeats for the third time, with a note of impatience in his voice. 'We leave in two minutes.'

The armoured bus, a robust metal box painted shiny black, is parked in front of the gate. Everyone is waiting for someone else to go first. Fed up, I get in, followed by my e-trolley. The scorching sun is filtered out by the small, darkened bulletproof windows, making it pleasantly cool inside. Instinctively I tuck myself away in the corner, in case there's an attack.

The bus fills up quickly. When all eight of us are in, two armed guards join us. As one of them slams the sliding door, I can't help feeling as if a prison door has been shut behind me. I'm totally at their mercy now. The driver speaks into the microphone. His voice is deep and serious, he sounds like a hero embarking on a dangerous mission. He probably plays up to it a bit, using the tone of his voice to let us know that, thanks to him, we are in safe hands. Philip once said they could charge us more if they put on a bit of a show.

If I hadn't done this before, I would be freaking out like the middle-aged couple at the other end of the bus, with a fully packed e-trolley. The woman has a thin face full of worry and clings to her husband, who is deathly pale. It's obvious they are first-timers. It's easy to spot who is here to visit a relative and who is the adrenaline seeker. I can see that most of them are family visitors like myself. Only a couple in their early twenties, each with a blue streak in their hair, are giggling and taking non-stop selfies, even while the driver is speaking. One of the guards gives them a look that would make me wither on the spot, but they carry on all the same.

We enter the Zone. The old London, like a living museum, unfolds before our eyes, with its endless narrow lanes and crumbling terraced houses, derelict streets, and collapsed escalators leading down to the abandoned underground stations where unfortunates live like rats, desperately trying to find shelter from the gangs. Burned-out skeletons of cars, with everything removable long stolen, line the roads. Though it promises to protect me from attack, the armoured bus cannot keep out the sense of despair that pervades the place.

My eyes are drawn to a group of children outside the window and my heart shrinks; suddenly I have the urge to cry. There are at least a dozen of them, huddled on the pavement, which is covered in broken glass, chipped tiles and other detritus. The children are watching our bus; blank fear is reflected in their vacant eyes. They don't come closer, knowing from experience that they won't be getting anything from this strange black vehicle. The middle-aged man in the corner turns even paler. The young couple with the blue hair are filming everything, erupting every now and then into harsh laughter.

One of the guards speaks into a microphone, giving us our money's worth. He talks about the socio-historical importance of the Zone, a remnant of the old system, of things that have been successfully eliminated from our affluent society. We need to be reminded of the wrong to appreciate the right, he says. I'm surprised by his elegant words and deep baritone voice. 'See, for example, those people on the roadside,' he says and points to a little group of unfortunates in ragged clothes, sitting on rain-soaked cardboard, with a large box in front of them. 'They rely on other people's mercy. In the old system when poverty was a sad reality, they were called beggars.'

'Wow!' the blue-haired girl exclaims and takes a few pictures as the bus comes to a halt, allowing the visitors to get a good look at these symbols of another century, a dark and backward time.

'Of course, money has no value to Zone residents,' the guard continues, 'so all they can hope for is food. But it's rare for beggars to survive longer than a week. Food is the most highly valued commodity in the Zone; no one gives it away for free.'

He warns us that feeding the unfortunates is strictly prohibited. 'If you wish to help them, please take items to the Visitor's Centre.'

The young man in black-framed glasses next to me speaks for the first time. Judging by his appearance he might be an arts student. 'So basically a human being is starving to death just meters away from me and I'm not allowed to help.'

'Like I said', says the guard in a mechanical tone, 'if you wish to help them–'

'Wouldn't it be easier to help the ones I can see here and now, rather than leaving things at the Distribution Centre where it's mostly the gangs who will pick them up?'

'Leave it', I murmur and nudge him with my elbow. 'They are just paid staff, they don't make the law.'

'There is a reason for this, young man', interjects the woman from the first-timer couple. 'They might look innocent. But they are very unpredictable. You never know what will happen if you open that window, even just an inch.'

The young man and I exchange glances. He shrugs and fervently types something into his notebook.

We continue our journey into the centre of the Zone.

'Is it true that some unfortunates eat corpses after digging them out of the mass graves?' the blue-haired girl asks the guard.

He pretends to pull a fed-up face, before answering in a mysterious voice.

'That's an urban legend. But in a place like this, anything is possible.' The passengers gasp in unison.

Our van now is getting closer to a structure that looks like a stadium when the guard confirms this.

'That used to be the Olympic Stadium. London hosted the Olympic Games in 2012 and the stadium was specifically built for the occasion.' The stadium has dirty grey walls and rails; some of the panels are hanging down on the side. Nearby stands a weird structure that looks like a large bent tower surrounded by a snake shaped metallic grid that used to be red. The van stops at a distance so we have a good view of both.

'We can't get any closer,' the guard announces. 'The stadium is now occupied by the Zone's most dangerous gang. Satellite pictures have shown that they are self-sufficient, having created an orchard and vegetable gardens in the centre of the stadium where the pitch used to be.'

'What's that ugly thing?' I ask, unable to tell if the weird tower is about to collapse or was designed that way.

'That was the so-called Orbit Tower. A big thing in its time. Again, built for the Olympic Games, it had a dramatic glass slide around it. On the top there were observation decks.'

A photo appears on the screen for us to see what it looked like when it was built. Yes, the grid was red and the structure wasn't covered with rust or ivy, but otherwise it didn't look much better. People in the old system had strange taste.

'Do people live in there, too?' someone asks.

'We don't know for sure, but it's unlikely. It has started to crumble. Large pieces can fall down anytime. Remember, since the new system started, nothing has been maintained or looked after here. For that reason, we are not allowed to go any closer.' We turn around and we are back in the narrow streets, but I keep looking through the window behind me, trying to imagine how this must have looked with all the visitors of the Olympic Games, the buzz, the glory, and how sadly it all ended.

Amid the mountains of rubble, Antonio's residence comes into view at the end of an abandoned street. It's a derelict factory building stretching for an entire block, harbouring a large courtyard inside its weather-worn walls. From the middle of the courtyard a long chimney rises like a lighthouse. Dust is flying up from the crumbling road. The ground floor windows are all boarded up, the first and second floor are protected by bars and dark curtains.

The driver shouts my name and stops the bus in front of the massive red-painted wooden gate. A red-painted gate or door in the Zone is a sign of warning to the gangs, a house where dangerous people can be found. People not to be messed around with. A guard knocks firmly on the gate, but minutes pass and no one appears. They're probably checking who it is from the top window. When the gate is finally opened, I climb out of the bus with my e-trolley. The guards stand on either side of me, offering protection. My feet are on the ground in the Zone; just the thought of it would frighten most people.

I find myself in an entirely different world, leaving the guards and the armoured bus behind. I can hear the bus rattling away along the bumpy road. Glancing at my watch, I realise I have over two hours before it returns to collect me.

I look around. The large courtyard with dozens of overlooking windows hasn't changed since I last came here with Philip. The little allotments are blooming with fruit and vegetables. Tomato vines climb their way up in pots covered with a plastic sheet to imitate a greenhouse. Every little niche or corner has been put to use for growing plants, not an inch has been wasted. There is a large secluded area just for potatoes, the most common food within these walls.

Haggard-looking men and women gather in the courtyard. They are wearing an odd combination of mismatched, ill-fitting clothes. They don't take their eyes off me but don't come any closer either. I grab my e-trolley, just in case. I seem to recognise one or two of the residents from the last time when I was here with Philip. So I was right, not everyone in the Zone dies within a year, and yet I was fired for saying it. Antonio approaches, wearing dark blue overalls, the kind workmen used to wear in my childhood. His shoulder-length hair is even wilder than usual. I can sense a mix of irritation and surprise in his gaze.

'What are you doing here?'

'I have to talk to you.'

'It's only three weeks till we meet in the Centre.'

'This can't wait.'

'Have you come to your senses and decided to join us?'

'Very funny.'

He ushers me through a low doorway. The shadowy room we enter functions as a kitchen. It has only one tiny window in the back, letting in just enough light to see. I can make out the silhouettes of other people, at least a dozen of them, sitting at a giant table made up of many smaller ones of different sizes. They sit in the semi-darkness, munching on something – boiled potatoes, I imagine. When they see me, the lively conversation dies out. They are all ogling my e-trolley with hungry eyes as it comes to a halt by my side.

'It's dark in here, but if we light a candle it will be too hot,' Antonio says while beckoning me to sit down. 'Most of us can find our own mouths, anyway.'

'I'd prefer somewhere a bit more private,' I say quietly, hoping the others will not take it as an insult. Carrying my e-trolley, I follow Antonio up the creaking stairs covered with patches of different carpets. I have to hold my breath. These carpets have never seen a vacuum cleaner.

We arrive on the second floor where his 'suite' is, a bedroom and living area separated by a wall from which the door has been removed. Half-finished paintings are scattered all over the place. Strangely there is some style, some art in the arrangement of the furniture, a mishmash of things collected from the Distribution Centre. On a long table next to the wall there are hundreds of old toys, mugs, broken picture frames, candleholders, and countless used books. These objects remind me of the old system. People were so poor they had to wear other people's used clothes, it was reported in a heartbreaking documentary on the Globe. There were even shops where they could buy them, so-called 'secondhand' shops. The way they were desperately, greedily pulling the items from the mountains of clothes bore a frightening resemblance to how Zone residents fight for items in the Distribution Centre.

I find a clean spot on the sofa and sit down. Antonio reaches behind a curtain, and fumbles with the window lock, trying to open it a bit more, but it doesn't give.

'Not much I can do against the heat up here,' he says. 'I have to be careful about opening the windows. They are at least fifty years old. If they break, we can't repair them.'

'Don't they leave window panes in the Distribution Centre?'

'Rarely and they are usually the wrong size. The gangs get them straight away. But while they have raw power, we have brains.' He taps his index finger against his temple. 'Plastic sheets are almost as good. And they are excellent as substitutes for green houses.'

He sits down on a chair opposite me, eyeing my e-trolley.

'I've seen your tomatoes. They could pass for Mediterranean ones.'

'You didn't come here to talk about my tomatoes. You're not safe here. Now, speak. I have a meeting in twenty minutes.'

'Meeting?'

'Without meticulous organisation, none of us here would still be alive, Alice.'

I take a deep breath. I don't know how to start.

'This will come as a shock to you, Antonio. But it's good news. Philip is alive. He is in a Dignitorium.'

I expect him to ask me to repeat myself, to move closer and examine my face to see if I'm lying. But he simply shrugs and leans back on the chair.

'I know,' he says.

'You…you know?'

'The Dignitorium was one of his choices. I have always thought it was the most likely one, given his weakness, the materialism you'd infected him with. He was too cowardly to move in here with us.'

I feel the room rotate around me.

'What…what do you mean? Did you know about this all along?'

His mouth curls and then slides into a mocking grin.

'Behold the epitome of perfect marriage as she finally discovers what everyone else knew about her husband.' He snorts. 'You should see your face now, bella.'

'What is it about Philip that everyone knew?' I don't recognise my own voice as it reaches a hysterical pitch.

'That he was going non-profit.'

'Non-profit?'

'He has advanced glaucoma. He's going blind.'

It simply doesn't make sense. Philip has never mentioned anything about his vision.

'How…? How do you know about this?'

'He visited me in October, totally devastated about his condition. Then he returned in November, saying he'd found a solution. I couldn't get any more out of him.'

'Why didn't you mention this to me?' I feel my blood pressure climbing rapidly.

'I hinted at it, I kept asking you to remarry,' he says, without any sign of guilt.

'You hinted at it.' I can barely get the words out now.

I pick up one of the porcelain bowls from the table and I'm about to smash it against the wall, but he twists it out of my hands and grabs my shoulders.

'Just let me finish, OK?'

'You're despicable!'

'He made me promise I would let you think he was dead. That was the whole point of what he did. All to please your selfish ego.'

I tear myself away from his grip.

'How dare you blame me?'

'He decided to withdraw because of you, Alice, to give up his place for another man who would be able to grant you your wish to have a child, your stupid dream family.'

It takes me a moment to catch my breath. I'm tempted to dismiss what I've just heard with a knee-jerk reaction. But his words, child and dream family, sting me to my very core.

'He wanted you to think him dead and remarry. It was you who sent him to the Dignitorium.'

I'm stammering – I feel like a trapped animal. 'How could he want me to find another man? Why couldn't he just BE that man?'

He snorts and for a moment I'm afraid the overwhelming scorn in his gaze will pour out and burn me.

'Typical,' he exclaims. 'Twelve years of marriage was not enough for you to listen, just once, to fucking listen to what your husband said, what he feared, what he believed. How he felt.' He kicks himself out of the chair and begins pacing the room; fury is crackling in the air around him like electricity.

'Listen? In the past few years there was nothing to listen to, he virtually stopped speaking.'

'That's when you should have really listened.' He stops, leans against the wall and scrutinises me with his cold grey eyes.

'You never change, do you, Alice? Bringing a consumer robot into this life that ends with premature slaughter in the Dignitorium. That's still your dream, isn't it?'

'We both wanted a family. How can you blame me for that?'

He shakes his head in disbelief.

'You know, I've never met your sister.' He walks over to the window and looks down onto the garden. 'I only heard about her from Filippo, the horror stories of what she did and how she fled to join the Owners. Entirely the opposite of what I would have done. But sometimes I think I can understand her. She must have realised the uselessness and triviality of the spender zones, your honey-coated Mid-Spender heaven that is slavery in disguise. I think she saw that. And she didn't want it.'

If he had slapped me in the face, he couldn't have delivered a bigger blow. I don't want to hear about Sofia. I don't want to hear this insane man, a useless, selfish father, praising her. I would leave this place for good now, if I could. But I'm a prisoner here for another hour.

'Suddenly you show a remarkable understanding towards Philip.' I spit.

He is still at the window, looking down.

'When he visited me in October, for the first time in his adult life Filippo opened up to me.' He speaks in a confessional tone. 'We kind of made up. He said I had been right all along. When he realised he couldn't afford the operation that would save his sight, he finally understood the system was designed to get rid of the sick. He felt he had failed you as a husband, though I did my best to tell him you're not worth the trouble and heartache.'

I swallow hard.

'He was inconsolable,' he continues. 'His illness made him realise the real danger of becoming non-profit: he saw through the system as it was, without your rose-tinted glasses. For the first time in decades we finally found a common voice.'

'Or a common enemy.'

'No, Alice. He never said a bad word about you. He wanted to give you what you have always dreamed of, even if it was only possible by getting out of the way. That's how much he loved you.'

I can't speak, I'm so close to tears. I don't want to believe a word Antonio says; I tell myself he's just trying to put me down and taking his petty revenge, but deep down I know that every single word is true.

'There is love that is constructive and wise, Alice,' he says, sitting down on his chair. 'And there is love that is just plain stupid.'

His words don't cut into me any more. There's no sense of aggression from him now; instead, his eyes are alive with pain and he looks at me with confusion rather than anger.

We are both silent, buried in our thoughts. What I feel is relief, a calm after the battle. He glances at his watch, an old-fashioned wristwatch with a leather strap that Philip gave him years ago. 'The meeting is about to start,' he says, and leaves. I'm suddenly left alone in this suffocating and untidy room where dead electric cables hang from the walls and ceiling, reminders of another era. I feel like picking up Antonio's ridiculous paintings and smashing them against the wall one by one. Instead I tiptoe downstairs, trying not to call attention to myself, as the meeting is about to start in the kitchen. I slip out to the yard. There are little paths of broken paving stones between the allotments, a mini maze through which I pace aimlessly, round and round, like a wind-up toy.

I love Philip, and I refuse to feel guilty for what Antonio accuses me of. I used to be a brainwashed consumer zombie, I admit that. I wasn't the wife Philip needed me to be, it's true. But how could I have known better? It was all I grew up with and saw around me until I became a Low Spender. Antonio is judging me too harshly, and that upsets me again. I resist the urge to burst in on the meeting and tell everyone that it was he who ruined Philip's life, crying out: 'Behold the man you so admire and rely on!' My steps become faster and faster. And he had the nerve to mention Sofia! Twenty years on and I'm still haunted by her words. For slowly but surely, her curse is fulfilling itself.

Suddenly my body is drained of strength and I drop down on a low brick wall. My brain is burning, my limbs trembling. I try to focus on the sounds around me. Birds are singing in the apple trees near the wall. Human voices drift out through the open kitchen door. I'll go mad if I'm left alone with my thoughts any longer. Even Antonio's company is more bearable than this, so I decide to go in.

They ignore me as I sit on a chair in a dark corner near the sink. Somewhere in the back of my turbulent mind I hear their conversation about food rations and other resources. I have to admit, the level of organisation is remarkable. They discuss the produce they will need for the following week and where to store it. Antonio is their leader, but they all have their own roles that they seem to take very seriously. Now there is a hearing and Antonio is the judge. An adolescent boy with wide, frightened eyes is accused of stealing tomatoes from the allotment at night.

'Are you aware, Alex, of the possible consequences of your actions?' Antonio's voice is calm and understanding but when he speaks, there is complete silence in the room.

Petrified, he hangs his head. He knows that if he's expelled from Antonio's residence, he's unlikely to survive even a week in the Zone.

'I take it you fully understand that what you did could have had a detrimental effect on your fellow residents.'

The boy's eyes are begging for mercy, and I can't help but feel sorry for him. He must be an orphan, one of far too many. Dumped in the Zone on his eighteenth birthday as a punishment for starting his adult life as non-profit .

Antonio concludes that from now on tomatoes and all other produce will be counted every evening, and guards will be set on night duty to watch over the garden. He gives the boy one more chance. Alex sneaks out of the kitchen, his face flushed with shame but also relief.

I notice a huge difference between how these people interact and how we used to communicate in the staff room at school or at Sunday Mass. Here, people pay attention to one another. It reminds me of the books I used to read as a child, nineteenth-century classics Dad got for me, in which people sat around fires and played cards or shared stories all evening.

The meeting continues, now on a more light-hearted note. Whenever there is a misunderstanding, Antonio smooths it out. If a conflict arises, he initiates a peaceful discussion, focusing on solutions. His eyes are glittering with excitement. He comes across as a brilliant, wise leader, responsible not only for the survival but also the wellbeing of his little community. His words still upset me but I can't see him as a deranged old man any more. This is not the Antonio I always knew, the person who struggled to make it as a spender, the father who let his family down. Ironically, the Zone has forced him to man up, and having given him his mission in life has transformed him for the better. He takes a gulp of water and when he puts the glass back on the table, he glances at me. For a moment our eyes meet but I turn away. I don't want him to see the respect in my eyes.

16 JUNE, 2050

The limousine approaches a set of black wrought-iron gates. They swing open automatically as the car slows and we pass through and make our way up the driveway. I look out of the window to my right. The red-brick Victorian mansion is a masterpiece of Gothic architecture, and exactly the kind of house I imagined as a child I might one day be mistress of, with servants attending to my every wish.

This seems less romantic now, though I have to face the bitter reality that Sofia is in fact living my dream, again. I force myself to stop thinking about it and focus on the task ahead of me.

The building is mesmerising, and as I look up, I notice something – or someone – in a second-floor window. The heavy drapery seems to move and from behind it I see a face. It's a child's face, white and eerie, but the tilt of the head indicates curiosity. I lean closer to the car window to get a better look, but it's gone. The curtain is still. So too, I notice, is the car. We have arrived.

BOOK TWO

ONE

The gates of the Scarborough Dignitorium stand at the end of a wide, tree-lined street. Why did Philip come so far? Surely there were suitable Dignitoriums in London. Was he allocated here or did he have a choice? Not that I care; I would go to the end of the earth to see him.

Last night, as I lay in bed, my phone rang. It was Edith, whispering into her ID Phone, telling me that Philip had read my letter and would like me to visit him as soon as possible. His six-month Honeymoon Period expires on the twenty-fifth. That's less than three weeks away.

For many hours, I battled with demons, brought to life by Antonio's words, before slumber finally overcame me. When I woke, as my head began to clear, the guilt came flooding back and clouded my mind as rapidly as black ink in a glass of water. I understand now the missing money – poor Philip struggling alone, spending all his savings on medication and then the unsuccessful laser operation. Even if he could afford a cure in an expensive hospital, it's too late. There's no way back from the Dignitorium. He has signed the contract.

After checking in, I'm inside the high surrounding walls, a feeling of serenity settles over me like a fine muslin blanket, making me wonder if the air itself is drugged. I try to shake it off. I can't stand the arrogance of the mock Victorian building in the middle of the park. The magnificent old trees are rustling in the breeze, their leaves dancing and inviting me to come nearer, like nymphs luring unsuspecting mortals to their death. But I can't stop seeing the decay behind the beauty, the death behind the peace. Experience has taught me that nature in a Dignitorium is not a symbol of spring and rebirth but of life's fragility and evanescence.

Most of the residents are old, in their sixties or early seventies, the right time to retire. I'm reminded of the missed opportunities in Philip's unfulfilled life and I can't entirely shake off the sense of blame. I only hope it's not too late. I can still be of use. I'll come every day. I'll make his final weeks worthwhile. I'll also come when he's sedated, I'll come…until the end. I don't want to think about what will be after the end.

It's time to make my way to the main building. In the marble-floored lobby, behind the dark wooden desk stands a young receptionist with a long black ponytail. The smile on her face never fades while she scans my ID Phone. My face appears on the screen, a photo that was taken some years ago, in which I'm smiling, glowing with optimism. It looks like someone else, someone I knew in a previous life.

I follow the receptionist through a spacious hall furnished with leather armchairs and antique-style standing lamps. The walls are covered with mahogany panels, on several of which hang screens. Each screen is showing the final Farewell Video of a different resident, reassuring us how gladly they are leaving this world behind. They talk over one another, male and female voices, high and low-pitched, a cacophony of happiness. They each sit in a cosy room with a period fireplace, its mantelpiece decked with flowers and photos of smiling grandchildren. Each resident holds up drawings, which have messages printed on them in a coloured font, such as 'Love You, Grandma' or 'For Grandad'. In the background, behind the sash window, stretches a magnificent landscape with rolling hills and fields of wildflowers.

I'm escorted to the Salon, a grand, rectangular room, reminiscent of old-fashioned drawing rooms. With its heavy curtains, antique fireplaces and gilded mirrors, it reminds me of the long galleries in period houses used for walking when the weather didn't permit going outdoors. From the walls, gargoyles and angels follow me with their dead stares. I drop into a robust armchair. It's burgundy and comfortingly soft to the touch. I still have ten minutes to wait, but already my heart is racing.

When the door opens, I glance up, hoping it's Philip. It's one of the carers, a woman of about my age, with auburn hair and pale skin. She stops in front of me and smiles widely, if somewhat automatically. A nametag is attached to her grass-green tunic. Next to the miniature Dignitorium logo is her name, Edith O'Connor.

'Edith? How nice to meet you finally! I'm so grateful for your help.' I jump up and reach out to shake her hand.

She doesn't take it, but stares at me with a look of astonishment. Her smile still frozen on her face, she remains formal, avoiding eye contact while she checks my identity on her mini-screen.

'Thank you again for everything.' I continue. 'Nurse Vogel spoke very highly of you.'

Again, there is absolutely no reaction apart from a barely noticeable flush of irritation. I'm beginning to feel like an idiot. She hands over a plastic wrist band with a mini screen on it. She asks me to put it on.

'You'll need this to leave the Salon and use the main entrance,' she says. I recognise her voice, it's definitely the same person I spoke to on the phone, yet she shows no sign of recognition. 'You are allowed to walk with your husband outside, anywhere in the grounds. If he needs medical assistance or any other kind of attention, press this button.' She points at a red button on the wrist band.

'You'll have a maximum of two hours with him and by the end of your visiting time you need to be back in this room, where he will be collected. After which you may leave.'

'There must be a misunderstanding here.' I struggle to contain the anxiety in my voice. 'My parents also retired in a Dignitorium and I had three hours with them every day.'

She doesn't bat an eyelid.

'These are the rules of our Dignitorium. Terms and conditions differ in each institution and are created solely by–'

'But why only two hours?'

'We pride ourselves on spending more time on our residents' preparation for their final departure. It is our greatest–'

'But–'

'Do you agree with our terms and conditions or would you prefer to leave the premises and return home?'

'I agree, of course. I'm sorry.'

I scan through the terms and conditions and I find that once a week the visitor is allowed to attend the bedroom of his or her loved one. My parents' Dignitorium never allowed anyone inside the living quarters. This rule appeals to me and I tell her this. I detect a hint of satisfaction at the corner of her mouth.

'We believe every visitor has the right to see the conditions in which their loved ones live. Sign here, please.'

Her smile is like dried honey and never leaves her face. No matter how hard I try to connect with the person behind it, her gaze strikes me as empty, inauthentic. How can this be the same

Edith Nurse Vogel said was helping me?

'You are not permitted to engage with others, be they patients or visitors,' she continues. 'If you have any questions, ask a member of staff.'

I nod again.

'You will see that there are no restricted places outdoors. You may walk everywhere, including to the Termination Wing. However, you must refrain from taking photos or any other activity that would disturb our terminal patients in any way. Many of them find joy in the view of the gardens in their final hours. For the safety of our residents, there are cameras outdoors, and you will be obliged to leave if you don't keep to the rules.'

I nod and she leaves.

Another five long minutes pass. My fingers are nervously scratching at the upholstery of the armchair, raking it in both directions. Finally I hear the door open. A man stands there with Philip's features, in Philip's clothes, staring at me. I jump up from my seat but something holds me back. Philip is a well-built, attractive man, but this man is haggard and painfully thin. Finally the eyes overcome my doubt; I know those eyes. There are several different urges rippling through my body; one is to scream at him, the other, much stronger, to hold him.

Our embrace is deep and quiet. We mould into each other and stay like that for God knows how long. Despite his unusual gauntness, I feel at home in his arms. He still smells like Philip. I can't find the words to describe my emotions. I let my tears flow.

We have been sitting on the sofa in front of the bay window for what feels like a long time, speechless. My left hand is pulsing in his right palm.

'Are they not looking after you well here?' I ask, looking him up and down, not hiding my surprise at his changed appearance.

'Quite the opposite. They're looking after me well. But my attention has turned away from earthly things like food.'

His docile eyes and the way he speaks in a low, melancholy voice, tell me his inner fire has waned.

'Why don't you ask me, Ali?'

'Ask what?'

'Your real questions.'

I hesitate. There's so much I want to know but there's so little I can think of right now.

'I was so relieved when I heard you were alive, Phil.'

'But?'

'But since then I can't stop asking myself: How could you do this to us?'

'Your letter. It was painful to read. I did it for you, Ali.'

'You still don't get it.' I sigh deeply. 'I'm now a Low Spender. I lost my career, our home. I could end up in a Dignitorium, like you.'

'I swear I never thought this would happen to you, Ali. You're more important to me than myself.'

I know he speaks the truth but why do his actions show otherwise?

'I went to see your father. He told me everything.'

'You went to the Zone, alone? Why?' He pulls me closer.

'To tell him you're alive. But our conversation didn't quite go to plan. It turned out he knew far more than I did.' I can't hide the disappointment in my voice.

'By the way, your dad is doing better than most of us. He told me about your glaucoma. Another thing you hid away from me.'

'I didn't want to trouble you.'

'How is it now?'

'It's in an early stage. But I've noticed some decrease in my peripheral vision.'

'Is it really that bad? Philip, is it really–?'

'Shush,' he says, wrapping an arm around my shoulder. 'Please, let's not bring this up again.'

'Maybe there's a new treatment or–'

'I've tried everything I could afford.'

'But it's your vision, for God's sake–'

'It doesn't matter as long as I can see you.'

'Can you see me well?'

'Just like before.'

I can't believe that this is happening. I have never felt so helpless. He is a useful member of society, a Mid Spender, a respected architect, so why can't the operation be more affordable? Do they really think if he drops out, there will be others to take his place? Are we no better than cattle, just another one of the herd? He squeezes my hand, probably reading my mind.

'Why the Dignitorium, Philip? Why not something else?'

'Like what?'

'Even moving to the Zone would have been better than this. Your father has created a little haven there. Surely he wouldn't mind–'

'Two more years.' His brooding voice carries a sad note.

'What do you mean?'

'In two years' time much of the Zone will be turned into a new major High Spender development. New mansions, a sports ground, recreational parks, a high speed race track and even a harbour for their bloody yachts.'

'They can't do that.'

'They can and they will.'

'Does this mean…?'

'Yes. Dad's residence will be gone, too. He doesn't know it yet. I haven't found a way to tell him.'

'You must, Philip. He needs to prepare, find a new place by then.'

'Do you really think one can just 'find' a place in the Zone like that?'

'I've seen how many derelict, empty houses there are.'

'Dad would need another fort-like structure to house his entire community.'

'So what will happen to them?'

'They need to break up into smaller groups. It means certain death.'

'This mustn't…it can't be true.' I shake my head. 'How do you know about this?'

'I was the one who was supposed to design it, Ali.'

I can't hide my shock. Where Antonio's home now gives shelter and food to dozens of people, High Spenders will be racing in their fancy sports cars. And the Zone residents will be crammed together even more tightly, more of them homeless, prey for the gangs. Is it really that easy to trade with the lives of thousands just because they are non-profit?

'You'll be fine, don't worry,' Philip says, resting his head against my shoulder. 'Now you can get married and have the kids you always wanted.'

'Is this what it's all about, Philip? Because if it is, you're wrong. I'll get you out, no matter what.'

I've just said goodbye to Philip, leaving him to attend a session called Eternal Peace. I'll be back tomorrow morning. I'm taking a final stroll before returning to the station. This Dignitorium feels different from those I've seen in London. There is more natural green here, not one coloured lake in sight, and its simplicity, with gardens of wild flowers, lends it a special charm. Once I get Philip out, we can go to the countryside again, back to Somerset, where we first experienced the natural world together, not long after our first date. The wild flowers there don't release the smell of death.

TWO

I've just arrived in Scarborough again. I'm observing the eclectic mix of modern and period buildings from the window of the local monorail. Scarborough is so different from the capital. I can't see the sea from here but I can still feel how close it is. Pedestrians – as if under its spell – radiate a certain joie de vivre. The original Scarborough was a small town that was then expanded into this megacity under the new system. Old terraced hotels were renovated. The majority of the buildings are built in red brick that lends warmth to the streets. I can't deny it feels good to be here, like being in a luxury holiday resort, carefree and sun-soaked. Maybe Philip chose to retire in Scarborough to hear the seagulls and smell the fresh salty air. Or to be as far away from me as possible.

It's early morning, but warming up quickly. When Philip enters the Salon, there's a wide smile on his face. He's shining with happiness, but the way he's walking worries me. Occasionally he holds a hand out in front of him as if he's struggling to find his way.

'Are you all right?'

'Of course.'

'No, you're not.'

'Ali, I'm fine. But you haven't seen my scar yet. Look.'

I touch the scar behind his left ear, where his tracker was removed on the first day of his retirement. It's so tiny it's barely visible.

'Did it hurt when they took it out?'

'Not at all,' he says. 'But Tiara Joy made a scene when hers was removed, as if she'd lost a limb.'

'Who?'

'You know, the *Elevate!* winner whom we managed to escape from at that awful party at Linda's. She has retired here and paid the Dignitorium enough to let her entourage in all day. You'll see – and hear – them for sure.'

'I don't think I particularly want to.'

I wonder why she is here. Two years ago, at the party, she was glorified. Maybe she has a terminal illness?

'Now, let me take you somewhere special.' He stands up and leads me out of the main building to the garden. We walk past a stone fountain and a little arboretum. Then I spot the lake.

A wooden gazebo stands at the lakeside, a jetty extending from it out over the water. All across its surface float colourful little rowing boats, like wrapped candies. Waves ripple on the shore.

'I love coming here alone, just looking at the water, and daydreaming about you sharing a boat with me,' Philip says. 'Even when I was sure I would never see you again, I still kept on dreaming.'

'This time it's real.' I squeeze his hand.

While we wait for the next boat to arrive back at the jetty, Philip stops on the middle of the bridge and leans against the wooden railing, looking down at our reflections in the crystal clear water.

223

I've never seen him this relaxed, like a general who has given up the battle, losing the war, but rejoicing in the wisdom that retreating and silencing the guns doesn't mean failure. He looks well in a dark green shirt, with his sleeves rolled up to his elbows. He's unshaven and I have to say stubble suits him. He never let it grow before – it wouldn't have been tolerated in the office.

A red boat arrives at the dock, carrying an elderly couple who are holding hands. They are both dressed in their best clothes, the woman in a blue silky dress and a matching hat. The man is wearing a black suit with polished shoes. Despite the solemnity on their faces, they emit the same strength and unity as my parents did on their final day. Without knowing anything about them, I am convinced they have retired together and will be terminated very soon.

Like a drop of oil, our boat slides out onto the water. The gentle rocking movement is immediately soothing. Philip rows until we get to the other side of the lake, to a chestnut tree that casts a shadow over the surface of the water. Here we stop.

'I'll get you out of here, whatever it takes,' I tell Philip and when he doesn't respond, I say it again. I can tell it makes him uncomfortable.

He reaches into the pocket of his jeans and takes a ball of paper tissue out. Before he unwraps it I know what will be inside. The ring with the snake swallowing its own tail hasn't lost its shine. Philip holds it up, rotating it slowly between two fingers.

'It has a whole new meaning now,' he says.

'Other than eternity?'

'The lifestyle we used to live, the madness, chasing whatever was there to chase but never really reaching it.'

'I'm so sorry, Phil.'

'I'm not blaming you.' He stares at me innocently.

'It's enough that I'm blaming myself. But when you're home

again everything will be different, I promise.'

Avoiding my gaze, he reaches out for my left hand and slides the ouroboros ring onto my finger.

'You don't seem to understand, Ali. There is no way out of the Dignitorium.'

He releases my hand and begins to row again.

'Yes, in normal circumstances,' I reply. 'But in this case it's a misunderstanding. You're too young.'

'I'm non-profit,' he says.

'You're not like most people here, unable to contribute to their Right To Reside, dangerously close to old age. You're—'

'It doesn't work like that, and you know it very well, Ali.'

'Once my visiting time's over, I'll ask at reception. I won't leave until they offer me a solution.'

He starts rowing again; I can sense his anger in the shortness and fierceness of his strokes. Other couples in nearby boats are staring at us, wondering what the reason is for our sudden increase in speed.

'What's your problem now?'

This comes out louder than I had intended. The stares around us are getting more curious. Philip points at a little folly at the top of a slope. It's definitely more private than the lake.

'Let's sit down there,' he says. 'I want to tell you something.'

I sense the irritation in his voice. I know what he'll tell me, that he wants me to give up, but I won't. This week I'll take him home.

As we arrive at the jetty, Philip hands the rope over to the two ladies waiting for our boat. He ignores their 'How are you today?' and after helping me climb out, he strides across the lawn in the direction of the stone folly.

At its centre stands a life-sized statue of a woman, praying. The dome-shaped, ivy-covered roof is supported by four pillars. We sit down on the cold stone steps. It's slightly cooler here than is comfortable and I put on my cardigan. We are watching the ducks floating on the water, quacking occasionally. I envy their carefree existence.

'I need you to promise you'll listen carefully,' Philip says, leaning against a pillar. I reach out my left hand to hold his right one, but he slowly pulls it away. He's looking at the lake with its glasslike surface.

'OK,' I reply.

'Nothing can be done about me or for me.' He speaks like a father explaining something of the utmost importance to his child. 'I want you to understand this, Ali. Even if by some miracle I could leave this place, I wouldn't be able to work for long because of my glaucoma, and then I would have to return here anyway.'

'But, for God's sake, it would give us a few more months together, and who knows, maybe a new, more affordable cure would become available.'

I could try borrowing from Linda, I think, but before I say it aloud I realise there is no Linda any more. She wouldn't recognise me if we met in the street, and she wouldn't answer my call. She would definitely not lend me – a fallen Low Spender¬ – any money.

'You're not listening.' Again, there's disappointment in his voice. 'There is no affordable cure. But more importantly, your parents' sacrifice would go to waste. Don't forget they died sooner than they had to so that we could have kids.'

'What does that have to do with this?'

'I'm not cut out to be a father; you were right all along.'

'I never said that.'

'You're only thirty-four, Ali. You can still have a family.'

'With someone to act like a stud horse, is that what you mean?'

'With someone who knows little enough of this world to want to bring children into it,' he says, and I open my mouth to argue with him, but I can't say a word.

The stone steps of the folly are so cold I would like to stand up, but instead I shuffle closer to Philip.

'Can you promise me you'll do it?' he asks. He can't be serious.

'Look, Philip, just relax and wait while I explain everything to the management. And I'm sure your boss will take you back if we tell him–'

He suddenly stands up and strolls across the lawn, down to the bridge. I follow him quickly.

'Philip, careful! It's too bumpy for you.'

'You think I can't cross a bloody lawn?'

'Look at the way you're walking, the way you hold your head–'

'Don't mention my eyesight. Please! Don't ever bring it up again, and stop worrying about it.'

I stand behind him, put my arms around his shoulders, but he's unmoving in my embrace, cold as a statue.

'You're only thinking about yourself again,' he murmurs. 'I want you to have a family. Would you grant me my last wish?'

'This can't be your last wish.'

'Why not?' His voice stiffens.

'Phil, we don't have much time.'

'You still don't understand. You never will.'

These words hurt, and I have to look away to hide the tears that are welling up.

'I won't be able to go in peace if you don't promise me you'll be happy,' he pleads.

I take a deep breath. This is the performance of my life and my audience is the only man who matters.

'I promise then.'

The tension in his posture eases immediately.

'Come, I'll show you my room.'

We are inside the main building, walking along wide corridors lit

227

with fake candles, our feet sinking into the thick carpet. Wherever we go, we're escorted by the fragrance of roses in enormous vases. Philip seems to know his way around this endless maze. Fluorescent signs help direct us, though sometimes I don't even understand the words written on them. One corridor leads to a 'Multi-sensory Studio', another one down to the cellar to the so-called 'Debodifying Caves'. People – staff, residents and visitors – pass us by, always with a smile, especially the carers who – with their humbleness – fit perfectly into the soft honey-coloured environment. On the second floor of the western wing, we turn right. Mahogany doors open onto private apartments. At the last door, we come to a halt. Philip scans his wrist band over the sensor, then turns the knob.

The high-ceilinged room we enter feels more like a luxury hotel suite than an institution for the retired. The space is divided into two; each resident has a single bed, a bedside cabinet, a desk and an in-built wardrobe with full-length mirrors for doors. All the furniture is made of heavy oak. In front of the enormous bay windows stand a coffee table and two imitation antique armchairs. The view is stunning; the room overlooks the western part of the gardens, with the lake in the near distance and a vast forest stretching beyond. On the right side of the room, behind an executive desk a gentleman is sitting with his back to us, wearing chunky headphones. His eyes are fixed on his mini-screen and he is saying words out loud in Italian. I shoot a glance at Philip.

'This is my room-mate, George,' he says. 'He's learning Italian.'

'Italian? What for?'

The words slip out and it's too late to take them back.

'To have a chat with me.' He chuckles.

George turns around and when he sees us he takes off his headphones. He jumps up to greet me. For a man who must be in his early sixties, he is very youthful. His brown eyes are bright with joy, and he shakes my hand, radiating warmth and honesty.

'George. George Dimitriadis,' he says.

'I'm Alice. Lovely to meet you, George.'

'We've become like an odd couple here, haven't we?' George glances at Philip.

'We neighbours have to stick together,' Philip agrees.

'Neighbours?' I ask.

'Well, I'm half-Italian, George is Greek, so we're neighbours, aren't we?'

I'm surprised that someone as full of life as George can be retired. I wonder if he has some illness that hasn't manifested itself yet. I'll ask Philip tomorrow. I'll also ask him why George is learning a language that he will have no use for. As if reading my mind, George turns to me.

'I'll learn till the very end, to improve myself,' he says. 'Until the last day. Which won't be too long, now, but I hate to be reminded.'

'George and I retired around the same time,' Philip turns to me.

'And we refuse to be dumbed down,' George adds.

'Yes,' Philip says, the sparkle returning to his eyes. 'Instead of going to the spa we try to have a conversation in Italian. Rather than wasting hours in the restaurant and bar, we go for walks in the gardens, contemplate life and discuss poetry.'

'I assumed you would have a sea view,' I say, standing at the window.

'Only the High Spenders have the privilege of seeing the sea from their rooms,' says George, and shrugs. 'Not that we care that much.'

'Why would a High Spender retire to a mixed-class Dignitorium?'

'You'll know the answer once you've seen Tara,' Philip replies in a sarcastic voice, and they both chuckle and pull faces like naughty schoolboys. Finding a close friend is the first positive outcome of this horrible situation, I'm thinking.

Out of the blue, Philip's wrist band reminds him that he has a meeting starting in five minutes. In the meantime, my wrist band starts blinking red, warning me to make my way down to the reception.

'A meeting?' I ask Philip.

'With the doctor. I have only two weeks left of my honeymoon period and they want to decide on the most suitable sedative.'

He says it with total ease as if he is discussing what he'll have for breakfast. I hope he doesn't notice the goose bumps suddenly appearing on my skin. George waves goodbye to me, then turns back to his desk and puts the headphones back on.

'Thank you, Ali, for understanding. You don't know how happy you've made me,' Philip whispers, holding me close.

We leave the room together, Philip and I. At the landing we kiss goodbye, then Philip goes straight ahead to the medical centre, through a frosted glass door beyond which I cannot pass. I carry on downstairs with a weight on my chest. Today the same receptionist is on duty, the young woman with the long ponytail. She doesn't stop smiling but it seems increasingly like a grimace. From the hall I can hear the cacophony of recorded voices, confirming their happiness in the Dignitorium.

'May I speak to a manager?' I ask, trying to force a smile.

'May I ask why?'

'I'm sorry, it's confidential.'

'I need to know the reason, Mrs Brunelli.'

'I'll discuss everything with the manager. If you would be kind enough to send them out.' It's difficult to hide my growing impatience.

'I'm the first point of contact, and no one can see a manager without talking to me first,' she says. Her mouth is still pulled upwards but her tone has turned frosty.

'Look, it was a misunderstanding that my husband retired, he was not supposed to be–'

'Pardon me?' she leans closer as if she hasn't heard correctly. Up close, her skin seems hard like a mask, due to the thick foundation she wears.

'I just…well, is there a way to get him out? He is still in his honeymoon period and–'

With her large green eyes she is staring at me as if I'm an alien applying for residency on planet Earth. She doesn't say a word, but without breaking eye contact she pushes a button on the wall. Soon the door behind the reception desk is thrown open and a woman in her early fifties, wearing a well-cut black velvet suit, appears. She has a stern expression on her face. She is holding a mini-screen.

'May I help?' Her smile is almost natural, she's definitely better at this than the receptionist, but I detect amusement in her eyes.

I repeat my problem, but halfway through she interrupts me and points at her mini- screen.

'Would you like to read it printed or on screen?'

'I skimmed most of the contract yesterday, thank you, but you have to understand that our case is entirely different and–'

'Your husband read the contract before he signed it, Mrs Brunelli. There's nothing else to add.'

'But you don't know our situation at all…'

The receptionist is shooting neurotic glances at us, pretending to do her job by pushing a pile of papers to the other side of her desk but always staying within hearing distance.

'I'm sorry, madam,' the manager says in a condescending voice, 'but if you keep forcing this, I will have to give you a warning.'

'A warning? What for?'

'Gaining two warnings disqualifies our visitors from entering the institution again,' she says with an air of victory.

'I understand, and sorry for the trouble.'

I turn on my heel and flee the building, not waiting for her reply.

In the garden I recognise the squeaking voice I heard two years ago from the pink heli-taxi. Tiara Joy is dining on the bar's terrace, surrounded by a dozen people who look like devoted fans, all women trying hard to copy her clothing and hair style. Unlike Philip's, her wristband is gold, sparkling in the sunlight, letting everyone around know she is a High Spender. On my way to the gates I see a few other High Spenders. All of them make sure, even those wearing long-sleeved tops, that their gold wristbands are clearly visible. Now I understand what Philip meant when I asked about the reason High Spenders retired here. In a Dignitorium that was exclusively for High Spenders, there would be no one to feel superior to. The gold wrist band is useless if everyone else is wearing it.

Sitting on the monorail back to London, I'm burdened with heavy, black thoughts. I had had to make Philip a promise I have no intention of fulfilling. It was a white lie, for his sake, but still a lie, the first I've ever told him. I don't know how long I can carry on pretending, without him reading the truth in my eyes. I wish I had Mum or Dad here to talk to. I ring Nurse Vogel, but again she doesn't answer. It's out of character that she didn't get back to me after my voicemail last night. There's no one else I can share today's failure with and my loneliness carries a new, acidic taste. I feel I'm hanging from the edge of a cliff with wet hands that will soon lose their grip. Maybe I should stop looking up for help and take the courage to look down in the deep, to prepare myself for the fall.

THREE

Today I'm up early and out of the house by eight. Crowds of people sweep past me on their way to work. I'm a loner, going against the masses, against the tide. I'm shivering, though it is hot already; apparently it will be the hottest day of the year so far. The perfect day for going to hell.

Just the thought of what happened yesterday frightens me, the possibility of not being allowed to visit Philip again. I am now approaching another Dignitorium, a familiar one that holds more positive memories. Saying goodbye to loved ones is a step everyone should take before leaving this world behind.

There is no one at the wall this early and my tears begin to flow. I feel Mum and Dad's love transmitted through the cold silver plaque as if they were trying to comfort me. We are connected and always will be. For several long minutes I soak up their presence and store it deep within me. I look around before I lift up my wrist to take some photos with my ID phone. They come out well: my smile seems genuine and my parents' names etched into the plaque are clearly visible behind me. The closest thing to a family selfie I can have these days.

I take a seemingly casual stroll around the park. I'm desperate to find any sign of Nurse Vogel. She still hasn't answered her phone. I have left several messages, but she hasn't responded. I can't wait to tell her about my meeting with Philip. It's strange how strong the power of beauty is. Even in my chaotic state of mind I can't help but stop for a minute to look up at the cream-white building before walking up the hill to go inside. At reception, I try to seem calm and collected.

'Is there anything I can help with?' the receptionist asks.

'I was just wondering if I could say hello to the ex-carer of my parents, the lovely Nurse Vogel, who is a dear friend of mine. If you could remind me of her shift for this week…'

She thinks I'm weird, I can see it in her eyes.

'I'm sorry I can't give you any information about staff,' she says, the uniform smile stretching across her immaculate face.

'All I want to know is what time to return to speak to her.'

'This is a place of work and any non-professional communication with staff is prohibited.'

Her eyes are starting to shoot arrows.

'Thank you, I'll contact her myself,' I say, before leaving.

On the monorail I'm trying to calm my fears about Nurse Vogel. In my mind's eye I see her being hauled away to the T-wing, turning her head back towards me, her eyes begging for help while her frail body is held up by two stocky guards. The monorail is now taking me to MN09, a place where no one greets me any more. No human being, at least. The apple tree my father planted, then replanted, means just as much to me as any human, and if I could pack it up and take it with me today, I would.

I wait for the young couple with a little boy and a baby to leave the house that used to be my home. Once they're out of sight, I take a last photo of the house, but it's the tree that means the most to me. It has grown since I last visited, its canopy above shading me like a parasol. It's the morning rush hour; the walkways are packed with people in black-and-white office wear, hurrying towards the monorail station as if charged up with electricity. I must look out of place wearing a simple T-shirt with a denim skirt, leaning my back against the tree and not rushing anywhere. As the rugged surface of the tree trunk presses into my spine, I imagine that Mum and Dad are with me, reassuring me that they support me and will be here for me forever. I take a few more selfies, then I move back a bit to get the whole tree in the picture. Before making my way back to the monorail station, I pick a leaf and slip it into my pocket. Sadly, it's too early for apples.

Ruth is not at home, so I don't have the chance to say farewell to her and Felicity. Maybe it's better this way. It would be too painful. Maybe Felicity's laughter would hold me back. They would probably try to change my mind. I'm sure Ruth would. In the apartment that I didn't even occupy long enough to call home, it takes no longer than ten minutes to pack my things. I won't need a lot. I'll commit the first crime in my life; I'll leave the place without clearing my old furniture out, without getting it ready for the next resident. It's not yet eleven when I leave this wretched Low-Spender area for the station, with one small e-suitcase following me like a faithful servant. Like yesterday and the day before, I use my ID Phone to buy a ticket for Scarborough. But today I don't buy a return ticket.

Now that I know I have limited time, my perception has changed. Past, present and future are concentrated in this moment. I only half-lived before, and probably half-loved, too. Everything that I experience is intensified: the flavour of the strawberry I've just finished, the bold purple colour of the shirt the woman opposite me is wearing, the grace of the rolling hills through the window.

The speaker on the train announces we'll be arriving shortly in Scarborough. It's a sweet female voice, wishing us a wonderful stay.

Philip is already in the garden, gazing at a glass statue of a frail old woman. From a distance Philip looks like an obedient schoolboy who has been told to sit quietly. He is listening to the sounds of nature around him, bliss is written across his face. He spots me straight away. I would have preferred him not to see me as there is still half an hour left until visiting time. I could have finished my business at reception then told him the good news. He comes to me, and we wrap our arms around each other.

'What have you brought me?' He is eyeing my e-suitcase. 'I don't need any more clothes.'

'It's not clothes. Not for you, at least.'

We sit down on an isolated bench at the top of a hill overlooking the lake. His skin is glowing, his eyes are shining and he seems relaxed. He must sense that I have something to say, as he's watching me impatiently.

'I have made a decision, Philip.' I swallow.

Continuing is far more difficult than I expected.

'It wasn't hard really. Given the circumstances, I think this is the only sane thing to do.'

'Is it to do with the contents of your luggage?' he asks, lifting his head, suddenly alert.

'So you guessed it?'

'If it's what it seems to be…you can't do this, Ali.'

'I'll speak to the manager, in fact if you hadn't spotted me, I would be already in the office. There would be no visiting time today. I would just join you, and never leave.'

He releases a painful sigh.

'So you were deceiving me yesterday when you promised to grant me my wish!'

'I needed time to think, Phil.'

'You didn't listen to me. You never listen, you just follow your own stubborn head, and you don't care how much it hurts me.'

I can see the tension rising in his shoulders. He's watching me with pain and disappointment in his eyes.

'But don't you see, it's good news. We'll have a wonderful two weeks together. Like Mum and Dad.'

'Stop this, please!'

'It's too late, Phil. I am not going back into that shithole, only to be alone and end up here anyway in a year's time, without you.'

'How can you say that? My God, look at yourself, you're young, you're in your prime.'

'In these two weeks ahead of us, we can make up for the bad times, together.'

His face turns red with anger.

'I don't want you in this place, do you understand that?'

A carer, a sturdy, square-shaped woman, marches towards us from the left. A guard from the gates approaches from the right.

'Philip, calm down. It's OK,' I whisper, trying to avoid calling any more attention to ourselves.

'It's not fucking OK!'

The guard and the carer reach us at the same time. It seems it's the first time they have heard him swear. And they are not impressed.

'Is there a problem, Mr Brunelli?' the carer asks.

'Oh, no. Everything is just fine. Marvellous that my wife has just decided to get herself killed.'

The carer shoots an annoyed glance at me, as if I'm a small child disrupting an important event.

'How come you're here so early?' she turns to me.

She checks something on her mini-screen.

'You are not allowed to visit for another fifteen minutes, Mrs Brunelli. I have to ask you to go to the reception area and check into the Salon.'

'But when I arrived Philip was already outside,' I say.

'It was his relaxing time and not an opportunity for anyone to disturb him.'

This word, disturb, is pronounced with an unpleasant stress.

'What kind of place is it that doesn't allow me to talk to my husband, as if he is a bloody prisoner?'

'Leave her alone,' Philip says to the carer. 'It was I who approached her at the gate. I apologise. For a moment I forgot I was in a Dignitorium.'

The carer ignores him; she's watching me like a hawk, expecting me to leave.

'What's in this luggage?' she asks.

'It's mine. I'm retiring today.'

'You're not retiring!' Philip raises his voice again.

'Please leave now, madam, or I will need to report you to security.' The guard turns to me. 'This may end in a warning.'

'If you ever loved me, promise me you won't do anything,' Philip yells as I make my way slowly towards the main building. 'Wait in the Salon, we'll discuss this.'

'Please, don't let her go to the office,' he begs to the carer.

'Don't upset yourself, Mr Brunelli. It takes more time than that to complete a registration.'

'Could you hurry up, please?' I can hear her raspy voice behind me. 'You're upsetting him.' The footsteps of the security guard to my right are speeding up.

The Salon feels like a hothouse; it has been soaking up the heat all morning. I can't wait for Philip to return or I will explode. It's infuriatingly noisy in here, for other families are also visiting. There's a large family in the corner; they are loud and cheerful, apparently celebrating some good news. Suddenly I see that it's George, Philip's roommate, surrounded by his family. He is very happy and cuddling one of his daughters. When he notices me he waves across the room. I reach out for the mineral water on the side table. The touch of the ice-cold glass is so refreshing, I'd like to pour the water all over my face. A few minutes later, Philip storms into the room. He spots me straight away.

'Don't you understand, if you upset me they won't let you in again,' he whispers. He drops into a chair on my left.

'What have you got against me moving in with you?'

He shakes his head in disbelief.

'Don't get upset. Just explain. Please.'

'This is my last wish. Is that satisfactory?'

'Philip, I–'

'I want you to live and find a good husband and have children. If you do this, the damage has been only half done. It's the only thing that can put my mind at rest.'

I take a deep breath before I reply.

'I promise then.'

I can't believe I managed to say it. This time I believed it. There's no other way, he would notice it if I faked it. He's at peace again; the tension gone from his body. He draws me closer and presses a kiss on my forehead. A kiss has never been so painful.

'I know it's not easy for you, Ali.' His tender voice breaks my heart.

'It takes some getting used to.'

Gratitude is pouring from him, walls and barriers collapsing. We keep quiet for a while. Philip gives me time to digest the truth. The truth is that this is it. No more silly hopes. He's got two weeks as Philip Brunelli, the man I have known and chosen for life. And the only thing I can do for him is grant him his last wish.

George's family are so loud, we decide to take a walk. Philip says he is taking me somewhere I'm going to like. We pass the rock garden, then the rose garden with its pink, red and yellow buds, then the lake with the fountain. All this reminds me of stories I read as a child in a Bible for young people, of the beautiful illustrations of the Paradise we all get to after the hardships of life on Earth. Walking here with Philip, hand in hand, evokes those pictures. Still, the external paradise can't silence the internal hell.

'I'm so happy you have found a lovely room-mate in George. What's his surname again?'

'Dimitriadis. He is extremely proud of it.'

'You've become good friends?'

'I would be so much lonelier without him. I would be the only one who asks annoying questions before Death Taster sessions.'

'Death Taster sessions?' I'm horrified. 'How could they call it such a thing!'

'Oh no.' He laughs. 'It's George who named it the Death Taster session. The official name is something like De-bodifying experience.'

I remember now the sign I saw for 'De-bodifying Caves'.

'It's a form of meditation, lying in warm water in a dark cave, which gives you the sensation of floating in space.'

'Like flotation tanks?'

'Similar, but much better. They guide us through with a mini-speaker implanted in our earplugs. You feel as if the voice is coming from inside your head, as if you don't have a body any more, though you are still alive and more content than ever.'

'Bloody hell!'

'It's quite pleasant, to be honest. I can only hope that death itself is similar.'

How can he be so casual about his own death? And what can I say to this?

'Mum and Dad didn't have it.'

'It's a fairly new thing. Someone local invented it. They're really proud of it and are selling the technology to other Dignitoriums. Of course, we get only two sessions per week, unlike High Spenders who get five.'

We turn onto a narrow, pebbly path that leads up to the top of the hill.

'What are the annoying questions you and George ask?'

'Things like "How does the inventor know real death will be the same? Has he died and returned?" The facilitators try to hide the fact that they don't know the answer. Most residents don't notice it, but we do.'

Maybe, in this case, it's better to be ignorant, I want to say, but I force my mouth shut. We're halfway up the hill. I stop and look back. I can see straight through a second-floor window of the Dignitorium, into the sunlit corner of a room. It's decorated like a palace, with gilded stucco walls and ceiling and a crystal chandelier in the middle. As the sunlight falls on it, it shimmers like diamonds. Philip follows my gaze.

'High Spenders,' he says with pursed lips.

How morbid! Even in the jaws of death High Spenders don't seem to give up their privileges. We turn around and continue our way up at a slower pace, panting heavily.

'Do you know why George is here?' I ask Philip.

'He had a so-called "charity" that went…"bankrupt".'

'What kind of charity?'

'He collected used items in the High-Spender areas, and redistributed them to the poorest Low Spenders.'

I don't get it. I've always thought helping the poor this way was counterproductive. We're considered worthless without consuming and being able to prove it.

'But what's the point of getting things for free? Without them going through the Buy-O-Meter and increasing our legal consumption?'

'Some people are so poor that they barely qualify for the Right To

Reside. For one reason or another – unemployment, redundancy, sickness – they are on the verge of becoming non-profit.' His voice is breaking up. 'Their savings are just enough to buy basics to keep the Right To Reside going for a while, but when something more expensive needs replacing, they can't afford it.'

'So with George's help they received thrown-away, barely used items for free.'

'Exactly.'

'I didn't even realise such situations can exist.'

'Most of us don't, Ali. They are the denied, the forgotten class.'

I remember people in rags I saw near Nurse Vogel's home, carrying a shiny red fridge freezer. They kept looking around as if they were afraid to be caught. For a moment I had the feeling they had stolen it from High Spenders, but now I understand.

'There are not many of these people left,' Philip says with resignation. 'Not for long, anyway.'

I can't help but shiver. I see myself in a year's time, alone, overcome by depression, trying to stretch out my miserable existence for as long as I can, just to ditch it all for the promised glory of the Dignitorium the next day.

'So they caught George in the end?'

'His tracker showed too much transition between the High Spender and Low Spender areas and it raised suspicion. They fined him, and he was unable to pay it off.'

'Fined him for what?'

'Impeding the economy, encouraging corruption, interfering with regulations. So he had to retire.'

'It's heartbreaking.'

Fury climbs up from the pit of my stomach, and I close my eyes. I'm nauseated by this Garden of Eden.

'He was still allowed the Right To Reside-free year in a family member's home,' Philip says, squeezing my hand. 'He is really grateful for that, as it could have been cancelled because his fine remained outstanding. The one free year expired in December. Then he moved in here, just a week after I did.'

'He doesn't seem to mind.'

Philip remains quiet.

'Or does he?'

'I don't think it's quite sunk in yet. But he's dreading the sedation period far more than the T-Wing. He talks to me about it in the evenings, after turning off the lights.'

'I thought the sedation period was really pleasant.'

'It's not that. He dreads senility more than anything. Most importantly, he dreads not recognising his family any more.'

This has never occurred to me, that it's not just pain we fear, but losing ourselves. Once my parents' drug therapy started, I still visited them every day, apprehensive at first, but when I saw the mellow joy they floated in, I relaxed. They were in a rainbow-coloured state but still able to talk and laugh. It was encouraging, almost tempting. Is George clinging too much to his mind, his ego, unable to let go? Is he right or wrong?

We've reached the top of the hill. It seems as if the whole world is under our feet. I look down at the main building of the Dignitorium and feel the bitterness flowing in my veins. Philip gently takes my shoulder to turn me around. Beyond the forest, down in the distance, I catch sight of the sea, endless and silvery blue.

'I like coming up here,' Philip says.

'Are there no seats?' I look around the little circular clearing.

He shakes his head.

'They probably don't want us to stay here too long and start realising what we're leaving behind,' he says sharply. 'They prefer us down there in the restaurant or in the spa. They prefer us even more in the T-wing.'

'Philip, it's not funny. Where is the T-wing anyway?'

He turns his back on the sea and we look down at the main building and the gardens again.

'That extension,' he says pointing his finger, 'at the back. That is the T-wing.'

'Why do they make them so small?'

'It's big enough to suit their purposes, for one or two terminations per day.'

I shiver and return to the sea view. It's much more pleasant. I link arms with Philip. I'm determined to keep him as happy as possible for the rest of his time here. I must avoid turning the management against me. I'll be good and grant him his last wish even if it costs me my sanity.

'Phil, I want you to know how sorry I am that I forced my image of a perfect family on you and never listened to you. I'm sorry for the lost years. For letting you down in the most difficult times.'

'Can you hear it?' he whispers and tilts his head to listen more closely. 'It's a woodpecker.'

'And if I could make it right and just have one year back, I would do everything differently.'

'We used to listen to birdsong when we were dating,' he says, smiling to himself. 'Do you remember, at the lakes, when we fell asleep on the grass and woke up the next morning, soaking wet from the dew?'

'I've realised you're more important than that imaginary lifestyle with that imaginary child.'

'We even wanted to record it, do you remember? But then we couldn't, because we didn't have our ID Phones with us. Do you remember those ID Phone-free Sundays we used to have? That was your idea.'

I'm transported back to those days, to my early twenties, to that carefree, optimistic young woman who came up with ideas. Ideas that were too little to get us in trouble but big enough to make us feel like rebels. What happened to that person?

Philip has just gone to his Death Taster session. I don't know how he can stay so cool about it. My legs won't take me to the exit yet. I need to try one more thing to make the most of our remaining time together. Philip doesn't have to know about it.

The receptionist with the long ponytail has 'here-comes-the-troublemaker-again' written behind her grin. I ask my question as politely as possible.

'Is there any way to make my visiting time just a tiny bit longer?'

'The rules and regulations cannot be amended under any circumstances by staff or by visitor request.'

'All right.' I take a deep breath. 'But surely you understand that I just started visiting my husband a few days ago, unlike others who have six months before their loved one's sedation period starts.'

'Rules and regulations cannot be amended under any circumstances by staff or visitor request. In case…'

I can see the growing tension in her face and I remember Philip's eyes begging me to grant his final wish.

'Forget it. Sorry for disturbing you.'

I'm outside. The irritating sound of Tiara Joy's voice squeaking from the bar's terrace reaches me, and I change my route and walk around the building to avoid her and her entourage. My blood pressure shoots up when I think about how she's allowed to break the rules while my modest request to see Philip for a bit longer has been denied.

The monorail rolls in to London. Looking at the affluent Mid and High Spender areas we pass by, I see it all with different eyes now. People are enjoying themselves to the full, making the most of all that society has to offer, not minding that they will end up like Philip or George. In the distance, miles away the sleek white tower of the Primavera Club reaches up to the sky. I feel disgust looking at it, exuding authority, although in reality its windowless walls reveal nothing, refuse to communicate. I have a sudden urge to go there and ask the Owners for help but I know they don't care about anything beyond their own decadent lifestyle. I don't have delusions any more. What I thought as a child to be a sophisticated, futuristic building hiding secrets I so craved to discover, tempting me with its mysterious treasures, I see now as a stone wall; unresponsive, impenetrable, indifferent, nihilistic.

It has been a long day, both for body and spirit. I'm crashed out on the sofa. Switching on the Globe, I flick through the channels, but it's one rubbish programme after another. On 'Elevate!' the female contestants are trying to out-dress each other. On 'Two' a documentary features a solemn man in his sixties, who sits in a solitary leather armchair in a studio, talking with tears in his eyes. He's remembering how his parents were neglected in a retirement home in the old system, their pleas to end their suffering denied as euthanasia was illegal. On 'Three' I catch the end of the news.

Yesterday a record number of non-profit people were captured in London. They should have retired or moved into the Zone but instead they were hiding in parks, in monorail stations. Some were even breaking through the red fence and escaping into the wolf-packed countryside until they were located via their trackers. Due to the gravity of the situation, PM Edward Finch is speaking live, introducing a new government initiative to assist the disadvantaged. 'Philanthropy will be better rewarded from now on,' he says with sincerity. 'If residents make a significant donation to the Zone Distribution Centre, they can gain months or even years of High Spender status. Everyone now has the chance to become a High Spender.'

Are people blind? Don't they see it's mostly the High Spenders who can donate enough in the first place? The PM stresses the importance of this initiative to build a fairer society. I watch his lips move. Previously his words would have lured me in, but now I can see Philip was right. It's a performance. But no matter how hard I try, I can't see any errors. He's pitch-perfect, and that makes him all the more frightening.

FOUR

Philip is almost victorious today, the way he lifts his chin, his eyes glowing as he stares into the distance, the wind ruffling his hair. He doesn't bring up yesterday's confrontation, as if it didn't happen at all. We're making our way to the restaurant and I do my best to put on a cheerful face.

I've just learned that I can have a complementary lunch with him, something every spouse of a Mid Spender is entitled to once a month. I find myself thinking of Mum and Dad, how happy they were in the Dignitorium, and how I didn't even doubt that when the time came, I would retire with Philip. Now that I've had a taste of it, my enthusiasm has gone.

'French, Greek, Japanese or steakhouse?' Philip asks.

'What do you mean?'

'For lunch. I'd like you to choose.'

'You're saying there are four different restaurants in this place?'

'No. There are many more – about fifteen, of different

nationalities and themes. But most of them only open for dinner.'

It amazes me how they pretend to really care for the residents' emotional wellbeing. The truth is they understand the risk of the residents getting bored, and work hard to maintain the illusion of novelty until their time comes to enter the T-wing. How cleverly thought out! And how sickening!

'You know which one I want to go to, don't you?'

He squeezes my hand and for a moment I'm that twenty-something-year-old girl again, who expected to cook Greek with her new boyfriend, but he had already cooked the meal.

'Will George be there, too?' I ask.

'That's the only one he goes to. He hasn't been to any other restaurant. Once we went to the steakhouse together but before the waiter arrived, George stood up and just left. I found him in the Greek tavern.'

'I can't stop thinking of how they mistreated him. And he remains such a positive person.'

'Not today.'

We make our way down a glass corridor to the dining area. Philip is walking again in a way that deeply unnerves me. My strong, talented husband has become an invalid. But I hold my tongue. At least this is one promise I can keep – I won't mention his illness ever again.

Above our heads, palm trees and other exotic plants are pressed to the outer side of the glass tube, the patterns creating the illusion of a living wallpaper. Bright green light seeps through the leaves. We emerge to find ourselves in a square where the buildings are arranged in a semi circle, connected by an open-air deck. Each house is built in a different style. They are all restaurants. Among them, there's a lovely-looking French bistro, an American diner and a traditional English pub.

The Greek tavern has white walls, blue window frames and doors, and a roof terrace which looks onto the lake, where the tiny colourful boats are out again. Whitewashed stone steps lead up to the terrace where tables covered with blue checked tablecloths are already waiting for their guests. There are fresh flowers in a blue-painted vase on each table. Philip pulls a straw parasol over from the corner, to protect us from the sun. So far the tavern is empty. The waiter greets us and hands us each a menu. The service is impeccable.

George Dimitriadis, wearing a perfectly ironed, short-sleeved white shirt and brown pleated trousers, comes running up the steps. I raise my hand to wave to him when I notice he is not even looking in our direction. He sits at the furthest table, right on the edge of the terrace, probably to have a full view of the lake. But he seems far away. Lost in his thoughts, he buries his face in his hands.

'Bad news?' I ask Philip.

He nods.

'He was so cheerful yesterday, with his family,' I whisper.

'It was yesterday. Then it sounded like good news.'

'What's happened?'

'His daughter is pregnant.'

'It's great news! What's wrong then?'

'He'll never live to see his grandchild.'

'What a shame! They were all so happy yesterday.'

'They weren't,' Philip says. 'He pretended, they pretended. They rejoiced but in the back of their minds they were all thinking the same thing: he will not live to see his grandchild. That's all he could keep repeating all night.'

The chardonnay turns bitter in my mouth though it is really good wine. We're munching on our nibbles, a selection of olives and warm rosemary flatbread, when we see George standing up from his chair. He is heading our way.

'Lovely morning we're having today, guys.' His voice sounds just as cheerful as usual.

'Are you OK, George?' Philip asks.

He nods, but avoids making eye contact.

'Have a seat,' Philip says, pulling out a chair for him.

George sits down, not saying a word. He looks around suspiciously then pulls his chair closer to us. He lowers his voice.

'Milan has disappeared.' He pauses for a moment to see the effect his words have on us, but whatever he's expecting, we don't deliver. I have no idea who this Milan is. 'Toby, his roommate, said he was removed from their room last night.' He leans even closer, his nostrils widening. Sweat trickles down his forehead.

'When Toby woke up this morning, Milan wasn't in their room,' he says, short of breath. 'Milan's bed was already made up for a new resident, all his stuff cleared out. Toby didn't make a big deal of it; we all know some people are quite abrupt about termination, change their minds overnight. But this morning he walked towards the screens at reception and there is no Farewell Video from Milan.' He is panting so hard, I am beginning to worry for him. Philip must be thinking the same as he offers him a glass of water, but George shakes his head.

'But where else could he be if he wasn't terminated?' I ask with pretended nonchalance while my hopes begin to rise.

George's face is glowing with excitement. 'Toby said Milan had been telling him quite mysteriously about a marriage between his daughter and a prominent High Spender and that it could change things for him, too.'

'We'll never know now, will we?' Philip says, and shrugs.

'I want to find Milan's family. They must know about the secret appendix to the contract.' The determination in George's voice is almost frightening. Philip reaches out to give him a comforting pat on his shoulder.

'Even if it were possible to buy your way out, nobody could afford it,' Philip says. 'That's why we're here in the first place, because we can't even afford the Right To Reside.' George doesn't seem to listen.

'We still don't know if it's a girl or a boy,' he mumbles to himself. 'I'll never know.'

'Of course you will, George,' and I want to say more comforting words but the lack of conviction in my voice would give me away.

'I'm here for you George, if there's anything I can do,' Phil says.

'Yes, but…' his dreamy eyes are staring into the distance, beyond the lake. 'Anyway, guys, I'll let you finish your meal.' He stands up abruptly and hurries down the stairs.

'Will he be OK?' I ask Philip.

'I don't know. I've never seen him this upset before. But tonight we have a Soul River session, which will help him relax.'

'What the heck is that?'

'It's very soothing indeed. It's a unique meditation with sensory overload. The sensation we feel is reminiscent of being carried by a gentle river.'

'Are you sure that's enough?' I turn my head away so he doesn't see me pulling a face.

He sighs. 'I hope so.'

Wild thoughts are spinning in my head. How could this Milan leave the Dignitorium? Is there really a secret appendix to the contract? If so, why is it not public? How did Milan's family learn about it? George is right, there is something dodgy about him disappearing from the room at night. What if Philip–?

'Alice. I know what you're thinking. Can you drop it, please?' Philip's hand stops just an inch away from his mouth, an olive rolls down from the toothpick and drops onto the table. It rolls to the edge, leaving a light trail of oil behind it.

'I'm not thinking of anything at all.'

'Yes, you are. And I want you to forget about it. You see, I can understand why Milan moved out secretly at night. The management doesn't want other residents and their families to speculate and build up our hopes for nothing.'

'I'm not speculating, I'm just thinking about it ¬ – it's interesting,' I say.

'Just drop it. Please.'

'I will. I have already. What are you having next?'

'Moussaka, I think.'

'I'll have the same then.'

The waiter, as if reading our minds, arrives and takes the order.

It takes no more than ten minutes for the food to arrive. It's delicious, but I can't enjoy even a bite. My thoughts are too preoccupied with what I've just heard from George. My heart goes out to him, to this real gentleman, whose simplest and greatest desire – to see his new-born grandchild – has been denied.

'Do we know, does anyone know for sure if it's possible to buy our way out? Has anyone read the full appendix?'

'No one really knows for sure,' Philip sighs. 'But that's not the point. The point is, it doesn't matter.'

'How can you say it doesn't matter?'

'Don't you understand, Ali? Even if there is a way to buy someone out, the cost has been deliberately made so high that you can't borrow it and you can never earn it.'

After finishing our moussaka, we are ready to look at the dessert menu. Now there are more residents around us, enjoying food and unlimited drinks. Men and women with immaculate hair, their faces riddled with wrinkles but still presentable, are chatting and laughing, holding a wine glass in their perfectly manicured hands, like the people you see in colourful cruise adverts. The women limp around in high heels like injured birds, blue roads of veins sticking out on their calves. If insecurity had a smell, the place would stink. Their well-cut, expensive clothes cover those areas of the body that are most prone to ageing. They are perfectly armed with illusions, pretending right up till the last minute. The meal has been excellent; the whole thing feels just as Mum described it, like being in a luxury resort where your senses are pampered in an almost hedonistic way.

The Salon is hotter than ever, even here in the corner in front of the bookshelf, where there is no direct sunlight. Nothing stirs in the stifling air. Next to us the grand piano's shiny chestnut surface is collecting dust, barely visible to the eye. Philip is holding my hand; I rest my head on his shoulder. Talking would only ruin this harmony we have so little left of. Our hands do the talking instead, his finger tracing circles on my palm.

My wrist band starts blinking. I don't want to go. We're counting the moments, trying to stretch them out one by one, before the nurse comes for Philip. We hold each other in a loving embrace. The nurse, a plump older lady with a round face, coughs once, then again a bit louder, and I can feel Philip slipping out of my arms.

He is gone. He has a course now, some kind of relaxation class where they are taught about the eternity of the soul. I hope he is already in the activity room. I don't want him to see me lurking around reception. I know I'm playing with fire but they can't give me a warning for inquiring.

'May I speak to a manager, please?'

'What is it about?' the receptionist with the ponytail asks. I could swear in her head she added 'again' to the end of the sentence.

Suddenly I feel like slapping that stupid grin off her face.

'I have some personal information about my husband I doubt he shared with the management.'

'Mr Brunelli has already informed us about his allergies and all other physical requirements the day he registered with us.'

'Yes, but…I have some things to discuss about his mental health.'

'You can tell me now and I'll put it in the system.' She lifts her hand, ready to type. I don't remember seeing her this eager.

'Well, it's a bit of a delicate matter, you know. His father tried to commit suicide several times and I'm worried about whether Philip told you that he also has the tendency.'

'Right, you can discuss this with our manager. Just a second.'

The manager I spoke to a few days ago, is soon at the desk, smiling widely, as if she has forgotten our previous conversation. She waves me into her office for a chat. The square-shaped, high-ceilinged room reminds me of a library from the Victorian era. With hundreds of leather-bound books on the floor-to-ceiling shelves, it smells like one, too. I sit down opposite her and immediately get to the point.

'Is there any way out of the Dignitorium, madam?'

'Are we at it again? I thought this was about Mr Brunelli's suicidal tendencies.'

'Is it true that there's a secret appendix to the contract no-one gets to read?'

She looks me up and down, clearly struggling to put me in a box.

'You never give up, do you?' She goes to a shelf in the corner and searches for something. She returns with a red folder.

'People love urban legends,' she says, taking out a large plastic envelope. She hands it over to me. 'This 'secret appendix' is one of them. It's not 'secret', anyone can read it. It's unbelievable how people read all kinds of rubbish but when it comes to their own life, they miss the most important text.' She clears her throat. 'This is your husband's full contract.'

I'm reading it; it's pages and pages of legal language until it gets to the part even I can understand. Nine months, yes, full board, yes, after six months the drug therapy starts, yes, euthanasia can be requested anytime when the resident feels the need, yes, two hours visiting time per day, yes, once in the Termination Wing no way to change mind, yes, Farewell video required with positive message before termination, using at least one of the following words: dignity, happiness, grateful, yes. I know all this. To the end of the contract an appendix with small letters is attached. It's so lengthy and dull that I understand why most residents just skip this part. While I'm reading it through, forcing myself to focus on the legal language, the manager doesn't take her eyes off me. In the final section it's explained that the cost of the used-up service can be calculated in cash. If the resident at any point before reaching the Termination Wing changes his mind and wants to leave, it is possible by paying that calculated cost and providing proof that the resident will have the means to contribute to society and will not become non-profit.

I look up at her. The total lack of any emotion, including impatience, unnerves me.

'So it's possible but the fee is astronomical, am I right?'

'You said it.'

Her face remains expressionless.

'You promise to withdraw from society, to stop becoming a burden,' she continues. 'In return you are provided with the highest standard of luxury for nine months. For how long exactly do you expect productive people to keep you?'

'If it's so unrealistically high, how could Milan's family pay it?'

'I shouldn't say this to you. It's confidential. But I hope if I tell you, you'll stop harassing us once and for all. Milan's family has come into unexpected wealth through marriage and they bought him out.'

'So if Philip came into unexpected money–?'

'Milan had only been with us for five weeks so his family had to pay a minimum length of service. Mr Brunelli's been with us for nearly six months. The cost of our services is substantial. Do you have the means to cover Mr Brunelli's fees?'

'No, but....'

She shrugs. We have nothing to discuss, her eyes say. She stands up.

'Could you, please…would you…?'

My voice is cracking up. I can't finish the sentence.

'Would you like me to calculate the amount your husband has used up so far?'

'If you would be so kind.'

'It will only give you unnecessary heartache and false hope.'

'Please.'

It doesn't take long, not more than twenty seconds, but they're the longest twenty seconds of my life and my palms are sweaty, my heart racing. When she finally speaks, the sum she tells me is higher than in my wildest dreams, it's fifteen years' worth of a Mid Spender's full salary. It's a hundred times more than what anyone would lend me. Philip will never be out of this place. In two weeks' time his new life of chemical happiness will begin. It's over. There's nothing I can do to save him.

FIVE

Today I arrive early again. It's 10am and I'm already outside the Dignitorium, just circling around the wall. I've come early on purpose to spend more time with Philip, if not in his company, then at least near him.

Cutting across the lawn in front of the main building, I notice a figure sitting on a bench covered with a pile of blankets, empty cocktail glasses by her side. It's Tiara. She's wearing a halter-neck summer dress and pink sunglasses. Her hair, falling on her shoulders, is immaculate as usual. For a change, she's alone.

I don't know what I'm thinking when, instead of entering the building to wait for Philip in the Salon, I take a sharp turn left and make my way over to Tiara. My legs seem to have taken control. When I stop in front of her, I don't wait for her to offer me a seat. As I drop down to her right, she ignores me, but I can sense a breeze of unpleasant surprise. I have no idea what to say to her.

'You don't know me, but I know you.' I blurt out. She continues to stare ahead, not acknowledging my presence.

'Just like millions of others,' she says finally.

I take a deep breath.

'My husband needs to get out of this place.'

She doesn't react at all. Like I'm not even there. I allow some desperation to creep into my voice.

'He shouldn't be here. It was a mistake.'

Still no reaction.

'You're the only person I can borrow money from, to save him.'

Not a word, not a movement of her head. I wait but she remains a statue. I'm only wasting my time here. I stand up and start walking in the direction of the main entrance when I hear her raspy voice behind me.

'Is that your husband you're always with? The dark-haired grumpy guy?'

I swallow hard and turn around.

'Yes.'

She gestures to me to sit. I obey.

'I can help you with that.'

'Would you really...?'

'I can put you in touch with some High Spenders; wealthy, lonely men. Some of my friends.'

'I don't understand—'

'This is what you want, isn't it?'

I'm struggling to believe my ears.

'It's what you all want, after all. A High Spender for a husband.'

I'm on the verge of bursting out with what I really think of her, that she's a common prostitute, an airhead, that she would never understand love. But I hold back. I can feel the hot liquid stinging the corner of my eyes and the trail of the tears burning my cheeks. I turn away from her and bury my face in my hands.

'Why does everyone assume I have money left?' she asks out of the blue. I glance at my ID Phone. In half an hour Philip will meet me in the Salon. I must pull myself together.

'You don't?' I try to hide the shock in my voice.

'You have no idea how much it costs to bribe a Dignitorium, sweetie, but if I couldn't have my fans here by my side, I would have requested instant euthanasia on the first day.'

She won't help me. How could I think she would – she can't even help herself. She is not taking her sunglasses off and she's not moving her head to look at me. I feel like a priest, used for those rare minutes of introspection and confession, the way she uses those fans for admiration. I'd like to leave now but my curiosity doesn't allow me to.

'Why are you here, then? You're a High Spender, a celebrity.'

'That was last year, sweetie.' She lowers her voice. 'Don't tell anyone, but this year they didn't even want me for hair-dye adverts.'

'So why don't you go back to your old life as a Mid Spender? There's so much more to life than being a celebrity.'

She fumbles for a cigarette in her pocket. She lights it and takes a long deep puff before she speaks again, with something like longing in her voice.

'Tell me, have you ever been loved?'

'Erm… My parents adored me. And my husband loves me–'

'Loved by millions. Admired. Don't answer! I know you haven't. Once you have, you can't live without it again.'

I turn to look at her. This is the first time I see her up close. Instead of glamour and glory all I see is sadness and defeat. She looks much older now, tired. Almost deflated. Deprived of the sparkle of life, an empty shell in a flowery dress. I can't help but feel genuinely sorry for her.

She is warming herself up for a lengthy monologue. It's something I would be happy to listen to in other circumstances.

Now it's becoming unbearably painful. I stand up.

'It was nice to meet you. And thank you for…'

'For what?'

'For making me feel better about myself.'

I have seen a lot of this place, but I haven't seen the most important part so I stroll towards the back of the main building. I walk past the western wing, then the little allotments that are kept for residents. Three residents are working despite the stifling heat, watering olive-coloured tomatoes or raking the damp soil. They're no different from the people we usually see at home in their gardens at weekends, working tirelessly with rolled up sleeves, bent backs, with heavy but determined motions.

I slow down involuntarily as if afraid of what's coming next. The brick-coloured extension that is the T-wing seems small even from up close. I try not to look directly but I notice that all six sash windows are covered with muslin curtains. In the meadow opposite, I sit down on a little rock and pretend to enjoy the view innocently while glancing over at the building I'm so curious about. I sense some movement behind a small frosted window, as if a hand is reaching up, but when I look closer, it's gone. I must be on the verge of a breakdown.

I had to see this place alone; I don't want to walk here with Philip. It would upset him even though he is calmer than ever these days. His skin is tighter and smoother, and he doesn't slouch the way he used to. He has an air of optimism and resolve which has already started to have an effect on me. Where does he get it from? Is it his inner strength or a mere result of the well-designed preparation, the palliative yoga, the relaxation classes, the spiritual guidance? I feel I lack the strength to fight; I've lost all hope to carry me through the battle. Every moment spent with him is a gift I should be grateful for.

Sometimes I want to slap my younger self, at other times I want to scream at Mum and Dad for bringing me up in a pink bubble, for not preparing me for real life. It's funny to think, but Sofia's final words to me seem truer than ever, the words that I put down to jealousy. She was right, after all, I really will never have any children or family of my own. Strangely, I don't believe any more that her curse is to blame. The powers pulling the strings here are untouchable, and we are no more than marionettes in their hands.

Now that it's time to meet Philip in the Salon, I'm relieved to leave the T-Wing behind me. There is nothing interesting here anyway. This little wing reaching out into the meadow of wild flowers is not any different from the rest of the building. Apart from one thing. It's deathly quiet.

Philip looks exhausted today, like someone who hasn't slept all night. As it turns out, he hasn't.

'That bitch Tiara threw a party. Nobody slept in the whole building.'

'It's outrageous that she can ruin other people's sleep. Is there no one here to give her a good kick up the arse?'

'There was a guard who confronted her. But she made a scene.'

'How long do you have to put up with her?'

'For the rest of my life.'

He laughs and my body freezes.

'Philip!'

'Seriously! She only arrived two months ago.'

I want to say something comforting but nothing comes to mind. We pass the park with the mermaid fountain and take a sharp turn left on the pebbled path.

'Let's walk behind the building,' Philip suggests and I know immediately where he wants to go.

'You know, the wine tasting session will start in a few minutes, do you want to have a look?' I ask, and grab his elbow, not waiting for his reaction.

'I want to see the T-wing.'

'I've just been there. It's nothing special, trust me. Why don't we–?'

'I want to face it, Ali.'

I give up. We stroll past the little allotments, arm in arm. There are six residents now, bending and cutting and watering, working tirelessly to sow seeds whose results they may never see. Philip is very quiet. I'm almost tricked into thinking it's because he's relaxed, but I can sense a hurricane beneath the placid mask.

'I know something is wrong, Phil. What is it?'

'George.'

'Did something happen to him?'

'We won't see him any more. He requested termination this morning.'

'Oh, no! Is it because of the grandchild he won't see?'

'Partly. But mostly it's the drug therapy.'

'I thought he still had three weeks till his sedation period starts.'

'He did.'

'So?'

'He refused it.'

I won't be able to get any more out of him for now. He is facing the T-wing like a condemned man facing his executioner, straight in the eye. He must be going through hell and he doesn't want to share it with me. We're in the meadow opposite the building, standing among the wild flowers that reach up to the knee. Philip takes off his sweater and lays it on the ground. We sit down then lie back, propping ourselves up with our elbows.

Watching the clouds floating idly in the undisturbed blue, I think of the missed opportunities in the past few years when I could have spent time like this with Philip, on weekends or during school holidays. We could have gone for a picnic or to the countryside and just been together, connected without words. I could have gotten into the depths of his mind, of his fears and worries. But I chose to follow the madness instead. Stuck in the consumer whirlpool I satisfied my yearning with shopping, dining out, going out. And now it's too late.

Suddenly the door of the T-wing opens and George runs out, breathing heavily. He looks around like a deer fleeing a hunter, but he doesn't notice us. He drops a dark green object on the ground that looks like a staff ID Phone worn by Dignitorium nurses. He stops at an oak tree, leans against the trunk and bends forward, as if he is about to vomit. He is panting, his face glistening with sweat. A young male carer follows. He quickly picks up the staff ID Phone and clips it around his wrist. We lie back in the tall grass and when the carer is not looking, we scramble over to behind a nearby bush to be fully concealed. The carer asks George whether he's ready to receive his family. He nods shortly. Now I understand what Nurse Vogel said about the staff who work at the T-wing. There is something sinister about them, though I can't quite put my finger on it. They might as well be robots, speaking, smiling and helpful ones, but without the sparkle of humanity. He whispers something into George's ear. George looks up at him, in awe. Philip stands up instinctively, ready to protect his friend if necessary. I pull him back.

'When can I see my family?' George asks the carer, his voice trembling. 'You said I could see them now and stay with them all evening.'

'Of course you can, George, don't worry. But first we just need a minute of your time.'

We listen intently, peering through the gaps in the bushes.

'Where are we going?' George asks the carer, who turns around, gently directing him towards the entrance of the T-wing.

'This is purely protocol. It'll only be a few minutes. Then I'll bring you back to the Salon to see your family.'

'Where are they? Are they here?' George looks around in panic, desperately hoping to catch sight of his family.

'Of course, they're all here, waiting for you in the Salon.'

'Are we going there then?'

'Yes, but we're going back to the T-wing first then we're going to the Salon to meet them.'

'Why can't I see them now?'

Seemingly out of nowhere, two other carers appear. One of them, a robust man with tattoos on his hands and wrists, grabs George by the arm.

'Mr Dimitriadis, let's not waste any more time,' he says brusquely. 'I thought you wanted to see your family as soon as possible. You'll see them once you've made the Farewell Video.'

'I'm not going to do it. I'm not going to lie to people.' George's voice is breaking up, his chest heaving rapidly.

'Sir, you have to calm down,' the carer says and puts a hand on George's shoulder. 'Unfortunately, you won't be able to see your family until the video is made.'

'You can't force me to say things that are not true.' George raises his voice. 'I'm not leaving with pleasure. I want to live longer, I don't want to die without seeing my grandchild's first steps, without hearing their first words.'

The carers exchange glances like he is a halfwit. One of them, a young, wiry man represses a smile.

'You confirmed yesterday, sir, that you were ready to go, and signed the papers,' says the tattooed carer to George.

'Because I have to, for God's sake. If I don't go today I have to within the next three weeks anyway, because I don't want the drug therapy. I said I was ready to go now because it feels I have a choice.' He wipes the sweat off his forehead with his sleeve. 'If I wait till the very last day, I won't have a choice. I will be dragged to the slaughterhouse, like an animal.' I suppress an urge to run to George and embrace him. As if sensing this, Philip grabs my arm and doesn't let go.

'So you're ready to go, then,' the carer says to George. 'I promise you it won't hurt. You'll just peacefully slip into unconsciousness.'

Other carers and security arrive from the T-wing. They quickly surround George. We can't see him now, we can only hear his muffled voice.

'I'm not going to do that video.'

'I'm afraid, you have to, sir. You signed the contract.'

'I had no choice, did I?' It's clear he's trying to force back tears. 'But it's not in the contract that I can't see my family if I don't do the video.'

'But this is how things work, Mr Dimitriadis,' the young carer says officiously.

'It's not in the contract, you bastards!'

'Unfortunately, sir, you won't be able to see your family if you don't do the video.'

'Fucking murderers!'

Now we hear a screeching female voice. It's almost painful to the ears.

'Mr Dimitriadis, I really can't see what the problem is. You've had a wonderful stay here, you've seen your family every day, you signed the contract gladly. The magical place you experienced during De-bodifying sessions is waiting for you over there. What else do you need?'

'I don't want to die yet. Not like this.'

We hear a commotion and a door slams loudly. Then there's quiet. I stand up cautiously. The white-painted wooden door of the T-wing is shut. There's absolutely no sign of life.

'Did you see that?' I ask Philip when he scrambles to his feet, brushing grass off his sweater.

'It must be the drugs,' he says. 'George is usually a very tranquil person.'

I stare at him, struggling to believe what I've heard.

'George has been tranquil; all he wanted was to live. And those beasts pushed him into the T-wing.'

'He was being very difficult; you have to admit that. If it's your time, you have to go with dignity. He seems to have forgotten that.'

I stop and face him to see if he's joking, but he's deadly serious.

'Are you out of your mind? How can you blame George for—?'

'I don't blame him. But you could tell he hadn't learned anything at the sessions. He still can't cope with death. He could have just agreed and done the video, said farewell to his family and accepted his termination. That's the only way.'

I'm aware that arguing with Philip will make the whole situation even more absurd, so I bite my lip and pray his attitude is down to tiredness. He asks me to take a walk up to the hilltop from where we can see the sea. Arriving up there, I turn my back to the Dignitorium. I sit down on a sunny spot next to Philip, watching and listening to the waves. I think about the fragility of the human psyche. I have no idea what Philip is thinking about.

Half an hour later, back inside the main building, we're walking down the corridor towards the Salon when we bump into the tattooed carer. He gives his usual grin to us and continues on his way but I block his path. I tell him we witnessed the scene with George. I ask what's happened to him.

'We had to calm him down as he started fighting after the video was made,' he says in a very professional manner. 'He practically attacked us. Now he is deeply sedated.'

'When will he be executed?' I ask.

'What are you talking about?' He looks at me, bewildered. 'No one is executed here, only terminated on request.'

'But you heard how he feels about his fucking termination, didn't you?'

I can feel Philip putting his hand on my shoulder.

'Oh, it happens,' the carer says with the arrogance of an all-knowing professional. 'Old people often don't know what they want. This is part of the deterioration process. But he signed, he enjoyed the services, and now he has to keep to the contract like everyone else.'

We enter the Salon. I grind my teeth and keep praying it's just a nightmare from which I'm soon going to wake up. Either it's me who's gone mad or everyone else around me. I feel as if I've been living in a dream, protected, like a child. Now that the real world has shown its true colours, I am finally an adult, but not in a way I ever wanted to be.

In the Salon, George's family, people of all ages, are sitting around a low coffee table in silence. Devastation casts a shadow over their faces and they hold each other's hands. Philip makes his way over to them. A plump lady with dark circles under her eyes, probably George's wife, stands up and gives Philip a hug.

'How are you, Helen?' Philip asks.

'I don't know how long I can bear it,' the lady says, wiping the corner of her eye. 'We've been waiting all morning, but now they've told us to come back tomorrow as he's not in his right mind.'

'It's not that bad, then. Tomorrow you can say a proper farewell.' Philip says in an optimistic tone, but the woman's face remains dark.

'They said he attacked some carers during the making of the Farewell Video so they had to sedate him. But we don't believe it; George would never do that. Not without good reason.'

At this moment Edith enters the Salon and makes her way over to George's family.

'As I said earlier, there is no reason for you to stay here any longer today. Please don't torture yourselves, I must ask you to go home and return tomorrow. After Mr Dimitriadis wakes up, you will be able to spend the whole evening with him and say goodbye properly.' There's a bite to her otherwise smooth and soft voice that tells me this is not a request but an order.

Edith waits as they file out, staring at each other in confusion. Once they're gone, Edith leaves, too.

Philip sits down next to me. I don't know what to say, my mind is still revolving around his change of personality. He couldn't have been serious. He must be fooling himself, too. Maybe even now, as he's sitting quietly to my right, doubt and dread are running through his mind, half-covered by a blanket of denial. Finally, when a nurse comes to collect him I feel a flush of relief. When I leave the Salon, heavy with grief, I'm so buried in my thoughts I hardly remember to breathe.

In the atrium my eyes are drawn to the dozens of screens on the wall. On one of them a miniature version of George Dimitriadis is speaking, with his familiar cheerful tone. He's wearing his favourite crisp white shirt. I move closer to hear him better. He says he is ready to go. He thanks his family; he thanks his carers. He is just like the others on the Farewell Videos, looking relaxed as he sits comfortably with his arms linked in front of him. Through the sash window behind him, poppies, cornflowers and daisies in the meadow are gently swaying in the light summer breeze.

SIX

I didn't sleep a wink, haunted by the image of George Dimitriadis pleading for his life. I managed to drift off at dawn but was awoken by the usual nightmare in which I see Dad lying face down, Mum leaning over him, crying and then screaming. This time the image was clearer. A woman with Sofia's features, but even paler and thinner, was peeking in through the window. When I woke, I was soaked in sweat. However, the idea was already perfectly formed in my mind and now I know this is the only option I have left. All I have to do is make sure it is what Philip wants, too.

It's after lunch when I arrive at the Scarborough Dignitorium. Somewhere in the distance Tara's laughing out loud, her booming voice followed by giggles of others. In the Salon, while waiting for Philip, I find George's family. The women's eyes are red and puffy; they hang on to each other and weep. The men stare ahead with a look of disbelief on their gaunt faces. I hesitate over whether to approach them. Maybe it's not the right time. A minute later, Philip enters the room, escorted by a carer, and after we greet each other, he goes over to George's family. George's wife, fighting back her tears, tells him that by the time they arrived this afternoon, George was pronounced dead.

'The carer said that after sobering up from the sedation he requested instant euthanasia, not wanting to cause pain to his family. But …' She can't continue, she's choking on her tears.

'I'm so sorry, Helen, I really am.' Philip is stroking her arm.

'We've been married almost forty years.' She cries. 'George would never do anything like this.'

'He wouldn't have missed it for the world, saying goodbye to us,' a young woman, probably his daughter, joins in. 'Something is just not right here.'

'Have you mentioned this to the management?' Philip asks.

'Yes. We demanded proof that he wanted to be terminated immediately,' she says. 'But all they kept showing us was his Farewell Video, which is an entirely different thing.'

'I know, Helen, that he loved his family more than anything. Maybe he really didn't want to cause you pain,' Philip says. 'Maybe after the sedation he wasn't really himself, and he didn't want you to remember him like that.'

Philip pats Helen's shoulder, then, not waiting for her reaction, he takes my hand and leads me out of the Salon, heading for the terrace where streamlined luxury loungers are lined up in the shade of the surrounding trees.

'You don't actually believe what you just said, do you?' I glare at him.

'Why not?'

'You know better than anyone else that George has been murdered.'

'Shush. Don't allow such terrible thoughts even to cross your mind.' He leans back on the lounger, closes his eyes and a look of bliss settles over his features.

'I don't know why you keep fooling yourself, Phil. What's the point—'

'I knew George better than you, Ali. His family meant everything to him. I can understand he didn't want them to see him in that state.' He pauses. 'They are not murderers, the Dignitorium staff. They are good, compassionate people.'

I will go mad if I have to stay sitting so I ask him to take a walk.

The slight breeze reduces the otherwise fatiguing heat, making the temperature ideal for light outdoor activities. Other residents must have realised this too, as they are out on the tennis courts, golf courses and bike tracks. With their suntanned limbs shiny with sunscreen, in snow-white T-shirts and shorts, they could be advocates of a fit and healthy lifestyle. Who would think that in nine months all that will be left of them is dust and ash? Philip is visibly irritated by the proximity of so many people. He takes my hand and leads me to the back of the garden. I know where he wants to go. We walk up the hill path, as if pulled by a magnetic force to the place he is so fond of. As we climb higher, the blue of the sky is outgrowing the green of the grounds and the little white figures of residents below, like ants, cease to trouble him.

At the top of the hill, I lie down with my head in his lap. He's watching the vapour trail of a plane high above us with indifferent eyes. Once, when we were in the little countryside area in Somerset, Philip said that he would like to be a bird for a day, just to see the world, the covered, hidden, fenced-off parts of the world belonging to Owners, where the wolves run free. Although Philip was free then, he longed to be even freer. Now, he is a prisoner, locked in a golden cage, and not once has he mentioned the desire to fly. What have they done to him in the Dignitorium?

'Are you thinking of George?' Philip asks.

'You, too?'

'His video was up by yesterday afternoon, and I watched it all over again.' He gently strokes my hair.

'You shouldn't have upset yourself with that,' I say.

'There was nothing upsetting about it. It was reassuring to see how peacefully it ends for all of us.'

'How can you say that?' I lift my head up, trying to catch his eye.

'I have been preparing well,' he says. 'I really enjoy the Death Taster sessions. And I attend the Soul River session every day. Sometimes even twice.'

My insides are in shreds. I hold back from screaming at him. I want to ask him where my Philip is, the Philip who prides himself on seeing through lies and deception, systems and propaganda, and who used to mock everyone who didn't share his vision. I remind myself again that he asked me to support him. It must be terrible for him, trying to rationalise his death. I let him believe. But does he? I almost think he does, but the odd twitch in his eye, the way he diverts his gaze, could mean that he doesn't, he is just desperate to do so.

'I'm glad you have calmed down and are ready to grant me my wish,' he says with childlike innocence.

He sounds so grateful, how could I have the heart to disappoint him?

'It's not easy, Phil.'

'I know. But let's just stay like this. It's a blessing.'

The pale face from my dream reappears in my head, like a reminder not to lose track. I can't bring myself to ask Philip's opinion about my plan. The last thing I want is to upset him. It would take him out of his fragile peace and raise false hopes that he has already put aside. I so want to tell him there is a way out, but I can't. What if my plan doesn't work?

I take a deep breath, trying to speak tenderly, for fear that he will crack otherwise.

'If you had been Milan, would you have returned home?'

The question clearly surprises him, and he takes a moment to think before answering.

'Milan was not going blind, Alice.'

'Yes, but…if we could – let's assume – pay the money that buys you out of the Dignitorium and pays for your eye surgery, would you come home with me?'

For a moment it looks as if he is considering it. Maybe he'll ask me to borrow. But he doesn't know that I know the exact fee. Nor that such an exorbitant amount cannot be borrowed. Now he sighs, with evident disappointment and anger. It's too late to take my question back.

'It was just an innocent question, my love. I was just asking.'

'Why? What good would it bring to know that if I had wings I could fly when I have no wings and never will have?'

'I see.' My voice is very gentle. But I know I've gone too far.

'Can I ask you to go home, Ali?' he says with a hint of impatience.

'But we still have twenty minutes.'

'You're upsetting me.'

'I'm not going to say a word.'

'You upset me with your presence, with your false expectations, with your restlessness.'

'I won't bring it up again.'

'Can you really not grant me my last wish, for God's sake? What I'm trying to do is incredibly hard, but the only way I can make it worthwhile is to accept the unacceptable.'

'I know, Phil, trust me, I know.'

'No, you have no idea how difficult it is to remain calm on the threshold of premature death. Sometimes I wish I could just go to the T-wing and request instant euthanasia. But I believe in humanity and I want to go through this stage gradually, alert and prepared, and to quote George, not be dragged to the T-wing like an animal to the slaughterhouse. I'm trying to make sense of all this, Ali, to give it a higher meaning.'

I keep nodding.

'In that sense I quite like what's going on here, the courses and training, the preparation – it really works. I've found peace through it. But I beg you, will you stop ruining it for me?'

'Philip, I–'

'Come back when you're ready.'

'I want to visit *you*, not a blissed-out zombie. But we have very little time left before your sedation period begins. Only eleven days.'

'I'll be waiting every day.'

I look back at him as I'm walking down the path. He is unresponsive, staring out at the sea, somewhere in the distance where the water becomes one with the sky. I am torn to pieces, I detest this beautiful and tranquil place that will become Philip's slaughterhouse no matter how hard he tries to transform it into something divine. As I walk past the fountain, I see the sign on the wall. Before I leave, I need to pay my respects to George.

There is no one else at the wall. In front of it, bunches of flowers are laid on top of each other like corpses in a mass grave. Under the fresh ones, the rest are dry and withered.

I don't have any flowers with me. I pick a bunch up from the top and say my little prayer for George, then place the flowers back down again. Among the masses of names it's easy to find the very last one. For a moment I struggle to believe what I see. Instead of George Dimitriadis, the name I see etched on the silver plaque is George Dimitriad. With a clear and pronounced dot at the end. Shortened, as if there was no space for the full name. The only thing holding me back from running to reception and protesting is that I will not see Philip any more if I make another scene. I stay a bit longer, to remember George. Quietly I thank him for making

Philip's last months more bearable and less lonely. Here lies George Dimitriadis, or at least his name, or at least most of it, father and grandfather-to-be, good friend, prolonger of life and violator of rules.

The monorail leaves behind the rows of red brick apartment blocks and mansions of Scarborough. Sitting by the window, I immediately search for a private detective on my ID Phone. There are hundreds, but I must find the best. Two hours later at home, I dial the number of a certain Mr Sikula. I was nearly put off by the high prices and his exaggerated website, which shows him sitting in a dimly lit library like a modern-day Sherlock Holmes. In his hand he holds a football-sized globe, with the slogan flashing above: 'As long as they are on this planet, I will find them.' But he has thirty-five years' experience, and reviews claiming he can perform miracles. He answers the phone immediately and I tell him my problem. My speech is wobbly and disorganised, but he keeps listening without interruption, nodding attentively.

'No problem, madam,' he says.

'But she is an Owner now. I know that makes it very hard because Owners don't have trackers in their bodies.'

'Not for me, madam. If you read my profile online you'll see that Owners are not a problem for Mr Sikula. It comes at a special fee, though.'

'I know, I know.'

Having checked the fee online, I ask him to confirm it, and I try to hold my breath when I hear it. If I pay Mr Sikula, there is no way back. It will require all my savings. We agree verbally, and soon I get an attachment that I need to fill in and send back. By five o'clock I have the contract in my hands. All it needs is my signature. It promises to find any living person's contact details within forty-eight hours. It does not guarantee that the found person will reply, though. I hesitate. What if he gives me a made-up phone number or email and claims it's not his fault if Sofia doesn't get back to me? I need to think it through first.

A cup of tea always tends to help, but on this occasion I make myself a double espresso. I can feel the effects immediately: the rapid heartbeat, the increased awareness, impatience verging on aggression. The urge to do something. I keep pacing up and down in the room, counting, calculating. The fee is ridiculously high; my savings will be gone. If he can't find Sofia… But in that case I won't need any money any more. In the Dignitorium the only currency is human life, my last remaining asset.

I slowly give in to the voice that keeps whispering to me. This is our last chance – Philip and I could still be together. There is still hope for us. I sit down at the table and stretch my hands out until they stop trembling and quickly scribble my signature at the bottom of the page.

It's done and it can't be reversed. If it doesn't work, I won't be able to afford to visit Philip for much longer. I just pray I can until his drug therapy starts, after which it won't matter much to him. I'll lie to him that I've found a new partner, I can even show him a fake profile on a dating website. I'll be the happiest future mother he's ever seen. I'll kiss him goodbye cheerfully, but behind my smile there will be invisible tears. Then I'll find a Dignitorium in London.

BOOK THREE

ONE

The large blind eyes of the Gothic windows of Sofia's mansion follow us as the limousine comes to a halt in front of the stone steps, gravel crunching under the heavy wheels. I've never felt so powerless in my life.

Despite its warm red-brick walls, the house exudes solemnity. The chauffeur jumps out to open the door for me. I clutch at the leather arm of the seat to steady myself, to gain some inner strength. The chauffeur helps me get out. As he reaches out a hand to me, I notice how immaculate his white gloves are.

When the cool sea breeze hits my face, my whole mission suddenly feels real. Maybe it's the aura of power and wealth that is palpable in the crisp morning air, maybe it's the chauffeur, who is avoiding my gaze and keeping his head bowed. He drives the car away. I'm surrounded by a silence I never thought existed. In front of the main entrance six servants stand in two rows like soldiers, wearing starched uniforms. I shiver. There's no way back from here, but the way ahead is just as frightening.

This is the first time I've seen an Owner's house in real life, not on the Globe or in a glossy magazine. It's far grander than I ever imagined. The red brick building towers above me menacingly, reminding me of my own insignificance. The front door is the biggest I've ever seen. It could swallow a whole army. On either side of the steps, a life-sized, white stone lion stands guard. I make a hesitant move, glancing at the servants for a nod of encouragement, the smallest sign, but they might as well be as lifeless as the stone lions. Only a trickle of sweat on the forehead of an older man reveals that they're flesh and bone like me. It strikes me that Sebastian's parents had their main residence near the sea in Cornwall and now I remember Sofia mentioning two lion statues in front of the house.

The forest surrounding the mansion is vast and ancient, and the highest branches sway in the heavy wind. From the distance I think I hear an owl hooting, though it's the wrong time of day for owls to be out. I scold myself for taking it as an omen, and force myself to walk slowly and steadily towards the house; Sofia might already be watching me on a camera somewhere. She can't see the cramp in my stomach or my madly pumping heart, but my fearful posture and hesitant body language might give me away. Knowing her, if she spots any sign of weakness, she will use it against me.

So far my entire reason for coming here has been Philip and the possibility that he might still be saved. But now, as I walk up the steps past the two lions, the silent guards, something changes. Memories start to flow, first a trickle, then a flood, one after the other. Feelings so intense I fear my nerves will get the better of me before I have the chance to speak.

First comes the jealousy paired with bitter helplessness I felt when I was thirteen and Sofia received a large bunch of black roses from the boy I had a secret crush on. After this I recall the joy and comradeship when I confided in Sofia that it had been me who accidentally spilled juice over Mum's precious table cloth, not the neighbour's cat, as I had claimed. Other feelings emerge, humiliation tinged with envy caused by Sofia scolding me in front of my friends in the playground, and again, admiration and even pride when she got herself into trouble for defending me from bullies at school. All this makes sense; I can relate these emotions to particular experiences. But another emotion rises up, so unexpectedly that I have no chance to fight it. It swells my chest with a warm, tender energy. I don't understand it; Sofia has never given me any reason to love her. I try to deny this misplaced emotion; love is the last thing I expected to feel and I don't want it. Not here, not now.

At the top of the steps, in front of the door, I stop. I'm surrounded by servants who keep their heads bowed and their eyes on the ground – they ignore me. The door swings open and I find myself in an entrance hall that boasts a meticulously polished marble floor. A gleaming chandelier hangs from the ceiling. It reminds me of an old-fashioned ballroom. A lavish red-carpeted stairway spirals upwards.

An elderly butler greets me. His steps are soundless and his appearance is immaculate. It feels as if he has been dropped here from the nineteenth century. He approaches me, stops at a good distance and bows with respect.

'Welcome, madam. Please, follow me.'

Without waiting for my reply, he is already walking up the stairway. We are passing through wood-panelled halls, long dark corridors, a large Victorian library that has the sweet, stale smell of ancient books, then we take two floors up in a lift that is completely over the top. It is carpeted, wall-papered and has two armchairs with cushions, gilded mirrors and an art deco floor lamp in the corner. We exit the lift to a reception area where a large white door stands before us.

'This is your key.' The butler says, holding up a silver wrist band. He scans it, and the door opens up slowly with a low buzzing sound. I can see there is something else he'd like to say before we enter. He clears his throat.

'I'm sorry, madam, but according to our house regulations, I need to take your ID Phone for the duration of your stay.'

It's absurd and I consider refusing. I look at him, and he holds my gaze. After a short hesitation, I take my ID Phone from my wrist and hand it over. He puts it in a transparent plastic bag which he seals and slides into the inner pocket of his jacket.

'This is the White Suite. Reserved for our very special guests,' he says with noticeable pride in his voice as we enter.

'This must be a mistake. I'm returning home today, after the meeting.'

'I'm only following instructions, madam.'

'Do you know when I can meet Sofia?'

'I'm sorry madam, I have no further information at the moment.'

It's a large rectangular room with rows of sash windows on both sides. It's ultramodern and chic. White is the only colour in the entire suite. In the middle, a frosted glass wall hides the bathroom. The giant oval bathtub is carved out of white marble. At the back is the bedroom area. An oversized sunken round bed sprawls on a circular stage. The living area is furnished with a set of velvet sofas and armchairs, built-in wardrobes, a white stone fireplace and giant vases. A balcony with a stone balustrade overlooks the forest.

The place should feel sterile, like a hospital, but instead it's pure and serene.

After the butler leaves, I allow myself to be conquered by the beauty, immersed in peace. Sofia gave me her most luxurious suite. Does it mean that she takes my visit seriously?

An hour later the butler returns. 'Is everything to your satisfaction, madam?' he asks, standing in the doorway.

It's on the tip of my tongue to tell him how nervous I am, how I don't give a damn about comfort.

'I must see Sofia right now.'

'Madam Sofia cannot see you today, I'm afraid.'

My heart sinks. She is playing with me, as I feared. She never had any intention of meeting me. It takes all my willpower to appear calm.

'Is there a problem? I have come a long way to meet her. It's very urgent.'

His eyes remain fixed, his manner as official as a bank clerk's.

'Madam Sofia will be available to see you tomorrow. It is her express wish that you stay the night.'

I want to say so many things, but all I do is clench my fists and force my voice to sound steady.

'I need my ID Phone back. I can't stay here without it.'

'I'm sorry, madam, I can only return it to you when you leave us. If you need to contact someone, there is a portable telephone in your suite.'

'Why can't I use my own phone then?'

'No photography or messaging is allowed in the territory of the estate, madam. If you need anything done that requires an ID Phone, please contact your personal maid for assistance.'

'I don't need anything at the moment.' I know I'm starting to sound hysterical but I can't help it. 'I must see Sofia. Today.'

'Madam Sofia will be available tomorrow. Thank you for your understanding.' He then turns on his heels and disappears into the lift.

I'm alone and trapped. Without an ID Phone I can't ask for help, and who would help me anyway? Who would believe me against an Owner's words? I force myself to stop thinking of all the worst things that could happen. A single day will not make much difference.

The afternoon has gone quickly. First, two maids brought up lunch on a silver trolley and I ate it on the balcony, with only birds and the warm breeze for company. It was a strange experience, almost surreal, to be surrounded by such silence. After lunch I dozed off and when I woke I was spaced out. I first thought Sofia had had something put into my lunch. But soon I realised I was simply in a state of peace. A peace one feels when things are entirely out of one's control. When surrender is the only way.

Now I'm outside, discovering the estate. I pass through a rose garden with a Victorian fountain in the middle, and walk along pebbled pathways bordered with exotic plants I don't recognise. Behind a wall I discover something that looks like a combination of a playground and an amusement park. It has endless slides, dodgem cars, a giant trampoline and even a Victorian-style carousel. I wonder if Sofia and Sebastian have a family or if it's just a part of what the estate has to offer for the children of their guests.

On the other side of the house, surrounded by a tall hedge, is the wing the butler told me to avoid. I stop at a distance. Next to the building I see a large swimming pool and a patio with outdoor dining furniture. A maid is clearing off the large wrought-iron table, while another one is sweeping the floor. I'm about to turn around when I hear something unexpected. The laughter of a child. When I look up, in a window of the second floor I see a woman in glasses, staring at me but quickly disappearing behind the curtain. It's the same window where I saw the child's face when I arrived in the limousine. I walk back to the park for a final stroll. It feels as if time has stopped here but for all its beauty and glamour it doesn't feel like a happy place.

A helicopter is about to land. From where I am, I have a perfect view over the landing pad. Three people, an older man and two younger women, get out. The man is carrying a doctor's bag. They are visibly in a hurry. The butler greets them and ushers them into the house. Not long after, a van arrives in front of the main entrance; the writing on the side says 'Fresh Seafood'. With the help of a servant, the driver carries ice boxes into the house. Having only seen the personnel, I have the impression people keep coming and putting things into an empty house as if they are feeding ghosts. And the house silently swallows them, wanting more and more. I don't have the strength to resist, either. I allow myself to be tempted to enter and let my curiosity drive me.

Like a phantom, I walk across corridors, halls, creaking wooden staircases, enjoying the lack of purpose, the sheer joy of aimless discovery. When I find myself in the Victorian library, I stop and allow it to take my breath away. I let the past talk to me through its thousands of old books, the scent created by ageing matter, the yellowed maps behind vitrines, the presence of a museum. When I'm ready to move on, I find myself in the entrance hall. Here I see a maid dusting the banister of the grand stairwell. She bows and curtsies to me but doesn't say a word. I stroll along a passage that connects two wings of the building. It resembles a cloister I saw once in a monastery. The arched windows are all stained with the most brilliant colours, depicting religious scenes. My steps are echoing on the stone and I feel lonely, but it's a peaceful loneliness, the quiet of the ancient stones washing away all worry.

At the end of the passage I arrive at the door that leads to the forbidden wing. Before turning around I eavesdrop. There's no sound but I know this is where Sofia and Sebastian live.

TWO

I'm on the balcony, still coming around. Last night I tossed and turned in bed, and once woke up to the hysterical laughter of a child. I'm not sure if it was a dream or reality. I feel lonely, totally bereft. My personal maid's smile is formulaic while she's pouring my coffee. She leaves me with my breakfast. I would like to connect with the world, check the news, anything on my ID Phone. I'm about to stand up to switch on the Globe in the living room when the portable telephone rings. It's the butler, telling me he will take me to see Sofia in half an hour.

The breakfast is even more abundant than my lunch and dinner were yesterday, with fruit juices in all the colours of the rainbow. I can barely touch it.

The butler arrives promptly. I follow him as he walks across hallways and rooms that I am already familiar with. We are in the ancient passage with the stained glass windows. I know where we are going. He opens the heavy wooden door at which I eavesdropped yesterday. This part of the house is more lived-in, and we stop in what must be the drawing room; its enormity is emphasised by the high ceiling and the long bay windows. The butler leaves without saying a word. I recognise Sofia's touch in the soft, luxurious furniture, the warm lamplight, the marble mantelpiece, and the abundance of red and gold. On the other hand, there is an element that is alien to Sofia, at least to the Sofia I know. A lack of finesse. What I see before me suggests the accumulation of valuable objects over many centuries, without any real understanding of their value. On the walls hang various paintings, even originals by Van Dyck and Constable, but they've been hung at random, in a way that doesn't allow you to really appreciate them. The room is also crammed with statues, male and female nudes in bronze and white marble. Besides, there is an abundance of small fossils. They are everywhere, on windowsills, on the shelves, around the fireplace, in groups of tens or alone, wherever a spot could be found for them.

Now I'm certain this is Sebastian's parents' house, the place Sofia moved to, where she found solace after her first escape. The place I dreamed of so often as a teenager, the place I yearned to visit and begged Sofia to bring me to, but she never did.

I can hear my heart beating in my throat; my head feels feverish and heavy. Hesitantly, I sit down on an upholstered chair in front of the fireplace. I'm alone. I listen to the creaking sounds that only old houses make, witnesses to hundreds of years of history.

I'm startled by a whistling noise.

The heavy armchair in front of the bay window slowly turns around. In it sits a woman wrapped in blankets, supported by cushions. Her long dark hair falls on her shoulders in knots. The armchair she sits in is so deep it could almost swallow her up. I move closer. I recognise the piercing almond-shaped eyes, the high porcelain forehead. But as I look at her hollow face, I'm fearful. Sofia is thirty-seven now, but the wreck of a woman before me looks much older. Her skin is ashen and lined with pain. I can't help but stare. She is fragile, the last word I would use to describe my sister. Her noble beauty has faded, her fire dwindled to ashes.

'Is that you, Sofia?'

There's no answer. Her eyes are quietly fixed on me.

'What's happened to you?'

She motions with her hand to the armchair opposite her inviting me to sit, but I hesitate. In the dim light I still can't see her face clearly. When she finally speaks, she sounds like someone who has just returned from the grave.

'I wasn't sure this day would come in time – that I would be still around,' she says, pausing to cough. 'But I'm glad it happened this way.' She scrutinises me, her eyes glinting with curiosity. I make as if to come closer, to give her a hug or kiss, but she lifts a hand that stops me in my tracks.

'Sofia. Are you sick?'

I'd still like to put my arms around her, but her reserve is like a force field, keeping me at bay. I want to ask so many things, like what she meant by still being around. Is she dying? Finally I take a seat in the armchair opposite her. We're close now, only separated by a low coffee table.

'I'm pleased to see you've become a fine young woman,' she says. 'Tell me about yourself.'

'I don't know where to start.'

'Are you married?'

'Yes, his name is Philip but–'

'Any children?'

I shake my head.

'I don't have anyone or anything now.'

'Is this what you came to tell me?'

'Where's Sebastian?'

'Wherever he is, you won't meet him there. Not for a long while,

I suppose.'

'He died? God, you should have contacted me. And I didn't know you were ill. You have always been so full of life, so confident. We thought you were happy, living the high life as an Owner.'

'We thought?'

'I mean Philip and I. Mum and Dad thought the same, but... They are gone now.'

'I know.' Her echoing voice is matter of fact, empty.

'You know?'

'Tell me more about your husband,' she says. She presses a button on her armrest, and the thick curtain opens behind her. Light pours in, transforming the heavily furnished room. Sofia's face hasn't become any lighter, though.

'Actually, Philip's the reason I've come—'

'I didn't think for a minute you were interested in me. You must be in deep shit, princess.'

The name princess awakes long-forgotten memories. Nothing has changed; she sees straight through me. I'm unable to say a word.

'So?'

'I'm honestly worried about you, Sofia. What has happened to you?

'It's money you want, isn't it?' She's evidently growing impatient.

'Look, Sofia.' I begin nervously. 'I know we had our misunderstandings and the way we parted was painful. I accept my responsibility for that. It still haunts me. I rarely had a day when I could breathe freely, without wanting to undo it. I'm truly, honestly sorry.'

'How much do you want?'

'Since then we've lost Mum and Dad. I'm an orphan and so are you, Sofia.'

'You would never have come here if I didn't have the money you need.' She wears her 'don't try to fool me' face, and finally I see something of the old Sofia.

I continue. 'And now that I've seen you, I'm really worried about you.'

She sighs deeply.

'I wish you would stop lying to me, princess. You're making it much harder for yourself.'

'Yes, I really need your help. It's a question of life and death.'

'Finally.' She reaches forward for a glass of amber-coloured liquid, but is overcome by her coughing. I begin to get out of my seat to try to help, but the coughing stops.

'To answer your question, yes, I'm dying,' she says. 'No!' She holds her hand up as in defence. 'Spare me your pity.'

I lean back in the armchair, forcing my shoulders to relax.

'What you said, about not having forgotten that day, it's the same for me, princess.' She pauses but I know there's more to come. 'On the day I left for good, after our fight, you destroyed my last chance of happiness. You gave me no other choice but to return here and become an Owner, become this. I find it amusing that you want my money in return.'

My skin turns cold.

'Do you think it was easy for me? Do you think it was for Mum and Dad after you fled?'

'After you forced me to flee.'

'I forced you?'

'Your behaviour, your hostility. Just wait till you hear the full story.'

'But you hated us and the way we lived, anyway. We had our fight, and yes, it was horrible, but then you returned to your glorious Owner life. What else is there to tell me?'

The storm comes unexpectedly, leaving the room dark. Sofia waves for more whiskey. I lean forward and pour an inch more of the golden liquid. She tells me to bring her some ice from the cabinet.

It's eerily quiet, the only sound in the room is the clinking of the ice cubes. With shaking hands, I hand over the drink to her, but she's not looking at me. She is watching a tree outside the window, a massive old oak tree, whose canopy is shaken and twisted by the raging gale. The wind whistles through the house.

'Put some more logs on the fire!' she says. 'I've become ridiculously old-fashioned these days.'

I have never lit a real fire. All the fireplaces I've ever seen were electric ones, even in the Dignitorium. Sofia has to talk me through the process. When it's done, I move away quickly. The fireplace is so big I feel I might fall into it if I'm not careful. I sit back down. Watching Sofia, I know she's collecting her thoughts to say something important, probably preparing for a long speech. My stomach is in knots and will stay so until she explains what she meant that I'd forced her to return to the Owners. Or is she playing with me? If she wants vengeance, there's no point in my being here.

The heat from the fire fills up the room and makes its way into my bones. This is the last chance for me and Philip. While I'm enjoying the warmth of this luxurious house, Philip is preparing for death. I won't leave until I get what I came for. I listen to the crackling of the fire and the ticking of the Edwardian clock in a wooden cabinet to my right.

'Pour yourself a drink,' she commands.

'I'm fine, thank you.'

'You'll need it, princess. This will take a while.'

I'd better not resist. I get up and go to the drinks cabinet. Dad used to call me princess. Princess Alice. But he said it so lovingly. It's been twenty years since I heard this other kind of princess, usually used for spoilt kids. I make myself a vodka with ice, not much, just enough to calm my ragged nerves. This might be a long war.

THREE

Sofia puts her feet up on a red velvet-covered footstool, leans back in her armchair and starts to speak.

'After my first escape from home, I found myself in a world most people can only dream of. This was before our fight. Even miles away, I could sense our parents' worry and your jealous curiosity. I enjoyed a lavish lifestyle with Sebastian, from the moment I moved with him into his city pad. He brought me here, to his parents' house. They seemed to like me, probably because I had a strong personality, unlike their son.'

'I often wondered how you were capable of doing such a thing.'

'What thing?'

'Marrying Sebastian for his wealth, while feeling contempt for him.'

'Here we go again. You're speaking of something you have no idea about.'

'Don't tell me you loved Sebastian for something other than his

Owner status.'

'You might find it hard to believe, but behind his extreme shyness, Sebastian was highly intelligent. He was passionate about the environment and geology, fossils for example.' She gestures around the room. 'We used to collect them together, travelling to the other end of the world wherever we could excavate them.'

'But you didn't love him for your common interest in fossils, did you?'

'You should drop the malice, princess. It doesn't suit you. Of course, I would have dated the devil himself for that lifestyle. But I wouldn't have married anyone just for that. Anyway, back to when I first escaped. Sebastian's gentle kindness had a calming effect on my turbulent nature. Also, his parents treated me like family; they welcomed me at their dinner parties. I was popular, because of my big mouth and my confident beauty. With Sebastian, I travelled around the world, along with an entourage of servants. We hopped on and off his private jet whenever a place took my fancy. What struck me was the way we were treated, with the greatest respect and admiration wherever we went. It took me years to figure out that it was no more than obedient fear. Oh, you have no idea what it feels like, coming from your mediocre lifestyle. It's like you're above everyone, like fresh and immortal blood has been injected into your veins.

'Sebastian's parents made regular visits to the Primavera Club. Do you remember how curious we were about the white windowless skyscraper as children? It turned out it was a place of mystery even for Sebastian. We were desperate to discover it, but there's no entry below the age of twenty-one. One day Sebastian had this crazy idea that we could sneak into the Primavera Club with fake IDs. It was more exciting than anything I expected from him.'

She peers out the window, squinting. Hearing the wind rattling the windows, she pulls her jumper tight around her waist. There's a long pause before she continues. When I realise how impatient I am to hear the rest of the story, I feel ashamed. While I'm listening to Scheherazade's tales, Philip is going through unimaginable agony, alone.

'What do you think there is? In the Primavera Clubs?' Sofia asks.

'Casinos, bars?'

She rolls her eyes.

'Spas?'

'Like everyone else, all I knew about the Primavera Clubs is that they were the playground of the Owners. Good fun, I thought, and I hoped there might be some exclusive form of entertainment based on futuristic technology and maybe some drugs that would restore the high, of which I urgently needed a fresh dose. I wanted to be a part of the elite.'

I lean closer. I'm so curious, I've almost forgotten what I came for. I don't have the courage to ask questions, we just listen to the fire and the wind and the creaking of the old building. The oak tree beyond the lawn looks as if it could be uprooted at any moment. Sofia's trying to find the right words, to make her speech as powerful as possible.

'We were wrong about the place.' There's triumph in her voice as she continues. 'All of us spenders were wrong about it all along. It's not a club for recreation, or at least not as we understand it. Sebastian managed to get two fake IDs. We were disappointed from the moment we arrived, for there was nothing glamorous about the white skyscraper. No spas, bars or anything glitzy. Just dark felt-lined corridors and a long line of doors, opening onto windowless rooms.

'The first room we went into was some kind of screening room. We joined a dozen others who were already in their seats. We sat in the corner, feeling disappointed that it was just a cinema. The other viewers were cheering on a hunter in the woods. Sebastian and I recognised the hunter as a friend of Sebastian's parents, Walter, an unlikeable, red-faced man. He wore a dark green uniform and was walking through the woods with a rifle. At first I wondered why he wasn't running after his prey. He was just sniffing around, wearing his usual grin. He circled around the trees, looked up and down, called out. He did nothing in a hurry. When he came to a red fence, I realised why. The forest was entirely surrounded and enclosed by the fence. The wolf had no chance. It was only a question of time. I found the film utterly boring and I was about to ask Sebastian if we could leave when I saw it. It was not a wolf. It was a young man, naked. He disappeared among the trees, and the hunter walked after him, slowly, clearly enjoying prolonging the man's suffering. Every time there was a glimpse of the victim, the audience cheered. Finally, Walter had him cornered by the fence. He still moved slowly, relishing the look of terror in the young man's eyes. The audience cheered and whistled even louder. I glanced at Sebastian. He was sickened by it, too. Then I saw him, the victim, from up close. He was a boy, not a man. He couldn't have been older than fourteen. His leg was bleeding heavily, but he was alive. Walter had shot him in the leg deliberately so that his agony could be enjoyed by the viewers for longer. That did it for me. I ran out through a small side door. It led to a tiny room, lined with marble sinks, into one of which I vomited. Part of me wanted to go home but I also found myself becoming bloodthirsty. I wanted to see more. I wanted to satisfy my curiosity, even if I had to force myself.

The second room we entered was a little theatre. On the stage a young woman sat tied to a chair. Next to her stood a man armed with surgical tools, who was following instructions from the audience. He worked slowly, deliberately, with an almost artistic precision. The woman's blood-curdling screams were amplified by speakers, for the amusement of the audience. Her hair was honey blonde, shoulder length, like yours. I couldn't stay long. The smell of fresh blood, thick in the air, was too much for me. Once again, I had to run out through a side door. Again, the sink was clean, unused before I left my stinking mark on it. That second room left me weak with shock. I understood straight away where the kidnapped people had gone. The reality made the idea of organ trafficking seem like a fairy tale.'

The hair rises on my skin.

'Everyone thinks that the Low Spenders are abducted for their organs. They blame the High Spenders,' she says, as if it's the most natural thing in the world. 'And that's how it should be: the truth will never come to light, and you Mid Spenders will always have a reason to hate and condemn High Spenders.'

It feels like a blow to the head. I remember Joshua, one of my favourite students, with his brown eyes that were always glowing with enthusiasm, his keenness to study hard to become a vet. And the other two kids in my school whom I hadn't taught, Samir Khan and his younger sister, Aliya. Were they separated? Or did the sicko prefer them to be tortured together? What was on Samir's mind in his last conscious moments? I can see him trying to protect Aliya until his dying breath. And the news, never saying but always suggesting that High Spenders had commissioned desperate Zone residents to carry out the abductions, for the organ trade.

'What's the truth, then?' My voice is breaking up.

She ignores my question.

'Sofia! That notorious kidnapping in the Mid-Spender area happened to kids from my school. One of the victims was my student.'

She nods.

'That was the day when the son of a prestigious Owner turned eighteen. And that was the birthday gift from his daddy.'

'Birthday gift?'

'Classier victims, not just Low Spenders as before.'

'So there are no organ robberies at all?'

'Why would there be? Organ transplants happen legally, in hospitals.'

'And the donors are Dignitorium residents, right? So all those poor kids had to die just to entertain Owners in the Primavera Club!'

'Finally you get it,' she says. 'But I've told you only the milder parts of what I saw. There are other rooms in the Primavera Clubs. I've seen them only briefly; they made me disgusted with humankind forever. I would give anything to be able to stop the visions haunting me.'

'How could this be allowed to happen?'

'I suppose it's a rhetorical question,' she says. 'Nevertheless, even the Owners are subject to restrictions. That birthday gift caused a big stir. The most powerful Owners got together and rebuked the father of the boy for being so irresponsible.'

'Irresponsible? That's all?'

'The incident shook spenders' faith in the system. And that couldn't be allowed to happen. Mid Spender areas must stay desirable otherwise they lose their attractiveness for the Low Spenders.'

'The attractiveness of the Mid Spender areas! Is that all that matters?'

Sofia ignores me. Her voice pulls me back to the present.

'With the taste of vomit still in my mouth, despite a part of me wanting to run away and never return, I followed Sebastian to another screening room. It was large, lit with vintage-style floor lamps in the corners. A thick scent of cigar smoke filled the air. The room was crowded with people sprawling on sofas. Sebastian ordered some caviar and champagne and we sat there for a long time with our feet up on a footstool. I was trying to convince myself that what I'd seen in the previous room was pretend, just for show, but I knew what I had witnessed with my own eyes and the smell of blood that filled the air couldn't be faked. I gulped down some champagne to recover, to try and forget. Other people chatted, ate and drank, their eyes occasionally drifting back to the huge screen. I thought they were using this room as a place to relax. I couldn't see any cause for excitement. The screen was divided into four smaller ones, each showing a different part of a period building. There were close-up shots of beds in different rooms but the cameras kept jumping to other parts of the building. In the corridors I occasionally saw a nurse walk past or what looked like patients, in bathrobes, most of them in their sixties or seventies, but some much younger. Sebastian pressed a small button on the side of the sofa and subtitles appeared on the screen: Termination Wing, Dignitorium, HS03 – Manchester, live broadcast.

'What?' I cry out. 'Hidden cameras in the T-wing?'

'You didn't suspect that, did you?'

'The bastards! The bloody bastards!'

I can't hold back the tears and I keep hitting the arm of the chair with my fist. Sofia drives her armchair out of the room and I'm left alone with my horrifying thoughts. Minutes pass, I don't know how many. When Sofia returns, I compose myself with what little composure remains. All I can think of is Philip, and how to get him out. I wipe my eyes and listen, fearing there's far worse to come, that Sofia has just started to enjoy this.

'Right now you look sicker than I do,' she remarks. 'Nothing very exciting happened in that room, as the odd infirm person was put to death. Occasionally there was an announcement to remind us in which Dignitorium the next termination would be and exactly when. The patients went to bed and fell asleep, forever. Before they went to bed, of course, there was often a scene with the patient refusing to make a Farewell Video, or begging the nurse to wait, wait just one more day, to see my son, daughter, grandchild, cat –

anything for another day. I'm too young to die, I'm only sixty-five, or fifty-eight, whatever.'

'I suppose it's one thing to agree to it when you're healthy, another thing to accept it when you're about to die.'

For the first time she nearly smiles, like we are in agreement.

'You know, that's why I enjoyed watching them. Their usual arrogance disappeared in a moment when they realised they had been deceived, that no sedatives were given before the poison, and they couldn't cheat death. High-Spenders were my favourite; I loved watching how their superiority collapsed in front of my very eyes. In their hospital gowns, with their messy hair and bulging eyes, they were unrecognisable. The piece of chocolate, given to them to take the taste of the poison away, was smeared across their horrified faces. It resembled dried shit. I have to admit, I couldn't wait to turn twenty-one just to be allowed to see their smug faces transformed again.'

'You're lying! They are sedated so that they gently slip into unconsciousness!'

'What would be the pleasure for us then?' She snorts. 'Silly little girl, still believes everything the adverts say.'

I feel vomit climbing up my throat. She continues without batting an eyelid and I feel filthy just for listening.

'After our first visit to the Club, I was in serious shock. Sebastian was also reluctant to return, haunted by nightmares in which he was the man being hunted in the woods. I had nightmares too, but they were far more sinister than Sebastian's. I kept being thrown among faceless demons, and they fought over my body, but after they had torn me to pieces I was still there, trapped alive in all of them simultaneously. The nightmares kept returning and I felt constantly sick.

'A few days later, Sebastian's parents were upstairs in their room getting ready for an outing to the Primavera Club. I was in the hall, the one you walked across. Walter, the hunter from the film we'd seen, was like a different person in his dark-blue tailored suit, with several golden rings on his fat fingers. He smiled at me like a predator, and asked me how I was. He walked closer to me as I sat at the table, browsing on my mini-screen. He knew he was not in the forest or at the Primavera Club this time; he had to behave himself. But he also knew I wasn't one of them, and never would be. He kept coming closer. He stopped just behind me. An icy current ran along my spine. There was a long wait, and I prayed that Sebastian's parents would come down. I heard a slight movement behind me, and I could sense Walter's thick, red fingers on the top of my chair. Then they slipped onto my shoulders. His heavy grip caused me some discomfort, but stronger was the fear I felt. In that moment I saw myself for what I was, without embellishment. I was nothing, a nobody. A pretty face, one among millions. Behind me stood an Owner, one of the wealthiest and most powerful men in the world, and a ruthless killer.

'His hands came up to my neck; he was only giving me a massage, I told myself. My heart was beating so strongly I feared he would hear it. His left hand slipped beneath my shirt, and cupped my right breast, with his rough, sweaty hands on my bare skin. I was paralysed. I waited. He waited. The next moment he squeezed my breast so hard, I screamed out in pain. Luckily, my scream was masked by the sound of a door opening and voices upstairs, and Walter moved away, unhurriedly, as if nothing had happened. He went over to the window and pretended to look outside. Sebastian's parents appeared in all their glory, heavily perfumed, ready for another night at the Primavera Club. His mum pressed a kiss on my cheek before joining the two men and wishing me good night. I watched them as they walked down the steps with their usual air of invincibility. I couldn't believe that these charming, well-dressed people were going to revel in child murder or human torture, and would enjoy a lavish dinner while doing so.

'Something died inside me that day. Do you remember when as kids we saw that film about the boy who put on his magic glasses and saw the world with ghosts and fairies in it? That's what happened to me, but instead of fairies I saw rot and decay on a whole new level.

'I'd witnessed my own defencelessness among the vultures. I didn't want to be an Owner any more, despite knowing what awaited me as a spender, that my premature death in the T-wing would provide delightful entertainment for Owners. Suddenly I realised I had a home. Somewhere in the Mid-Spender area of north London I had a family waiting for me to return. I knew I wasn't good enough for that family, but for the Owners I wasn't bad enough. I belonged nowhere.

'Once the helicopter carrying the three of them had disappeared, I could breathe again. But the terror didn't leave me. I knew I had been lucky to escape Walter, but I might not be so lucky the next time. I've never known such homesickness before or since; all I wanted was to flee, to belong. I would have rather been an average Mid Spender than at the bottom of the Owners' ladder.

'That night I begged Sebastian to fly back to London, which we did, but even in his penthouse I didn't feel safe. It dawned on me that I'd brought this upon myself, I'd chosen this over the security of my family. The next day I fled Sebastian's city pad in panic while he was in the bath.

'I wandered in Hyde Park for hours, watching people go about their simple pleasures, playing games, cycling, chatting, walking their dogs. I fought the urge to go up and warn them of what awaited them. But I knew they wouldn't believe me. Eventually the dark clouds that had been lingering ominously gave way to torrential rain. Not thinking of anyone else but themselves and their kids, the people let their masks of civility slip, as if washed away by the storm. They pushed each other out of the way in their haste to find shelter. That's when I saw them for what they were, and I couldn't bring myself to care about the herd any more. I just wanted to go to the only place where I felt safe. It was like the return of the prodigal son. I snuck back into our home that evening, burning to tell you all what the Owners were really about, to warn you. To be your hero. To give you another chance. I wanted you all around, to listen to me, to protect me, to tell me it had all been a nightmare. To assure me I would never again be valued for my market price.

'I got home late in the afternoon. I had imagined the scenes of warm hugs and forgiveness for which my heart ached so badly. All I wanted was to sit on my favourite seat in the conservatory, and be surrounded by loving family. But when I arrived, you were sitting there already, being admired. You, the spoiled princess, the perfect girl dreaming up the perfect life, a good husband, happy children, everything I didn't have and didn't want. And whatever I tried to do, I would always remain a second-class daughter. It was like an attack, right in my face. I sensed your superiority, that you were better than me. That I was excluded from the family idyll. I also sensed your discomfort that I had returned. Your gloating words, hoping I had broken up with Sebastian, have always haunted me. When I needed the most support, that's when you let me down.'

She reaches for her drink, and gulps it down with trembling hands.

It's on the tip of my tongue to ask why she didn't tell me this there and then, but I quickly realise she's right. I wouldn't have cared.

'Sofia, we were children. I was barely thirteen. I was immature, I know.'

She looks at me as if I'm a strange exotic animal.

'You really want this money, don't you?'

'It's because—'

'I'm not interested.'

'The sum is pocket money to you, but it would save our lives.'

'Our lives?'

'I spent all my savings to find you. To cut a long story short, if you don't help me, the Dignitorium remains my only choice.'

Her face is unmoved. She asks me to pour her a fresh glass of water and I relish focusing on such an ordinary task for a moment.

'Maybe you're lucky,' she says after taking a sip. 'I might even grant you your wish. By now, any anger or desire for revenge have long gone.'

'Time heals all kinds of wounds, doesn't it?'

'Time has just made things worse, magnified the painful memories,' she says with irritation. 'No. It's because I finally found my gratification for all you lot have done to me.'

'Gratification?'

She leans back on the chair, covers her feet with the blanket and tugs its edges around them. I empty my glass and prepare myself for another blow.

'I had mixed feelings about the Primavera Club. I never had the stomach to re-visit the torture rooms or the hunter film. But I became a regular in the screening room that broadcasts live from the Termination Wings. What I found dull and uneventful at first, I quickly developed a taste for. I can't even explain why. Was it cruelty or just nostalgia? A desire to feel after the long years of the numbness which all Owners experience sooner or later? Who knows?

'Anyway, I found my gratification on the morning of a mild autumn day, four years ago. In my favourite screening room, with a tray of junk food on my lap, I watched the live broadcast from the Termination Wing of the Dignitorium in MN09.'

My heart stops beating, and cold sweat runs down the back of my neck. She reads my face.

'Yes, princess. It's what you're thinking. I saw them when you couldn't, and while you were weeping on the bench in front of the main building – there's a camera right above the bench – Mum and Dad slipped into unconsciousness, not at all as peacefully as they'd been made to believe. They begged the nurse, like all the others, to give them one more day, to see their only daughter again – I never forgave them for that word, 'only'. In fact, as a revenge for that one word alone I like re-watching the tape. I asked for a copy. You want to see it?'

'No!'

'You should. You should see the way they held each other's hands, how Mum cried on Dad's shoulder and the nurse nudged them to hurry up. World-class entertainment. The shock on their faces when it turned out that no sedation would ease the panic of their final minutes. How Dad tried to negotiate with the nurse, and when all else failed, asked for a double bed which they were given by pushing two single ones together. Once the nurse administered the poison – unlike in the adverts – there was no cuddling and hand holding, not a human word of consolation. The nurse just left the room and never returned. Dad died first, but Mum was still alive and awake. She crouched above Dad's lifeless body and kept shaking him. She panicked and howled but no-one came, and then she was sick on the bedside and died in agony.'

I remember the dreams that have been haunting me for years, but I always pushed them out of my mind. Instead I believed what Dad had promised me, that they would leave happily, with smile on their faces.

'No! Stop it!'

'You have no idea, princess, how long I've waited to see your lofty little world crumble and collapse.'

I can hardly breathe. I choke on my tears and turn away from her.

'Will you watch it?'

'No! Never!'

'Fine,' she says and drives her wheelchair to the door. With her finger above the button that opens the door, she glances back at me. 'But you have to bear the consequences.'

I don't know how long I've been crying, I've lost all sense of time. My knees are wet with my tears; I feel I have no strength in my body. I've lost. It's over and Philip will die, just as my parents died, abandoned, howling, watched by the hungry eyes of the Owners.

FOUR

It's ice cold in here, despite the crackling flames in the fireplace. The storm is still raging outside and the room has turned dim and cave-like, an orange patch of light flickering on the ceiling, reflected from the fireplace below. Sofia hasn't returned yet. I can see Mum and Dad on the bed, dying then dead; I don't have to watch the video to have it engraved in my mind's eye. I want to scream, but I fear I won't be able to stop. I want to run, to ease this unbearable pain that is eating my insides away. There's nothing for me here.

I jump up from the chair and scurry out of the room, across the hall, ignoring my echoing steps on the floor. I press the button on the wall. When the door starts opening, slowly and heavily, I squeeze myself out and rush down the stone steps. I feel the eyes of the lions on my back, the eyes that have seen it all.

I cross the lawn, making for the dense forest. I run along on a narrow path, not knowing where I will end up. All I know is that I have to get away from here. Sofia won't give me a lift; she wants to continue spewing out her venom, but it's too much to take.

I don't know how long I have been running. When I look back, I can't see the house or anything else outside the forest. It's semi-dark, particularly so beneath the ancient trees. I hear an owl, again. It must be right above me. There should be birdsong, but there's nothing. I'm panting so heavily that I stop and lean against a tree trunk. It seems no one is following me.

I hear a noise behind me; it could be an animal – a wolf! I start running out of sheer terror, into the depths of the forest. I force myself to think rationally about what Sofia said about Walter and other hunters. Does it mean there are no wolves; was it all just a cover-up by the Owners to disguise their sick murders? Or to control the places where spenders can go? But she didn't confirm it. I must know for sure if I want to be safe. I look around but everywhere it's only dark green, so dark it's almost black.

It hurts me to admit it but returning to Sofia is the only – if extremely slim – chance to save Philip. I sacrificed so much to get here; I won't give up on him now. I tiptoe to the edge of the forest, where trees are sparse and it's lighter. I picture Walter in front of me, his thick fingers clutching at his rifle. Now my steps are quieter, to avoid the attention of whatever is out there, a wolf or a hunter. I don't know which I should be more afraid of.

When I see the silhouette of the house and its many chimneys, I'm almost relieved. I move closer, carefully, so as not to disturb anything underfoot. Leaving the forest, I come to a clearing, just a stone's throw away from Sofia's mansion. I'm facing the back of the forbidden wing now, where the patio is. It's a picture perfect view, but knowing the things that went on here, I find it hard to appreciate the architecture.

The sun has banished the black clouds; the sky is now still and impossibly blue. Sofia sits in her electric armchair on the sun-soaked patio, wearing oversized sunglasses. How different she is now! The way she's holding her head, slightly tilted to one side, her mouth pulled into a smile, she almost looks carefree. There is gentleness on her face, something I would never expect in her. There must be someone with her, the way she is looking. She speaks but I'm too far away to hear what she's saying. Maybe it's safe for me go over, now that she has company. I cut across the clearing, and I see a little girl of about six in the swimming pool. At this moment Sofia notices me.

'I hope your makeup is not smudged,' she says, while I'm climbing up the steps.

'I don't wear makeup these days.'

'I remember how keen you were on it,' she says. 'You even nicked a lipstick from a beauty salon we went to with Mum.'

'I must have been about five.'

'More than that. At least nine.'

She waves at the chair on the opposite side of the table. I hesitate; I don't want the niceties, I just want to get what I came for and go back to Philip as soon as possible.

'What are you having?'

'Nothing, thank you.'

As if she hasn't heard what I said, she presses a button on her wheelchair and immediately a waiter appears. He's an older man, dressed like a butler in a period drama, immaculate and attentive. Sofia orders two sparkling waters, not moving her head an inch to look at him. The waiter leaves without a word. However hard I try, I can't get out of my head what I've heard earlier. This place makes me sick to the core.

We're interrupted by a splashing sound in the swimming pool behind me. I turn around and I recognise the dark eyes, the well-formed lips, the chalk-white forehead. For a moment I forget why I came here. I don't dare ask, I just watch the girl throw a bathrobe on, remove her swimming cap, shake out her dark curly locks, before running over to Sofia and giving her a kiss on the cheek. There's an untamed playfulness in her every move, but I can also sense a budding awareness. She calls my sister Auntie Sofia. What the hell is going on?

Sofia puts her palm on the girl's shoulder.

'This is Alice. Alice, this is Maya.'

I shake the girl's outstretched hand. Maya lowers her gaze, clearly not accustomed to meeting strangers. She says good morning in a sweet, girly voice before scampering off into the house.

I wish I could just leave, before I get attached to this lovely little girl, before it fully sinks in that she's my niece. The closest thing to a child of my own.

FIVE

'We haven't finished yet,' Sofia says when I get up from the chair.

'You said everything you wanted. I can't take any more.'

'I haven't said everything. I'm not going to give you a lift to the station until you let me finish my story. You may go anytime, but you'll have to walk.'

'Are there any wolves?'

'I hope when we've finished, you'll be able to figure it out for yourself.' She rings for the maid, who appears immediately. She instructs her to show me out to the helicopter. She tells me we're going to the beach.

'Sofia, please tell me they didn't suffer. Tell me it was just anger speaking.'

She doesn't reply. All she says is that she will follow in a few minutes. The beach can only be a few miles away. It's strange that she takes the helicopter to get there, but I should have learned by now that Owners do everything differently.

The wind has subsided but there is still a breeze, cool and refreshing. The crisp air invigorates me; I hope it will help to clear my head after the things I've heard. I follow the maid down the steps and across the lawn to get to the clearing where the snow-white chopper stands. There's not a spot on its smooth surface. The pilot greets me with a nod of his head, and shows me to my seat. Inside the helicopter is also spotless, from the velvet-covered seats to the curved and polished wooden panels.

Soon Maya turns up with a docile young woman whom she introduces half-formally as her nanny. She has fair skin, long mousy hair and is wearing a long, shapeless linen dress. She is wearing glasses. In her I recognise the woman I saw yesterday in the window. They get in with complete ease as if they have been doing this forever. We're only waiting for Sofia now. Maya shoots shy glances at me, and whispers into her nanny's ear, but when I look at her, she turns her head away.

Finally Sofia arrives, driving her electric armchair across the lawn, her hair flying behind her. With the help of the pilot, she gets into the helicopter without getting out of the chair. She is placed just opposite me. She stares ahead, avoiding my gaze as we take off. I'm surprised how much quieter this helicopter is than those used as taxis in the city. We fly towards the sea that lies beyond the forest.

I am reminded of the last time we were in a helicopter together. It was twenty-five years ago when we returned home after taking Grandma to the Dignitorium. Then it was the city beneath us, being redeveloped. Sofia pointed out the difference between old areas and the new ones. I remember seeing overcrowded quarters turned into spacious and sophisticated neighbourhoods. What I see now, twenty-five years later, is the by-product. Now I understand why we have taken a helicopter. There is no road to the beach. There are almost no roads at all. When the helicopter turns around, I catch a glimpse of Sofia's house and the road I arrived on, winding through the old trees, but it's the only one in sight.

As we get closer to the beach, I'm surprised to see the ruins of a small town a few miles from the coast. The town was presumably abandoned like all the rest when the population had to move into the megacities at the beginning of the new system. I can see the remnants of old roads, by now almost completely grown over with weeds, the derelict terraced and detached houses rising up like gravestones, monuments to a bygone era. Weatherworn cars with deflated tyres line the narrow streets. In the centre of town stands a church with a half-collapsed spire, slates from the roof lying shattered on the pavement. Sadness lingers over this ghost town, declaring the victory of natural destruction.

'Why hasn't this place been renovated into a nice seaside resort?' I ask Sofia.

She looks down nonchalantly.

'Why would it be? There are so many already, dozens of them, just in this area. Fifteen miles west of here, I have another beautiful mansion that used to be a seaside spa hotel. It's crumbling away, but there is absolutely no reason to renovate it. Nobody would use it.'

'Why not sell it to the High Spenders?'

'Sell? You forget that they can't own land. Their Right To Reside is only valid in the cities.'

'Yes, but if they bought property, that would bring in extra income for the Owners.'

'We don't need any more income. We are already suffocated by what we have. And no amount of money would make up for the noise and the mess that spenders would create, or for their increasing demands. The more you give them, the more they want.'

I shiver but I can't keep my eyes off the sad view below, the town that has been abandoned for almost three decades, a leaking time capsule. How many children like Felicity could live there? How many lives from the Zone could be saved?

I can't describe the joy of standing on the beach, a long-forgotten experience. The waves are licking at my toes; the quiet roaring of the sea sounds as if it comes from the very depths of the earth. From our holidays, I remember the beaches being fairly crowded, covered with people in beachwear and kids with plastic toys, the sand etched with their footprints. This is entirely different, for there's no one here but us. It's as if we've landed on an uninhabited planet. The white sandy beach with its smooth, untouched surface stretches out in both directions. Once my feet touch the sand and I breathe in the salty air, a long-forgotten joy returns. I drop my bag and start to run along the water's edge, where I can feel the mixture of seawater and sand under my feet and between my toes. Seagulls are floating right above my head, making the cooing sound I haven't heard for years.

As the waves curl up to my ankles, they seem to wash away the shock of the past few hours. I don't want to think of tomorrow, when sour reality will strike me in the face. For now, I just let myself forget. Without any warning, Dad's face appears in front of me, his gentle, hazel eyes and his mouth that so easily turned into a smile.

I stayed on the bench. He and Mum arrived at the entrance of the T-wing. Through my tears I watched them, hoping they would look at me one last time. The carer at the doorway gently led Mum in, and I didn't see her any more. But Dad stopped for a moment before crossing the threshold and turned to look back at me. I couldn't control myself; I jumped up from the bench and ran to him for our final embrace. Something was bubbling up from deep inside me. I was shaking. Dad held me away from him for a moment and looked deep into my eyes. 'I promised you, didn't I?' He released my arm and turned around. The next thing I remember is the slam of the door, the impenetrable white wooden surface an inch from my face. I didn't stop crying but these were tears of joy. He would leave happily; he would go to a good and safe place as he promised. All through the years I knew he hadn't lied. No matter what Sofia claims to have seen, I am certain Dad kept his promise. Something ascends from my soul, like a captured bird released.

After the walk I return to the others, rejuvenated. Sofia, wearing her sunglasses and with a light white scarf wrapped around her head, ignores everyone else. Her feet are up on a chair. Her head is tilted to one side, she is either staring into the distance or sleeping. Maya approaches me holding her hand out, and pulls me away from the others. 'Come,' she says, pointing at the row of beach huts in the distance.

I look back at Sofia, but she seems to be asleep. Maya's nanny smiles at me, making eye contact for the first time. 'She likes you,' she says. Maya's pull is getting stronger and when the nanny nods I let her drag me away.

'Are you from the city?' she asks, looking up at me.

'Yes, I'm from London. Have you ever been to London?'

'Once every year Auntie Sofia takes me there, to show me the Christmas Fayre. Then she takes me to the puppet theatre.' There is undeniable longing in her voice.

'Do you like it?'

'I like the people and the other children in the puppet theatre. And once we had a yacht ride on the Thames, just me and Auntie Sofia; that was lovely.'

'Do you go to school?'

'No, it's the school that comes to me. I have five teachers.'

But no class, no classmates, I find myself thinking. How lonely she must be here, at the end of the world, with only adults for company.

'Do you have any friends, Maya?'

'I see other children six days a week. Auntie Sofia invites them to come and play and talk with me. Will you stay and play and talk with me?'

'I will stay for a bit but I have to go home soon.'

We arrive at the row of wooden beach huts, painted turquoise and cream. They are in surprisingly good condition; someone is definitely looking after them. Maya runs to the first one and opens the door. She waves at me to follow her. Standing in the doorway, I'm amazed by the number of dolls and toys piled up in the hut.

'What do you think?' she asks.

'Wow! Why are they here?'

'I come here to play with nanny, or sometimes with my friends.'

She runs out and opens the door of the next hut. I'm surprised for a second that these huts are unlocked, but then I realise, who would come here? In this hut, loungers and parasols are kept, in the third one, mattresses, beach balls and blankets, in the fourth one, more toys. When we turn back, she holds out her hand for mine.

'Can you not stay for another day?' she asks.

'I'd really like to. But I can't.'

'I'll ask Auntie Sofia to pay you.'

'It's not about that, honey.' I ruffle her hair. 'I have something urgent to do. But I'll come back another time.'

She must sense a false note in my voice, for her smile fades.

'Catch me!' she yells.

She runs away, screaming with joy, and I run after her and try to catch her. When I get close, I pretend to fall over so she has the advantage. But when she sees I'm on the ground, with apparent pain on my face, she scurries over to me and reaches a hand out to try and help me up. She runs up to the top of a dune, her feet sinking down to the ankle in the fine sand. Once at the top, she throws herself onto the sand and starts rolling down, squealing. Once down, she runs up again. I follow her and we roll down several times, laughing and screaming, until I'm so dizzy that I can't take any more. Her nanny and Sofia are watching us from the distance, but when I wave to them, it's only the nanny who waves back. Sofia turns her head towards the rumbling sea.

We're back with the others. Sofia sits up on her lounger and nods to the nanny to take Maya away. They're playing with a multi-coloured beach ball; I can hear Maya's screams in the background. From time to time she checks if I'm watching.

'What do you think of her?' Sofia asks.

'She's lovely. Why does she call you auntie?'

'She seems to like you.'

'I like her too.'

Now that the sun has hidden away again, she removes the white scarf from her head, revealing her dark, messy hair. It's still long and frames her face and shoulders but has lost its healthy shine.

'You're looking a bit better,' she says. 'I was afraid you would faint. I've never seen you that pale.'

'I just don't understand.' I burst out. 'How could anyone find pleasure in other people's death? And I don't mean it in a naïve way, I know there are some cruel people. But what on earth does an Owner have against unfortunate dying people that makes them enjoy their agony? Like a morbid reality show.'

'Despite having everything they could ever dream of, most Owners are hollow inside and have ceased to feel any real emotion,' she says. 'Watching others suffer and die is the only way they can recharge that long-empty battery, I'm afraid.'

Mum and Dad appear in my mind, again, like in my dream but more vividly. I have a powerful urge to leave; I can't let Sofia see me weak and disturbed. She won't give me the money. She wouldn't give it even if I watched the recording of my parents' termination.

What if this is just a trap, and she'll never let me go home? She may hold me back by force, like when I wanted to leave her room, on that night twenty years ago, but she didn't let me, not until she finished what she wanted to say. I may be a prisoner here, while

Philip gets closer to the final date, without me there beside him. And there's nothing I can do to save him. Like Nurse Vogel couldn't save herself. She was right in the end.

'So the old system was really better than this,' I say, more to myself than to Sofia.

'There were Owners then, too, they just had a different name.'

'But at least people were protected, non-profits didn't have to die, they had benefits and pensions to rely on.'

'Benefits? Pensions?' Sofia stares at me, bewildered. 'That's absurd. It's not as if humanity is a rare species that needs to be protected from extinction. Why do people still feel they deserve to receive anything? Your petty little life is absolutely irrelevant to society as a whole.' The colour has returned to her face, and her eyes are like darting flames. 'You don't do anyone a favour by living, princess; quite the contrary, you use up energy and resources, actively contributing to the decay of this overpopulated planet. Apart from those few who are personally attached to you, no one gives a shit about you.'

I get it, Sofia, how could I have been so stupid to think otherwise, I want to say, but I don't have the strength to argue.

'Have you finished your story?'

'I'll finish it when we return home.'

Her eyelids are drooping, and her movements are sluggish; it's probably the sun. I don't want to hear what else she has to say. I simply can't take any more.

She calls out to the pilot, who has been sitting barefoot on the beach, watching the sea. She tells me to fetch Maya. Maya's eyes are shining as she grabs my hand and we stroll back along the golden beach. We stop at intervals, turning to look at the trail of footprints behind. Maya doesn't stop chatting about a starfish she and her nanny have found in the sand. We climb into the helicopter, Sofia first. On the way back, I try to avoid looking down at the abandoned town below.

SIX

Back in the house, Sofia and I sit at the table on the terrace, overlooking the forest. The waiter sets the table for afternoon tea.
'I'm surrounded by useless people,' Sofia says all of a sudden. 'Not even one of them is worth a penny. Useless bunch of fucking Owners. You've got a husband, then?'

My hopes are rekindled and I find an official photo of Philip on the mini-screen on the table. It was taken when he took on the Paradise project. He was glowing, wearing a bespoke black suit with red tie, smiling with confidence. I hold it up in front of her.

'This is Philip.'

I sit there quietly, telling myself that all is not lost, or maybe it is and I must go before I become the victim of another tantrum. She looks at the photo for a while then leans back on the chair.

'He will do,' she says. 'He will be perfect.'

'Perfect for what?'

'We've got similar tastes in men, did you not know that?'

'I don't understand, Sofia, what—'

'Everyone will think she's his. Maya included. The dark eyes, the features. And she's got your nose. Good.' She smiles to herself.

Something turns inside me. I'm glad she can't see my trembling hands beneath the table. If I ask her to explain herself, I might ruin the moment or she might take it back or say I've misunderstood something. What the hell is she talking about? Why is it so easy to resuscitate hope? I stare at her, but I can't read her expression.

'I couldn't be further from what you call a good mother,' she says. It sounds like a confession. 'You with your Philip, you could give her a fresh start. A different fate, unlike mine and Sebastian's.'

'You're speaking in riddles, Sofia.'

'Now that Sebastian is gone, Maya is a half-orphan. Soon she'll be a full one.'

'Don't talk like that.'

'The drugs and pleasures of the Primavera Club did the damage, and it's far more than just physical. You don't know the half of it, Alice. I'm burned out, to the extreme.'

'How long do you have left?'

'One month, maybe two. Unlike our parents, I will go in peace. Like them, I cannot cheat death, but I can make mine beautiful, free of panic and throwing up. Living like an Owner is not nearly as good as it seems from the outside. Dying like an Owner, however, is the only way I want to go. Unobserved.'

The waiter's arrival interrupts us. He is pushing a chrome food trolley, packed with sandwiches, cakes and tea, all on gold-plated bone china. He places everything on the table, slowly, one by one. His white gloves are just as spotless as those of the chauffeur. When finished, he leaves, without making a sound. Sofia doesn't touch the food and I'm still too upset to have an appetite, though I haven't eaten since breakfast.

'As I said, you're lucky I'm surrounded with useless people,' Sofia continues. 'I truly think you would make a good mother. You must have noticed she called me auntie.'

'I was wondering why –'

'I brought her up to believe I was her aunt. I told her one day her mother would come and take her home. If you agree to be that mother, I'll tell her today that you and your Philip are her real parents.'

'Why didn't you tell her you're her mother?'

'I'm so un-motherly,' she says with a deep sigh, 'even she wouldn't believe the truth. So I'm just Auntie Sofia.'

So many questions are whirling in my head; I don't know which one to ask. I want to know whether she's serious. If she is, it means, or it may mean, that Philip will live.

'There's no one else I can trust with Maya. If you stay, because you still look like you're about to leave, I'll call my lawyer and make the arrangements now.'

I don't know what to say, I'm paralysed by the fear that this is just a dream and if I move, it will all dissolve into thin air.

'I will forgive you if you do me this favour.' Her voice has softened. 'If you let me die in peace.'

'Don't be so melodramatic, Sofia. Of course you'll go in peace. But what happened to Sebastian?'

'His so-called friends got him into heavy drugs – out of fun. They often mocked him but he never noticed. He died during a private party in the London Primavera Club.'

'Poor Sebastian. He didn't deserve to die like that.'

'How do you know what he deserved?'

'He was always nice to me, never made me feel inferior. That's enough for me to judge someone's character.'

'In a way, he wasn't any different from other Owners' children,' she says, broodily. 'Overfed but undernourished, over-pampered but under-loved. But he had a heart. As he got older, the typical

Owner lifestyle took its toll on him. He even stopped being interested in the fossils. He gradually became a wreck, both morally and physically. I believe his passing was his salvation.'

I shiver. This is not how I imagined the lifestyle of the Owners, admired and envied by everyone.

'I just can't get my head around it. What is their problem?'

'Just promise me, you'll stay out of contact with any Owners and do everything to keep Maya safe from them too.'

'Are all of them like this? Pathetic drug users? How can these losers manage ruling the world?'

'Not all Owners are the same, Ali. Sebastian's uncle used to be my favourite, a jokey, easy-going type, good company on those annual occasions when he came here to visit the family. He would often predict what would happen in the world. Political events, like who would be the next leader in any given country. I was eighteen when I first witnessed one of his predictions. He shared with us during dinner in the great dining room that the retirement in the Dignitoriums would soon be limited, that after maximum of five years all residents would be euthanised.'

'I remember this being announced in the news.'

'Uncle Andrew wasn't a genius or a psychic. He was simply a member of The Society, a secret board of the most powerful Owners who were and are ruling the world. One word from them is enough to start a war and cause the death of millions. They have the power to shape history and humanity. They're playing with lives as if it's only a game of chess.'

'How clever they are to manipulate unlimited retirement gradually to nine months, so people never realised!'

'Of course, then five years seemed a perfect time to enjoy retirement to the full before your body starts to break down. Nobody thought there was anything wrong with it then. Now, people have got used to the nine months the same way.'

'The bastards! Will they have the cheek to cut it even more?'

'I'll ask Uncle Andrew for you, right? Maybe if I ask nicely, he will discuss with his board and they will put a stop to euthanasia and let everybody live happily ever after.' Her coarse, rusty laughter is cutting into the air.

My fear has turned to honest compassion for Sofia. It has just started to dawn on me that it was my behaviour that afternoon that gave her no other option but to return to this lifestyle. How would our lives have been without that one fight? Would things have been any different? If I had been the sister she needed me to be, maybe she would have stayed. Perhaps we would have become close after her trauma, closer than ever before. I could have turned her life around. She could have had a normal life, become a scientist, like she had always wanted. If so, she is right to hold a grudge against me, but I don't think she is angry any longer.

'Will you go to an Owners' Dignitorium?'

'They expect me to. But I'm dreading it.'

'It'll be a relief to leave this harsh world behind–'

'I'm not afraid of the place where I'm going. Not the one after my death.'

I'm left speechless for a moment when I realise what she means by this.

'I'll go with you if it helps,' I say softly.

She snorts.

'You're not going anywhere. You're looking after Maya.'

I nod.

'I'm not a coward,' she says. 'I'm ready to face whatever is waiting for me.'

The sun is coming out again. Finally I find the appetite to take a gulp of my tea.

'I'm so glad I came in time, Sofia,' I burst out. 'That I've found you.'

'You've found me?'

'Well, it was the detective but –'

'Owners can be found only if they want to be, Alice, you should know that by now.'

Suddenly something dawns on me.

'Have you...have you been tracking me? Following my life?'

A gentle breeze rustles through the canopy of trees and Sofia turns to observe, pausing for a moment before answering.

'Only after I found out that my illness was fatal. I had to know I could trust you. Who else should I leave Maya to after I'm gone?

'So if I hadn't found you, you'd have found me, is that it?'

There is a knowing glint in Sofia's eyes.

'Strange, isn't it how fate saved your life and your husband's too?'

She rings for the maid and asks her to bring Maya. Then she calls her lawyer. While she's on the phone, I wait for Maya to arrive and meet her mother. This will be the whitest lie I've ever told.

SEVEN

It's dark outside, past eleven. The house is silent as a crypt, all its inhabitants are sleeping. I was given my ID Phone back and I feel safe and complete with it gently pressing at my wrist.

Earlier I put Maya to bed. She listened intently as I read her a story. Then she wanted another, and another.

'Why did it take you so long, Mummy?' she asked.

'What took so long, honey?'

'To come back.'

'I wanted to come earlier. Much earlier. But I couldn't.'

'Why?'

'I'll tell you all when you're a bit bigger. All right?'

She nodded and patted the pillow next to her to indicate that I should lie down. Once I was comfortable and holding her soft little hand between my palms, she asked me where I had been all her life.

'In the city.'

'Is my father still there?'

For a moment, my heart jumped. I could change into the role of her mother surprisingly easily, almost to the point where I believed it myself, but I hadn't prepared what to say about her father.

'He will be joining us soon. You have no idea how much he's been wanting to see you. He'll be over the moon.'

'What is he like?'

I found some recent photos of Philip on my ID Phone and showed them to her. She didn't take her eyes off him as if she was mesmerised.

'You'll like him.'

She looked at him a while longer, then put her head on my shoulder and cuddled up to me tightly. So this is how it feels, I thought. This is what it's like when the heart is alive.

It has been a long day. Soon Philip will be collected by Sofia's people. He doesn't know it yet but the arrangements are made. He is saved, just like Antonio and Ruth and Felicity, who will all share our new home with us. I wish Nurse Vogel could join them, now that I have the means to help her. But I fear she can't be helped any more.

In the afternoon, the lawyer came and I signed the legal documents. I'm an Owner now, technically. And Maya's official mother. It feels as if a delicate soul has been handed to me, to nurture.

There's a knock at the door.

'Come in,' I say.

The maid enters hesitantly. She waits at the door, timidly, as if I am her employer.

'Madam would like to see you, miss.'

'Right now?'

'She requested you immediately, miss.'

'Is there anything wrong? Is she unwell?'

'No, miss.'

I follow her along the seemingly endless corridors, where lines of ancestral paintings hang on the walls. On the second floor, the maid opens up a mahogany door for me. I enter and hear the door close softly behind me.

The room I'm in is surprisingly small. The dimmed light of a bedside lamp illuminates a corner; otherwise it's dark. The heavy burgundy curtain is drawn. Sofia is sitting up in bed, leaning back on a pile of cushions. She resembles Snow White as she's lying there, her black hair cascading over the pillow, her face as white as marble.

'Come and sit with me, I have something to say,' she whispers.

'Are you OK, Sofia?'

'I'm tired and I don't have much time left. I've called you here because I want to share something intimate.'

I sit down at the end of her bed, and place my hand on her blanket over her knee.

'I'm listening.'

'I said earlier that I'm happy to face whatever is waiting for me in the Owners' Dignitorium. I lied. Maybe it's easy to speak so confidently in the daylight, but when the dark cloak of the night covers the sky, I find myself filled with dread. I'm ready to go, Alice, but I'm afraid. I'll need your help.'

'Don't make me do this, Sofia. I beg you.'

'I've given you my daughter and my fortune; I expect obedience in return. I want this done as soon as possible.'

'What do you want me to do? I'm not a doctor.' I feel my heart skip a beat.

'All I ask is for you to stay with me, till the end. Don't let them near me.'

'Let who near you?'

'Those who want to watch me die.'

'I won't.'

'Good.'

'But maybe…we could have some more time together. Now that we finally–'

She's not listening.

'This is where I want to die. And I want you to be by my side and give me the piece of chocolate spenders are given in the T-wing to ease the bitterness of the poison.'

She smiles to herself. 'Chocolate must be an incredibly important thing if that's the last thing people want before they die,' she mumbles to herself.

'Before you go…we could spend a few days together. You, me, Philip and Maya.'

'No.'

'It would be easier for Maya.'

'You know I have always been a selfish person. I love Maya more than anything but I can't do more for her.'

'You haven't even met Philip.'

'The way you fight for him, makes me admire you. I'm glad to see you've grown up. Answering your question, I don't want anyone to see me like this. You should know me better, Ali. And I want you to hold my hand throughout and to make sure no-one's watching.'

'Sofia–'

'Can you promise me that?'

This is the most important decision of my life. Now that we have met after decades apart, we could finally be together. We could have some moments of joy before she leaves this world. I don't want her to go yet. But I try to imagine how it would feel to be trapped and helpless in a T-Wing, with no one to hold my hand, only the sound of the door slamming, and hundreds, maybe thousands of invisible eyes upon me.

'I promise. I'll make sure you go in peace, Sofia.'

She reaches out for my hand and squeezes it. Her trembling hand is ice-cold. I see gratitude on her face, and it softens and melts her features.

'Whatever you wish, I'll do it,' I tell her, clasping her hand. 'And I won't leave your side.'

She gently smiles and mumbles 'thank you'. While her eyelids droop heavily and she drifts into the realm of dreams, the painful memories within me begin to melt away.

EIGHT

I haven't left Sofia's bedside all night. She's sleeping, occasionally moaning in her dreams. It's dawning outside, but I'm just sitting here, by the orange light of the night lamp. I let the memories come; memories that I thought were long buried. I see us as little girls: I'm five, she's eight and we're wearing matching dresses, red polka dot with an oversized ribbon at the waist. We're holding hands, standing at the roadside, and Mum is screaming behind us, screaming at me, but it's too late and my feet are on the busy road. I don't look around, I assume the cars are far away, and I know I can get over to the other side where I see something shiny in a shop window. Sofia's arm is suddenly pulling me back and Mum reaches us, flying, her bag dropping on the pavement, but she doesn't mind; she just gives us a big hug, with me on her left, Sofia on her right.

As soon as Sofia wakes up and comes around, she asks me to go to the cupboard and get out a little bottle. It has a dark brown tint so I can't see what's in it but it's so light I'd have thought it empty.

'We'll do it later today,' she says. On her face I see the joy and excitement children feel before setting out on a long and exotic trip. 'I need to sort out some paperwork.'

She must see that I haven't slept all night because she sends me away to have a nap.

Back in my suite I'm lying on the bed with my eyes closed, but sleep doesn't come. I think about how my life will change now that I have become an Owner. I will spend my time and energy on charitable work. I will use my newfound wealth and influence for the good of the less fortunate in our society. I will keep my promises to Sofia and protect Maya from the hedonistic lifestyle of other Owners. I'm not like them and will never be.

Sofia, Maya and I have lunch together on the terrace, pretending it isn't the last one. When finished, Sofia holds Maya close to her and struggles to let her go. Maya doesn't understand why Sofia is so emotional today, but gives her a long hug before she's released to return to her teacher.

'Mummy, can you take me up to Ms Fischer?'

Instinctively I glance at Sofia, waiting for her reaction before I realise that Maya is talking to me. My heart nearly exploding with tender joy, I take her hand and we walk, through endless corridors and staircases, to her classroom.

The evening has arrived too early. In Sofia's room, the same little room we spoke in last night, Sofia asks me to help her lie down on the bed. She's in her long white nightgown and tucks herself under the duvet, as if she is just going for a little sleep. The brown bottle on her side table, stands where I put it earlier, like a warning sign. I sit on the side of Sofia's bed to hold her hand, but I can't help shooting nervous glances at the brown bottle.

'You'll find a way to explain this to Maya, won't you?'

'I will.'

'I'm ready, Ali,' she says with ease. Her strength – coming from somewhere deep inside her – calms me. No mortal could possess this kind of strength without the help of a spiritual force.

'How does this work?' I ask, rolling the bottle between two fingers.

'Its a formula, and far superior to what they use in Dignitoriums,' she explains. 'You can't go wrong with this. It's perfect.'

'Still bitter?'

'That's not a problem.'

'Do you want some chocolate?'

'No. I just want you to open it.'

'But maybe you want some biscuits,' I say and jump up from my seat to get the tray of biscuits from the top of the drawer.

'Ali, put the biscuits down.'

'Okay, then I'll bring you some…'

'You still don't understand, Ali. I don't trust the Owners' Dignitorium. They expect me to turn up in there, to feast their eyes on me while I'm dying. I must go before they arrive. They are here, very close by.'

'I'm the only one here, there's no one else.'

'They'll be here soon. So open it.'

I slowly and deliberately turn the cap like delaying time could give us precious extra moments. When it's done, I hand the bottle over to Sofia. I'm about to stand up to get a glass, but Sofia gestures for me to sit back.

'I don't need a fancy glass to gulp this down,' she says and without hesitation she drinks up the liquid. I forget to breathe.

When she looks at me, her eyes say 'I've won.'

'Don't stare at me like that,' she says. 'We have almost an hour before it sends me to sleep.'

'What do you feel?'

'Nothing.'

Sofia reminisces over childhood stories. I was about ten when we had a guest with a baby and Sofia found the little screaming thing annoying. But when I picked it up, it stopped crying.

'You had so much love for it,' she says, 'I was just watching you and wondering where all that love was coming from. You were so tender, so nurturing.'

'I don't even remember.'

'Luckily I do. And this memory of you convinced me that you could be the right mother for Maya.'

Then she moves onto the next memory, of Auntie Joanne when she came to visit. The way she always lectured us about how eating sweets was bad for us, and she even spied on us. So we would hide in Sofia's wardrobe and eat them secretly. When Sofia recalls Auntie Joanne, she cracks up. We laugh together but my laughter is heavier than hers.

It takes a good half an hour before her speech begins to slow, and her eyelids become heavy.

'Can I have that chocolate?' she asks with mischief in her eyes.

I open the drawer and take out a small piece of milk chocolate. Her face is pure joy while she places it in her mouth, letting it melt.

'Ever since I saw what happens at the Primavera Clubs, I have been afraid to die,' she says, lifting a feeble hand up to me. 'I knew they would do it to me, too. But I've won, Alice. I've managed to go freely, unobserved.'

I stay with her, still holding her hand for a long, long time, until it's dark outside, and I can hardly see. I check her pulse with my ID phone. There is none. Sofia's face is peaceful and I say my quiet farewell to her. I know she's still around. Finally, we can have some time together. If Dad is watching from above, he must be happy with the outcome, how the war concluded.

NINE

'I have to tell you something, Maya.'

I'm in her room, gently taking a doll out of her hands. I lift her up and sit her on my lap. She must sense it's something important as her eyes are locked on mine.

'Auntie Sofia had to go to a better place. She won't come back.'

'Has she died?'

'Yes. I'm so sorry, honey.'

She cuddles up to me. She's so fragile. I mustn't cry.

'Please, Mummy, don't leave me again.'

'I will never leave you. I promise.'

I can't help the tears, and she notices it.

'Are you crying because of Auntie Sofia?'

'She's in a good place and I said my farewell to her. No, honey, I'm crying because I feel bad about how long I was away. I wanted to come back sooner.'

'It's OK.' The way she says it, like an adult, is funny. 'Your letters were with me all the time. I read them every evening before bedtime. Or at night when I couldn't sleep.'

'Letters?

'Auntie Sofia had a special case made for them. Look!'

She reaches under her bed and takes out a leather case that looks like a document bag. She unzips it and I see hundreds of letters organised neatly, all addressed to her. The lump in my throat is growing.

'This is my favourite.' She takes out an envelope covered in unicorn stickers. There is a note and a letter inside. The note is a message from her 'mum'. It's short, only a few sentences, full of good wishes and love, promises of coming home to her when she can. The letter attached was written by Snow White, personally for Maya, and posted to her mum who forwarded it to Auntie Sofia. It's a fairy tale, a sweet story about a little girl adopting a unicorn. It's handwritten – in a different script from the note – but there is more than writing. There are tiny drawings along the side, stickers and even rose petals, there are perfume patches with a strong fragrance, and a drawing of a blonde woman with hair down to the waist, widely set blue eyes and a dimple in her cheek. An arrow points to it, saying 'Your Mummy'.

'Why have you had your hair cut, Mummy?'

'It's just… I don't know really. It's more practical. If you like it that long I can grow it again.'

Maya takes out more letters, other favourites, as she calls them, all with different decoration, some hand-drawn, some cut out from magazines. In each envelope, there is a note from her mum and a fairy tale from Snow White. The stories are imaginative, and always see good triumphing over evil. Maya is staring at me, as I weep and shake uncontrollably. I let her believe it's because I hadn't seen her for such a long time. My heart is aching for the Sofia I am only just starting to get to know, the sister I so misunderstood.

I have just spoken to Philip on the phone. He is on his way. He is being flown here by helicopter; it will be another hour. For the day after tomorrow he's already booked into the world's best eye clinic in Switzerland. Antonio and his commune will soon be evacuated from the Zone. Ruth and Felicity are arriving tomorrow. It's only Nurse Vogel who won't be with us. Sofia's head of security has done everything to save her. But it was too late. 'Our people couldn't get to the old lady in time,' he said.

I walk up the narrow stone steps to the roof of the mansion. I want to take in the view. To think things over, to fully understand my power. To make space for Maya's unexpected love in my heart. I move carefully among the dozens of chimneys, with my ID Phone providing light. I stop at the ridge and switch off the light. Now I just stand here in the near pitch-dark, so deep and infinite. The deathly silence sobers me up. A cool breeze touches my face, bringing with it the scent of the sea. In the distance I hear the trees swaying in the wind. The sky is a dark blanket, the same shade of midnight blue I would gaze at from my childhood bed.

As I survey the land – now my land – for an instant the extraordinary feeling of power overwhelms me. It's frightening, but there's a sweetness to it that I find seductive. This is my house and my land, but does it mean the sea beyond the forest is mine, too? Or the stars shining in the black velvet of the sky? I might not be able to withstand all this alone, but I know Philip will have the strength for both of us. I can rely on him. He won't let me become just another wolf among the pack.

END